ASHES FROM A BURNING CORPSE

A Novel based on a true crime

By Noel Hynd

Published by Red Cat Tales, LLC, Publishing, PO Box 34313, Los Angeles, CA. 90034

Email: Red.cat.Tales.publishing@gmail.com

AUTHOR'S NOTE

My late father, Alan Hynd, was a true crime writer in the United States for more than fifty years, starting in the 1920's and ending in the 1970's. He covered more than a thousand cases in his career. The *New York Times* in 1952 (*) called him "probably the most successful financially" of fact crime writers of the day.

Of those thousand cases, three stand out as having had the most impact upon him both personally and professionally. The first was the case of the swindler Charles Ponzi in Boston in 1920. The second was the kidnapping of Charles Lindbergh's son in 1932 and the execution of Bruno Richard Hauptmann in 1936. The third, which follows here, was the horrific depraved murder of Sir Harry Oakes in The Bahamas in 1943.

Oakes at the time was one of the wealthiest men in the world. Alan Hynd's frank coverage of the case resulted in his being permanently banned from the Bahamas and his life being threatened.

I've set about to use my father's material, his reporting, his work, the many conversations he and I had about these cases long ago, and his first-person voice, as the basis of three novels that will form a trilogy: ***An American True Crime Reporter in the 20th Century***. These works are not so much about the cases as they are about the profound effects they had on a reporter who covered them. This is the first of those novels, though it's chronologically the third.

Enjoy.

Noel Hynd

October 2017

(*) NY Times, October 12, 1952, Book Section, Page 31

3

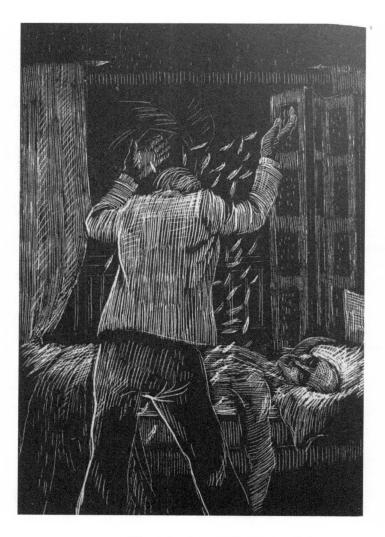

The Murder of Sir Harry Oakes

For

Jeremy Noel Hynd,

Alan's grandson

CHAPTER 1

I'm going to tell you about a murder—or several murders, plus some attempts that failed. The murder in question took place on a stormy early morning of the eighth day of July 1943, in a mansion known as Westbourne, a sprawling baronial luxury home in Nassau, the Bahamas, once owned by a woman named Maxine Elliott, who was a celebrated American actress. The property faced the sea in the western part of Nassau.

On the night the crime was committed, there were no servants in the main house. The victim was a man named Sir Harry Oakes, a well-known gold mining executive reputed to be one of the wealthiest men in the world. The only other person on the premises was one of Sir Harry's closest friends, Harold Christie, a governing official of Nassau and maybe the island's second wealthiest and best-known citizen. Christie, who had spent the night with Sir Harry to wrap up some business transactions in which they were jointly involved, said he discovered the body about seven o'clock in the morning. He put through telephone calls to the police and to Dr. Hugh Arnley Quackenbush, a prominent Nassau physician. The Doctor arrived at Westbourne about seven-thirty. Not long afterwards, another man arrived: Major Herbert Pemberton, the deputy commissioner of the Nassau police.

Sir Harry, or what remained of him, lay face-up on a bed in a luxurious second floor chamber that overlooked the beach. There were four wounds behind his left ear, triangular gashes about half an inch wide at the most. It was Dr. Quackenbush's opinion that the wounds had been made by the end of a sharp metal instrument. Whoever had handled the weapon had probably been a person of unusual strength.

Each wound was more than a quarter of an inch in depth. The four wounds appeared to be the cause of a quick and sudden death. The left side of the victim's head had been shattered. Blood coated his face. The stench of burning flesh hung in the air. Someone had tried to incinerate the body.

Oakes had been dead between two-and-a-half and five hours, Quackenbush decided when he examined the body, fixing his death between two-thirty and five o'clock in the morning. As Quackenbush conducted his initial exam, the bedchamber remained heavy with smoke. Part of a rug was smoldering. The head of the bed and part of the mattress had been burned, as had the corpse. There was a second bed in the room, but it was empty aside from a pair of pants and a white shirt that the victim had worn the previous evening. Between the beds was a small table on which lay a pair of reading glasses, a set of false teeth, and a lamp. There was also a Chinese screen in the room, a five-section piece that was currently stylish. There was a print design on the screen, but the piece had been charred and scorched by the fire.

Sir Harry had been the target of an intense flame, particularly around the eyes and his genitals. It appeared he had been burned both before and after death. His body contained wet blisters which arise only when a person is still alive, and dry ones which occur only after death.

As if all this weren't enough, the corpse on the bed had been sprinkled with feathers taken from the pillows. The feathers were not burned, so they must have been put there after the fire was out.

The Superintendent of Police, Colonel R. A. Erskine-Lindop, reached the scene shortly after Dr. Quackenbush and Major Pemberton, perhaps around eight o'clock. The police knew at a glance that they were facing something horrific and depraved. The concentrated flame that had been applied around the eyes and the genitals smacked of an uncivilized hatred; the feathers gave the crime a touch of witchcraft, voodoo or some form of the occult. The outer islands around Nassau were thick with native men whose familiarity with primitive jungle ritual of one kind or another was far from extinct. No perverse explanation could be eliminated.

At eleven o'clock in the morning, some four hours after Harold Christie had reported finding Sir Harry Oakes' body, His Royal Highness the Duke of Windsor, Governor of the Bahamas,

7

having been notified of his close friend's untimely death, sat in Government House trying to arrive at a grave decision.

The Duke, formerly King Edward VIII of England, was rusty in arriving at important decisions, having been free of the necessity of making any important ones since he decided to forego his crown a few years previously. His problem now was whether to entrust the local constabulary with the formalities to be performed about the passing of an important citizen. His option was to call in out-of-the-country cops.

With a few exceptions, the Bahamian cops would have warmed the heart of Mack Sennett, the old-time Hollywood movie maker whose Keystone Kops supplied nickelodeon patrons with belly laughs a third of a century before. So the Duke decided that the local boys might need some help. He picked up a telephone and put through a call to the United States to the Miami, Florida, Police Department. There the Duke connected with Captain Edward Melchen, chief of the Homicide Department. The Duke was personally acquainted with Captain Melchen, who had previously arranged special guards for him when Windsor had passed through Miami.

"A very prominent citizen is dead here," said the Duke to Melchen, "and it might be suicide. Can you come at once?" Captain Melchen said he would catch the next plane. The Duke, for reasons unexplained, was apparently not in possession of much clear information about the discovery of Sir Harry's body when he made the call.

Obviously, this was no suicide.

The Duke's mistake in reporting Sir Harry's death as a suicide rather than a murder proved to be, as the Duke himself later put it, "most unfortunate." An investigator sets out with considerably more equipment to investigate a murder than he takes with him to consider a suicide. Gas, poison, or shooting causes most suicides. So, when Captain Melchen, Chief of Detectives in Miami, accompanied by his pal Captain James Barker, head of the Miami Police Identification Department—the fingerprint unit—left on the eleven fifty a.m. airplane, they were carrying with them equipment for investigating only those three methods of self-destruction. Fingerprints, as it turned out, were to be of the utmost importance in the investigation, but

8

Captain Barker was carrying only a small portable fingerprint kit and no fingerprint camera, the standard equipment of the day.

Melchen and Barker landed in The Bahamas with solid credentials. First, they were said to be the handpicked choices of the Duke, which gave them a bit of luster. Second, there were their resumés. Melchen, aged fifty and hefty to the point of being porky, was the head of Miami's Homicide Bureau, a busy unit considering the heat, tempers and fast money for which that city was noted. Barker was eight inches taller than Melchen and a solid good-looking American southerner with accent to match. He dressed well, usually in a good suit, and habitually wore a homburg. He had worked fingerprints on more than five hundred cases and had been President for one term of the International Association for Identification, the most prestigious forensics organization in the United States. By any accepted standards, Barker was an accomplished fingerprint expert.

Melchen and Barker arrived in Nassau at one thirty-five in the afternoon. Local police drove them directly to Westbourne. As soon as they saw the murder room, of course, they realized the Duke's message had started them off on the wrong foot. But that wasn't all. Though the murder room and the immediate vicinity were jumping with bloody finger and handprints, everything was so damp from the heavy storm of the night before that dusting for prints was out of the question. A fingerprint is comprised of one percent body oil and 99 percent water. The body oils do not show up under conditions of extreme dampness, so Barker said he would wait until the following day, when he hoped to be able to develop prints.

The Miami cops took a good look at Sir Harry's body, which had been left in place pending their arrival. They decided that somebody must have poured some highly flammable agent over Oakes, and in the process, the killer might well have received some burns himself, because of proximity to the blaze. They thought exclusively in terms of a male suspect or suspects. The force of the blows on the skull ruled out from the beginning a likelihood that the crime had been committed by a woman.

As a matter of normal police routine, Harold Christie, as the only other known occupant of Westbourne at the time of the murder, was subjected to a microscopic examination to determine whether he had any singed hairs on his head, his face, or his hands and arms. He hadn't.

During the examination, the affable but shaken Christie informed the police on the situation at Westbourne. Lady Oakes and the five Oakes children were in the United States, having gone North sometime before to escape the suffocating heat of the summer months in Nassau. They did this every year. The fact that this year, 1943, was a dark year during World War Two did nothing to discourage them. To the contrary, for a wealthy family, the mainland of the United States was a safer haven than an island off the east coast of Florida where German U-Boats prowled.

Christie, at the invitation of Sir Harry, had come over to Westbourne to stay with him while finalizing some business matters until Sir Harry was ready to go on a business trip to South America. Sir Harry's trip had been scheduled for that very morning.

On the previous evening, according to Christie, Sir Harry had thrown a party for himself at Westbourne, a farewell party. It was a comparatively small get-together of friends, including the Duke and Duchess of Windsor. It broke up quietly about midnight.

Then Sir Harry and Christie had another drink or two by themselves while the servants cleared away the debris left after the festivities. The servants finished putting the house back in order by about one o'clock, and left for the nearby cabins in which they lived. Christie and Sir Harry had then said goodnight to each other and gone to their respective rooms.

Shortly thereafter, somebody or several somebodies murdered Sir Harry Oakes as he slept peacefully in his own bed.

CHAPTER 2

Two evenings after the murder, I was at home in my Manhattan apartment with my wife and eighteen-month-old daughter, savoring true big-time financial success, a modest bit of fame as an author—I had had a book titled *Passport to Treason* on the New York *Times* Best Seller list for a good part of that year—and a wonderful second marriage. We lived at 530 Park Avenue on the eighth floor. We had a gorgeous nine-room spread, with a study that overlooked the corner of Sixty-First Street and Park Avenue. My specialties were true crime and espionage, and I had done very well writing about both. Financial success lands a man in some nice places: not all the time, but most of the time.

"Alan?" asked the voice on the line.

The caller was Kenneth Gelb, my most senior editor at Fawcett Publications and Editor in Chief at *True* Magazine. Fawcett had a magazine empire perched in New York's West Forties, a not unpleasant walk from where I was living. As miserable as life was for most of the world in 1943, life was rosy for me.

I was not directly in the war, and there were three reasons. I was forty years old. I had a shattered knee cap from an auto accident and still sometimes limped along with a cane. I'd tried to volunteer after Pearl Harbor, but was given 4-F due to my age and my leg. I was helping the war effort in my own way—writing, propagandizing, whatever you want to call it. I was selling the victory line in any publication that I sold to and trying to add to the effort on the home front. It didn't seem like much compared to the guys who were fighting in Europe and the South Pacific, but it was what fate sent my way. We all get by as we can, and I was getting by much better than most.

My call from Ken Gelb piqued my interest from the get-go. It ran twenty-five minutes, and then the call ended. My wife appeared at the door to my study. She sensed something, as women do when they know you too well. I said nothing.

Outside there was a warm rain falling. The world was going to hell. Canadian, American and British forces had just established beachheads in Sicily and were starting the long slog northward that would hopefully lead to Rome and toppling the little tinhorn dictator Mussolini, Hitler's pal. Men were fighting and dying and bleeding.

I rose from my desk in my apartment and lifted my daughter. I put an arm around my wife. It was bedtime for the little girl and I was a lucky man.

"What was the phone call?" my wife said to me.

"Ken Gelb at Fawcett publications. It's an assignment."

"What and where?" she asked.

I bounced the little girl.

"A murder case. The Bahamas."

She blinked. "Not *the* murder case?" she asked.

"Yes. That one," I said. "Fawcett's wants reports every three days, if possible."

Like anyone else in the civilized world who could read or hear, she knew all about the Oakes slaying. It had been not just all over the news, it had been *the* news, the story that had pushed the war aside. The Bahamian crime—like another case that I had covered, the Lindbergh case in New Jersey years before—was populated with a distinguished, sordid and colorful cast of characters of which the deceased was the star.

Sir Harry Oakes himself, as Ken Gelb described it, had been a belligerent man of sixty-eight who had more enemies per square foot of Bahama real estate than any other man in the islands. Not the least of which among Sir Harry's enemies were a legion of husbands of occasionally straying local wives. Then there were so many of his questionable business dealings. The fact that Sir Harry had attained his sixty-eighth birthday without being knocked off earlier was as much of a mystery as the murder itself. He had for much of his life been accumulating enemies and asking for it.

Or so said my editor.

Oakes was a notable character not only in the Bahamas, but also in the United States, Canada, England and South America. His fortune was estimated to be in the range of two hundred million dollars at the time of his death. Oakes circulated only in the rarified precincts of the social world and participated in events with such high-profile figures as the Duke and Duchess of Windsor, whom he counted as close friends. His death by malice aforethought thus became a world-wide sensation even during a global war.

"Nassau?" she asked. "Nassau!"

"Nassau," I said.

"Isn't Nassau dangerous? Isn't *travel* dangerous?"

"*Life* is dangerous," I said. "And I can't sit at home." I shrugged. "I'll probably be back in two weeks."

"Two weeks often turns into six weeks," she said after a few moments of silence.

She had a point. Often, she did.

We put my daughter to bed.

"How much money did he offer you?" she asked.

The average guy earned two thousand dollars a year at the time.

"Four hundred dollars a week," I said. I was the highest paid true crime writer in the country, and my editors knew they had to pay. My readers wanted to know what I had to say. That's how it worked.

"Wow," she said softly.

"Yes," I said.

My wife said little more to me that night. The case didn't seem like a good idea to her, money notwithstanding. She must have had an instinct. I should have known better, too.

Two days later, I left for Nassau.

CHAPTER 3

I took a train from New York to Atlanta, then another hot rattling wartime peasant wagon to Miami. I hated flying and feared for my safety every time I went aloft in a plane, but I had no choice. The murder of Sir Harry Oakes had already become the biggest story on the planet outside of the war. I needed to get to Nassau while there were still lodgings available, ahead of the rest of the world. To do that I needed to fly, at least part of the way.

I arrived in Nassau by air from Miami four days after Oakes had been murdered. Already all hell was breaking out, particularly on the Bahamian island of New Providence where Nassau sat as the colonial capital. On my way in from the airport, I was already sensing the mood. My taxi driver's name was Felix, a pleasant man of about thirty with skin the hue of light coffee. He wore a noisy tropical shirt and a straw hat and smiled easily. I struck up a casual conversation with him and steered it to the death of Sir Harry Oakes.

Felix told me that Harry's genitals had been mutilated by a blow torch, something I hadn't heard yet and which was not part of any information that had been released to the public. But this was why I liked to talk to cab drivers.

"What did that suggest?" he asked me. "Destroying a man's power center?"

"The obvious," I said. "Jealousy. Revenge, maybe."

Felix laughed. "Of course," he said.

My driver took me to the British Colonial Hotel, a comfortable place that was aptly named. As I paid him and tipped him, he wrote out his three-digit phone number.

"You need any rides around the island," he said, "I can drive you. I can be your guide."

I thanked him again and booked into the hotel, carefully putting Felix's phone number in my billfold.

The hotel was on Bay Street. I took a walk shortly after my arrival to familiarize myself with the area. Bay Street was the widest and toniest thoroughfare on this overheated island two hundred miles east of Miami. Bay Street was also where the money was and where the power resided. Bay ran from the hotel on its west end to the glimmering Yacht Club and beyond in the east. There were banks and government buildings. Lawyers. Real estate developers. Insurance agents. There were shops and bars jammed-packed one-by-one next to each other, few with entrances wider than sixteen feet.

Pastel-colored canvas canopies in pinks and blues and green, much of them faded and weathered, fluttered above the pavements and softened the look of the sides of the street. Some of the better canopies were tiled and more secure, or had iron pillars supporting them. The sun could be hard and so could the drenching rains. No merchant wanted to deter a wealthy shopper.

My new best friend, Felix, had told me just before arrival that some of these iron pillars had once been used as hitching posts for horses and then were reshaped and repositioned during the 1930's when automobiles began to make their presence on the island. Felix appeared correct.

On the lesser end of Bay Street and around the corners, these same pillars were horizontal. Farmers and contractors who still drove buggies used them as depots to bring their wares into Nassau. To my eye, they gave the town the look and feel of the American Old West.

On each block, there were outdoor stairways that led to the second floors above the shops. I glanced upward, and saw that the doors on the upstairs landings bore cryptic names of discreet businesses. These were registered companies with non-descript names painted in gold letters on solid black doors. Anyone who was anyone in Nassau had a portal here—lawyers and accountants mostly, above the businesses. Bay Street was where finances took place, where you spent it, where you transferred it, where you protected it. The upstairs people, the financial operators, were like puppeteers above their storefront marionettes. Probably everyone behind these doors had known Sir Harry. Probably everyone had a theory as to what had happened and why. I knew already that no one was going to take very kindly to strangers, much less a busybody reporter from New York.

I was exhausted from travel, and so I retreated to my hotel for a six-p.m. dinner, then sat in the hotel bar. I listened to what people were talking about, and spoke to no one first. I didn't want to seem too anxious. I would respond when someone asked my opinion of some aspect of the case, but mostly I listened and sipped rum Cokes with plenty of ice. I heard more stories and parts of stories than I could count, and many probably had some truth to them. It was hard not to hear stories, since the murder was all anyone was talking about.

Sir Harry had looked upon the world as his oyster and he had a gargantuan appetite. He was a ham-fisted gent and, despite his age, he packed a wallop. He delighted in bullying his presumed social inferiors. If a shopkeeper did something to displease him, he would clear his throat and spit on the man. His servant turnover was brisk.

Of course, he was known to everyone in Nassau. How could he not have been? On any given day, hot, tepid, rainy or sunny, he would walk along Bay Street, clad in high boots and a prospector's rumpled jacket, hands buried in his baggy pockets. His hat was jammed on his head. He'd whistle tunelessly, nodding a greeting here, grunting a good morning there, striking up casual conversations in a sharp nasal voice. He could easily have been a gold miner—which he once had been—setting out for another day's desperate prospecting. This was the image he wore like a suit of armor for decades.

15

I also heard that Oakes was in the habit of going down to the wharves wearing white pants and a loud sports jacket to cast an eye on the unattached females that came down the gangplanks from the tourist ships. When he saw something tasty, the chase was on. It was hardly a secret in Nassau that more than one fair tourist, after being spotted by the old huntsman, had experiences not mentioned in the tourist literature. The talk around Nassau was incessant: Sir Harry had dished out favors both financial and amatory to certain ladies in permanent residence on the island. Any one of these cuckolded men would have been a logical suspect.

I quickly caught on to something else. The islands were strictly segregated. White Bahamians had raised the old-time master-servant attitudes to an art form. Nonwhites on the islands had been consistently denied any political or economic power. The "colored," as they were politely but condescendingly called, still constituted the classes who provided dirt-cheap labor. They lived at a lower standard of living than any whites on the island. In 1943, when I arrived, non-white people were routinely denied access to downtown hotels, restaurants and theatres. The Bahamas were an extension of the American south of the late Nineteenth Century, but with a British colonial accent, hotter weather, and worse insects.

Deep trouble simmered beneath the surface, as it often does in repressive places. The islands, I knew, had the potential to blow sky high. The white minority had the electoral power locked up because they denied voting to nonwhites. The geography of the island made subsistence farming almost impossible. The whites then used the non-white population as a captive market for the merchandise imported by traders from Europe and North America and other points around the Caribbean. As nonwhites were not allowed to be merchants, only whites could sell to blacks. Hence, white Bahamians arrogantly extorted generations of profits from their less fortunate countrymen with no hint of shame. Why would there have been? Many among them felt that the "colored" were incapable of living in a civilized way. The Bay Street Boys, the term for the white power elite on the islands, were doing something wonderful by exploiting them.

Despite the prevailing and rampant atmosphere of stuffy British colonialism, Nassau was a place unto itself. The standards of

16

other British colonies didn't always apply. Adultery, boozing, gambling, philandering, any combination of the aforesaid, was fair game.

***

Later that same night, I found a favorite bar not far from the hotel. It was named Dirty Dicks. It became my new hangout. I spent my first few evenings there, falling into conversation with anyone who would talk to me. I didn't initiate talk. I let others do it.

I wasn't naïve about what went on in the West Indies, however. I'd heard plenty of stories from a man I knew named Bill McCoy, who was once the subject of one of my true crime articles but who had also become a friend over the years.

Bill McCoy had been one of the great "gentleman smugglers" from the Prohibition Era. Bill was a handsome bastard who liked to call himself, "The Real McCoy." He stood six feet tall plus a couple of inches. He had a powerful build, a voice like a fog horn and genial Ivy League good looks.

Bill owned a twenty-foot boat called *The Tamoka*. Prior to Prohibition, Bill and his industrious brother Ben ran a boat yard and taxi boat service in Holly Hill, Jacksonville, Florida, but they weren't having much success. Bill was a few weeks away from bankruptcy when a friendly gangster approached him and his brother—you can meet anyone along the coast, after all—and asked if they'd be interested in accepting a hundred bucks to sail a liquor shipment ashore through Rum Row, the Prohibition-era line of ships loaded with liquor anchored beyond the maritime limit of the United States. The maritime limit was three miles prior to April 21, 1924, and twelve miles thereafter.

They said no. But an idea was born.

Collecting together the last of his savings, Bill began his smuggler's career by investing in the 90-foot schooner *Henry L. Marshall*, which he soon sailed to Nassau. There he loaded his ship with fifteen hundred cases of Canadian whiskey. Three days later the *Marshall* entered back into US waters via St. Catherine's Sound, twenty miles south of Savannah, Georgia. They sold the booze for $15,000 in tax free funds.

It was early 1921. Bill McCoy had re-invented himself.

On a regular basis, McCoy began to smuggle whiskey into the U.S., sailing from Nassau and Bimini in the Bahamas to the east coast of the United States, spending most time dealing on Rum Row off New Jersey. After a few successful trips smuggling liquor off the coast of the United States, Bill McCoy had enough money to buy a 130-foot schooner named *Arethusa*, the "waterer" in Greek mythology. A man of sound business principles, and himself a teetotaler, McCoy soon expanded the operation. He hired a second captain for the *Marshall* and purchased a new flagship of his own and refitted it as a "floating liquor store."

Recognizing the potential for legal trade just outside America's three-mile marine border, Bill anchored his fully laden vessels just inside international waters and arranged for thirsty boating enthusiasts to make their way through Rum Row to purchase liquor from his floating stores.

McCoy took precautions, of course. Only two potential buyers would be permitted aboard at any one time. And all trading vessels would be under the scrutiny of a swivel machine gun on the *Arethusa*'s prow to deter anyone with funny hijacking ideas. Bill, a former US Navy man who had been aboard the *Olivette* in Havana Harbor in 1898 when *The Maine* exploded, employed Great War veterans behind his guns.

Despite the ugly security needs, Bill was a gracious host on board ship. He developed wonderful rapport with his customers, often inviting them to remain aboard for evening cocktails and parties.

Bill also developed the "smuggler's ham," an innovative way of transporting liquor between vessels. A "ham" consisted of a pyramid of six bottles arranged triangularly and bound tightly in straw and burlap. The bundles stacked conveniently and were easier to move between vessels than the stodgy old wooden cases of twelve. Most hams were stuffed with salt which, if Bill's ship was about to be boarded by authorities, could be thrown overboard where they would sink with the weight of the salt, hiding any incriminating evidence.

Later the salt would dissolve and the sack would float back to the surface when McCoy's people came looking for it.

Bill was a busy man in the early 1920's, zipping up and down the east coast of the United States with his contraband cargo. He transported eight-dollar cases of liquor from the Bahamas to Martha's Vineyard on the *Arethusa*, making $300,000 in profit for each trip. It was a great business.

Bill's first clash with the authorities occurred on August 2nd, 1921. The *Marshall*, along with its captain and crew, were nabbed off New Jersey by the US Coast Guard with fourteen hundred cases of whiskey aboard. The surprise was the vessel's seizure in international waters outside of the legal three-mile boundary.

Authorities filed two writs against the vessel, dredging up an old Maritime Act of 1790 which implied a twelve-mile limit of approach for any vessels engaged in fraudulent pursuits. The discovery of the old act set a new legal precedent for the maritime border, causing a major blow to smugglers working on the Rum Row.

Initially the owner of the *Marshall* could not be identified, but once Bill was labelled responsible, he became one of the most wanted men of the Prohibition era. To safeguard against any further surprises, Bill re-registered the *Arethusa* under British sovereignty as the *Tamoka* and French sovereignty as the *Marie Celeste*. Foreign registration offered a degree of protection as US authorities were less likely to board international vessels in international waters.

For Bill, however, his smuggling days came to an end in 1923 while on a night run in November. The *Tamoka* with Bill aboard was seized six and a half miles off the coast of Seabright, New Jersey. The USCG flagship *Seneca* was the captor, the same ship as had busted Bill in 1921. Despite McCoy's attempt to outrun the *Seneca*, a warning shot from one of her four 6-pounder guns convinced McCoy to surrender.

With plenty of connections and savings behind him, McCoy remained on bail for two years thanks to a sympathetic judge—a drinking man, no doubt—who allowed a monitored confinement in a New Jersey hotel room. Bill had freedom to come and go as he pleased. It was then that I met him and interviewed him over lunch at The Algonquin on West Forty-fourth Street in Manhattan. The interview formed the basis of a two-part piece I wrote on him for *The American Mercury*.

"I'm an honest lawbreaker, Alan," Bill explained to me. "I'm somewhat like John Hancock and John Adams before the American Revolution."

"Nonetheless, you may go to jail," I said to him.

He shrugged. "So did David Thoreau," he said. "What irks me is I was legally in international waters when the *Seneca* attacked me. Never trust your own government, hear me?"

Eventually Bill served nine months in a New Jersey jail after pleading guilty to all counts of illegal smuggling. Once his time was finished, having been out of the game for so long and with his savings eaten into due to legal fees, Bill decided it was best not to compete with the developing crime syndicates. He moved back to Florida, investing in real estate and a boat-building business with his brother Ben.

I learned some lessons from Bill McCoy that served me again these days as I watched the crowd at Dirty Dick's.

When the rum running and smuggling was full blown during the Prohibition years of 1920 to 1933, business boomed in Nassau. Hotels and bars, notably the enticingly named Bucket of Blood, opened in Nassau to soak up the fortunes being made. Men gambled at dice for fifty dollars a throw. New luxury houses sprang up where there had once been beachfront farms, and each July brought the Bootleggers Ball, the centerpiece of the social season.

Between 1918 and 1922, as tonnage at the port went up tenfold, re-export duty on alcohol at Nassau leaped twenty-fold. The money was used to fund much-needed improvements to the islands' communications and infrastructure. The harbor was dredged, electricity brought in and proper plumbing installed. Surplus funds were put towards the reconstruction of the British Colonial following a fire, and the building of a golf course—the precursor of Sir Harry's links—to attract tourists and the Canadian distillers who had started to take advantage of the islands' favorable banking regime.

Rum-running and bootlegging first established the potential of the Bahamas as a tax haven. The principal beneficiary of this bonanza, however, was not any individual, but the British Government.

I had learned more than my share of lessons over a career in reporting crime, particularly in the case of the affable Bill McCoy. Foremost among those lessons: It was always wise, when approaching a case, to look at where the money was going and where people were making profits.

CHAPTER 4

By the day after my arrival, the Nassau government had given official local authority to the cops from Miami, Melchen and Barker. The cops began nosing around for a suspect. They quickly filled themselves in on local scuttlebutt. I followed along in their path, posing mostly as a curiosity seeker and a tourist. There were plenty of those, so I could blend in well. For a while, no one paid any attention to me.

Melchen and Barker were already in charge of the investigation. The more the Miami cops listened, the clearer it became that if they were going to try to do a thorough checking job on everybody who might have had a motive for bumping off Sir Harry, they would be in Nassau for the rest of their lives.

Besides motives, the opportunity to kill Harry had been unlimited. Despite the palatial aspect of the Oakes home, guardianship of it was entrusted to a local watchman or two, casually making rounds through the night hours. The security, or lack of it, furnished by this arrangement was such that a prowler would practically have had to make an appointment with the watchman to get caught entering the place. Sir Harry, who could have afforded to maintain a standing army of guards, had never bothered. For most of his life, he had never had the slightest doubt that he was able to take care of himself.

Conveniently in the foreground of their inquiries was one suspect who might have been called "the natural." He was Count

Marie Alfred Fouquereaux de Marigny, a tall, thin, handsome fellow of thirty-seven, and Sir Harry's son-in-law. Less than a year before the murder, he had married eighteen-year-old Nancy Oakes, the oldest of Sir Harry's five children and the apple of Papa's eye. The Count, a French native of the island of Mauritius in the Indian Ocean, had never been Sir Harry's favorite boy. He was not at all Sir Harry's type. Nancy Oakes was his third wife, and before his second wife divorced him, he had borrowed a big chunk of money from her. The sum was reputed to have been more than a hundred thousand dollars and he had never got around to returning it. In the eyes of the cops and Sir Harry himself, the Count was a classic example of the oily no-good European fortune hunter.

At the time of his murder, the rumors insisted, Oakes had been concentrating on some way to see that de Marigny would never lay hands on any of his two hundred million dollars. This project, naturally, did nothing to inspire the Count with affection for his father-in-law. The Count and Oakes had not been on speaking terms for several months, according to local gossip. At the time of the murder, de Marigny was living in a cottage about five miles from Westbourne. In another part of the island, he had a profitable farm where he raised chickens.

I asked some questions. I had learned long ago to never believe the official version of anything, so I wanted to know what people were saying on the street. I got an earful pretty fast.

De Marigny, despite his dubious title, was more a man of the people than most other white residents. At his chicken farm, he employed many black laborers. He had the reputation for treating them fairly. The non-white population also viewed him as a fellow outsider because it was obvious he was not as English as much of the other ruling class.

Equally, he was not a favorite of the white power structure. He was, in fact, a thorn in the side of the staid white power structure. He had from time to time chided the wealthy white Bahamians on their "pirate mentality," alluding to the fact that very few of them had ever made any significant money on their own, and that most of them were indeed descended from wealthy pirates. Captain Morgan and Blackbeard had all been successful local pirates, as had a couple of notorious females named Mary Read and the Irishwoman, Anne Bonney, who made Nassau their home port in the early Seventeen Hundreds when the Bahamas were known as The Republic of Pirates.

While de Marigny had a point, he was only partially correct. The white residents of the Bahamas were mostly descendants of the British settlers in North America who had been loyal to the Crown during the Revolutionary War. After Washington's victory at Yorktown in 1781, these settlers had moved south to the Bahamas, bringing slaves or other non-white household retainers with them. These old-line Bahamians had also been joined by freed or runaway slaves fleeing the American south after the civil war. And here in the Bahamas, the two groups, whites and non-whites, re-established themselves in much the same social relationship: servant and master.

De Marigny seemed at odds with the island. He was too slick, "too French," the Anglo-white people said in their braying colonial accents, and only became an English subject when Great Britain took over the partial administration rule of Mauritius from France in the 1930's. He drove around New Providence, the eighty-square mile island where Nassau was located, in a flashy new Lincoln imported from the United States. Nobody did malaise and nonchalance like a Frenchman, and most of the Anglo locals didn't care for it.

In stores, at the yacht clubs, at the bars of the Hotel George or the British Colonial he was always the most debonair man in the room. Often, before marrying Nancy Oakes, he had been found in the company of beautiful females imported from America or France.

De Marigny had also made a powerful enemy on the island: The Duke of Windsor. Exactly when the two men developed bad blood between them was unclear, but there was plenty of it. It probably began when they had first laid eyes on each other, shortly after Windsor's arrival in 1940. It continued with some perceived snubs by de Marigny aimed at the Duchess, followed by retaliatory snubs in which the royal couple avoided any social events planned by the Count. Then there was some ongoing petty stuff, one episode involving treatment of some Frenchmen in the Bahamas who were escapees from Devil's Island, another involving de Marigny refusing to sell a prized bottle of cognac to Windsor, and another involving de Marigny's desire to get a travel visa for a German friend, the application for which Windsor personally nixed. Eventually, the ex-King—or the "moth-eaten prince," as the New York *Mirror* now called him—had described de Marigny as, "an unscrupulous adventurer with an evil reputation for immoral conduct with young girls." Heaven forbid!

Thus, was it any surprise when the two American detectives, brought in specially by the Governor, took a meeting on arrival with the Duke and then quickly focused on de Marigny as their chief suspect, as if instructed to do so?

De Marigny's guilt thus agreed on, the next question centered on his motive.

The two Miami cops, pondering what they were hearing about de Marigny from the Duke, became excited. But not nearly so excited as when they heard about a remark the Count had made the morning the news of the murder spread through Nassau. "It's about time that somebody killed the old bastard," the Count had muttered to a local man who had informed him that Sir Harry had been murdered.

From that moment forward, Count Alfred de Marigny's goose was in the oven.

CHAPTER 5

If de Marigny's goose was cooking, it didn't take Melchen and Barker long to turn up the heat, pulling the lapdog local cops along with them. That next afternoon, my fourth in Nassau, Melchen and Barker and a couple of Nassau cops leaned on the Count.

"Why don't you come clean and tell us what you know about the murder?" Melchen asked.

"That won't take long. I don't know anything," de Marigny answered. "Why would I?"

"Where were you between two thirty and five that morning?" Barker asked.

"Same as you," said de Marigny. "Home. Asleep."

One of the cops noticed that the hair on the Count's hands looked singed. De Marigny was asked to roll up his shirt sleeves. When he did, it was apparent that the hair on his arms was singed, too. The Count had a little pointed beard of the type that some local dolls considered cute. That, too, was singed at the point. Considering the bonfire that had taken place in the deceased's bedroom, this discovery was not good news for Monsieur de Marigny.

Barker pressed on. Would de Marigny be kind enough to explain how he had come to get his hands, arms, and beard singed? And while he was at it, Barker pressed, would he oblige with an alibi that could be corroborated for his whereabouts during the vital time span?

De Marigny favored the cops with what one of them later described as a sneer. But he would be glad to explain everything so long as they were so damned insistent.

This, then, was how De Marigny explained:

Early on the evening before the murder, de Marigny, not having been invited to Sir Harry's going-away party, was busy preparing to throw a small party of his own. He and a house guest of his, a thirtyish French marquis by the name of Maxim Louis Georges de Visdelou-Guimbeau, a friend from their native island in the Indian Ocean, were going to have a quiet dinner for a few friends. Two of the guests were ladies who were married to Englishmen training in Nassau for the Royal Air Force.

De Marigny's bride, the former Nancy Oakes, was conveniently in the United States with her mother and the other Oakes children.

The party was to be held on the lawn behind the de Marigny cottage. The Count went out and lit four hurricane lamps, and in the process, he singed the point of his beard and the hair on the backs of both hands and both forearms, since he was ambidextrous. But after de Marigny lit the lamps, he noticed the mosquitoes were particularly bad, and decided to entertain indoors.

Three guests remained after midnight: the two wives of the R.A.F. pilots and a gorgeous young blonde usherette at the local Savoy movie theater, Betty Roberts. The Count's friend, the Marquis, was attentive to Miss Roberts who, any way one looked at her, was well worth attention.

The five of them sat around talking and drinking until ten minutes after one. The fliers' wives said they must be going. De

Marigny offered to drive them home. The Count had three cars: a Lincoln, a Packard, and a Chevrolet. He pulled the rumbling Chevy out of a garage behind the cottage and drove off with the fliers' wives, conveniently leaving Miss Roberts and the Marquis alone in the cottage. The aviators' wives were staying a ten-minute drive from de Marigny's cottage and not far from Westbourne.

The Count had to pass Westbourne to take them to where they were staying. As they passed the Oakes property, de Marigny recalled to the Miami police, that the two ladies noticed that the estate was in total darkness.

De Marigny dropped the women at their door, then returned to his cottage, getting back around one thirty or a little later, some twenty or twenty-five minutes after he had left.

The Marquis and the blonde were nowhere in sight.

The Marquis owned a black male Persian cat, a very intelligent animal that the Count had given him. The cat was roaming around, having left the Marquis' rooms, where it usually stayed either of its own accord or by request. The Count retired to his own apartment, but the cat followed him in and began to annoy him. It continued to annoy him, and at three in the morning Count knocked on the door of the Marquis' apartment and asked him to keep the cat.

Miss Roberts was still there. Marquis explained that he had been taking a little nap and that he was now going to drive the girl back to the hotel where she was staying.

De Marigny didn't bat a Gallic eyelash. "Use the Chevrolet," said the Count. "It's in the driveway."

That was about three thirty, de Marigny recounted. The Marquis returned shortly after four o'clock, He left the Chevy at the cottage, alongside a door leading to a flight of stairs to the second floor.

"That's what happened. That's where I was when Sir Harry was murdered," de Marigny concluded to the police. "And the Marquis will back me up."

But the Marquis didn't back him up. Not entirely, anyway.

The Marquis didn't mention the blonde at all in accounting for the previous night. He said that Miss Roberts had departed by herself. He added that de Marigny had come in around one thirty, after taking the two ladies home, and that such had been the last he had seen of him until he saw him driving away in the Chevrolet around seven in the morning. Since the murder had been committed between two thirty and five o'clock, that left de Marigny with no alibi whatever for the important window of time during which Sir Harry was snuffed.

That, plus the fact that his hands, forearms, and beard were singed, looked very bad.

There are four different kinds or degrees of burned hair. In the first stage, the hair becomes more brilliant than usual. This is caused by the natural oils coming to the surface. The second stage causes the hair to curl. In the third stage, the tip of the hair, thinner than the base, crusts while the part near the base becomes either curly or brilliant. The fourth stage, caused by intense heat, causes the hair to burn, leaving only a carbon ash.

The Count had all four degrees on his beard, hands, and forearms. By way of buttressing his claim that his singed hair had come about under noncriminal circumstances, de Marigny said he could have acquired some of the burns while working in scalding water at his chicken farm.

The cops pointed out that that would hardly account for the burned hair on his beard. The Count seemed stumped, but only for a moment. Brightening up, he said he had had the Van Dyke singed by a barber. Just what barber? And when had the singeing been done to the beard?

De Marigny couldn't recall. He was a busy man, he said immodestly, what with one thing and another, and he didn't keep an account of visits to barbers.

A local cop, a Lieutenant John Douglas, was assigned to keep an eye on the Count, twenty-four hours a day, from this point on.

The Miami cops came right back at de Marigny. They had talked with every barber in Nassau and none of the tonsorial artists recalled putting fire to the Count's cute beard.

"This begins to look pretty bad for you," said Captain Melchen, with a heavy gift of understatement. The Count was in no position to argue.

In the meantime, Westbourne was crawling with police. The place had dried out from the storm and the July humidity that came with it. Captain Barker got busy dusting for fingerprints in and around the murder chamber on the second floor.

De Marigny was told to sit in a drawing room on the first floor to await the attention of the cops. Lieutenant Douglas, the man assigned to keep an eye on the Count, was sticking with it except, of course, to make an occasional trip to a bathroom and get the Count an occasional glass of water in deference to the heat. The Count had to go to the bathroom occasionally, too. Aside from that, the two men chatted amiably.

There was a large five-paneled folding Chinese screen in the murder chamber, the kind used occasionally as a room divider. Sir Harry had frequently used this screen close to his bed to protect himself from drafts. It had been put to such use the night of the murder. The screen, made of paper with a floral design, was smudged with smoke from the fire in the room.

In the afternoon, Captain Barker escorted de Marigny to a different room on the second floor and fingerprinted him. Soon thereafter, the Captain announced that a print of the little finger of de Marigny's right hand had been found on the screen in Sir Harry's room.

The Captain explained that he had removed the print from the screen by means of applying a strip of Scotch tape to it and then transferring the print from the Scotch tape to a piece of portable surface. After removing the print from the screen, the Captain further explained, he circled with a pencil the approximate spot from which he had removed the print. Things were beginning to heat up for de Marigny, who was now a lot less talkative.

The two Miami detectives openly put forth the notion that de Marigny had murdered his father-in-law. He could have done it, they decided, out of sheer hatred for Sir Harry, or he could have done it to protect his interests in the Oakes estate before Sir Harry completed legal steps to make sure that his son-in-law would never get a pound of his money.

The Miami cops could not find the murder weapon, a somewhat important piece of evidence in a homicide. They were not even certain what kind of lethal instrument had been used. But it didn't matter. The Miami boys went before Police Superintendent Colonel Erskine-Lindop and quickly placed their findings before him.

Colonel Erskine-Lindop ordered Count Marie Alfred Fouquereaux de Marigny arrested for the murder of Sir Harry Oakes in the name of His Majesty, the King, the Duke of Windsor's stammering younger brother. Confronted with the accumulated evidence against him, de Marigny made a simple statement to the police.

"I didn't do it," he said.

Nonetheless, de Marigny was locked up tight in Nassau's rickety and fetid old jail. His cell was something out of the Middle Ages: narrow and low-ceilinged, it barely contained him. There was a heavy door, an overhead light that remained on at all hours, a camp cot with a short mattress, and a dented aluminum bucket to serve as a toilet. At this moment, the Count finally understood the gravity of his situation.

There were only two ways out of his current predicament: the charges against him could be dismissed, or he could be led to the gallows to be executed for murdering his father-in-law.

Nancy Oakes returned to Nassau. The police permitted her to talk with her husband in the jailhouse. He convinced her of his innocence. It was a good thing, for she was the last person of influence who could help him.

CHAPTER 6

There was no way in the world that I could ever have stayed away from the Oakes case.

My career as a writer began as a reporter. In 1920 *The Boston Post* hire me at the age of seventeen. On a Monday, they gave me a note pad, the phone numbers of the city editors, and sent me out on the street. They told me to make my own luck or I'd be fired by Friday. I started out on police beats. On my first week, I covered four crimes. All four got into print. So, I could stay for a second week. I kept getting in print so *The Boston Post* gave me a regular job. It was official: I was a crime reporter, the youngest one in the city. At the time, *The Boston Post* was a big deal, the largest selling paper in New England.

I dealt with the lowest of the low in a metropolis which in the 1920's had no limits to the depth if its depravity. I covered rapes and stabbings, bank robberies and street stick-ups. Bootlegging. Domestic assaults. Arsons. Bank frauds. Gambling dens. Prostitution. Opium deaths in Chinatown. Mob stuff. Shootings. Strangulations. There was no shortage of horrible stuff that people wanted to read about. Some days I hit a half dozen or more crime scenes. Almost everyone I talked to had a weapon. Almost everywhere I went there was blood.

The homicides were a category by themselves. I wasn't a young man prone to violence, as many were, particularly in the years after the Great War. But I had no trouble writing about violence. My editors and I discovered I even had a certain flare for it. My bosses started to give me the most horrifying murders in the tenements and on the streets of Boston and I gave them juicy reports. It worked out just fine. I was happy to have a job. I was sending money home to help my parents, who lived in Trenton, New Jersey. They were immigrants from Dunfermline, Scotland, an old gray town perched on the high ground three miles above the northern shore of the Firth of Forth.

In the late summer of 1920, *The Boston Post* bumped me up a few notches and threw me and an army of other writers on a major case: a then-unknown North End swindler named Carlo Pietro Giovanni Guglielmo Tebaldo Ponzi, better known locally as Charles Ponzi. The Ponzi case was bigger than any one reporter or any team of reporters. But I was on it. I did good work. I got some interviews, including with the swindler himself. I kept getting promoted and kept getting my by-line in print. I covered Charlie Ponzi through his trial and conviction.

At the time, *The Boston Post* was the top selling daily paper in New England, but the Hearst papers were now competing with it. Newsstands were war zones. Some papers hired thugs to throw acid on the competing papers or to slash the tires of the competitors' trucks or rough up each other's reporters. Prohibition was in full force but one never would have known it from the newsrooms or the speakeasies, which were everywhere. I would arrive at work at six in the morning and wrap up my day's assignments at two p.m. After that, a lot of us would pile into taxis and go see the Red Sox at Fenway or the Braves at Braves Field. All of us had hip flasks. Some of us had guns. I had a pair of brass knuckles, just in case. We had a lot of friends. We had a lot of enemies. Sometimes the distinction between the two was vague. There were fights and brawls. It was rough work but exhilarating, a good time to be alive and a young man in what seemed like a limitless America.

I liked my peers. I even liked my work, gory as it sometimes was. Who would have known? Before I even knew it had happened, I had become a "fact crime" reporter.

I was offered better jobs with better money in other cities. I left The Boston *Post* in 1923 at the age of twenty. I signed on with for a stint in Philadelphia on the *Public Ledger* and then *The Philadelphia North American.*

I made a fair bit of money, invested in the booming stock market and made more money. Taxes were low. I was restless. I wanted to see the world. I got a passport, quit my reporting job in Philly and travelled to Europe by steamship. I arrived in Paris on May 3, 1924, my twenty-first birthday. I enjoyed that city in its jazz age best and stayed in a sleazy walk-up residence on the rue Delambre. There was an inspired Japanese artist named Foujita who lived upstairs and an American style bar across the street called the Dingo that was open all night. I went to the Louvre, sat in the cafes, heard great music and was witness to several great fistfights at La Coupole and outside of Le Select.

After six weeks, I moved along to Florence and then Rome. There, Mussolini had just dropped all pretense of democracy and set up a legal dictatorship. I saw the right monuments and left Rome quickly, not being terribly fond of the obnoxious Fascists marching up and down the streets.

When I returned to America, I found a small apartment on Riverside Drive in New York City. It was the heyday of newspapers in the big city. I had a solid reputation from Boston and Philadelphia. I had no trouble finding a job. I took some night courses at Columbia

University to improve myself and I went to work on a scurrilous late afternoon newspaper named *The New York Evening Graphic*.

The *Graphic* was a world and a story unto itself.

The New York Evening Graphic was a tabloid newspaper founded in 1924 by Bernarr MacFadden. MacFadden was a rival and mortal enemy of William Randolph Hearst. He was a bodybuilder and a publisher, an odd mix. The paper was new, young; an upstart. It elevated breathless sensationalized reporting into an art form and defined tabloid journalism in its day. It was even printed on pink paper so that the yokels who paid a nickel for it could spot it quickly on the newsstands.

The *Graphic* had the nerve to display the slogan, "Nothing But the Truth" up on the front page each day beneath the paper's flag, but then its writers and editors proceeded to never let the truth get in the way of a lurid story. Suffice it to say that I covered crime, organized and disorganized, for that paper, interspersed with the occasional society sex scandal. If the two elements were in the same story, so much the better, and I had a front pager.

I should admit: it was a disgraceful venture. I loved working there. I savored it, every rotten disreputable moment of it.

Sometimes the lurid stories needed no embellishment. When I first arrived, the editors at the *Graphic* baptized me by giving me an underworld beat. I filed stories but, by agreement, I never used my real name. The newspaper was careful. I phoned in everything and only my editor knew who I was. We used the by-line of Allen West so that I wouldn't turn up in the Hudson some morning wearing concrete boots.

By 1928 I was regularly on the front page. I had a hell of an undercover story.

A mobster named Joey Noe had opened the Hub Social Club, a small hole-in-the-wall speakeasy in the Bronx. He hired a guy named Fleigenheimer to work as a bouncer and enforcer. Fleigenheimer had a reputation for beating people to a pulp within sixty seconds. I went up to the Bronx one night with a couple of other thirsty reporters and we witnessed this.

It wasn't pretty but it was impressive.

Eventually, Noe made his strong-arm guy a partner, maybe out of self-defense. Noe and Fleigenheimer soon opened more joints up and down Gun Hill Road and Bruckner Boulevard. To avoid the high delivery costs of beer, they bought their own trucks. A brewery owner on Utica Avenue in Brooklyn supplied their beer. Fleigenheimer rode shotgun to protect the beer trucks from other gangs.

There were two Manzi brothers, Calabrians, who already controlled an operation in the Bronx. They refused to buy suds from Noe and Fleigenheimer. The Manzi brothers didn't know what they were dealing with. Eventually, the elder brother, Johnny Manzi, agreed to cooperate, but younger brother Louie balked. One night the Noe-Fleigenheimer gang grabbed him off the street. They beat with a tie iron and hung him by his thumbs from a meat hook. Then they wrapped his eyes in a tight bandage smeared with discharge from a gonorrhea infection. His family ransomed him for fifty grand. Shortly after his release, he went blind. From then on, the Noe-Fleigenheimer gang met little opposition as they expanded to control the beer supply for the entire Bronx.

No arrests. No prosecution. The cops were all on the pad.

I wrote this one up in the *Graphic*. We couldn't print the part about the gonorrhea or the cops being on the pad. The notion of the crooked corrupt cop was unknown to the American middle class at the time. It was ironic. There was a lot of made-up stuff that we could print and a lot of true stuff that we had to lay off.

But our audiences loved it, laughing and chortling as they moved their fingers and lips as the read along. The Noe-Fleigenheimer gang loved it, too, because it served as a warning for their ongoing 'customers.' I was now launched in the big city. And by that time Fleigenheimer was known as his tabloid name, Dutch Schultz.

Dutch sold a lot of papers for us. He also liked reading about himself. He made it known that the *Graphic* was his favorite daily. One time he sent over a thank you note with a case of Canadian Club.

With the end of Prohibition, Dutch Schultz sought illegal income elsewhere. His answer came in two forms: Otto Berman, and the Harlem numbers racket. The numbers racket required players to choose three numbers which were determined at the end of each day by the last three digits of the amount race track bettors placed on races at either Aqueduct or Belmont Racetrack.

Otto Berman, nicknamed "Abbadabba," was a middle-aged accounting whiz who aligned himself with Schultz. In a matter of seconds, Berman could mentally calculate the minimum amount of money Schultz would need to bet at the track at the last minute to alter the odds, thereby ensuring that he always controlled which numbers won. Berman would last longer than Noe and Fleigenheimer, by the way, as mob assassins caught up to them in 1931 and 1933, respectively.

The *Graphic* pioneered a new form of telling the news, influenced directly by a 'confession' magazine called *True Story*, which McFadden had also founded and which had produced for him a great fortune. The magazine devoted itself entirely to stories of human experiences told in the first person. As applied in the *Evening Graphic*, the account of a woman who had murdered her husband was to be written in a breathlessly frantic first-person voice.

The real-life suspect was to be interviewed in jail—anything was possible if a reporter spread around enough of his boss's ten-dollar bills at a detention facility—and her 'confession' was to be published under her own signature.

The headline over such a story might have been:

**I BUTCHERED MY HUSBAND
BECAUSE HE STANK
OF ANOTHER GIRL'S
TEN CENT PERFUME!**

While I worked there, the *Graphic*'s circulation rocketed to a million copies sold each day. They were a 'picture' newspaper before the *New York Daily News* and *The New York Mirror*. They, or I should say *we*, had pictures that no one else could get. We had these pictures that no one else had for one reason—these pictures didn't exist: the guys down in the press room had invented something called "the composograph."

The composograph created "photographs" of events which had never been photographed, such as Rudolph Valentino's corpse in

34

1926. That one sold so many papers that the next day they had a "photo" of Valentino's spirit being greeted in heaven by Enrico Caruso. The concept of a camera in Heaven didn't bother the *Graphic's* readers because, in all objectivity, they were morons and believed in such things. They seemed reassured that such things existed, bless them. Exploitative and mendacious, we were referred to as The PornoGraphic.

The other newspapers were irate with us. They hated us. They berated us. They blasted us while morning papers stole news from our evening editions. Eventually, the other tabloids swiped most of our techniques, except for *The New York Times* and the *Herald-Tribune* which were for better educated readers and were above such things.

We were a genuinely disreputable rag, but we had some fine young talent.

From the beginning, the paper featured a gossip column by a young guy not yet thirty years old named Walter Winchell. Another young guy named Ed Sullivan wrote a sports column entitled *Sport Whirl*. Later Sullivan wrote a show biz column called *Ed Sullivan Sees Broadway*.

There was another writer named Sam Fuller who worked for the *Graphic* as a one of the other crime reporters. As a young crime reporter with the *Graphic*, he was shown how-to by veteran crime reporter Rhea Gore, the wife of actor Walter Huston and the mother of John Huston. Fuller's first big "scoop" was when he became the first journalist to report the death of Jeanne Eagels, a movie and Broadway star who'd fallen victim to a narcotics habit that thrilled our readers.

Fuller was the American-born son of Russian-Jewish immigrants named Rabonovitch. They changed their surname to Fuller in tribute to a doctor named Sam Fuller who came to the U.S. on the Mayflower. Sam served as a rifleman in the U.S. 1st Infantry Division during World War II. Fuller saw action in North Africa, Sicily, Omaha Beach on D-Day, and then on through Europe to Czechoslovakia. He was awarded the Silver Star, Bronze Star, and Purple Heart. He later used many of his war experiences in Hollywood to write war and crime movies.

There was an artist named Ernie Bushmiller, the son of a Bronx bartender. Ernie started as a copy boy for the guys who drew the comics, but it turned out he was a brilliant artist. He had the soul of a comedian, the hands of a great artist and the instincts of a steely-eyed accountant. For the *Evening Graphic*, he created a successful comic strip titled *Mac the Manager*. Later Ernie made a ton of money creating and drawing the comic strip *Nancy*. God bless him, the strip would run for decades.

We also had a daily horse racing tout panel called "Asparagus Tipps" which selected the best wager of the day at any eastern track. It was usually provided by a weaselly little man named Irv Papp, who quietly arrived each day and drew the panel and left. But the actual pick was provided by an immense mobbed-up fat guy who was known only as Tony and who everyone sane was afraid of.

Winchell and Sullivan. Fuller and Bushmiller. I knew them professionally and they were friends. I knew Irv and Tony, too, but cut them some careful distance.

I hung around with the *Graphic* through the stock market crash of 1929 and into the 1930's. I married for the first time and lived with my wife, June, in Tudor City, just south of where they would eventually build the United Nations. By then I had moved on from the newspapers to writing and editing the major true crime magazines while picking up a book contract or two in the process.

Over those years, I drank too much and smoked like a chimney. But it went with the territory. I could be fussy and nervous and cantankerous. I frittered away my first marriage after eight years simply by ceasing to work on it or give it proper attention. On the way home from work, there were too many bars or earlier speakeasies.

In 1937, I got lucky. I was driving one night and a drunk ran a red light and smashed into the car I was driving. My right knee was shattered. I would never walk quite straight again, but would use a cane. I booked a cruise along the St. Lawrence River in Canada as part of my recovery, and on that cruise, not yet exactly divorced, I met a wonderful woman from a fine family of home builders in northern New Jersey.

She was engaged to someone else at the time. She told me so and showed me the ring when I sat down at her table to chat with her. "Is your fiancé on the ship?" I asked her.

"No."

"Well, that was damned careless of him," I said.

"I beg your pardon!"

"I'm going to marry you."

She, not yet exactly married, stared at me. "What do you do for a living?" she asked.

"I'm a true crime writer. Possibly the best in America."

"You think so, do you?"

"A lot of people think so."

"You're the most conceited man I've ever met in my life," she said. She stood up and left the table. Well, it was a start. I pursued. I turned up the heat of my charm. I made my case. When the ship returned to port, she returned the ring. We were married in Stamford, Connecticut, January 15, 1938, much to the grudging chagrin of her family who were devout Christians and not happy about a divorced man.

My new bride and I went to Hollywood in 1940. I sold some stories to the movie and radio people. Crime stuff. My new wife and I stayed at the St. James on Sunset. The skies were blue. Every day was a great day. I met producers, actors, directors and other writers. It's like that when you're on a roll.

I got to know some producers and film men. Joe Mankiewicz was a favorite, a college man and a class guy. Joe was doing well this year, too. He had just been nominated for *The Philadelphia Story* for the Academy Award for Best Picture in 1941. Now he was writing his own stuff and directing it, too. Joe had his themes, his topics. He liked the clash of aristocrat with commoner. That one always worked.

I got to know a man named Joe Schenk. Joe was a whip-smart Jewish Russian guy who built a carnival and amusement ride place call Palisades Park in New Jersey. You can see it from Manhattan. Joe later went into the film business and founded Vitagraph Studios. Vitagraph was a big deal twenty years ago.

He once spotted a cutie on one of his sets. He couldn't take his eyes off her. Her name was Norma Talmadge, a top young star with

Vitagraph. She has since had three husbands and still counting, but Joe was the first. In 1917, when he was married to Norma, they formed the Norma Talmadge Film Corporation, which made a lot of dough, even during the Depression. They divorced in 1934.

Schenck then built a home out in the desert. When I was in California with my second wife, Joe invited us out to his place and we stayed out in Palm Springs. He reminded me of Meir Lansky, and that's a compliment. Joe had learned how to behave like a gentleman.

Appearances were always important in Hollywood.

In 1933 Joe partnered with Darryl Zanuck to create Twentieth Century Pictures. The latter merged with Fox Film Corporation in 1935. As chairman of the new Twentieth Century Fox, he was one of the most powerful people in the business.

Then there was big trouble. Caught in a payoff scheme to buy peace with the militant unions, Joe was convicted of income tax evasion and spent time in prison before being granted a presidential pardon. Joe rarely granted interviews. I was honored when he granted me a long one in 1940 and *Liberty* Magazine prominently published it.

I had a producer friend downstairs, also, when I finally moved to 530 Park Avenue. His name was Mike Todd. He was crude, obnoxious, brutish, charmingly crooked and a fine friend. Mike had been producing stuff on Broadway since the thirties. He used to tell me how he had burned through a million dollars of other people's money before he was twenty-one. Twice.

Mike began his career in the construction business, where he made, and subsequently lost, his first fortune. He opened the College of Bricklaying of America, buying the materials to teach bricklaying on credit. The school was forced to close when the Bricklayers' Union did not view the college as an accepted place of study. Todd and his brother, Frank, next opened their own construction company. They served as contractors to Hollywood studios, soundproofing production stages during the transition from silent pictures to sound. Their company went belly-up when its financial backing failed in first year of the Depression. There went his second fortune.

But Mike was a stubborn son of a bitch.

During the big Century of Progress Exposition in Chicago ten years ago, Todd produced a girlie attraction called the *Flame Dance*. In this production, the best looking female dancers he could find were sent on stage to flaunt their stuff while a big band played music. As the number went along, gas jets on stage would burn off parts of the ladies' attire, leaving them looking naked. It was a dandy new variation on a strip tease, something that never goes out of style.

Mike hit a big-dollar bulls-eye with that one. The act was a big hit, all anyone could talk about at the Century of Progress. Mike moved his show to the Casino de Paree nightclub in New York City, over on West Fifty Fourth Street at Broadway. The Casino de Paree was a theater and restaurant known for its revues, dancing, and side shows. There were fire eaters and animal acts in addition to the pretty girls. Mike's timing was sagacious. His show opened just in time for the end of Prohibition.

Mike got his first taste of Broadway and then started to produce shows. He moved into the building I was in a few years before me. We'd say hello in the lobby and the elevator. We became friends.

Friends. From writing and entertainment, I had some interesting ones.

Enemies, too. From writing about some other people, I had some nasty ones. Most of them just said spell the name right and don't say I did something I didn't do. And they'd cut you a break.

But it didn't always work out that way.

In terms of my own professional success, it had taken me damned close to a quarter of a century, from scrounging a job in Boston in 1919 looking at corpses in tenement apartments to being a best-selling author living on Park Avenue in 1943 to being sent to cover a high-profile murder case in Nassau.

There were many reasons that my editors in New York chose me to cover the Sir Harry Oakes case. I was no stranger to crime, even the most brutal ones. I had been working crime beats for twenty-five years. I was also no stranger to some nasty people. I'd been roughed up and threatened. Loaded guns had been pointed at me by people who were ready to pull the trigger. It was part of the job.

I also had dealt with people of wealth and influence, some of whom had been born to it and others who had earned it. Added into the equation, I was also very skeptical about people who had been born with money. And I wasn't easily intimated. Not by anyone.

In terms of my being sent to Nassau on the Sir Harry Oakes case, let's face it: it was a perfect fit.

CHAPTER 7

The arrest of Alfred de Marigny did nothing to calm the island. To the contrary, it turned Nassau onto a sharper edge than it had already been on. One could feel a change on the streets. There was a new tension and it was heavily racial, even though de Marigny was white. There was also an additional presence of soldiers and police.

I asked questions and began to hear several accounts of the events that had marked 1942. Several white Bahamians told me that the black people had "gotten out of hand" and "had to be put back in their place." From the accounts that I was getting, the ungrateful black population had risen for no reason to bite the hands of the kindly wealthy people who fed them.

I wasn't any Marxist, but I wasn't buying that explanation. I went over to the local newspaper, *The Nassau Tribune*. I reviewed the front pages of the previous summer. There had been some "labor disturbances" involving work at the local airport. There were pictures of angry black crowds in the main streets being confronted by white policeman and white soldiers. Nowhere could I find an explanation of what had started the trouble.

I put the newspapers away. When I was alone with the front desk librarian, a white woman, I asked about the disturbances. She looked at me as if I had just arrived from outer space. "You're American?" she asked.

"I'm American," I said.

"Then don't come here and cause trouble," she said.

She got up and left. I knew better than to ask the man who replaced her at the desk.

I wandered back to the British Colonial Hotel, using my pocket handkerchief to mop the sweat from my forehead. It was already ninety-five degrees, judging by a thermometer on the front of a grocery store. The humidity matched.

I found my new best friend Felix, the taxi driver, at the hack stand near the hotel. "Busy?" I asked.

"Not for you, sir," he said.

I asked him to show me around the island.

"What do you want to see, sir?" he asked.

"How about you just drive me around?" I said. "We can chat."

"Yes, sir."

He held the door open to the rear seat of his richly dented '36 Hudson. I climbed in. He stepped around to the driver's side and started his engine.

"Where would you like to go?" he asked.

"Oh, show me the town. Then maybe some shoreline. Beaches. Ocean air, know what I mean? We can both cool off a little."

"Yes, sir. Very good, sir," he said.

He drove me around Nassau. He gave me the official tourist showcase. I listened patiently and quietly. He fed me the official lines for the tourists.

Finally, "May I ask you something, Felix?" I asked.

"Of course, sir."

"How does everyone feel about having the former King of England here as your Crown Governor?"

There was a pause.

"We are very proud of having the Duke and Duchess here, sir," he said.

His eyes were upon me via the rearview mirror. He turned off Bay Street and onto West Street.

I smiled. "Oh, come on," I finally said.

"We are *deeply* honored by the Duke's presence and leadership, sir," he said.

"Sure," I answered.

He looked back to the road and continued farther.

"Let's find some cooler air, Felix," I said. "Maybe the shoreline."

"Yes, sir."

Maybe the heat was pushing me forward, but there was a small protocol here that was uncomfortable for me. In my book, one man was as good as another.

"You don't need to call me, 'sir,' Felix," I said. "I'm an ordinary man, same as you. You might think I'm a wealthy American, and I've done okay. But my parents were immigrants from Scotland. My father was a potter and my first job was at age eleven bringing buckets of water to a bunch of nasty Italian laborers on a construction site in Trenton, New Jersey. I'd appreciate it if you'd call me by my first name. It's 'Alan.'"

He tried to suppress a smile, but wasn't able. I reached across the back of the front seat and offered a handshake. He accepted it.

"Thank you, Mr. Alan," he said, taking my suggestion halfway.

We passed the Fort Montagu Hotel. I noted an unusual presence of British soldiers in front of and around the building. A few minutes later we were on a sparsely populated beach road. Out of nowhere, a convoy of British army vehicles passed us, heading in the opposite direction. I counted seven vehicles, including a command Jeep at the front.

I grabbed the moment.

"What happened here last summer, Felix?" I asked. "Tell me. I'll keep it between us."

"What do you mean, Mr. Alan?"

"The demonstrations. The labor problems," I said. I pulled an American twenty-dollar bill from my wallet and passed it across to the front seat. He accepted it.

There was a long pause, then he unloaded.

"All right. I will tell you," he said.

There had been a construction project at the local airfield, the same one as where I had landed, the previous summer. Non-white Bahamian laborers had been employed at a stingy four shillings a day to fulfill a government contract to enlarge the landing strip. This way, newly minted warplanes from American factories could land. Some troublemaker leaked to the workers the information that dozens of white Americans working on the same job were being paid eighty shillings a day, twenty times the wage for a non-white worker.

For some reason, the exploited blacks took violent offence at being paid five percent of what white Americans were paid. They rioted.

"And," said Felix with a deep laugh, "it was a hell of a great riot, man."

The demonstrators overturned buses and threw rocks through windows on Bay Street. They set fire to cars. They smashed open the private liquor shops near the expensive whites-only hotels and they angrily drank themselves into an even greater and more uncontrolled fury.

A rambling seething mob closed in the seat of the government. White residents fled. Others, who couldn't get out of the Bay Street shopping district fast enough, pulled up the steps and stood nervously on their second-floor promenades with shotguns.

The rioters cleaned out the shops. They were armed with sharpened machetes, their onetime tools for clearing the underbrush at the expanded airfields.

They pillaged everything in sight. The rioting continued into a second day. The Duke of Windsor, making a rare decision, mobilized a garrison of British troops stationed at the Fort Montagu Hotel. These troops were ostensibly Windsor's private security detail, but they arrived in town in battle gear and with fixed bayonets. The white soldiers formed fighting squares and confronted the rampaging black mobs. The soldiers showed every intention of being anxious to spill some blood.

For several long hours, a stand-off existed on the streets. Then, toward evening, cooler heads prevailed. The demonstration ebbed and the rioters dispersed.

The disturbances had caused close to a million dollars of damage and financial losses for the merchants of Bay Street. But something even more valuable was lost also by the white power structure.

For generations, Bahamian blacks had apparently accepted a subservience based in part on their background as the descendants of freed slaves. But now, for the first time since the islands had first been settled, the social structure had been challenged. The British Army had restored surface order, but the island had not forgotten.

The Duke had put the arm on the Exchequer back in London and decreed that the laborers would now receive a whopping five shillings a day, plus a free lunch each day. Snarling, still at bayonet point, the airport laborers returned to work, hacking at stubborn underbrush all day in the blazing sun. They also got to keep everything that they had ripped out of the posh stores.

They had scored a victory—a lawless one, but a victory. The white power structure shuddered at the thought of the black mobs ever getting out of control again. It was common currency that one more good reason to riot, real or imagined, would set off the mobs once again.

Hence now when Count Alfred de Marigny was arrested, the Duke took what he felt was a wise precaution. He again had called out his garrison of soldiers and stationed them in town as peacekeepers. Nassau was essentially under martial law. The convoy of soldiers and armaments that had passed Felix and me on its way into the capital had been part of that armed reinforcement.

The afternoon was waning, but it was still plenty hot. I asked Felix if there was a place where we could get some ocean breeze and wait for the day to cool down.

"I know a place, Mr. Alan."

Felix drove me to a strip of beach which I guessed was ten miles west of Nassau. There were native kids playing on it and a few people swimming, some spear fishing, presumably for dinner. There was a small refreshment stand. Its owner knew Felix and waved to him. Felix returned the wave.

"Does your friend have cold drinks?" I asked.

"He does, Mr. Alan."

"Let's have some Cokes," I said. "I'm buying."

"How long do you plan to be in Nassau?" he asked as we walked toward the small wooden stand. It was shaded by a canvas awning and there were battered metal chairs.

"A few weeks," I said.

"And you'll be traveling around the island? Different places?"

"Probably."

"Then I wish to show you something, Mr. Alan," he said. "May I?"

"Of course."

Felix tapped my arm and pointed. We changed directions. "Come look," he said. "But do not touch. Or stand too close. Breathe lightly, Mr. Alan."

He beckoned me to a nearby grove of trees. I thought he was going to confide something to me about the case I was there to investigate. I was wrong. It started out as what seemed to be a horticultural tip, but turned into more.

Several of the trees were marked with red X's. Someone had come along and slashed them with crisscrossed strokes of paint. Felix led me to within fifty feet then held out his sturdy brown arm and halted my progress. Before us stood a row of trees, each maybe twenty to forty feet high. The shrubbery was pleasant enough to look at, a vibrant green, beachy in its way. Some were laden with tempting looking small greenish-yellow fruits that looked not unlike apples. The larger trees had reddish-greyish bark, small greenish-yellow flowers, and shiny green leaves. The leaves were finely serrated or toothed. The grove swept down to the shore.

"Manchineel trees," he said.

"So?"

"The fruit might tempt you," he said. "The red X's are your only warning. Do not eat the fruit. Do not touch it. You might want to rest your hand on the trunk, or touch a branch. Do not touch the tree trunk or any branches. Please, my good friend, do not stand under or even near the tree for any length of time whatsoever. Do not touch your eyes while near the tree. If you want to slowly but firmly back away from this tree, you would not find any argument from any botanist who has studied it."

"Poisonous?" I asked.

"Very. After all, it is rumored to have killed the famed explorer, Juan Ponce de Leon."

Others tress were marked with a painted red band a few feet above the ground. A few of the younger trees were unmarked.

"In the old days, Bahamians were known to poison the water supply of their enemies with Manchineel leaves. Spanish explorer Juan Ponce de León was struck by an arrow that had been poisoned with manchineel sap during battle with the Calusa in Florida, He died thereafter. Ever since, the Spanish speaking people on the islands call it *la manzanilla de la muerte*," Felix said. "The apple of death. Or the *arbol de la muerte*. The tree of death."

"I guess what was bad for Ponce de Leon would be equally bad for me," I said.

"Very so, Mr. Alan," he said.

"Thank you for showing me, Felix," I said. "You're a smart young man. How do you know so much?"

"I read a lot."

"It shows. Good for you."

"Thank you, sir."

He led me back to the refreshment stand. Felix introduced me to his friend, whose name was Andrew, a trim agile black man in his thirties. We sat indoors. There was a big lazy ceiling fan that circulated the air. It wasn't cool, but it was tolerable, a relief. There was a big red Coca-Cola cooler packed with ice where Andrew kept his stock. We drank iced soft drinks. We each ate a cold homemade chicken patty, which Andrew sold to us.

Felix and I chatted. He seemed to relax more. I edged to things I had already seen about which I wanted to know more.

"All those soldiers that we saw," I asked. "Are they all billeted at the Hotel Montagu?"

"No, Mr. Alan. There's a British fort out of town. It's off limits to people of color. I can't show you."

"I don't need to see the fort," I said. "I'm curious about all the troops at the hotel."

"Those are guards."

"What are they guarding?" I asked.

"The guards are for the Duke of Windsor. They're billeted at the Fort Montagu, Mr. Alan."

"Doesn't the Duke have his own official residence?" I asked.

"The Duke fears that the Germans will come to Nassau to kidnap him."

"They're just going to march in and grab him?" I scoffed.

"That's what His Highness thinks," Felix said.

"I think his Highness might be flattering himself," I said.

Felix laughed. "U-boats, Mr. Alan," he said, adding some seriousness. He indicated the water beyond the refreshment stand. "Our fishermen see periscopes all the time. My brother was on a skiff the other Tuesday. Saw a hefty sixteen feet of pipe watching from half a knot, about a mile off-shore. Dangerous out there, Mr. Alan. Never know."

"Ah," I said. "I see."

Everyone knew about the Duchess of Windsor's extreme terror over airplanes. In April 1916, the Duchess had met her first husband, Earl Winfield Spencer, Jr., a U.S. Navy aviator, at Pensacola, Florida, while visiting a cousin. It was at this time that Wallis Simpson, the future Duchess, witnessed two airplane crashes two weeks apart, resulting in a lifelong fear of flying. According to current island lore, the Duke had a similarly visceral dislike of submerging in a submarine.

Further scuttlebutt that was all over the smarter circles but which never appeared in any newspaper had it that the one-time king of England and his twice-divorced wife may have been guilty of collaborating with the Nazis in the summer of 1940. This would have been as a prelude to Hitler returning him to the throne as a "puppet king" in the wake of the expected German victory over the British in 1940 or 1941. Like many other sure bets of history, this one had never happened, either.

"Why would they kidnap the Duke?" I asked.

"Hess, Mr. Alan. That's what the Duke thinks. The Duke thinks the Germans would abduct him, take him to Germany and ransom him for Rudolf Hess."

I was quiet as I listened.

Hess, Hitler's batty Deputy Fuhrer, had swiped a Messerschmitt and landed in Scotland in May of 1941. Hess was still in the United Kingdom, still locked up in the tower of London, if rumors could be believed.

47

I angled. "That's an actual piece of intelligence or it's what Windsor thinks?" I asked.

"It's what we hear," Felix said. He made a gesture with his hand imitating idle chatter and loose talk, loose jaws. His brown eyes danced. Then he raised a finger and put it to his lips in the best I-never-said-it-and-don't-repeat-it gesture.

"So, it's what your friends who work in good places overhear?" I said.

A pause, then, "Very correct, Mr. Alan," he said. "That could be so."

I smiled in response. "Well, I can see how a former king might not take too kindly to the prospect of being captured," I said, "much less the rigors of a long submarine trip. It would make all those cockroaches and termites in the governor's mansion look good in comparison, wouldn't it?"

Felix gave me a long chuckle. "Yes, Mr. Alan. Very good and very correct, my friend."

When the Duke and Duchess of Windsor had first arrived in Nassau, their first concern had been the state of their own would-be residence, named Government House. The building dated back at least a hundred years, was rickety and infested with termites, mice and roaches the size of small birds. The furnishings were faded and shabby, dating from the Victorian era. Windows were cracked, broken and grimy. After a week of swatting insects, The Duke and Duchess hired exterminators, carpenters, and painters. Then they fled.

The Duke wished to take an extended vacation to a cattle ranch he owned in Alberta, Canada. But the British government in London, busy ducking Hitler's bombs and preparing for a possible land invasion, was chilly to the Duke's wishes. Departure for Canada would create the appearance that the royal couple were abandoning the Bahamas within weeks of accepting the post. The Duke and Duchess ultimately accepted the hospitality of Harry Oakes, who hosted the royal couple at his mansion, Westbourne, in Nassau.

Felix and I finished our refreshments. He brought me back to the hotel late in the afternoon, just when the heat of the day was starting to ebb. The martial presence had been intensified. It gave me the creeps. The Bahamas struck me as a type of small time fascist state. I took a brief walk around, wondering what else I might uncover.

Even this late in the afternoon, I saw black women dispensing flowers and homemade foods to grocers. The black people seemed to all know each other, their own little colonial and subjugated community. Near the shops, down a little from the administrative buildings, there was a brigade of chauffeurs, every one of them black because white men didn't take these jobs. They wore sharply starched white uniforms, complete with jackets and ties in the eighty-five-degree heat. The drivers waited patiently on the right side of a fleet of new Fords, Chryslers and Buicks while their white employers—mostly British, American, Canadian and a few South African—shopped, chatted in the shade or dined. They stood in the crushing sunlight as their employers dined on cold meats and sipped iced drinks under ceiling fans.

I arrived back at my hotel. My room was stuffy so I went back to the lobby. Then that evening, I sat in the dining room, nursed a couple of drinks and picked at a dinner. I missed my wife and daughter. I missed New York, even with the wartime blackouts. I missed the United States.

But work was work. There was a murder to cover. I was already starting to ask myself some odd questions about why everyone seemed so anxious to walk the little Frenchman up to the gallows and hang him.

I soon learned that I was not the only one entertaining such seditious thoughts.

CHAPTER 8

Seven scorching days after arrival in the Bahamas, I filed my first dispatch to my editors in New York. I wrote about the arrest of Alfred de Marigny and his protestations of innocence. I wrote about Sir Harry and who he had been, and how he had obtained the position in life that he had been in when he was murdered.

Despite speculation on how and why he might have been murdered, I tried to stay away from those aspects of the crime. For the time being, I left the speculation for other scribblers. There were plenty of them who seized the opportunity.

That morning, Lady Oakes had departed to the United States, taking her husband's body for burial. The plan was to fly to Palm Beach and then board a train to Maine to return Harry to his boyhood home town. But therein lay an odd complication and a new set of rumors sweeping Nassau. Apparently, once the private aircraft carrying the body to the United States was aloft, a call came from Nassau demanding that the aircraft return. The pilot complied. Thereupon, according to the local gossips, it had been returned to Deputy Commissioner Pemberton and subjected to a new autopsy, or maybe even an initial autopsy. Or something. Then it had been shipped north again.

This bizarre turn-around was done in the utmost secrecy. No one "unofficial" was supposed to know. I only knew because I'd overheard a couple of housekeepers talking in the hotel lobby. Apparently, some aircraft workers had seen the corpse return—they recognized the expensive casket and knew from the weight of it that it still had an inhabitant—and chattered to friends. Other eyes and ears on the street had seen the strange cargo arrive at the morgue a second time and then take off again.

What the hell was this all about? Wasn't the case strange enough already without medical examiners treating a corpse like a yo-yo? I started to ask a few questions. No one who knew much wanted to say much. Nothing unusual there.

Then there was an even more macabre wrinkle: Nassau had already ordered, and received, a special sturdy hemp rope to be used for the hanging of de Marigny once he was convicted. I'd never seen a place in such a rush to put a man on the gallows. Why not just skip the trial completely?

That evening, a thirst was upon me that matched my curiosity and my distaste for much that was going on. I had already chosen my favorite watering hole, Dirty Dick's.

I took off for a stroll to the bar. I followed some narrow passageways and twisting alleys between the buildings that led to less salubrious dwellings behind the pretty pastel-colored facades that fronted Bay Street. There was a scent of garbage and sewage that was distinctive of Nassau, as it was foul and spoiled and yet had the hint of rotting jasmine or roses. The stench was strong by the entrances to these side conduits. This being mid-summer, I still had plenty of daylight.

I looked down a few alleys. More local charm.

Gulls picked at trash, rats roamed in the late sunlight, and scavenging black crabs clicked along jagged off-kilter flagstones. I found the contrast between the exteriors of Bay Street and what lay just a few paces beyond it more than a little ironic. I'd covered crime for twenty-five years. It was my beat. I was under no more illusions here than anywhere else. Most of Nassau's fortunes and more notable families had dark histories, pasts that were as questionable as their finances. No one chose to live here. This was a place of convenience as much as a flag of convenience on the stern of a suspicious ship. Much like the robber-barons of the United States of the 1890's, only time could sanctify some wealth.

At the far eastern end of Bay Street, within blue-and-silver reflections and the fresh salty scent of the harbor, there was a statue of Queen Victoria, dour and unforgiving as ever. Beyond there stood the Bahamian Assembly building with its white pillars, pink-washed walls, and green shutters. Before it was an open area with a massive sprawling cotton tree that cast welcome shade over a tidy town square.

This tree stood in the administrative center of the capital. On one side was the Post Office; on another, Fire Brigade headquarters and the Central Police Station—green wooden verandah, white shutters, Victorian police lamp with blue glass. Next to this stood the Supreme Court, another impressive old building, but smaller than the Assembly House.

Beyond that, mercifully, there was the hotel that hosted Dirty Dick's. I ducked under a maroon canopy that led to the street. I walked in, parched. Never mind one drink, I was ready for a triple.

The air was cooler, thanks to a series of fans, including a big one sweeping the ceiling. The walls were white. The beams across the ceiling were dark wood. There was a sea of round tables and chairs of the same dark finish as the beams. There were maybe two dozen people drinking, mostly men. Those seated at the tables were white. The staff was black. A black gentleman with a sweaty brow and a formal dark red coat gave me a bow as I entered.

"Good evening, sir," he said in a lilting accent.

"Thank you," I said. "To you, also."

He seemed surprised, pleased, by the response.

"Welcome back," he said.

I gave him an appreciative nod.

Heads turned toward me. I went to the bar. Conveniently, there was a space toward the near end. There was a crisp mirror behind the bar. Where I stood, there was also a glass case where the best Cuban and Dominican cigars were on display. I reached to my own pocket, found a pack of Chesterfields and my lighter. I lit up.

A barman appeared in front of me. His service jacket bore the name, Charles, green stitched lettering on deep burgundy.

"Rum and Coke," I said. "A mighty big one. On ice."

"Double shot of rum, sir?" he asked.

"Definitely. Thank you," I said. "You're a mind reader."

He gave me a wide smile. "Right away, sir," he said.

He went to work. His selected a double-sized glass. His hand came to rest above a bottle of Bacardi's. Cuba's best. He made my drink and presented it to me.

"I haven't had enough money changed yet. American currency is okay?" I asked.

He said it was. I put two dollars on the bar. "Keep it," I said.

He banked it fast into a jar.

I sipped. I sipped a second time and felt the excitement of the cold bubbling Coke and the double shot of booze hitting my throat and stomach. Then I heard a voice from the other end of the bar.

"Alan!" someone barked. "Hey! Alan!"

I had to lean forward. I looked to my left. I saw a stout ruddy-faced silver-haired gentleman in a tropical seersucker suit. White shirt, blue and red regimental tie. He flashed me a wide familiar smile. My friend withdrew from the gentlemen with whom he'd been speaking and walked toward me, cutting behind the other drinkers.

"Alan! I'll be damned!" he said. "I should have known you'd be here!"

Raymond Schindler. Ray was one of the greatest detectives in the world, and probably the most famous. He lumbered toward me, his hand outstretched. He stood around six feet but looked bigger: a jolly genial giant of a man.

"Ray! Well, well!" I said, happy to see a friend, particularly this one in this place.

He pumped my hand and it turned into a clasp of the elbow. He was a smooth, ruddy man in his early sixties, graying hair, with an impressive paunch from the better life,

"Come over here and sit down," he said, jerking his head toward an empty table. "Let me get away from these bores and poseurs," he said in lowered tones. "I want to know *exactly* why you're here."

"I might ask you the same," I answered.

Ray already had me by the arm and was guiding me along, dismissing his previous partners with a curt wave. "That's what bars are for, aren't they?" he asked.

I grabbed my hard-earned drink and followed.

"It's one of their functions," I allowed. "And I think it's obvious why were both here."

"Of course, of course," he said. "But the Devil is in the details, isn't it? Come. Talk."

We went to a table toward the front. It was in a corner so we could watch the door and the saloon activity at the same time. Mr. Schindler put a five-pound note on the table. Our glasses were not allowed to be empty, the ice not allowed to melt. Someone turned on a radio. Bing Crosby warbled.

Ray and I had known each other since New York in the 1920's. We had worked on some of the same cases, he as a private detective, I as a reporter, particularly when I was with the *Evening Graphic.* We were kindred souls: men who had created our destinies in the tumult of the America of the first three and a half decades of the Twentieth Century.

Ray had grown up poor in a one-horse town in Oswego County in upper New York State near Lake Ontario and the Canadian border. He hadn't had much of a formal education, same as I, but had set out early to escape the rural doldrums and make his fortune. He had worked as a typewriter salesman, then went to California as a prospector when he was about twenty, ironically much like Harry Oakes. Ray had made himself some luck, struck a modest amount of gold, and for five years operated a small gold mine in the northern part of the state. He did okay, mined the gold out, but never amassed the fortune that he was hoping for or that Harry Oakes had eventually attained. Ray sold out his mining interests and went to San Francisco, arriving on April 19, 1906, the day after the big quake.

Nosing around for a job, he struck up a friendship with William J. Burns, who owned a private eye agency in San Francisco. He went to work for Billy Burns personally, investigating insurance claims to see if they were quake damage, fire damage, or bookkeeper lightning.

Four years later, Burns sent him to New York. He opened a chain of Burns offices, and was quickly in the headlines, cracking cases that the cops couldn't solve. There was the murder of a ten-year-old girl named Marie Smith in Asbury Park, New Jersey. The year was 1911 and it was Raymond's first capital case. The cops claimed a Negro named Black Diamond, a local troublemaker, had assaulted and killed her. Ray wasn't buying it: he didn't like official stories any more than I did. The cops were incompetent. Ray nailed a drifter in a rooming house and got a confession.

The next year, he cracked the Arthur Warren Waite murder case. Waite was a bad apple dentist in New York City who shared his luxury apartment on Riverside Drive with his wife's retired parents. His father-in-law, John Peck, had built up a sizeable fortune after a career as a pharmacist in the Middle West. Waite longed to inherit as much of the money as possible.

Neither parent seemed in poor health. It occurred to Waite to give nature a helping hand by causing Peck to ingest harmful bacteria which would trigger an entirely convincing onset of a serious disease, followed by a severe physical decline and ultimate death, without anyone being held responsible.

Waite succeeded with his wife's mother, then couldn't quite knock off the older man. He boosted the poison to arsenic instead of ordinary bacteria. Schindler got involved and Waite eventually traded his dentist's chair for the electric one at Sing Sing.

The newspapers made Raymond a hero, which he was, not to Dr. Waite but to everyone else.

In 1912, Ray left Burns and opened his own agency, R.C. Schindler and Company at 7 West 44th Street. Now, two decades later, Raymond Schindler was the country's leading private sleuth. His specialties were jewel theft and high-society blackmail, but he would entertain any case that was legal. He celebrated his own fame as much as the tabloids did. He liked posh places and smart people. He made much money and spent oodles of it. His principal client these days was Anna Gould, daughter of the notorious robber baron Jay Gould. Schindler currently lived on the Gould estate in a New York suburb. His residence was a guest cottage that was so lavish that it had its own bowling alley and swimming pool.

Now, here in Nassau, Raymond Schindler was still savoring the peak of his career. He was a New York personality wherever he went. He was a party giver and a club guy. He had a reserved table at the "21 Club" and The Stork Club, hosted by our charming old bootlegger pal from Oklahoma, Sherman Billingsly. He was president of the Adventurers Club of New York, the president of the International Investigators, a fellow of the American Geological Society, the British Detectives Association and the American Polar Society. It went on forever. Or it could have.

We travelled in different circles, the truth of it was, even though each of us was often on the clean edge of some dirty doings. And yet we were close friends. Our friendship fed off each other in the best possible way.

By the time 1943 had arrived, after a quarter century, I had seen close-up maybe a thousand cases. I was a beer sort of guy. Ray, on the other hand, was a champagne sort of guy, even back during Prohibition. He worked on big cases. Maybe fifteen or twenty a year.

So here was where we helped each other, the reason we often talked by phone. I had the street experience. There were few things I hadn't seen, including many that I wished I hadn't. Ray would phone me with a case and tell me about it and ask if it rang any bells, where I thought a suspect might be lurking, what threads of investigation to follow. I'd tell him what I felt. He would consider my ideas. Sometimes my tips and theories helped him, sometimes they didn't. But he was always grateful.

When he was close to resolving an investigation, he'd get back to me. I'd get the inside story. In return, I'd write it up. I'd stick to the facts, but I made sure Ray looked good because, after all, he was a pal and he deserved to look good.

He was also a well-read man. He liked books and he liked writers. He always wanted to talk about books, the theatre and sports. He wanted to know who I knew, who I'd read, if I'd been to the big Dempsey or Joe Louis fight or if I'd been out to the Polo Grounds to watch Hubbell and Bill Terry or to Yankee Stadium to see Ruth or Joe DiMaggio. We talked each other's language.

There was one final aspect to it, strange as it sounds: mentor, protégé. Ray was twenty years old than I, almost exactly. I was the kid reporter, and he was the experienced teacher, or at least that's how it had started out. Now perhaps we were equals, but the two decades of age difference still loomed between us. I always listened and was ready to learn. He was like an uncle with consistently solid advice.

Now, here in Nassau Town, at our small round table in Dirty Dick's, he pushed back his jacket sleeve from a powerful forearm and wrist. He lifted his perspiring glass with an equally sweaty hand.

"Here's to you, Alan," he said. "Congratulations, my young friend."

I laughed. "For what? Arriving here safely?"

"I keep an eye on you. You're a bigshot best-selling author," he said.

I was flattered. "I got lucky," I said.

"We all hit luck from time to time. Good luck, bad luck. It's like being dealt cards. It's how you play things after your hand is dealt. *Passport To Treason*. That's the name of your book, right?"

"It is," he said. As usual, Ray was correct. I'd spent 1942 writing a non-fiction expose on Nazi German espionage in the United States leading up to the current world war. The book had been published early this year, 1943. Then the great voice of American news radio, Walter Winchell, my old acquaintance from The *Evening*

Graphic, had picked up the book and ballyhooed it on his radio show as a headline.

"A book every good American should read!" he breathlessly proclaimed.

Within a week, the stores were sold out. The publisher, McBride & Company, was falling over itself to reprint, and signed me fast to write another big spy exposé. Meanwhile, *Passport to Treason* hit the *New York Times* Best Seller list in May.

It was gratifying. It was more than gratifying. I'd gone from a magazine editor-writer to a best-selling author overnight. Overnight, that is, after many years of pounding true crime beats in Trenton, Boston, Philadelphia and New York.

"You deserve the success," he said. "Got another one in the pipeline?"

"Damned right," I said.

"What's it called?"

"It doesn't have a title yet."

"What's it about? Criminals? Spies? Tell all."

"It's about our other enemy, the Imperial Japanese. Spy rings in the United States leading up to the war. From San Francisco to New York."

"Ah! Incendiary," he said with a wink. "Sounds good. Should do well with our crazy wartime mentality."

"I've got a few nibbles from Hollywood already," I said.

"You know some producers out there, don't you?" he asked.

"A few. I wrote and narrated a radio show on NBC a few years ago. A series called *Wanted: Armed and Dangerous!* True crime. Criminals at large. I was the radio voice. It was produced by a man named Aaron Fairstein."

"Ah! I know Aaron," Schindler said. "Are you two still friends?"

"Very much so," I said.

"Yes, yes, I now recall. Well, listen, Alan, when the dice are hot, the dice are hot," he said, draining his glass. "Keep rolling them." His eyes left me for a moment and he surveyed the room.

He lowered his voice. "Those two men over there," he said, indicating with his eyes two white men in the opposite corner, "work for Governor Christie. Security people. Very unofficial. Dumb as mules but equally stubborn. That's what you get down here in the inbred tropics. It's okay, you can glance."

I turned and looked toward the bar, catching a view at the same time.

"I've had my antenna up ever since I arrived," Schindler said. "I can honestly tell you that I feel as welcome here in Nassau as a good island-wide outbreak of bubonic plague." He laughed.

"Sorry about that, Ray," I said.

"Ah," he said, dismissing it. "I'm used to it. They've got a salt and pepper team following me, also," Schindler said. "The colored one is outside in a green Buick. The white guy is down at the second table with two women. They don't think I spotted them yet, but they followed me from the airport yesterday. Now that they've seen me with you, you might have a tail, also. Or we can stay together and they can follow us both at once."

"We'll see," I said.

"Look at those security people again when you can, Alan," he said. "Look at their shoes."

I stole a glance. "Okay. So?" I said.

"Police shoes. Standard issue for the Bahamian police. Even the flatfoots out there conducting traffic have the same footwear. That's how dumb they are. They don't even realize that I can pick out the undercover people by glancing at their feet." He paused. "Now, you can, too. Cheers," he said, lifting a refreshed drink.

"Cheers," I said, reciprocating with the drink.

"On the street, they work teams of five, two at a time. The overall direction seems to come from a mulatto thug in a farm-stand truck, as if I'm not supposed to notice. Each one has a sun visor turned down on the passenger side so they can spot each other. I'm not supposed to spot these either, I suppose. Keep your eyes open, Alan. If you make yourself unpopular enough, you'll draw a team or two, also. I assume you're here on the Oakes case," he said.

"Correct."

"Who sent you?"

"*True* Magazine. Fawcett Publications," I said. "Not a literary journal like *The American Mercury* which I also work for, but they have a solid checkbook and it pays the rent."

He nodded. He knew them. Everyone did. *True* was a man's magazine. Action, adventure, crime and sanitized pictures of wholesome girlies in peril. It was hot on the newsstands and popular in barber shops. People also sent it to their soldiers overseas.

"At the end of the day, what else matters?" he asked. Schindler's eyes found me again. "So how long have you been down here in Nassau?" he asked. "When did you arrive?"

"More than a week ago. Seems like a month."

"Have you had your eyes open?"

"It would be dangerous not to, wouldn't it?"

"What do you think?" he asked. "Bring me up to date. And for God's sake keep your dulcet voice down in this place."

"I think there are a lot of loose pieces with the case against Alfred de Marigny," I began. "You know as well as I do, a murder case, any major crime, has its own logic or even a logical strain of illogic. I don't see it here. Not yet."

"The money angle," Ray said. "The potential inheritance? There's a story that Oakes was going to cut him off, or already did."

"Sure," I said. "But there's still Lady Oakes and Nancy and a bunch of sibling, so the wealth isn't going to flow through that cleanly."

"Tell me more."

"I've done a little pencil and paperwork," I said. "Not with the official versions, but with what people are saying. If the Count gave a true summary of his movements the night of the crime, he would have had to be a magician to transport himself from his cottage to Westbourne to commit the crime."

"He could be lying."

"He could also be telling the truth. There are other problems, too. Is the Count the type of fellow to slug and burn Sir Harry, then stick around to sprinkle him with feathers, with Sir Harry's good friend Harold Christie snoring in the next room? I can't picture it."

"Money will drive many men to extremes. And we know the Count likes money."

"For whatever else his faults are," I said, "and he has plenty, nothing de Marigny's past indicates that de Marigny is a violent man. Far from it. And, come on, Ray, what about the feathers, anyway? That feather business was strictly dark-of-the-moon stuff. De Marigny is a light-of-the-moon character, whatever else you might think of him."

"Valid points," Schindler said. He laughed.

"Further, why are they so fast to order a noose and build a case against him? Did you hear about that? They've already ordered a rope to hang the man."

"I heard. What do you think of those Miami gumshoes that His Highness the Duke of Windsor hired?"

"Not much."

"Keep talking."

"In my opinion, these Miami dicks are a couple of burned out hacks. If they were ever any good as cops, they don't seem to be flashing any brilliance these days. They arrived without fingerprint equipment, did you hear that?"

"I heard. Anything else?"

"About the cops? Sure. Miami has one of the most corrupt departments in the country. It's a Mafia town and seven eights of the department are probably on the pad."

"And the crime itself?"

"I'm not convinced Sir Harry was killed in his bed. He may have been killed elsewhere and the body was moved. Don't know. Then a fire was set to cover the crime, but the killer failed to set an efficient fire. Forget about that part for now. Harry was a big man. De Marigny hit him four times, then moved the body by himself? I'm not able to envision that, either. So, who helped him? His wife? Servants? Harold Christie? It's preposterous, Ray. There's too much here that doesn't fit."

Schindler's head tiled back and he laughed. "That's what I always liked about you, Alan. You could smell the bull crap a mile away."

"Let's just say the stench is pretty strong here," I said. "Now, you talk. Why are you here? I don't know you to be travelling pro bono in wartime."

"I don't," he said. "Why would I?"

Just then, the decibel level in the bar dropped by half. Ray and I looked around to see what had caused it. Bing Crosby still crooned from the radio, but something had changed the room tone and even the atmospheric pressure.

It didn't take long to spot the reason. Two men, one big and hefty the other small and wiry, had come through the door from the outside. Everyone else in the bar seemed to know who they were. They sauntered past us, gave us a long look as if to suggest that they didn't like the fact that they didn't recognize us. But they kept going.

They were in tropical suits and walked with their arms folded behind their backs. The wiry one walked a few steps in front of his partner. I knew plainclothes security people when I saw them and these were them. Whose was another question.

The wiry one wore a yellow tie and a straw boater. His suit jacket was soaked. He had slightly tinted glasses and a sharp face like a weasel, dark eyes and an unbending expression. His partner was half a head taller in a canvas pith helmet. He wore the map of Ireland. He had a broad open face with some of the small broken veins of a man who drank heavily. His gaze was locked on me. His face looked like ten pounds of corned beef floating in beer. The two of them exuded menace, each in their own way. They were as subtle as a couple of deep belches.

They did a brief tour of the place. Almost imperceptibly, the small one gave a short nod to one of the cops that Ray had indicated at the table near the bar. The cop gave a little gesture back. No words were spoken.

I glanced at their footwear. Police shoes. No surprise.

They shot us another glance when they were on the way out. Then they were gone.

"It's wartime," I said to Ray.

"It's always wartime in the colonies," Ray answered. "Be careful in the Bahamas Alan. Everything you say, everything you hear, everything you see, chances are someone's watching."

Another drink arrived for each of us. Ray leaned forward. He lowered his voice yet again, keeping beneath the din of the room so that only I could hear him.

"When Nancy Oakes was in the United States," he said, "to take her husband to his burial in Maine, a mutual friend came to my office. Dr. Paul Zahl. He's a New York physician and very friendly with Nancy. They travel in the same social sets. Know him?"

"Too wealthy for my circles," I said.

"Nancy Oakes de Marigny is in a tough squeeze," Schindler said. "The girl loved her father and she loves her husband. One of her loves is charged with murdering the other. She can't believe that her husband is guilty of the murder, or that he even had the slightest knowledge of it. So Paul Zahl came to see me. He asked me to get into the case."

Schindler was a natural recommendation, considering the society in which Nancy Oakes moved.

"Alan, I'd been reading about the murder in the papers," Schindler said thoughtfully. "I didn't jump at the proposition offered by Dr. Zahl on behalf of the slain man's daughter. It's another country, another justice system, another system of power and wealth lurking beneath the surface. This is a sunny place for shady people, the Bahamas. From the ex-King, who's a long way away from being the smartest member of a particularly stupid royal family, right down to the colored kids selling funny cigarettes down at the far end of Bay Street. And if you don't like what you see here in Nassau, you should get a gander at what goes down on the other islands. You've got colored men out there that are barely civilized. The grandsons of slaves, living on islands which have no electricity or running water, much less indoor plumbing. So first, I told Zahl, I'd have to get a letter from Nancy de Marigny saying that if, while investigating the case, I find her husband guilty instead of innocent, I have permission to turn the results of my investigation over to the Crown, via Nassau authorities. Dr. Zahl flew to Nassau and returned with a suitable letter. Then the question of fee was discussed. I come at a high price, everyone knows that. Nancy de Marigny has the money to afford me plus a lot more. Meanwhile, I'd gone to the Pacific Coast on another case. My brother phoned me in California, I suspended the West Coast investigation and flew here. I arrived yesterday and met with Nancy."

"So, you're working for Nancy?"

"Let me tell you what she told me, Alan. Those two Miami clowns Barker and Melchen cornered the widow a few hours after her husband was buried. It was up in Maine. They flew up there just to lean on her, from what I can see. They summarized the murder for her, their opinion. They claimed an intruder came onto the Oakes estate, picked up a sharp stick or object from the outdoors, came into Harry's bedroom and attacked him. Then the intruder poured some flammable liquid on him, maybe kerosene, maybe insecticide, and set him on fire. Then they claim Harry woke up screaming, rose up and tried to fight back. The Chinese screen got knocked onto the intruder, who grabbed it, then Harry was overcome by flames, settled back onto his bed, roasted and died. And the fire was relit."

"By the Frenchman all by himself? That doesn't work."

"That's their case. The cops claim de Marigny's fingerprints were on the screen."

"If that's even true, who knows how and when the fingerprints got there?" I asked. "De Marigny was Harry's son-in-law. He had been to Westbourne before."

"Exactly," Ray said. "Nancy also said that Barker and Melchen's explanation of the crime was thoroughly unconvincing: a halfwit Punch and Judy show."

"And what about Harold Christie sleeping in the next room?" I asked. "He didn't hear anything?"

Ray's eyes went to his drink. He swirled it in his glass. He looked back up at me.

"Christie's an immensely powerful man here, Alan," he said. "Be careful when you stroll in that direction."

I was taken aback by his change of tone. I was about to follow up his warning with a question, but he continued too quickly.

"Miami," he sniffed. "I was in Miami in 1929. I had to visit a police station to interview a potential client. The police officers, the detectives, they all knew me, of course, thanks to gentlemen like you, Alan, who write me up so graciously." He winked. "I arrived there by taxi but they gave me a motorcycle escort to the main train station. It was a terrifying ride." He paused. "They were drunk. All drunk. My driver and the motorcycle escort. It seemed that they were all buddies with some bootleggers. A bunch of busybody revenue agents had just seized several trucks full of booze. They'd turned over half of it to the cops who were going to give it back to the rum runners. But the mob guys are generous souls, as you know, and take great pleasure in helping working men. They'd left ten cases in the police headquarters and the boys had been sampling it. Never mind whether real police work was being done. Between us, Alan, the fact that these two dicks are brass in Miami doesn't impress me goddam one bit, even if it impresses the featherbrained Crown Governor. In fact, just the opposite! Cheers."

Ray lifted his glass and we drank to the thought. Then he leaned back and seemed to study me.

"What are you doing tomorrow, Alan?" he asked.

"Hanging around hot and sweaty Nassau to see what develops," I said.

"Alan, let me ask you something. Do you know my friend, Joe Cook?

"The vaudeville entertainer?" I asked.

"The one and only," Schindler said.

"I know who he is. Everyone does. I don't know him personally."

Schindler had many glittery friends. Cook was just one of scores. Joe Cook, who'd been born out in the heartland somewhere under the name of Joe Lopez, had risen to the highest levels of vaudeville, headlining at New York's famed Palace Theatre. He later conquered Broadway and then radio. In the 1920s and 1930s, when he'd played the most prestigious houses from New York to San Francisco plus the sweaty midwestern metropolises in between, Cook was one of America's most popular entertainers.

I had seen Joe Cook perform in New York many times. Joe's talents were endless. He could ride a unicycle, juggle Indian clubs and skip across a tightrope while telling hilarious stories that made audiences howl with laughter. My friend Walter Winchell once noted in his Broadway column, that "Joe Cook is certainly one of the musical theatre's three geniuses. I can't at the moment think of the other two."

I knew from my pal Mike Todd that Joe had recently made a couple of movies. I also knew he had been ill and his performances had been curtailed.

"Joe lives out in New Jersey," Schindler said. "Lake Hopatcong. When we get off this lousy sand bar and back to civilization," Schindler said, "we'll make a Sunday date and drive out. Bring your wife and daughter. We call Joe's house 'Sleepless Hollow,' mostly for the celebrities and the parties. The place is gag-infested. You'll see."

"How can a house be gag-infested?"

"Joe has a three-hole golf course. On hole two, you tee off onto a clear fairway, but the ball rebounds back at you. Joe camouflaged a boulder with green paint. The last green is a trip to duffer's heaven: the green is a funnel. No matter where your ball lands it rolls into the cup. Conditions inside Joe's mansion are similarly cock-eyed," Ray continued. "He employs old vaudeville friends who've fallen on hard times. He's got a Swedish maid who's a midget. A butler who's a contortionist. A chauffeur who's an acrobat. You always keep your eyes open."

We shared the laughter. Heads turned and watched us from the other side of the room.

"Why are you mentioning this?" I asked. "What's it got to do with the Bahamas?"

"Everything." Ray leaned forward. His low tone of voice went even lower. "Why don't you come along with me while I nose around and ask some questions. Just be in the background. Keep your eyes and ears open. I could use the extra set of both. What do you say?"

"Work with you?"

"Accompany me. Observe. I like the way you think."

"May I write about what I see?'

"Within limits. Someday, of course, everything. For now, we'll work it out."

"I'm game," I said.

We shook. I was flattered, working with the great one. But I was no fool. Ray liked to have a publicist as well as a witness. It was a deal that worked well in both directions.

"Listen," Ray said as we split the bill and stood up to leave. "I'm working for Nancy. But let me be clear. My job is not to find the killer. My job is to keep her husband's neck out of that noose that they've already tied for him."

I waited a moment.

"Think he's innocent?" I asked.

"Ha! What a question, Alan. I *know* he's innocent. But cancelling that date with the hangman? *That* is another story!"

CHAPTER 9

With de Marigny arrested, people seemed willing to talk. A complex portrait emerged of the dead man.

Harry Oakes was not, as many people thought, an Englishman. He was an American from Sangerville, Maine, the son of a surveyor. Harry's professional career was pluck-and-luck stuff in the Horatio Alger tradition with one exception. The Alger heroes who climbed from the bottom to the top, snagging a pretty woman during the ascent, were tough and sometimes rough but never nasty. Oakes, on the other hand, bore a resemblance to the storied bachelor who was despondent because he didn't have a daughter to throw out into a raging snowstorm.

As Oakes grew into his teens he decided that Maine was not for him. He didn't like potatoes or lobster and he wasn't fond of hunting or fishing. He saw a possible escape through a sound education at Bowdoin College, where he earned expenses by playing semipro baseball and waiting on tables. He graduated in 1896 at the age of twenty-one. Like everyone else in the civilized world who could read or hear, he had become interested in the fortunes that were being made by prospectors for gold in the Klondike. He kissed Maine goodbye and set to blaze a trail north, to a land that made Maine in the winter look like a summer resort.

He encountered everything the Klondike and Alaska had to offer except gold. The dogs pulling his supply sled died in the white wilderness and Oakes had to snowshoe it for uncounted days. His feet froze. He lost his moneybag. Men with less moxie cracked up under tests far less severe, but Oakes emerged from the crucible with flinty eyes and a jutting jaw. He had hit the North too late to get his share of the shiny stuff but by God, he would find it someplace else. He was young and the world was wide.

The scuttlebutt around the camps was that the Philippines were loaded and just pining for smart diggers. He bummed his way to San Francisco, looking and smelling like a fugitive from a garbage dump. He shipped to Manila as a galley cook. As in Alaska, he arrived too late. Next stop: West Africa. It was the same story there; the pay dirt fields had already been staked out.

Harry Oakes was twenty-eight when, in 1903, he showed up in Australia, still on the prowl for the yellow stuff. But he found something else. In Sydney, where he took odd jobs to meet expenses, he stayed at a boardinghouse where a pretty girl who sat across the groaning board began to put him off his feed. He wondered why. He came to the realization that, for the first time in his life, the little guy with the bow and arrow had shot him straight through the heart.

The girl, who was almost ten years younger than Oakes, was an attractive doll named Eunice McIntyre. She worked in a jewelry store. She was gentle and sweet. Caught up in the mysterious attraction of opposites, the stony, barrel-chested adventurer enchanted her.

But Oakes didn't have the cash to tie the knot. For the first time in his life, the lad from Maine found himself riddled by indecision. He wanted to marry Eunice McIntyre and he wanted to lay hands on a quick fortune in gold. He couldn't have both, for there wasn't any gold in Australia. At least, not for him.

His boarding house bill began to pile up, and he couldn't find a job anywhere in Sydney. Oakes had a lumberman's appetite. The woman who ran the boardinghouse, sensing that he would eventually eat her into insolvency, lowered the boom on him. He would either pay up, she informed him, or get the old heave-ho.

Miss McIntyre paid up for him. Moreover, she lent him money for passage back to America. "I'll never forget you for this, Eunice," he assured her. "When I make a strike, I'll come back and marry you."

For several years after leaving Australia, Oakes followed his nose around the world. In 1911, when he was as far as ever from the end of the rainbow, he got wind of gold deposits in northern Ontario, near Porcupine Lake. He was in Nevada at the time, broke as usual. He bummed his way to the Middle West, then struck north toward his destination. He was riding in a rattling passenger train in Ontario, bound for Porcupine Lake, with no money and no ticket. When the conductor came through and asked for his ticket, Oakes went through the motions of searching his pockets for it.

"Well, what do you know about that?" he said. "I seem to have lost it."

That was no dandruff out of the conductor's hair. The passenger could pay cash. But the passenger didn't have any cash. The conductor studied Oakes with all the enthusiasm of a loan shark studying questionable collateral, left the car, and returned with two brakemen. The train came to a stop and the man who one day was to be knighted by the King of England was tossed to hell off.

Oakes stood in the Ontario wilderness watching the train disappearing into the distance. He walked many miles to the nearest settlement, a place called Kirkland Lake. He gave the landlady of a boardinghouse there a song and dance, moved in, then went out on the town to rustle up something, anything.

He fell into conversations with some locals. He heard tales about gold thought to be in the vicinity. Oakes rubbed his chin. By God, maybe this was it. He went into the local hardware store and began a pitch to the proprietor to let him have some digging equipment on credit. The proprietor, a large and powerful man, tossed Oakes out the door, the future baronet's second heave-ho in two days.

The proprietor of the local laundry, a Chinese immigrant bearing the celebrated moniker of Lee, happened to be passing as Oakes flew into the street. He helped Oakes to his feet and inquired as to the nature of the difficulty. The Asian gentleman was fascinated by Oakes' recital of the long string of events leading up to the tossola. He offered to grubstake Oakes.

Oakes accepted.

On the shores of Kirkland Lake in 1912, Oakes struck gold. Not just gold, but one of the great mother lodes of North America. He established a mining company, and almost overnight, Harry Oakes was transformed from a hobo into a man worth more than three hundred thousand dollars. He sold his holdings, pocketed his cash, and then promptly did three things.

First, he went to the Chinese man who had grubstaked him, Mr. Lee, and paid him off in full. Then Oakes asked him what it was he would like to have more than anything else. Mr. Lee, for some obscure reason, had all his life dearly wished to own a movie theatre.

Oakes may have been somewhat startled to hear of this unusual ambition, but he didn't let that stand in his way. He ordered construction begun at once, and as soon as the theatre was finished he made a present of it, free and clear, to his benefactor.

Second, out of spite, he built a hardware store right next to that of the man who had so enthusiastically thrown him out into the fresh air, and made a policy of selling everything below cost. In about three months his enemy was out of business.

Third, he looked up the conductor who had tossed him off the train and put him on a pension for life. By the Oakes reasoning, if this conductor had not had him bounced off the train at that point, he would have ridden past the town where he struck his first gold.

With his grudge settled and his debts paid, Oakes went on the prowl for another and bigger strike. Soon the lightning struck again. He found gold in another Canadian spot, christened the mine the Lake Shore, and, almost before he realized it, was a multimillionaire.

Lake Shore Mines soon became the second largest gold mine in the world. Now, in 1923, at the age of forty-eight, Harry Oakes lit out for Australia. In Sydney, he headed straight for Eunice McIntyre, the girl who had, two decades before, given him enough money to get out of the boardinghouse, out of town, and out of the country. He had corresponded with her all that time. In storybook fashion, she had believed in him and waited for him. They were married.

As a wedding present, Oakes presented his wife with a half million-dollar mansion on the Canadian side of Niagara Falls. But one address, even though it was a mansion, was not enough for Harry Oakes. He built a house in Newport and another in Palm Beach, and began to circulate among the wealthy elites. He learned to sip tea with the little finger of his right hand stiffly perpendicular, to carry on a conversation without swearing, and to give his seat to a lady. At heart, he was still a roughneck, but he was a most acceptable gentleman in circles where money was more important than anything else, for by this time he was worth several million dollars.

By 1935, after he had been married for twelve years, Harry Oakes, sixty years old, had sired five children: two daughters, of whom Nancy was the elder, and three sons, all younger. Although Oakes, everything considered, was a loving father, he was especially devoted to his eldest child, Nancy.

Now, with millions piling upon millions from the gold mine, with a devoted wife and a fine family, plus the home in Canada and two in the United States, Harry Oakes decided to go to England. There he purchased a magnificent town house in London, a country estate, and a hunting lodge in Scotland. He began to make lavish gifts to English charities. Then in June of 1937, when he was sixty-two, he was created a baronet on the King's Birthday Honors List. Thus, the onetime boy from the backwoods of Maine became Sir Harry Oakes.

Early in 1938, Sir Harry received a visitor at his town house in London.

The caller was a dark eyed, moonfaced man of middle years by the name of Harold Christie. Christie, by this time a highly successful real-estate operator in the Bahamas, boasted that he could accommodate a land buyer with anything from a lot to an island. This meeting between Oakes and Christie was to be the beginning of a fine and lucrative friendship.

It was real estate that Christie had come to see Sir Harry about. Real estate and taxes.

The Second World War was already looming. Income taxes in Britain were becoming increasingly tough and were likely to become even tougher. Sir Harry's income was about three million dollars a year and as a British subject, he was wide open to taxes that would confiscate practically all of it. Sir Harry had perhaps fifty million dollars scattered here and there around the globe by this time, but he still turned purple every time he thought of the amount of dough he was forking over every year to the Chancellor of the Exchequer.

"Why not come to Nassau, become a resident, and take advantage of the practically nonexistent tax on large incomes that we have there?" Christie suggested.

Sir Harry blinked. "Really?" he asked.

"Really!" Harold Christie said.

Sir Harry was more than interested.

Christie, ever the shrewd businessman, had just the property to sell: a twenty-bedroom estate once owned by Maxine Elliott, the noted American actress. Brother Christie could let Sir Harry have the place for a song: say the equivalent of five hundred thousand dollars. Sir Harry and Lady Oakes took off for Nassau by steamship to look the place over.

They were enchanted by it, and bought it for cash. That was in 1939.

Once in Nassau, Sir Harry and Lady Oakes quickly became socialites in a very society- minded neck of the world. They tossed lavish parties, with buckets of champagne and tubs of caviar. Sir Harry's belligerent attitude, however, had not diminished with the years, even if his manners had improved. One night he went into the British Colonial Hotel, Nassau's largest, and became incensed at the headwaiter because the headwaiter—new and not familiar with Sir Harry's little ways—seated the Oakes party at an inferior table.

Now Sir Harry, according to Lady Oakes, did something that many men have wished they could do to even a score. He made a telephone call to New York next morning to the Munson Steamship Company, the owners of the hotel. He closed a deal for the purchase of the hotel for one million dollars in cash. That night he went back to the hotel, deliberately late so that the best tables were already taken, and ran into the same headwaiter.

Sir Harry pointed to a choice table. "Seat me there!" he said.

"But that table is occupied, Sir Harry," said the waiter.

"So what?" said Sir Harry. "Throw those people out."

The headwaiter said he couldn't do that.

"No?" said Oakes. "Well, I bought this damned place this morning and you're fired!"

The longer Sir Harry Oakes lived in Nassau, the better he liked the place. Although he made occasional trips out of the country, he spent as much time as possible at Westbourne, even in the hot summer months. All the while he was engaging in various business enterprises, mostly real estate, with Harold Christie. Christie, rising in power and importance, became one of the governors of the Bahamas. Eventually the two men—Sir Harry with his tremendous wealth and Christie with his official position and general know-how—were, between them, practically running the islands.

Then along came a major quirk in history.

Edward VIII was King of the United Kingdom and the Dominions of the British Empire, and Emperor of India, from January 20, 1936 until his abdication on December 11 of the same year. He was the eldest son of George V and Mary of Teck. He became king on his father's death in early 1936. However, he had never shown much fondness for royal protocol. Months into his reign, he caused a constitutional crisis by proposing marriage to Wallis Simpson, already his mistress, a strong-willed American from Baltimore who had divorced her first husband and was seeking a divorce from her second.

The prime ministers of the United Kingdom and the Dominions opposed the marriage, arguing that a divorced woman with two living ex-husbands was politically and socially unacceptable as a prospective queen consort. Additionally, such a marriage would have conflicted with Edward's status as the titular head of the Church of England, which at the time disapproved of remarriage after divorce if a former spouse was still alive.

Edward knew that the British government, led by Prime Minister Stanley Baldwin, would resign if the marriage went ahead, which could have forced a general election and would ruin his status as a politically neutral constitutional monarch. When it became apparent that he could not marry Wallis and remain on the throne, Edward abdicated.

He was succeeded by his younger brother, George VI, a frail youth with a severe speech impediment who appeared not up for the role history was about to cast upon him.

After his abdication, the former Edward VIII was created Duke of Windsor. He married Wallis in France on June third, 1937, after her second divorce became final. Later that year, the couple toured Germany.

During the Second World War, he was at first stationed with the British Military Mission to France but, after private accusations that he held Nazi sympathies, he was appointed Governor of the Bahamas. Thus, the exiled Duke and Duchess of Windsor arrived in Nassau on August 17, 1940.

Local officials met them, along with an honor guard of local police, starchily resplendent in pith helmets and tunics. The ex-King wore a khaki uniform and peaked military cap. He looked uncomfortable in the soaking humidity and scorching heat. The Duchess wore a light linen dress in a floral pattern and smiled easily. She was also, like her husband, sweating profusely. The reception was warm, however, in every way.

As was usually the case in the realms of power and politics, appearances deceived. Most Bahamians felt the Duke was there voluntarily. He was not. He was there privately kicking and screaming. The Duke had referred privately to the posting in the Bahamas as "third rate." But the couple was seen as the victims of official snootiness on the part of the Crown. He had given up his kingdom for the woman he loved. That was the official story line, believed by a dismayingly large segment of the gullible public.

Inability to accept personal responsibility or make a cogent decision were themes excised from public discussion. He arrived as a handsome rebellious figure, thwarted from the possibility of becoming a dynamic monarch, an instrument of great influence and social change, all because of his devotion to the woman he loved.

Little could have been farther from the truth. Windsor was wealthy beyond reason, privileged beyond description. He was well known privately for ducking out on entertainment expenses such as dinner and parties, not paying private contractors who didn't dare pursue the money involved, and even slipping out of debts run up at casinos in France and Monte Carlo. He had been trained for a lifetime to accept the position of King and he had walked away from it in his mid-thirties, leaving his younger brother, who became George VI, sobbing on the shoulder of his mother, Queen Mary.

The truth of the matter: the royal couple were a royal pain to the royal family, and always would be. They had been assigned to a remote posting on the other side of the Atlantic because to have them on the loose in Europe would be to sabotage the allied war effort against Mussolini and Hitler. The Nassau assignment had been thrust upon the Duke by Winston Churchill who privately referred to the couple as "feckless and reckless."

Few members of the public at large knew at the time how much the Windsors had compromised themselves with their political leanings in the late 1930s. On a 1937 trip to Germany, Edward—then the Prince of Wales—had met with Hitler.

Hitler enthralled the Prince. Windsor wasn't an astute student of history, or anything else, but he had arrived at some uncomfortable conclusions over the events of the Twentieth Century. The Bolshevik Revolution of 1917, for example, had proven to the world that the monarchies of Europe were vulnerable to the downtrodden masses. The execution of the Russian royal family had put an exclamation point on it. Repercussions troubled the royal heads of London, who didn't take kindly to the notion of suffering the same fate as the royal family in France in the Seventeen Nineties.

The Russian revolution, and the spread of Bolshevism that it enabled, was a fear that the crowned heads of western Europe shared every day. There was a possible new order out there and it was ready to do away with The Duke and others like him. The unwashed masses were equally ready to dismantle their royal properties and holdings. The rise of the new Labor Party in England was further proof.

It would be generous to say that the Duke was not a towering intellect. And to him, Hitler was a refreshing antidote to the leftward march of history. Hitler was an anti-Communist. He was also a vicious anti-Semite. There again he scored points with the Duke. The most powerful merchant bankers of Europe were mostly Jewish families, clever scheming foreigners with hidden agendas, in the Duke's view. They too were parvenu and posed yet another threat to the established social and economic order. Hitler's glorified militarism and brand of Fascism was also a thrill for Windsor. The dual goals of blocking the scourge of communism and the spread of

Jewish influence, combined with raw military power, was electrifying.

Edward was joined in this fascination by his bride-to-be, Wallis Simpson, who was even more of a Fascist than he was. Wallis Simson was nominally from Baltimore, but resolutely southern in her ancestry, upbringing and attitudes.

"Southerners know how to treat colored people," was a pearl of wisdom she hissed to friends on frequent occasions. She was enthralled by Nazi goose-stepping, arrogance and posturing and said so publicly. The Nazis offered a system that claimed it uplifted the strong, where she included herself, against the undeserving weak, which meant non-whites and non-Christians in general.

In so many ways, she and Edward made a perfect couple. The Duke privately fostered a routinely dismissive attitude toward what he referred to as "the non-white" races. He considered people of color as shiftless, untrustworthy and inherently dishonest, well in keeping with the condescending upper class racial toxins of the day. It was but natural then for the Duke of Windsor and his wife to become friendly with Sir Harry when the Duke arrived to take over his dull chores as governor general of the Bahamas.

Sir Harry saw to it that the Duke's tenure in the Bahamas would be as merry as possible. There were some big balls at Westbourne during the Duke's residence there. His Royal Highness had a swell time except on those occasions when the Duchess, focusing a cold glare on her husband's tenth champagne refill, would say to him, using the boyhood name by which the family still addressed him, "That will be quite enough, David!"

Then at one of these parties at Westbourne, there appeared a tall, slim fellow in his middle thirties. When things had reached the high decibel level, Sir Harry pointed toward the fellow and inquired of Lady Oakes, "Who the hell's that?"

"I'm sure I don't know," said Lady Oakes. "I thought perhaps you knew."

"Never saw him before in my life," said Sir Harry. "He's spending an awful lot of time with Nancy. Find out who he is."

Nancy, seventeen now, heiress to more money than she would ever be able to count, and within a year of the age when she could marry without parental consent, had eyes filled with stars. Her friend, she told her mother, was Freddie or, to be more specific, Count Marie Alfred Fouquereaux de Marigny. Freddie was a charmer, no doubt about that. He was staying with friends in Nassau. She had been introduced to Freddie quite properly, she assured her mother, but just hadn't got around to introducing him to her parents.

Freddie was handsomely turned out and gave the impression of a lad who had a way with women, and knew it. When Lady Oakes passed this intelligence along to Sir Harry, the baronet was all for throwing the Count out. He would do it himself or he would have his security squad do it. But it would be done. Pronto.

Lady Oakes restrained him.

"All right," said Sir Harry, "but I'm looking the son-of-a-bitch up first thing in the morning."

What Sir Harry found out about Count Alfred de Marigny wasn't at all to his liking. He learned about the Count's two divorces and the hundred thousand dollars that his second wife had given him at the time her knot with him was untied.

Lady Oakes told her daughter about this. Nancy was unimpressed. "Your father never wants you to see that man again," said the mother. Nancy was still unimpressed. Nancy said she thought she would take a trip to New York to visit friends. She didn't expect to see the Count again, she told her mother. So, she left for New York. De Marigny followed her a couple of days later.

Sir Harry put detectives on the trail of the two. The dicks sniffed out their quarry too late: Nancy and de Marigny had left for California with a young married couple as chaperons. By the time the gumshoes got to California, the quartet had lit out for Mexico.

In Mexico City, Nancy ate some food that proved to be tainted. She came down with typhoid fever. She almost died. Upon her recovery, she and de Marigny went to New York. There, in January 1943, two days after Nancy's eighteenth birthday, she and de Marigny were married by a magistrate.

Not long after the marriage, Nancy de Marigny discovered that she was pregnant. She was not a robust girl and she was in an especially rundown condition after her siege of illness in Mexico.

Several doctors decided that if the pregnancy continued, her life might be endangered.

An immediate operation was recommended. The Count went to Florida with Nancy. She checked into the Good Samaritan Hospital in West Palm Beach. De Marigny took a room next to his wife's and decided, if he was in the hospital anyway, that he would have his tonsils removed.

The day after the Count had his operation, Sir Harry and Lady Oakes came over from Nassau to see their daughter. While Sir Harry was about it, he stopped into the next room to voice his opinion of the Count for knocking up his daughter right after her siege of typhoid.

It was far from flattering.

"And if you don't get out of this room, away from Nancy," declared Sir Harry in closing, "I'll pick you up and throw you to hell out, myself!"

The Count quietly got out. Burning up, he wrote a letter to Sydney Oakes, Sir Harry's eldest son, then only fifteen, a letter that Lady Oakes was one day to describe as "the most diabolical letter a man could write to a child of fifteen about his parents."

While Sir Harry was in West Palm Beach he consulted his attorney. The lawyer quietly drew up a new will which cut off all his children from any inheritance until they reached thirty years of age.

Somehow or other, de Marigny got wind of the change and figured he and Nancy had been cut out of Harry's financial picture. It didn't take a genius to arrive at that conclusion.

De Marigny stormed into the lawyer's office and demanded to know precisely what was up. The lawyer wouldn't tell him, but De Marigny did find out something else. His second wife, upon hearing that de Marigny was interested in Nancy Oakes, had written a letter to Sir Harry and Lady Oakes, putting a hex, a nix and a chilly blast on the Count. Naturally, the letter dwelt on the Count's habit of squandering large sums of money. All this hardly improved Sir Harry's feeling toward de Marigny.

Nancy's illness, however, somehow changed conditions, at least for a time. In love with her husband, she made her parents promise that they would let bygones be bygones if she regained her health. They promised. Nancy got better. And so, after a time, everybody returned to Nassau together, one big, almost happy highly dysfunctional family.

One day Sir Harry had a couple of whiskeys in him at a Nassau social event. He asked the Count what he could do except chase girls with money. The Count said he had a chicken farm. It was five miles from Westbourne. Soon thereafter, he and Nancy took up residence there.

Sydney, the Oakes' eldest boy, had taken quite a liking to the Count. He often visited the chicken farm and remained overnight with the Count and his sister at the cottage.

Sir Harry, violently objecting to his eldest son's attachment to the worldly Count, much less his daughter's, went to the cottage one night while Sydney was there. He ordered Sydney off the premises.

"And if you ever set foot in this place again," Sir Harry roared, "I'll disinherit you! One in the family's enough to have anything to do with this character."

That wrapped it up, but good, between the Count and the Baronet.

A few weeks later, Sir Harry would be murdered on a hot stormy night.

CHAPTER 10

Raymond Schindler was too clever to stay in a local hotel.

On arrival, he had checked into luxurious quarters in the home of the Baroness Marie af Trolle and her husband, a Swedish nobleman with business interests on the island. They were socialites and friends of Nancy.

He began reading the local newspaper accounts of the case. The newspaper stories didn't make things look any too good for the Count. Schindler called at the offices of a handsome fellow by the name of Godfrey Higgs, a soft-spoken affable chain-smoking thirty-five-year-old lawyer who had handled some commercial paperwork for de Marigny in the past. The son of a local sponge merchant, he had been sent away to private schools in England. He now passed for an old-line British Bahamian. It did him no damage.

Nancy de Marigny had hired Higgs to defend her husband. He was an odd choice, and also a second choice. De Marigny had wanted to hire a man named Alfred Adderley. Adderley, though black, had cunningly navigated the oppressive and racist system in the colonies. He had become the top legal mind on the island. Naturally, the Crown had gotten to him first and hired him to prosecute de Marigny.

Schindler liked Higgs and Higgs liked Schindler at their first meeting. Whatever the outcome of the whole business, these two would get along fine.

"Higgs has a good mind," Ray said to me about to attorney. "He's the type of man whom the other side might underestimate."

"Think he can pull off a big upset in court?" I asked.

"I think he can," Ray said. "Whether or not he will might depend on how rigged the court system is."

Higgs was already in possession of most of the background information that the police had picked up before putting the collar on the Count. They disclosed that there were many people on the island who might have had a motive for killing Sir Harry, from disgruntled husbands to people who thought Harry had fleeced them in a business deal. But the way Higgs saw it, and the way Ray Schindler and I were coming to see it, the cops had found a suspect whom they fitted to the evidence rather than finding evidence and then fitting it to a suspect.

"The Count's reputation is against him," Higgs said to Schindler. "The problems start there."

Logically, the Count's reputation should have had no influence on the investigation of the case. But obviously, it had. The Miami cops had gone to work building a case that led to the gallows for the Count, throwing away all the wood that might have been used to build one for somebody else.

Higgs showed Schindler the ghastly police photographs of the corpse of Sir Harry. The tableau was as gruesome as it was extensive. But the pictures made it doubly clear to the detective that this had not been a murder for profit.

"When a man kills for money," Schindler said to me at one of our many seances at Dirty Dick's, "he commits the crime as quickly and simply as possible and then gets away. This killer had not been in a hurry. He had deliberately taken time to stick around and concentrate an intense flame on Oakes' eyes and genitals. This suggested hatred, perhaps over a woman. The sprinkling of feathers over the corpse after death suggested a cultish ritual of some kind. The feather sprinkling might have been done by a crazed Bahama native or, more likely, by someone who wanted to make the crime look as if it had been committed by a native."

"Either way," I agreed, "it was plainly no hit-and-run job."

Schindler now devoted his attention to the time element in de Marigny's alibi. If everything de Marigny said was true, it would have been impossible for him to be at Westbourne between two thirty and five o'clock in the morning.

According to the Count, the only time he would have had to leave his cottage, commit the crime and return, without being observed by anyone or at least heard by the Marquis, would have been during the half hour when the Marquis had taken Betty Roberts home.

"But more than half an hour would have been needed, Ray," I said, "for the Count to have done everything the murderer had done."

"Exactly," Ray agreed.

It had been storming violently during the night of the crime, something right out of Sherlock Holmes or Agatha Christie: torrential rain, thunder and lightning. Fast driving had been out of the question. But even if the Count had needed only ten minutes to cover the five miles between his cottage and Westbourne, the round trip would have eaten up twenty minutes of the half hour. That would have left less than ten minutes to commit the crime. It seemed to Schindler that more than ten minutes and perhaps a good deal more than ten minutes would have been required to do everything that had been done in the Oakes mansion.

"If de Marigny did it," Ray said to me as we chewed over the case, "he would have had to have moved around like greased lightning for that half hour. Even at that, his timing would have had to be desperately close."

The trouble was that the Marquis' story of the night's events differed slightly from that of the Count. De Marigny said Miss

Roberts had spent some two hours in the Marquis' rooms, leaving only after three in the morning. The Marquis said nothing of the kind.

Schindler figured that the Marquis was chivalrously shielding the good name of the blonde. Schindler put it up to the Marquis in clear terms. Which was more important, a blonde's good name or a friend's life?

The Marquis decided the life was more important. He corroborated everything the Count had stated about his movements the night of the crime, a big break for de Marigny if it stood up.

It thus seemed increasingly unlikely that the Count could have committed the crime. If he hadn't committed it while the Marquis was taking the blonde home, he would have run a chance of being detected by the Marquis had he left in a car after the Marquis returned. Schindler also established the fact that the Marquis was a very light sleeper.

Now Schindler, who wanted to instruct himself in on everything possible before talking to de Marigny, decided it was time to go through Westbourne. Bahama regulations called for him to be accompanied by several cops. Schindler thought as much of that as he would have of a mickey in his drink. But he had no choice. He asked if he could bring an assistant, a second pair of eyes and ears, and someone to take notes, as needed. His request was grudgingly granted. I was officially in the ball game.

We visited the crime scene on Wednesday morning, July 21. I mostly kept my mouth shut. The flatfeet buzzed around us like native flies and mosquitoes, and almost in matching numbers and aggregate annoyance: another reason to keep my mouth shut.

The whole area of the crime struck Schindler as having been crudely torched, rather than merely burned. I had seen many arson cases in New York, Boston and Philadelphia and concurred with Ray's assessment, which he later shared.

The bed on which the roasted Baronet was found had been subjected to a flame so intense that it could have come only from a torch. There were marks on the rugs, on the floor, and on doors and woodwork between the murder rooms and the first floor. The marks looked as if they had been made by a torch carried by the killer. It was one thing to hear the details of a murder and a murder scene; it was quite something else to see it, smell it and practically taste it, as well as picture the inhumane violence that had transpired.

I suppressed more than one shudder and more than one urge to vomit. I had seen many venues of mayhem over the course of a quarter century. But this one was in a category by itself.

Every time Schindler or I turned our heads, we saw bloody finger and handprints—either intact or smudged. Even the French telephone in Sir Harry's room, the one that Harold Christie had used to summon aid at seven in the morning, was bloodstained. So was a phone book near it. There was also a big bloody fingerprint on a door leading to Christie's room. This was understandable. According to his own account, Christie had touched his friend's body to determine whether Oakes was dead and, in his agitation, had naturally picked up some blood.

There were also bloody hand marks on the wall of the murder room that had not
been of any interest to the police. The marks were near two windows, as if the killer, after the first phase of the murder, had gone to the windows to look out to see if anyone was around, placing his bloody hands on the wall while he did so.

"Okay," Schindler finally said to the cops with us. "I've seen enough."

Out on the street when we were alone, Ray spoke to me.

"Did you see those prints on the window?" Ray asked.

"I saw them."

"The prints were made by a short, stubby hand. The Count's hands are long and thin, like the rest of him, as far as anyone knows."

"What about Harold Christie?" I asked.

"I'm here to keep de Marigny's neck out of a noose, not to put someone else's neck in it. Stop asking about anyone else."

"I'll try to remind myself."

"You should. And here's something else to think about. Do you know how much the top man earns in the Nassau police department, Alan? I did some asking around. Top man makes about seven hundred fifty pounds sterling a year. About fifty dollars a week, American. That's the Commissioner. Imagine what the guy on the street makes. Maybe seven dollars. Think he won't take the occasional backhander out of someone's reptile fund, twenty to fifty pounds, to feed his family? I'd say he'd be crazy not to."

"You're saying they're all corrupt?" I asked.

"I'm saying they're not very good and they're poorly paid," he whispered. "*And* they're corrupt."

The next day, Thursday the twenty-second, was time for Schindler to talk to the man he was to prove either innocent or guilty.

Schindler had measured many murderers in his career. His first impression of the Count was that he just wasn't the type to take to murder. The Count may have been a slayer of the ladies, but he didn't impress Schindler as a killer of men. He was too fond of good living to ever do anything, for whatever reason, that would lay that good life on the line. Moreover, he sounded sincere to a man who had been measuring sincerity for a third of a century.

Schindler had heard a story that the Count had asked one of the cops guarding him at Westbourne if a man could be hanged on circumstantial evidence. "What about that?" Schindler wanted to know when he spoke to de Marigny.

The Count just smiled and shrugged. "Wasn't it, considering my position, a natural question?" he countered.

"It may have been a natural question, but it wasn't a smart one," Schindler answered.

The singed hairs on his hands, arms, and the beard? What about that, Schindler asked.

His friend the Marquis would corroborate the Count's story of hand and arm burns from the hurricane lamps, and the chicken singeing chores.

"I'm told that no barber in Nassau can remember singeing your beard," Ray pressed. "What do you say to that?"

"Well, perhaps not. Maybe I singed it myself and got confused when the police were pummeling me with questions."

"What about the fingerprint on the Chinese screen?" Ray asked.

Here de Marigny was adamant and animated.

"Listen!" he snapped. "I visited that house many times. The screen could have been somewhere else and I touched it. I don't remember. What I can tell you is that I was not in the old bastard's bedroom during or after the murder! The print of my little finger on the screen in Sir Harry's room might have been faked! Yes, faked! Those two American cops, and most of the local cops, have just been too damned eager to pin the rap on me! Why the devil didn't they look around a bit? I could name a dozen people who had a lot to explain but hadn't even been questioned!"

With that, guards appeared. They announced that de Marigny's allotted time with his visitor had expired. They led him back to his cell.

The next morning a wave of paranoia overcame me.

I had developed a sense over the years, one that comes from asking unpopular questions sometimes, being punched, cursed at threated, menaced with firearms, not to mention the threatening mail, most of it with Bronx and Brooklyn postmarks. There was always the notion that someone was watching, someone would someday suddenly demand a moment of reckoning, either out of a story from the past or one smack in current day. And I had that feeling now. I decided to run a little gambit, a newspaperman's test that I'd picked up in Philadelphia on the 1920's working on the case of a guy who was engraving plates to make five-dollar bills in his basement.

I wasn't planning to see Ray that day. But I decided to do some of my own detective work. I went downstairs to the dining room where I had a light breakfast. Then I stopped in the lobby where I found the bell captain, a man named Sonny.

"Is Felix here?" I asked Sonny, inquiring after my driver.

"He's outside."

"Does he have his hack?"

"Assuredly, sir," Sonny said.

Before I could stop him, Sonny put his sturdy fingers between his teeth and shrilled a whistle that could have raised the dead. Felix came in with a determined trot.

"Could you take me for a ride? In maybe twenty minutes?" I asked.

"Where to, sir?" Felix asked.

"The church. The big one. The one everyone says I must see. Near the open-air market."

"I'll be ready, sir," Felix said.

"What's the address?" I asked.

"Montrose Road, near George Street."

"That will be fine," I said.

Felix went out to the street to stand by his '36 Hudson. I went upstairs to my room. There was a phone directory of only thirty-six pages; there weren't that many folks who had phones. I opened the directory. I choose a name at random. I called.

A man answered. I didn't even introduce myself. I just spoke quickly.

"We're meeting in front of St. Ambrose church in thirty minutes," I said. "Just as you suggested. I'm bringing the money, all of it."

I rang off before the individual on the other end could say anything. I repeated the procedure with two more numbers. Random calls, random recipients. Then I hustled down the stairs to Felix's hack. I confirmed the address. I sat in the back while Felix drove. The streets were hot but there was little traffic due to gasoline rationing. We were within sight of the church within seven minutes. I asked Felix to stop three blocks away and wait.

"Yes, Mr. Alan," he said.

I stepped out, drew a breath and walked in the direction of the church, looking as much as a Yank tourist as I could. I conspicuously carried a guidebook. There were trees and some construction; I took advantage of cover as best I could. When I came to the last side street, I glanced down it. I saw what I had expected: one police car hovering next to a hydrant. I made a point of taking in the church's architecture. With my peripheral view, I saw two men in a café across the street. They weren't talking. They were just watching in my direction. I bought two pieces of chilled fruit at a market next to the church. I ate one as I walked back to the taxi.

I was quiet as I stepped back into hot cab. I handed Felix the second piece of fruit. A gift. He was surprised. "Thank you, sir."

"Anyone come by to bother you?" I asked. "Or ask questions?"

"No, Mr. Alan."

"Good," I said. "Then we're going back to the hotel, Felix."

"Excellent, Mr. Alan."

We rode back in silence. But that didn't mean my mind wasn't in overdrive.

My telephone was tapped. Someone knew exactly where I was going. And someone involved with the murder of Sir Harry Oakes was getting official protection. Both were already undeniable.

CHAPTER 11

One way that Ray Schindler operated was to do the unexpected as often as possible. I knew how he worked but he surprised even me with his next move.

"I'm leaving Nassau," he told me one evening during the last week of July.

"What?"

"All the phones here are tapped," he said. "Or at least the ones I'd have access to are. I need to get off this island, confer with some experts and maybe bring in some further assistance."

"Makes sense," I said.

"What about you?" he asked. "Sick of this place yet?"

"You want an honest answer or a polite answer?" I asked.

"Honest. Always."

"I'd love to get home and see my wife and daughter," I said. "I know, I know: not good to walk away from the story. But we seem bogged down right now in pre-trial procedure and investigation. There hasn't been much new in the last few days."

"True enough," he said.

"And I really miss my family," I confessed.

"I can tell."

"Can you?"

"It's written all over your face," he said. "Listen. I'll go for a short time, then we'll figure a time for you to go. You cover for me, keep your eyes and ears open and your head down. We compare notes, then I'll cover for you. How's that?"

"Deal!" I said.

We shook on it. We drank to it. We smoked Chesterfields to it.

"So where are you headed?" I asked.

"New Orleans and Chicago," he said. "Maybe with quick stops in New York and Washington."

"What are you up to?" I asked.

"Off the record?"

"Off the record," I promised.

Ray's eyes narrowed. "If you examine what we've heard so far," he said, "the Crown has a tenuous case against Nancy's husband. There's a lot of hearsay, a world of bias and a mountain of ill will. But there's not much evidence other than one thing."

"The fingerprint?" I asked.

"Exactly. That's what our side needs to attack."

***

Two days later, telling no one other than his hosts and me, Ray left Nassau by air to Miami, then he connected to New Orleans and Chicago. Realizing the importance that fingerprint evidence was to assume in the investigation, Schindler sought the best talent possible. Within two days, he had contacted the men he needed. Then he continued to Washington where he conferred with another old friend and working contact, Homer S. Cummings, a former United States Attorney General of the United States under Franklin Roosevelt.

Schindler wanted Cummings' advice about what he had found, and Cummings was just the man to give it. Years before, when he was a prosecuting attorney in Connecticut, the Attorney General had found himself in a unique situation. A young fellow was accused of a murder, and although it was up to Cummings to prosecute, he was convinced that the fellow had not committed the crime. So instead of prosecuting, Cummings set out to prove that the defendant was innocent. And he did prove the fellow's innocence—the defendant had been a victim of mistaken identity.

When Cummings heard Schindler's story, he said, "Ray, I think Count de Marigny is innocent. If there's anything I can do to help, just let me know."

I didn't realize it at the time, but a consensus was emerging about de Marigny's innocence. Whether it would keep him off the gallows in Nassau was beside the point.

Then Ray was back up to New York City to keep an eye on his office and meet other aids and confidants.

***

Just as Ray had predicted, little of substance was transpiring in hot sleepy Nassau during August. I was starting to wish for a respite from the island and its miseries, also.

One day had been particularly harsh. There had been no new developments in the Oakes case and no announcements from the prosecution or the police. That evening, I looked into Dirty Dick's and didn't see much of promise, nor did any other gin mills on the side streets appear inviting. My inclination was to go back to the hotel for dinner. I also knew shaking up my pattern was a good thing.

There was a little Mexican place called Juanita's Cantina, one door down on Kent Street. I eyeballed it from the door. It looked cozy and there was the enticing sound of south-of-the border music. A dozen tables were going and about a dozen empty. I walked in. The smell of tamales greeted me. A moment later, so did Juanita. She was a pretty woman in her mid-twenties with a lovely face and lovely skin the color of a milky coffee. There was also a bar, populated by white people only. Behind the bar was a fierce looking man with a droopy moustache, a white shirt and a red scarf. He kept a sharp eye on Juanita and the front door. I had a feeling that he was the security system as well as the barkeep. I assumed he had a pistol. I had already noticed that most people who had to work nights or go home late in Nassau carried artillery.

"A table by yourself, señor?" she asked in English.

"Yes. Please," I said.

I hadn't taken two steps before a nearby voice barked at me from a partially obscured table in the rear.

"Alan! Hey, partner! Join us!" a voice bellowed.

After an eight-day absence, Raymond Schindler had re-appeared.

Ray had a table in the corner, seated with his back to the wall, so that with equal ease he could watch the room and the window that gave onto the street. It was a table for four, but one of the other chairs was not yet taken. He beckoned me and indicated that I should sit in the empty chair to his left, the one that was also against a wall. I caught on quickly.

"How did you find us?" he asked. "I thought *I* was the detective."

"The same way a lot of reporters find things," I said. "Pure dumb luck."

"Ha! No such thing, Listen, I want you to meet some people," Ray said, indicating his guests. "I didn't want to phone you, of course. I don't think there's any surveillance here but Bay Street will catch on quickly. Sit. Meet my associates."

With him were his two fingerprint men whom he had imported from the United States. Like Schindler, they were as welcome to the Nassau police as ants in a picnic sandwich.

They were Captain Maurice B. O'Neil, chief of the Bureau of Identification of the New Orleans Police Department and Professor Leonarde B. Keeler, executive director of the State of Illinois Crime Bureau.

I was honored to be included at the table. From having written true crime for almost a quarter of a century, I knew well who these men were, yet until now, I had never had the pleasure of meeting them.

Captain O'Neil was recognized in official circles throughout the United States as one of the country's top fingerprint experts. He was a thoroughly honest and professional policeman, having supervised one of the most important departments in New Orleans for two decades. He had made his reputation in using fingerprints to clear an eccentrically cuckoo couple in the Goat Castle murder case in Natchez, Mississippi in 1932, a case I had written up for *Colliers.*

"That was quite a case," I said. It involved the brutal shooting of a spinster recluse named Jennie Surget Merrill. The case had been all over the tabloid newspapers, with details of wealth, beautiful women, European royalty, Southern aristocracy, army generals and ambassadors, plus madness, incest, racism, bitter internecine feuds, mind-boggling tumbles from grace and a hefty dose of overall perversity. All of this in huge helpings. I hated to think how many trees had been cut down to print all the newspapers the case sold.

"That case got me into the International Association for Identification," O'Neil said.

"Isn't that the same organization that James Barker is in?" I asked. "One of the cops that the Duke called in."

"It is," O'Neil said.

"Do you know Barker?"

"I know him."

"He's a friend of yours?" I asked, intrigued.

"No," O'Neil said with a heavy pause. "I know him."

I read the eyes around the table. I changed the subject.

The other man at the table, Leonarde Keeler, was a quiet, handsome man in his early forties. Named after Leonardo di Vinci, he had more than lived up to his namesake. Keeler was the co-inventor of the lie detector and an authority on scientific crime detection. He had been a partner of the famous John Augustus Larson, a cerebral Police Officer in Berkeley, California, United States. Larson was the first American police officer to have an academic doctorate and to use polygraph in criminal investigations. In February of 1935, he conducted the first use of their invention, the Keeler Polygraph, on two criminals in Portage, Wisconsin. They were later convicted of assault when the lie detector results were introduced in court.

Both Keeler and O'Neil were old friends of Schindler.

I shook hands with both men and settled in. It appeared as if Ray and his friends had just been served their meal. Juanita stayed with us, menus in her hand.

"What are we drinking tonight?" I asked around the table.

"Tequila. Iced," Ray said. "Try it."

"I'm more of a rum drinker. Or Scotch."

Ray turned to Juanita. "Alan will have a tequila, also. We must educate the young man. Open his worldview, what do you think?" My muffled protest was ignored. The others laughed. "Tequila will put some hair on your chest, Alan," Schindler said. "Shut up. This isn't tea time."

I didn't bother to protest a second time.

"Something to eat, sir?" Juanita asked me.

"Yes, definitely."

She offered me a menu. Ray intercepted it and handed it back to her.

"Alan will have the same as I have. Corn tamales with hot sauce. Delicious."

I shrugged to the very pretty young woman. "He's the boss," I said.

"Damned right I am and don't any of you forget it," he said good naturedly.

Juanita winked to me and disappeared. Then Ray set to work on his food, taking several mouthfuls. My drink arrived quickly. I tried it and liked it, though by that point on this day I was predisposed to enjoy anything chilled with an alcoholic content.

The four of us exchanged small talk around the table and some banter about the Oakes case. I was flattered anew when both Keeler and O'Neil revealed that they had read many of my stories. Captain O'Neil asked me what had been the strangest case I'd ever written up.

"That's an easy one," I answered. "It's the one I called *The Case of the Attic Lover*. It involved a woman named Wanda Walburger who kept a paramour in her attic for ten years without her husband finding out. The lover came downstairs when Wanda was having a fight with her husband and shot him."

"I remember that one," O'Neil said.

"Did she get convicted?" Keeler asked.

"What do you think?" I laughed.

"No," Keeler said.

"Correct," I said.

My meal arrived. Ray looked up. "This Mexican stuff is pretty good. You'll like it."

"I've had it before. My wife and I went to Acapulco after we were first married."

"You like it?'

"Which? The Mexican food or Acapulco?"

"Either."

"Both," I said. "Also, the marriage."

"Wise man. Smart man," Ray said. His eyes twinkled.

"Are we alone in here tonight," I asked, "or do we have a shadow?"

"You never know, but I seem to have shaken off my usual armada of bumbling busybodies," Schindler said. "It won't last long. They'll find out where I went tonight, who I was with, and they'll be in here tomorrow. So maybe I'll come in to let them think they're smart, which they're not, or maybe I'll give them the slip again. We'll see."

"I'm sure we will," I said.

"Tell me something I've always wondered about, Alan," Captain O'Neil then asked me. "How did you get started in crime writing?"

"I was assigned to it," he said. "By my editor. A tough guy Irishman like yourself named Eddie Dunn. City editor on *The Boston Post*."

"Tell me about it," he said.

"My second day on *The Boston Post*," I answered, "there was this laborer in the South End. O'Hara, I think his name was. He was arrested at the tenement house on D Street where he lived with his brother-in-law, a man named McDermott. O'Hara used a straight razor to cut McDermott's throat. When the police arrived, they found blood all over the walls and on a table. Both men had been drunk. O'Hara claimed he was lying in bed asleep with his wife when McDermott broke down the door to their two-room apartment, came in, brandished a hammer and threatened to kill both. Apparently, O'Hara slept with a straight razor under his mattress—it was that type of neighborhood. O'Hara came up with the razor, slashed at his brother-in-law and caught him clean and hard across the front of the throat. The wife supported her husband's account. I remember standing there listening to O'Hara give his account to the police. The dead man was still lying there and the cops were laughing. I remember looking down at the floor and seeing all the blood. I'd been standing there for half an hour without moving. Transfixed. And my shoes were sticking to the floor because the blood was drying."

"And that was your start?"

"Yes, sir. Eddie Dunn, the editor, sent me from tenement to tenement. Deaths in small hotel rooms, rapes and murders in basements. Slashings in elevators, shootings in gambling dens, stabbings in open air markets. There was no limit to the variety, no depths to the depravity or brutality. Looking back, I wonder if Mr. Dunn and the other editors were having a game with me, wanting to see if I'd quit or could take it. Next thing I knew, after maybe a hundred homicides, the editors changed. Mr. Dunn promoted me and I was put on a higher issue of crime. Bank robbery, forgeries. From there I landed on the Ponzi case, one of several reporters. That was 1920."

Ray lit a cigarette. I joined him.

"You know," I continued, "I'm not a college guy. I didn't finish eighth grade. Did you know that? My father told me to quit school and work. He was an ignorant man who had no use for education. What I know is what I've learned. I've read books. I have a huge library back in Manhattan. I'd like to show it to you someday. To some degree I think a man's profession finds him. Ray, yours found you in San Francisco. The quake opened the opportunity. Investigation suited you. You excel at it. But there's something to me that's fascinating about the mind of a criminal. I'm a bit like the bookish little man who lives in an attic, never travels, but writes adventures about the South Sea Islands. Or the old lady spinster who writes great romances. Murder, it's something I would never do. But it fascinates me: the mindset, the commission of the crime. The attempt to get away with it, frequently successful, sometimes not."

"A parallel reality. A fantasy world," Ray suggested as he sipped.

"You could call it that," I said.

"The study of murder is the study of the human heart at its coldest strangest moments," Keeler said. "That's what Edmond Pearson wrote in *The New Yorker* twenty years ago. Almost every major writer has investigated homicide. Shakespeare. Balzac. Fitzgerald. Tolstoy. Dostoyevsky. Dickens. I think what we're all looking for is a way to throw some light on the darkest places of the human soul."

"Did you know an Englishman wrote the first critical essay on the subject?" Schindler volunteered. "Thomas de Quincey. It was called, *On Murder Considered as One of the Fine Arts*. Eighteen twenties, I believe."

"De Quincey was also an opium eater, if I recall, Ray," I said.

"I have no doubts that he was. Me. I'll stick to whiskey," O'Neil said.

"Cheers," Keeler said. He lifted his shot glass. I lifted mine. We clicked them.

Dinner concluded shortly before ten p.m. Schindler paid for all of us, or maybe Nancy de Marigny did. It was vague.

"Thank you, Mr. Schindler," Juanita said, as we stood and assembled ourselves.

"You're welcome," he answered.

She cleared the table and left us. We started toward the door.

"Aren't you afraid that you're getting a little too well known in Nassau?" I asked.

"Too well known? Oh, hell, no! That's just the way I want it," Ray said, speaking softly.

There was a big console radio near the bar. It was tuned to a live radio show from Mexico City. It was enough to cover our conversation.

"Many people quietly hate the government and the power structure in Nassau," Ray said. "De Marigny also has friends. A lot of the colored like him a hell of a lot more than the Crown. Somebody in this place is going to resent the way the deck is being stacked against the Frenchman. I'm hoping that person will eventually contact me on the sly. So, I stay accessible. Visible."

I nodded.

"We both work the same way," I said. "From the ground up."

CHAPTER 12

In the days that followed, Schindler studied a copy of the Crown's picture of de Marigny's fingerprint that had been developed by Barker, the Miami cop. Ray noticed that the print had been developed against a background of small circles. The circles looked to

Schindler as if they had come from a glass surface rather than a paper one. According to the official investigation, the print had been taken from the dislodged and scorched Chinese screen in the murder room. The screen was made from a light Asian wood like bamboo, and decorated with paper.

Schindler showed the fingerprint photograph to Professor Keeler and Captain O'Neil.

"There's not one chance in ten million," said Keeler, "that this print came from that screen."

O'Neil agreed.

Just to make sure, Keeler took a photograph of that part of the screen where Barker, the Miami cop, said he had developed the Count's print. Sometimes a photo would reveal something not visible to the naked eye. But not in this case.

"Bring me a pile of Bibles," Keeler said to Schindler, "and I'll swear on them that that print did not come from this screen."

So far as Schindler could learn, that fingerprint remained the most important piece of physical evidence that the Crown had against the Count. Schindler had a couple of Scotches on that. "What about other fingerprints?" asked Captain O'Neil.

"Good question," Schindler answered.

Captain O'Neil's jaw dropped when Schindler explained how the Nassau police had conducted their forensic inquiries.

The day the murder was discovered, and the following day, Ray explained, some busybody had washed the walls of the murder room, thus removing fingerprints and hand prints. The phone directory in Sir Harry's bed chamber had not been removed, and it still had blood splotches all over it. But prior to Schindler's arrival to begin his probe, dozens of persons had picked up the phonebook, so it was not possible to get a fingerprint that meant anything.

Schindler, who had been gathering information via casual throwaway questions as he went along, had learned that when the Nassau police had first arrived on the murder scene they had found a loaded revolver lying on top of a pile of bills on a dresser. The weapon had since vanished. From all Schindler could learn, Sir Harry had not until recently owned a revolver. This begged the question: from whom had Harry obtained the weapon? And why? Handguns were not easy to come by in the British colonies. Schindler asked if he could see the gun so that he could trace its origin. But an official in the police department informed him that the weapon had been destroyed.

"Keeping it would only have confused the whole investigation. After all," the official explained, "Sir Harry was not shot."

"Confused the whole investigation, indeed!" snarled Schindler.

"And 'not shot'?" I said.

Ray shrugged. So far, the Crown had not offered an official explanation as to exactly how Oakes had been murdered. Barker and Melchen had spun a sordid tale in private to Nancy Oakes, but nothing official had been forthcoming.

Schindler figured Oakes might have carried the gun as part of his personal equipment. If that were so, it might indicate that the Baronet had had some potent reason to fear for his personal safety, since he had still been a good man with his fists. Had Oakes feared somebody—man or woman—enough to think that his life was in immediate danger?

If so, who? Schindler would have paid a high price for that gun. He could have run down its origin from its serial number. He could have established where and when and under what conditions Oakes had come into possession of it. If Oakes had acquired it recently, that would suggest a specific threat of recent origin.

It would have been very easy for anyone to reach Sir Harry's bed the night he was murdered. The violent rain and windstorm with lightning and thunder blasted away most of the night. Outside stairs led to the upper porches that practically surrounded the house. All one had to do was walk upstairs and open the door. No one could have heard an approach and the doors were not usually locked. There were also several other furnished bedrooms nearby, but curiously the mattresses and covers were not on the beds.

Like the professional detective that he was, Schindler had a burning curiosity about what was going on in Westbourne in the days and hours leading up to the murder. It was his notion, and one I shared, that the mood and events that played out in the mansion could foreshadow the crime.

To this end, Schindler used a local intermediary to set up secret meetings in the homes of two of the servants who had worked for Sir Harry. He plied them with Jamaican rum and a small stack of British five-pound notes. He got them talking and picked up some gems of information.

For example, apparently on two or three occasions during the week before he was murdered, Sir Harry walked along the upper porch to go into one of these other bedrooms, pulled off the beddings and slept on a mattress on the floor. Sometimes, the servants found his bedcovers in these other rooms. Sir Harry would move them without anyone's knowledge. It was obvious to Schindler that the man had been in fear, hiding out in case someone came to his bedroom.

"He probably had his pistol tucked into the waistband of his pajamas," I suggested.

"There's a good chance," Ray answered.

Moreover, Ray speculated to me one morning, it was within the realm of possibility that Sir Harry could have been drugged before going to bed. If Oakes had not been drugged, and had been awakened by his attacker, Sir Harry would have put up one hell of a fight. He could have yelled for his friend and business associate in the other bedroom. Christie was a strong and capable man as well.

"But I don't think it worked that way," Ray said, and I agreed.

Despite the tale that the Miami cops had spun to Oakes' daughter and widow, we believed that the intruder had reached the bed without waking Oakes and killed him, then stayed to torch him and sprinkle him with feathers.

Schindler would have given a year of his life to have had a good look at the corpse of Sir Harry Oakes right after the murder. He could have followed through, by way of an autopsy and a scientific examination of the vital organs, on the possibility that Oakes had been drugged before death. He could have had a good look at the Baronet's head, particularly at those four wounds. But the body had been whisked away quickly before anyone could ask any nosy or inconvenient questions. The body had even been sent beyond Bahamian jurisdiction.

Yet oddly enough, the Bahamian police, not known for their exacting competence, had done one thing well. They had taken excellent photographs of that part of the victim's head containing the wounds. Schindler got hold of copies of the photographs and the medical reports. The pattern of the four wounds was rectangular about two inches wide and a little longer. The police hadn't the slightest idea what sort of instrument had been used by the murderer.

Neither did Schindler. Neither did I.

Although the wound pattern formed a sort of rectangle, it was not possible to determine whether the four wounds had been made by four separate blows, each blow making one mark, or by two blows with a two-pronged instrument.

One end of the cradle of a European telephone, if brought down four times on a man's head, could have produced the murder wounds. Although there had been such a telephone in the murder bedroom, it was too far from the Baronet's bed to have been used for such a purpose and it was anchored to the wall the morning the murder was reported.

No one had ever accounted for another inexplicable detail of the murder. The wounds to Sir Harry were behind his ear and theoretically had been made while he slept. Yet pictures showed that blood covered his face. Why had the blood flowed upwards in defiance of gravity? Why, unless the murder had happened elsewhere and the body had been moved?

One afternoon in mid-August, Ray and I went over to Westbourne to see if we could manage an extra walk-around. There was a lone guard whom Ray had previously befriended who gave us a big smile. Ray slipped him two of those ever-useful five-pound notes.

Schindler and I searched through Westbourne for the possibility that any other French phone had been yanked from a wall. Nothing doing. Nor did we seriously entertain the idea that someone intending to commit a murder would show up without a weapon and then improvise.

In the garage behind Westbourne, we came across something interesting. There was a stack of short wooden railings, two inches by two inches in thickness. Ray had previously learned from an Oakes servant that such a railing had been found, the morning after the murder, leaning against one of Sir Harry's cars, which he had left parked in a driveway behind the house.

Out of curiosity, the servant had kept the railing. Schindler examined it. There were no indications of blood on the wood. Schindler questioned the servant as to just how the railing had been leaning against the car when it was found, and he learned that had been leaning against one of the wheels.

Schindler figured the railing business as this possibility: The murderer, going into the garage in search of some kind of weapon that could not be traced to him, had picked up a couple of railings. On his way to the house itself, the murderer had decided that one railing would be enough for his purpose. So, he had discarded the second railing. In landing on the ground, it had struck the wheel of the car while still in an upright position, and it had stayed that way until the servant came across it the next morning.

Although in one respect the railing—one point of the end of it used four times—sounded good to Schindler, in another way it didn't. The superior investigator has a singular digestive apparatus; he can't, somehow, stomach a piece of evidence that just doesn't seem appetizing.

"A murderer armed with a piece of railing would be likely to use it as a club," Ray explained. "The weapon that was used was used to poke his victim like a sword." Schindler was not discarding the railing, but he wasn't swallowing it, either.

We left Westbourne with nothing new.

Meanwhile, Leonarde Keeler, the Chicago criminologist, was devoting himself to the development of scientific clues. He took pieces of the rug in the murder room, and pieces of the burned woodwork at the head of the bed, and began to conduct experiments in the home of the Baroness af Trolle.

He concluded that the killer had used a torch while going about his grisly business. De Marigny didn't own a torch and had never had reason to use one on the chicken farm. The Baroness af Trolle, eager to see Schindler and Keeler develop any evidence favorable to the Count, nonetheless must have looked on the discoveries of the two dicks with mixed feelings. Keeler, experimenting with different kinds of flame produced by different kinds of fuel, stank up her lovely home on a regular basis. To top things off, one shaft of flame got out of control and ruined a chunk of priceless furniture.

Since a blowtorch had been used in the crime, Schindler wanted to check the entire island to find out who owned blowtorches. Such equipment was rare on the island except in one place where wartime building operations were going on. Schindler wanted permission to question the workmen on such projects. Permission was denied.

Every person arriving at or leaving Nassau had his name and address recorded in official records, along with his reason for coming or going, and the dates of his arrival and departure. Schindler wanted a look at those records. Permission was denied.

Ray and I began to bite our nails and sprinkle a little more profanity than usual into our speech. We were getting a message, loud and clear.

With the revised testimony of the Marquis and the evidence he and O'Neil had developed regarding the fingerprint, Schindler was confident that the case against de Marigny could be smashed to splinters when it came to trial. As that was what he had been hired for, he had already earned his fee. But he wanted to do more. Having satisfied himself based on provable facts that de Marigny did not commit the murder, Schindler at this point was more than a little curious to know who did.

We learned that Oakes had another home in another part of Nassau that was not as large or pretentious as Westbourne. Sir Harry had sometimes entertained married women at this other home since it was more private. Arrival and departure could be more discreet. We visited. Incredibly, the place was unlocked and had no watchman.

Sir Harry, the one-time gold prospector, liked to tinker with tools, and in the rear of this second residence was a tool house. Schindler found a detailed list of the equipment supposed to be in the tool house, and checked the tools in the shed against the list. Everything was there except one thing: a prospector's pick, a heavy, short handled piece of hardware with an odd triangular point. Prospectors use it to take samples from veins of ore, but a prospector's pick could have been just the thing to do in Sir Harry. Its triangular point would have produced just the kind of wounds that had been found in Sir Harry's noggin.

Sir Harry didn't occupy this second home very often. When he wasn't there, it was deserted. A watchman kept an eye on it at night, but it would have been possible for anybody, studying the watchman's routine, to go into the tool house and come out with the pick.

"I think," Ray said to me when we left this second home, "that we now know what the murder weapon was. The remaining question," he said, "is—?"

"—who used it?" I continued.

Ray winked. "Let's go for drinks," he said. "We've earned it."

CHAPTER 13

Two afternoons later, a thick storm rolled in from the Caribbean and pounded Nassau with hard fat raindrops. I was on Bay Street a block from my hotel when the deluge began. I took immediate refuge under the covered arcade outside a row of merchants. The humidity made my knee ache, however, as did all the pavement pounding I was doing. I reckoned I'd make a run for it and head to the hotel. Then I realized that I was half again closer to Dirty Dick's and would only get half-soaked if I jogged in that direction.

The place was full. I had not been the only person to react this way to the storm. The tobacco smoke was thick and the conversations were loud. Getting a drink would be a challenge and finding a seat impossible. I approached it the way I might approach a questionable Turkish bath on a hot August afternoon. I entered, pushing my way through a crowd in the general direction of the bar and cigarette case. Halfway there, I felt a felt a sharp tug on my sleeve.

"Alan!" came a voice that travelled up from a table. "Hey! Right here!"

I gave in to the tug, turned, and should have known.

Schindler, as usual, was there at a narrow table. This time he was with an older gentleman. Ray had spotted me, turned, and reached out with his unavoidable long arm and tight grasp.

"Join us," Schindler said. By chance or by choice, he had held open a third wooden chair. "You must meet my local friend." I settled into the free chair, happy to take a load off my feet, happier still that I'd avoided getting completely soaked.

Ray introduced me to a jowly fiftyish Englishman and now Nassau resident who went by the name of Colonel Abraham Chalmers, late of the British Army. We shook hands, the colonel and I. The colonel's paw was fleshy and moist, more from sweat than the rain. He had a grayish white mane, a droopy moustache that matched, and worried eyes under bushy brows. He wore a pale suit with many buttonholes. The shoulders of the suit, nicely tailored to the colonel's bulbous form, were pockmarked with raindrops which told me that the colonel hadn't been there for more than fifteen minutes. Maybe twenty. Beside him, braced against his chair and the table was a tall walking stick, carved presumably from a friendlier local wood than the manchineel tree.

Schindler introduced me by name. I quickly gained the impression that if I was okay with Ray Schindler, I was okay with the colonel.

"My friend Alan here is the new Edmund Lester Pearson," Schindler said. "Finest true crime writer in America today," he continued with undue flattery, "especially following Pearson's death in 1937." The colonel studied me. "Alan has a bestseller on *The New York Times* list as we speak."

The colonel's bushy brows shot toward the sky.

"Pleasure to meet you, sir," Chalmers said, speaking in a too-dignified upper-class bellow that on another occasion might have encouraged me to turn and run. But I had already picked up signals from Ray. He wanted me to meet the colonel and hear what the old buzzard had to say. The colonel pumped my hand again and didn't want to give it back. "Pleasure," he said again.

"Ray is overly generous in his praise," I demurred. "I had a bestseller earlier this year. It dropped off the list after five weeks."

"Ah, but it was *there*." the Englishman said.

"It was there."

"Crime? Murders?" the colonel asked.

"Nazi espionage. I'm concerned with the war effort, as we all are."

"But you write about murders?" Colonel Chalmers pressed.

"I do, sir."

"Of what sort? Do tell?"

"Well, I should say that I favor what I might call 'cerebral true crime' over the more mundane 'real life' killer books," I began. "The appeal of the latter seems often wallow in low horror. What intrigues me in a case, what I prefer to write about, are cases in which there is the allure of the puzzle: what made someone kill someone and how they did or didn't get away with it and why. Who they are. What complexities drove them to commit a heinous crime. In my work, the victim is often the most fascinating character."

"And what you write is factual?"

"It's true crime, sir. Non-fiction. A literary cousin, perhaps, of the Golden Age detective fiction," I suggested. "But a literary form of its own." I paused. The colonel wanted more, I could tell. "I believe in justice for victims of murders," I said. "That includes the death penalty for the guilty. Too many tears are shed in America for persons accused of murder or convicted of murder."

The colonel nodded. We now seemed to be friends. "Couldn't agree with you more," he harrumphed. "Jolly!" Mercifully, the barman returned with a rum and Coke for me. "Bloody good," the colonel said, sipping his own drink.

The colonel took a time out and dabbed at the sweat on his face with a handkerchief. He blinked and rubbed his eyes. Sweat had come through his silk shirt, also. For an instant, he looked like a man coming around. Then he was back again. His eyes found me.

"Colonel Chalmers was no stranger to violence and blood when he was a younger man," Schindler said, leading the conversation.

"Quite right, sir," the old soldier agreed. "Unfortunately."

The colonel started on what was apparently his third gin. My reporter's instincts kicked in. I fed him a few questions and sounded him out on his own past. Schindler leaned back, watched and listened.

Colonel Chalmers, it turned out, had been the eldest son in a landowning family in the English Midlands, but had come by his rank the hard way. He had grown up in Warwickshire, he recounted quickly. As any patriotic young man would have, had joined the British Army at the outbreak of the Great War. His unit was the 48th South Midland Division. He and his comrades were sent to France in March 1915. They fought in the Battle of the Somme in 1916, the Battle of Pozières and the Third Battle of Ypres on the western front. In November 1917, colonel's division continued to Italy. On the Asiago Plateau in June of 1918, the colonel lost a third of his right foot to a bullet and another third to gangrene. That didn't leave much.

"That's why I use a stick," he told me, indicating the walking staff beside him. He gave me a wide grin then thrust out a prosthetic boot that served as the lower half of his right leg.

I nodded. I understood.

"I was one of the lucky ones in Asiago," he said. "It was all mountain fighting where I was. Three hundred thousand Italian soldiers died in six weeks. Poor buggers. I sat out the armistice in a hospital."

The old coot was starting to appear to me as more of an owl than a buzzard.

"I was in a field hospital for two months. Wounds to the extremities were so severe that hundreds of British soldiers had to have limbs amputated. There was a French doctor, a devil named Tourino. He had a small guillotine, a variation on the type used to cut off royal heads in the Frog Revolution. He used it to amputate limbs. You could hear the blade falling all day and the men screaming. Chop, chop, chop. But it saved lives. It often precluded infection."

I grimaced. He sipped his iced drink.

"Infection was a serious complication. My foot was infected, and I thought the blade was going to drop on me. No antibiotics. There was an Irish doctor who had this sodding practice of 'debridement.' I chose the Irishman to do my leg. The tissue around my wound was cut away and carbolic lotion was used to wash it. Then they wrapped it in gauze soaked in the same solution. No anesthetic, I'm grateful. They saved a third of my foot. I went home, then moved here in '39. Not boring you, old man, am I?" he asked me.

"Not in the slightest, Colonel," I said.

Across the table, Schindler winked to me. The colonel was a windbag. But Schindler found it informative to keep him talking. Detectives like people who talk too much.

"The colonel was amusing me with stories about 'David,'" when you happened in," Schindler said, guiding the conversation back to where it had been.

"David?"

"The Duke of Windsor," said Schindler.

"Our revered and much beloved former monarch," said the colonel acidly. "And now our esteemed Governor. 'David' is the name the chap is called within the royal family. To the rest of the world, as King, he was Edward VIII."

"I see," I said.

"The Colonel knows the Duke personally," Schindler said. Ray held up a hand with two fingers crossed, suggesting the Colonel had tight knowledge of the governor and was ready to unload privately. I took the hint.

"And how do you find him?" I asked. "The newspapers in America used to find him quite charming, but now some of them see him as a wealthy bore."

With pique and a harsh rattle of ice cubes, the colonel quaffed the end of his drink with a single gulp. He chewed on the ice for a moment, swallowed it and was ready to talk.

He started with the small stuff. Grist for the mill: The Governor of the Bahamas was notorious for never tipping his golf caddies or settling his gambling debts. He had ducked out of millions in gambling losses and luxury restaurant bills. He had always been that way.

"David may be the undisputed darling of the conservative American press and the dominions," the colonel began, "but it's all a pernicious charade played out before the naive public. I happen to like the man personally. But I also find him vacuous, vainglorious and effete," he said.

"Effete?" I asked. It never ceased to amaze me how much some people would say to a writer given sufficient alcoholic lubrication. "Meaning what, sir?" I asked.

"Do you know the stories about the future King and the French prostitutes?" he asked.

"No, but I'm sure I'd enjoy hearing them," I answered.

Ray winked at me when the colonel wasn't looking.

"Ha! Raised as a Victorian, you know. 'Filthy and revolting' was his description of the naked prostitutes he once saw posing in a Calais brothel. His grew up fundamentally afraid of women. In July 1917, his equerries hired a French prostitute named Paulette helped him overcome his fears. A subsequent six-month affair with a Parisian courtesan named Marguerite Alibert gave the Prince a healthy appetite for sex."

The colonel laughed. "From there on," he said, "David has never rarely ever been out from between a woman's legs. Often those legs have been married, the most recent two belong to the current Duchess. From the outset, this unusual woman has enchanted poor David. We used to see him getting down on hands and knees like a canine to paint her toe nails."

Long before he met Wallis, Edward's freewheeling bachelor lifestyle had become a great concern to the King and Queen. They were already concerned about his bisexual brother Prince George, who had become addicted to cocaine and morphine thanks to his relationship with the American socialite Kiki Preston, known as "the girl with the silver syringe."

The colonel spared us no compromising detail. He recounted the good days of the 1930's in England, good for the upper crust at least, when Mayfair society was agog with lurid speculation about her various liaisons and exploits, including her time spent learning curious sexual techniques in the brothels of Shanghai, as well as a leathery affair with an Italian diplomat named Count Gian Galeazzo Ciano, who later became foreign minister and Mussolini's son-in-law. It was even thought that Wallis, in her free time, had seduced the Nazi diplomat Joachim von Ribbentrop, who had once famously given her a bouquet of seventeen carnations. Queen Mary, Edward's mother, thought her a sexual hypnotist. A chronicle of these sexual adventures was apparently contained in an infamous document called "The China Dossier," which was prepared years later for Prime Minister Stanley Baldwin and King George V.

"You know, when David was first appointed Governor of the Bahamas," rambled the colonel, "Edward called it a third rate posting. He refused to come here unless Churchill agreed to allow two soldiers to be released from Army service to act as his personal servants. Poor Winnie was grappling with the fallout from the Dunkirk evacuation and David's having a hissy fit. Meanwhile, Wallis was concerned that their fine bedlinens be protected. She sent her maid to Nazi-controlled Paris to save them. On the quiet, Edward has hired Nazis in France to protect his various properties. He also insisted that they first sail to New York—so that his wife could go shopping along Madison Avenue. That said, in person they are a charming couple. They have a few kinks. We all do, don't you know? What are yours, Alan?"

"I'm joyfully monogamous," I said.

Colonel Chalmers didn't hear my response. He was midway into another tale, the one about how angry the Duke had been in Bermuda when loyal female subjects receiving them had not curtsied to the Duchess. No grievance was too petty to be expressed to the counselor staff.

But then, his eyes continually scanning the bar, the Colonel fell silent. He switched his conversation to British cricket and how he had learned an off-drive from an underling in Coventry. At the same time, the decibel level in Dirty Dick's dropped by half as patrons observed an ominous new double presence. I turned, glanced, and recognized the two-man surveillance team. I saw two gentlemen, one hefty and one wiry. I use the term "gentlemen" very loosely. They were in tropical suits and walked with their arms folded behind their backs. I had seen them once before and liked them even less now. The wiry one wore the same yellow tie, straw hat and cheap tropical suit. His partner was the hefty taller man in the canvas pith helmet.

They approached our table and stopped.

"Good afternoon, Colonel," the smaller wiry one said. "Who are your guests?"

Schindler folded his arms. I noted his wariness.

The colonel hesitated for a moment, then answered.

"This is Mr. Raymond Schindler from New York," Colonel Chalmers said. "He's here to help defend Monsieur de Marigny. As you know, Mr. Greywater," he said.

Schindler offered a hand in greeting. It was ignored. He withdrew it.

"De Marigny's going to hang," our visitor said.

"We'll see," Schindler couldn't resist saying.

The little man—I'd say he was about five and a half feet—ignored Ray's comment. His gray eyes slid over to me. I could feel the disapproval.

"Who's this?" he asked.

Schindler introduced me by name as a friend from New York.

"This guy works for you?" the little sawed-off guy asked.

"No," Ray answered quickly.

"What brings you here?" the smaller meaner one asked me.

"A vacation," I lied.

"Funny time and place for a vacation," he said.

"I think it's a swell place and a great time," I offered.

"Military?" he asked.

"Civilian," I said.

"What do you do for a living?"

"I write books. About spies," I said, sticking to a larger truth.

"You're American? Canadian?"

"American."

"Do you have identification?"

"May I ask why are you—?" I began.

"Just show him, Alan," the colonel said in a friendly murmur. "Mr. Graywater here is with the government and is making a reasonable and friendly request."

"Of course," I said. "Happy to oblige."

I produced my United States passport and handed it to him. Graywater flicked through the pages, found my picture, then glanced back and forth to be sure it was me. He examined the passport sideways, studying the stitching and the printing, searching for flaws.

"If you're here as a tourist, why are you with this detective?" Graywater asked.

"We're friends," I said. "We know each other from New York."

He took a second look at my passport.

He treated the document roughly. Then he snapped it shut.

"It's legal to be friends," I said.

"Not always," he said. He tossed the passport onto the table, rather than handing it back. "Watch yourself. Stay out of trouble," he said. His voice, aside from the ice in my drink, was the coldest thing I had encountered since arrival.

"Of course," I said. "Thank you, sir."

No response. They turned to continue through the room.

"Good day, gentlemen," the Colonel said.

The old soldier released his staff. I could see his body slump. Graywater made no reaction. The fat one gave me a harsh eye and then a short nod. As he passed, I noticed for the first time that he carried a truncheon.

The two men made a tour of the room, asking another question here, another there. Then they went back out into the rain, which had ebbed but continued in its steadiness.

"The small one's name, the one with the yellow necktie, is Julius Greywater," the colonel said, when they were beyond earshot. "His mother was a local octoroon who owned a cat house on Eleuthera, his father was a disgraced Australian solicitor from Singapore. The old man moved here in the Thirties and was a notorious pimp."

The colonel's blue eyes tracked the pair through the room.

"The big one is Felipe McBruey. They both grew up here. Security. The powers that be send them around to make sure everyone knows that no one at the top table in the Bahamas is going soft."

"Police?" I asked.

"It's vague," said the Colonel.

"Private security?"

"It's complicated. You're happier having not anything to do with it. Or not knowing."

"I came here to know things, Colonel."

"Be careful who you say that to."

Conversation hesitantly resumed around the room. A feeling of relief washed through the bar. The rain had eased enough so that an extra window or two could be opened and a slight breeze wafted through. The breeze felt even better when Graywater and McBruey disappeared out the front door.

"This 'top table,' you mentioned," I asked. "Who sits at that?"

"The Bay Street Boys," he said. "The lawyers. The merchants. The bankers. The real estate people. The Bahamas is about money, how to make it and how to keep it. The islands are run by the people who make those decisions."

"You must have a few names," I said. "I'd love to meet some of these folks."

Pointedly, Colonel Chalmers didn't hear my inquiry, much less address it.

"Where do these security gorillas fit in with the local power structure?" I asked.

"At the top of the heap. Or that bottom, depending how you want to look at it," Ray said. "Straight out in-your-face street intimidation. Think in terms of a visit from the Gestapo. Same style. Same intent."

"Are they actually official police?"

"I don't know. I ask people who live here and they answer by saying that order must be kept, the colored must know their place, and the economic security of the islands must be looked after. No one wants to answer that question."

I eased back and looked away. "Okay," I said. "I get it. I think."

I glanced at the colonel. "Can you tell us anything about those guys?" I asked. "Who they work for?"

"None of my business," the colonel said.

A waiter reappeared unrequested. He looked as relieved as the rest of us. He had refreshed our drinks without even our asking.

The colonel eventually regathered himself.

"These islands can be dark and intimidating sometimes," he said. "It's a warm bright place but with some very dark corners. Sometimes there's fear. There's contradiction. Sir Harry, God rest his soul, kept his doors unlocked but even he was worried recently. For the first time on the Bahamas he had recently acquired a gun."

"He *did?*" Schindler asked, playing dumb.

"Yes. It was a little Smith and Wesson 'Victory' model. Six shots. Thirty-eight caliber."

"How do you know?"

"I saw it. I taught him how to use it. We went out to one of his orchards a month before he died. Harry didn't say why he wanted it. I asked twice. He only said, 'Chalmie, it's wartime, old chap. What if the God damn Huns come up out of the ocean to steal my coins?' making a joke of it, sort of."

I exchanged a glance with Ray. Then the Colonel read our minds and posed the same question that we were thinking.

"Why he didn't use it the night he was murdered," Colonel Chalmers said. "That's what I don't understand. Something to think about, isn't it?"

Ray leaned back. It was a body language gesture between us that we had used before. It was my turn to push my nose into the questioning if I cared to.

"Know what happened to it?" I asked.

"I suppose the constables took it," Chalmers said. "Can't say. Don't want a weapon flying around loose, you know. Someone could get hurt."

The colonel, it seemed, was starting to feel his distilled spirits.

"It's difficult to get a firearm in the Bahamas, isn't it?" I asked.

"Too bloody right," Chalmers said.

"So, who was Sir Harry's armorer?" I asked.

Chalmers laughed.

"He probably bought it from one of the Devil's Island boys," he said.

"Who?" I asked.

Schindler leaned forward with interest.

"Right," said Chalmers. "There are four escapees from Devil's Island hiding on one of the out islands," Chalmers said. "They deal in contraband, so I hear. Maybe Harry bought a gun from one of them. Who knows?"

"Where would we find these men?" Schindler asked.

"Ha!" Chalmers said. "Not too bloody hard to arrange! Should I inquire?"

Schindler reached to his wallet and peeled off two twenty-pound notes and handed them over.

"Yes," he said. "Discreetly. And right away."

111

CHAPTER 14

For years Schindler had been an exponent of the clever professional diversion. So Schindler decided to use a trick from comedian Joe Cook's playbook and have some fun one evening with the not-so-sharp Nassau cops. He stopped his car in the center of town, ran into an alleyway, studied a blank wall with a magnifying glass, placed a chalk circle around a small spot, ran out of the alley, jumped into his car, and drove away. One member of the Nassau cops spent a week in the alley trying to figure out what the circle on the wall indicated.

His high visibility remained. Sure enough, I was walking with Ray one night and a white woman walking behind us drew abreast of him and, in appearing to brush against him, slipped a note into his hand. She hastened on her way.

Schindler had known that we were being followed by local security but did not know whether our tails had seen the woman slipping him the note. It happened so quickly that I didn't even realize what had happened until he spoke.

"Keep walking," he said. "I just got a special delivery."

We played it smart. We sauntered around town for fully an hour. Then we got into his car. He dropped me at my hotel, then drove back to the villa of the Baroness. It was only then that he read the note that had been slipped to him.

The note was from a prominent woman in Nassau whose name Schindler had come to know. He was to come to her home the following night at ten o'clock. He asked me if I would go with him. I said I would. He referred to her as Lady Estelle and it was understood between us that it was not her real name

The next night Schindler gave his tails the slip. He hired a different car and picked me up in the alley behind my own hotel where I'd given my own watchers the slip. His driver then took us through a maze of back streets and then a dark country road. I assumed it was as much to deter pursuers as it was to keep me from knowing where we were going or had been. Ray had obviously promised to protect his source. I understood.

We arrived at his destination undetected. A large residential building lay at the end of a gravel driveway that looked to be part of an estate. From what I could see in the light of a half moon, the main structure may have been a farmhouse and the estate was part of a working farm. I saw a corral but no livestock.

We were met at the front door by a butler. I was not admitted to the meeting with Ray's contact. Nor did I ever see her. Rather, I sat in the front foyer, watching for any unexpected visitors. I was to notify Ray with a sharp knock if I saw trouble. Fortunately, we had no additional company.

As I sat and waited, Ray cleverly left the door slightly ajar to the salon where he was meeting his newest best friend. I could hear the whole conversation. At one point the butler brought me a glass of ice water and a sandwich.

Ray found the note passer a conservative person, very intelligent, and not, he judged, given to going off halfcocked.

"Did you know," she asked Schindler over Remy Martin and American cigarettes, "that Sir Harry Oakes had a cache of gold coins on the island of Eleuthera?"

Schindler had heard about such a gold cache, but had not learned the detail of the precise island where the stuff was reputedly stashed. Gold was hot stuff, as always. The British government had asked all citizens to turn in their privately held gold to finance the war effort. Many people had been witless enough to do so.

"Yes," the woman continued, "Sir Harry had several million pounds sterling hidden on Eleuthera."

"In a bank? In a vault?" Ray asked.

"No. Hidden. Just hidden."

Eleuthera was one of the largest of the Bahamian islands, some seventy miles east of Nassau. Schindler asked how his informant had come into possession of the information.

"Why," she laughed, drawing suggestively on a Lucky Strike, "*practically everybody* in Nassau knows it."

Schindler was hardly able to check that statement. Suddenly Schindler became conscious of the fact that the woman was telling him that Oakes *had had* gold cached on Eleuthera.

"You're speaking of it in the past," he noted. "It's not there anymore?"

"No."

I could hear a bottle hitting the rim of a glass. Another drink was being poured. "Could you explain?" Ray asked.

"Draw your own conclusions, Mr. Schindler," she said in a throaty voice. "But I think if you go over there you will find colored natives selling gold coins at about half their face value."

Schindler had already learned that Sir Harry Oakes, shortly before his death, had made several trips to Eleuthera, both by boat and by small aircraft. Such trips by a man of Sir Harry's prominence would have aroused suspicion both in Nassau and on Eleuthera itself, an island that remained remote and primitive in its interior and along the more remote sections of its shoreline. It would have been entirely possible for some of the rougher elements on the island—and there were some very rough ones—to have become curious about the Baronet's visits and followed him. Discovering the gold cache, if it were unprotected—buried or stashed in a cave—they could have taken it into their heads to help themselves to it.

Then, being discovered and possibly confronted by Sir Harry, they might have feared he would use his influence to have them imprisoned.

"Never mind the fact that Harry had violated the law by not declaring the gold when the British government asked their subjects to turn in privately held gold to finance the war effort," Ray said to me as we were walking back to the car and out of earshot of our driver. "A man like Harry would have bought his way out of any legal trouble for stashing the gold. But the colored men who had stolen it, they would have gone to prison."

"So," I said, "just speculating, hypothesizing, fearing Oakes' reprisals, the thieves could have crossed to Nassau by boat in the night, crept into Westbourne, and done Sir Harry in?"

"The savagery of the crime, the burning of the eyes and the sex organs, did have distinct overtones of primitive ritual," Ray conceded. "I believe Harry had hidden an amount of gold somewhere. It's what he would have done. I'm not sure I'm buying gold thieves as murderers but we can't dismiss it."

"The circle of possible suspects is getting bigger all the time, isn't it?" I said.

"Don't you wonder why the police aren't thinking the same way?"

It was a question that hung unresolved in the air between us. Quickly, however, we were on to other things.

Major Chalmers had left a message for Ray with the trustworthy Marie af Trolle. He had contacted a certain French citizen who was vacationing nearby, and arrangements would be made to meet. It would cost another hundred pounds sterling, but Ray barely flinched.

He could afford to grin. It was Nancy's money he was spending, after all, not his own. And Nancy didn't care how he spread it around if eventually he got an acquittal.

Back in New York, however, my editors were not as copacetic. My book editor had galleys of my next book which I needed to read and edit. My magazine editors had more pressing issues: the expenses in Nassau were adding up and his boss was getting cranky. The pre-trial stage of the Oakes murder case had hit a dry period and there wasn't much new to write about. I kept filing reports, they kept printing them, but with a lull in the events, it was hard to maintain the heat and sex appeal of the murder case, much as I was doing my best.

Both editors were starting to suggest that it might be beneficial that I came back to New York until the trial started. I was not unreceptive to the idea. But I continued to resist the trip back. I knew from experience that when you left was just when the big news broke and others would scoop it.

I didn't want anyone else to own that scoop.

So, for the time being, I stayed where I was.

CHAPTER 15

No one was quite sure whether three or five recent escapees from Devil's Island had made it to the Bahamas. What was apparent was that a small band of them were holding up at a remote residence on Grand Bahama, about a hundred thirty miles north of Nassau. The British government had no interest in returning them to the penal colony in French Guiana. The penal colony was now under the control of the Vichy French, who were collaborating with Hitler's Germany. So why help the Vichy French in any way large or small, much less potentially provide for them a few more soldiers?

"Want to come along to meet these cutthroats?" Schindler asked me. They would cautiously meet with the right people, and Schindler had secured a meeting.

"I'd be crazy," I answered.

"That means you're coming, right?"

"I'd be nuts," I emphasized.

Ray hired a small airplane. The pilot was a stocky mocha-skinned man with wild unkempt hair that fell beyond his collar. It was not dissimilar to a mane. Hence, I assumed, his *nom de vol*. Ray introduced him as "Lion," which was the only name Ray knew him by. I gathered that he worked within the gray area of the law and did odd jobs therein, such as this one. If he had a pilot's license I never saw it, but things could be casual in this part of the world.

We flew to Grand Bahama on Lion's rickety old aircraft, probably never more than five hundred feet above the water. We met three escapees—they were all Frenchmen—in a waterfront bar. Neither Ray nor I spoke French and the ex-prisoners spoke no English. Conveniently, however, the Frenchman who seemed to be the leader had brought along a local Haitian émigré named Henri-Claude to serve as an interpreter.

Ray sat at a table with the man whose name was Francois. The two others watched the door. I assumed they were armed. I sat several feet behind Ray and listened. Francois was a rough unshaven man in a dark blue shirt and soiled khakis. He had a powerful body, like a wild animal. A deep scar marked his left temple.

Ray inquired about the gun. Through the interpreter, Francois said he knew nothing about selling any weapons. Ray asked if any of the escapees had ever met Oakes. Francois said they hadn't, then added that none of them had tempted fate enough to go to Paradise Island which was the seat of the government.

No, Francois said, none of them had any idea who might have murdered Harry and no, they were not inclined to do much other than sit out the war in peace and maybe move along to the United States or Canada once the war ended. They sure as hell were not returning to France, Francois said; they were still wanted there for murder and other violent crimes and had no desire to be sent back to Guiana.

Francois talked a good ball game. We knew that men like this could lie in your face and then stab you in the back two seconds later. We also knew it remained possible that this group of convicts had discovered the gold cached in Eleuthera, helped themselves to it, and then learned that Sir Harry was after them. Knowing of the man's power on the Bahamas, they would have had ample reason to do him in.

Schindler put the question right up to them a second time as he was concluding the meeting: Did any of them know anything about the murder of Sir Harry Oakes? Through long experience, Schindler had solid instincts about when a man or potential witness was lying or spinning. He decided that the Devil's Island alumni had nothing to do with a murder in Nassau and didn't have any knowledge of it.

Then Ray turned the tables on the Frenchmen. As he was moving to conclude the meeting, he dropped a casual question. "As someone who had nothing to do with the crime," Schindler asked, "what's your theory? Why was Sir Harry killed?"

Ray waited as the interpreter phrased the question in French. We expected a shrug and a non-answer. But Francois was more forthcoming.

"Money," he said. "Someone stood to gain a lot of money."

"Like who?" Ray asked.

"American Mafia, maybe?" the Frenchman said through Henri-Claude, the interpreter. "Business here after the war? Casinos? Hotels? I don't know. I only guess."

"What about a sexual angle?" Ray asked.

"A jealous husband?"

All three Frenchmen laughed. A crime of this much violence just didn't fit that motive, they all agreed. There was more laughter. They suggested that any man's wife would enjoy getting naked and getting a little frisky if she was ignored long enough. Women were like that, the Frenchmen maintained.

We thanked our new acquaintances for the life lesson about females. We boarded the sea plane back to Nassau.

"I've been hearing this more than a few times," Ray mused in the small plane as we flew back to Nassau. Ray produced a small flask of Scotch and we shared it. "Gambling interests. Mob guys from Cuba and southern Florida," he said. "They've got an eye on the Bahamas after Germany and Japan are defeated."

"Is there credibility to that?" I asked.

He shrugged. "Who knows? I suppose it makes some sense. It's the type of thing that Christie would have been for and Sir Harry against," he said with a moment's thought. He shrugged again and fastened his seatbelt as we hit some bumps over the dark and turbulent high waves of water between Grand Bahama and New Providence. "But I'm playing Devil's advocate. I have no evidence." He paused then concluded. "Plus, remember: I'm here to acquit de Marigny. One man's life is enough of a responsibility. The Bahamian authorities will have to live with whatever comes next. We don't. It's not our circus and these people we are dealing with aren't our monkeys."

"Right," I said, without too much conviction.

In the dark plane, Ray's eyes narrowed. "How are you bearing up?" he asked.

"What do you mean?"

"You're starting to look beaten up," he said. "These cases, these long assignments, they wear you down, don't they?"

"I'm all right," he said.

"No, you're not. You'd like to go home."

"I'm a writer. I have an assignment here," I said.

Ray was about to answer when the pilot turned to us. "Seat belts tight, gentlemen," he said. "Starting descent to land."

"I'll say this about this flight," I said. "At least it was short."

The pilot, Lion, laughed. He knocked back a gulp of booze and gave us a thumbs-up. Then we took a few bounces through some low wind shear and found our final approach for Nassau, accompanied all around by a final swig of Scotch.

CHAPTER 16

By the fifth of September, Ray and I began to recapitulate what we had discovered.

We were convinced de Marigny had not committed the crime. We were further satisfied that the murder could have been committed by any of several enemies Sir Harry had acquired before or since his arrival in Nassau. And it could have been done by robbers from the outer islands.

But we had also been hearing a lot of local gossip. We had learned the identities of the husbands of women at whom Sir Harry had successfully and unsuccessfully made passes. Schindler had, in fact, met some of these men at parties he had been invited to because of his connection with the Baron and Baroness af Trolle. Here was a valid angle. Yet none of the wronged husbands seemed to fill the bill as a suspect.

Schindler decided to go back to the beginning, or to a few days before the beginning. If he took things step by step, he figured he might come across something he had not previously considered. Investigations are that way.

What we knew for certain was that week before the murder, Sir Harry's pal Harold Christie had moved into Westbourne, ostensibly to keep him company, but also, according to what people told us, to work on many pressing business situations in which they were jointly involved. The two men were alone in the big place at night, as the servants slept out. Christie occupied a room on the second floor, about eighteen feet from the nearest wall to Sir Harry's room. In that immediate section of the mansion, there were two other rooms: a small dressing room and a bathroom. It was thus possible for someone to walk from Christie's room into Sir Harry's by passing through a door that led from Christie's room into the small adjoining room. From there one would continue through a door leading into the bathroom, then out another bathroom door into Sir Harry's room.

There was also another way of going from Christie's room into Sir Harry's. A screen door led from Christie's room onto a veranda that ran the entire width of the house. A similar door in Sir Harry's room led onto this veranda. It was the habit of the two men, when they alone remained at Westbourne, to go out through the screen doors of their respective rooms and meet on the veranda for breakfast in the morning.

On the night of July sixth, twenty-four hours before the murder, Sir Harry and Christie sat out on this veranda sipping drinks made of native rum, sugar, and fresh lime juice, a pleasant nightcap. Then the two men retired.

On the morning of the seventh they had breakfast on the veranda. Then they spent a busy day together, preparing for Sir Harry's departure the next day on a business trip to South America. They returned to Westbourne around five in the afternoon, played a couple of games of tennis and had some drinks. Then they washed and dressed for Sir Harry's farewell party that night. The party broke up about midnight. The servants straightened up and left Westbourne for the night.

Christie and Sir Harry had a couple of more drinks and then went to their respective rooms. All during the night it stormed. In the morning, when Sir Harry did not show up on the veranda for breakfast, Christie walked into his chamber and discovered the body.

Exactly what had happened between the time Christie and Oakes parted for the night and the time Christie walked from the veranda into the Baronet's chamber in the morning was the key question.

Since his arrival in Nassau, Schindler had occasionally run into Christie in the street or at a party. The two men had never spoken to each other, just nodded in a stiff sort of way. After all, they were on opposite sides of the official fence, Christie was to be a witness for the Crown and Schindler was trying to knock down the Crown's case. They couldn't have been much more opposed than that. But even had they not been on opposite sides of the fence, they probably wouldn't have liked one another. It was a case of chemistry: the two men just didn't click. Now Schindler began to drop a few questions about Christie. Everyone on the island had a good word for the man. Or so it seemed. Or maybe sometimes just a good word and then they would stop talking or flee the conversation.

No one revealed much about his background. Or at least no one wanted to chat in detail about it. He had, apparently, just materialized in Nassau as an adult and over the years come to be a power in the place.

Schindler began to catch whispers. So did I. Some residents of the island who had come from faraway places and bought property from Christie weren't satisfied with it. Some of Christie's real-estate clients were, in fact, downright dissatisfied with their purchases. But they didn't complain. For some reason, many people seemed to be afraid of Harold Christie.

Schindler began getting interested. He had developed some trusting local contacts by this time, particularly among the non-white non-power people of both Paradise Island, Grand Bahama and the nearer inhabited islands. Again, the Bahamas were an insular little collection of islands where everyone knew everyone else's business. Nassau itself was a small town on a remote coral reef.

Pretty soon, after talking on the QT to several locals, a more sinister portrait emerged of the local top citizen.

Christie had been born to an old Bahamian family that dated back to the Tory flight to the islands following the American Revolution. His old man had been a local character who fathered eight children—out of twenty pregnancies—to Harold's long-suffering mother, who was called Madge. The old man had been a successful merchant when he'd cared to pay attention to life's economic duties, but like many other whites on the island he was complacent, sometimes to the point of indolence. As young Harold grew to manhood, his father all but abandoned financial support of the family. Madge ran the household, kept the books, and operated her husband's businesses for him, to the extent that there were any. Meanwhile, dad spent his time in evangelical studies, praising God and Jesus and writing bad uninspired poetry.

To his credit, young Harold didn't care much for this. When World War One broke out he found his way to Canada and enlisted in the Royal Air Force. He took well to the big world beyond the Bahamas. Then in 1920 the moralists and puritans in the United States handed Harold Christie a gift on a golden platter: the Volstead Act, which banned the sale of booze in the United States.

"Ha! I'll drink to that," Christie reportedly laughed to friends.

Apparently, many others would also. Using his newly found knowledge of boats, small aircraft and the geography of North America, Christie became an engaging and friendly conduit between Nassau's liquor wholesalers and their speakeasy customers in the United States. The business was hugely profitable. Christie was still in his twenties, young and ambitious, and he was starting to make serious money, little of which was being peeled away by Uncle Sam. He was, recall, not subject to American taxes. It was a splendid situation for Christie, cozy and profitable in more ways than any man could count.

I was intrigued when Ray explained all this background to me one day in mid-September over lunch. But I must have yawned or something because suddenly Ray changed the subject.

"Alan," he said in his friendliest most avuncular voice. "I'm going to ask you something as your longtime friend. Why don't you get to hell out of Nassau?"

"What?" I asked.

"Take a break from the overheated murder, mayhem and mystery down here in the damned colonies. Go home for a couple of weeks."

"This discussion again?" I asked.

"Probably for the last time," he said. "Why are you trying to tough it out? Hell, I've left the islands three times since I first arrived. It does a man good to refresh. Explain to me: why are you not taking a break?"

"Ray, you know how it works. The moment you leave, something big happens."

"I'll cover for you."

"I appreciate that, but—"

"Look," he answered. "You're in a miserable state. Your family misses you. Your magazine publisher is hounding you and chaffing at the expenses. Your book publisher wants to see you in person. You told me so yourself. You're strung out and overextended."

I reached for my drink and finished it. I tapped another cigarette out of its pack and lit it. "Leave and come back when the trial's ready to start," he advised. "I'll bring you up to date on everything you miss. I'll telegraph you some stuff you can use for articles and you can write from your home. You'll come back refreshed, ready to work. You'll make everyone happy, including yourself."

I thought about it.

Ray leaned in closer. "Alan, I got a tip today from the courthouse. There's a nice lady in the register's office. She feeds me information in exchange for five-pound notes. The trial date has been set for October 18. It won't be announced till the first day of the month. Today is September 20. You should leave and try to be back by October fifteen to be safe. Make a hotel reservation before you go. The outside press is going to pour into this place. Okay?"

"Do I seem that miserable?" I asked.

"You *are* that miserable. Start packing."

"You can get along without your extra man?" I asked.

"I'll do fine. I don't want to see you here in twenty-four hours. But I do want to see you when the trial starts. Now get the hell out of here."

After a moment, I asked, "What do you think is going to happen to de Marigny?"

"He could very possibly hang."

"Jesus," I said softly.

"It's the job of my lifetime to make sure he doesn't," Schindler said. "It's your job, too, as a writer, to promote the truth, unlike the various hack journalists who have invaded this island and who are feeding pap to the Hearst papers."

"Jesus," I said again.

"If anything critical happens I'll send you a Western Union. Any sane man needs a break from this hot crazy place. Get out of here, Alan," he said emphatically. "Go spend time with your wife and family. You won't regret it. Go! Now!"

I went back to the hotel. I sat for a moment on the edge of my bed. I wondered whether to take Ray's advice—I was stuck in a terrible place, not knowing whether to move forward or back, but knowing I had to move. I felt like I was walking off the story. But the break made sense. The defense was lining up its best artillery. The prosecution had lined up theirs. Ray was right. The first shots wouldn't be fired until court convened.

I stood. I packed.

The next morning, I went downstairs and announced my check-out, booking a new reservation at the same time. I left one bag of clothes at the hotel. The staff would launder everything and hold my possessions for me till I returned, unless of course it got stolen. I booked my return for October fifteenth as Ray had suggested. If the trial began on the eighteenth, a few days of recovery and lead time would be precious.

I went to the Nassau airport with one suitcase and caught a Bahama Airlines Curtiss C-46 to Miami. It was a nerve-wracking forty-seat transport that offered reasonable comfort. The weather provided no comfort, however, as we flew right into one of those sudden late afternoon tropical thunderstorms. I had been wise enough not to eat before the flight. When we bounced to a rough landing in Miami an hour and a half after take-off, those passengers who still had anything left applauded.

I couldn't tolerate another flight. And wartime travel restrictions didn't make finding one any easier, so I took an overnight train to Washington's Union Station. I had two hours between rail connections, had lunch, went out to the front steps of the station and gazed at the wartime capital.

I felt a corny little thrill—I hadn't realized how much I had missed just being in my own country. And now here I was right in the heart of power, the nerve center of the western anti-Axis world. I bought a *Washington Star*. The front page was all war news: British midget submarines had attacked and crippled the German battleship

Tirpirtz, at anchor in a Norwegian fjord. The Soviet Red Army had retaken Smolensk. Take that, you Nazi bastards.

I boarded a train for New York. It crept through the mid-Atlantic region, then hit Philadelphia. I got out to stretch my legs; the stop was twenty minutes. Then we were back chugging northward. I saw my old home town of Trenton, and had to turn away from the window. There was too much baggage. Same with northern New Jersey: I had mixed blessings there because on the upside, my wife and her family were from the Bernardsville area, good solid industrious God-fearing Americans, but it was also not far from Hopewell, where I'd worked on the Lindbergh case and lost whatever had ever remained of my innocence in my thirties.

The train arrived at New York's Pennsylvania Station around nine p.m. The tracks were two or three stories underground. I climbed the stone steps and came up into the spacious lobby with the huge columns which rose to the ceiling murals. There's an old newspaper saying: a city gets what it wants, is willing to pay for, and ultimately deserves. Penn Station was one such treasure.

There was still a florist open. I bought two dozen red roses for my wife and found a taxi on Seventh Avenue. He drove east on Thirty-Fourth Street, then drove up Park Avenue to Sixty-First Street. 530 Park Avenue. Home.

The door staff greeted me warmly and the elevator man took me up. I knocked on my door and fumbled with a key but the door came open before I could turn the lock.

I fell into my wife's arms and she into mine. I fought back tears. I hugged her as I had hugged no other person ever in my life. It was not until I saw her that I realized how much the case had ripped into my soul and torn me apart. I admitted to myself that I found the murder case in the Bahamas, in all its primal violence and aura of corruption and compromised justice, as repugnant as anything I'd ever written about. I dreaded going back. And I was nowhere close to the end of my involvement.

CHAPTER 17

In the first days that followed, I spent a lot of time on little things, like straightening my desk, having quiet lunches on Madison Avenue with my wife, answering mail, and taking my daughter to Central Park. The carousel and the zoo were pleasures that I had never fully appreciated. A war was raging far away on many different fronts, but I turned my eyes away from it. For one of the few times in my life, I avoided the news and newspapers.

Gradually, I got around to business. I had lunch twice with my pal Aaron Fairstein, who had produced the radio show, *Wanted: Armed and Dangerous!* that I had narrated. Aaron was a small intense gnome-like man in his sixties. He looked and acted like a deranged elf. He always had a dozen or more projects on his drawing board, hoping that one would come to fruition. We talked about some new ideas, but I was non-committal until I could see my way through current assignments. "Just let me get through this Oakes thing and my next book," I said. "Then we can talk about anything."

"Reasonable enough, kiddo" he answered. Aaron was remarkable. His underworld contacts were extensive. He had grown up on the Lower East Side of Manhattan and he knew some terrifying people. He used to brag that some of the best episodes that he produced on *Wanted and Dangerous!* were on guys with whom he had gone to grade school.

My book publisher, McBride and Company, sent over the galleys of my second work of non-fiction. The title was now *Betrayal From the East*. It had a nasty cover of an evil-looking Japanese man, or the artist's version of such, a clumsy caricature which would embarrass me far into the future.

The advance orders were great. For a forty-year-old writer who had never finished high school, I reminded myself again what a lucky man I was. But there were trade-offs. Sometimes successful book publishing was like prostitution; and on certain occasions, the distinctions were vague. This was one of those times. I could be a stickler about language and facts, and it disturbed me that I found some of my own writing rushed, ragged and—dare I say—from time to time inventive.

I phoned McBride. I talked to my book editor, a surly no-nonsense guy named Bob Farnsworth, not to ever be confused with my day-to-day magazine editors at Fawcett Publications. "Is there time to fix some of this?" I asked.

"Why the hell would you want to, Alan?" Farnsworth replied.

"The book could be a lot better."

"So what? It doesn't matter. What matters is that needs to hit the goddam bookstores by Christmas. Are you finished with that murder case in Cuba?"

"It's in the Bahamas, and no, I'm not. I'm just in town for a few days."

"Well, come in and say hello to our staff. They always enjoy seeing you. I don't know why, but they do. We'll have lunch, okay?"

"Okay," I said. Lunch would mean at a little French place called Monsieur Laurent near Union Square. It was right around the corner from the publisher's office on East Sixteenth Street.

And that's how it went. Outwardly, I was calm, walking on air. Inwardly, I was set to explode. I needed to release. When I started to put the events of Nassau in perspective, they began to wake me up at two a.m. and then again at four and six. I couldn't get them out of my mind. Now that I had pulled myself away from the legal proceedings in Nassau, I could see what a sham they were.

Sometimes it made me feel ill. Other times I would break a sweat. And it wasn't even my neck that was going to be in the noose.

"What's wrong?" my wife asked, sensing my distress.

"This is a rough case in Nassau," I said. "Somebody bashed in the head of one of the world's richest men. Now they're planning to hang an innocent man for it."

"Oh," she said softly.

"Yeah," I said.

"Why do you think he's innocent?" she asked.

"That's what my guts are telling me," I said. "Plus, there's no real evidence."

I had only known my wife for six years. I didn't want to go into how many times, covering the vilest forms of human behavior for a quarter century, I'd seen variations on the same event: an innocent man accused. An innocent man jailed. An innocent man convicted. An innocent man executed.

The American justice system was probably better and fairer than any other in the world, but it was far from perfect. Mistakes were made by overzealous prosecutors, overeager or corrupt cops, dumb juries, alcoholic judges and crooked lawyers. The last thing any innocent man or woman wanted to do was get caught up in the system. The system would chew you up and spit you out, battered and broken, ruined or dead.

On a few evenings, booze helped me shove these thoughts aside. Worse, while I was back in New York, I fell into an old pattern that had cost me my first marriage. I'd hit some bars after business hours and sometimes not managed to get up and head home until after midnight. I'll confess: sometimes I was too looped to do much more than stagger and hang on a lamppost on Lexington or Third Avenue.

But I'd be smart enough to tie a load on in my own neighborhood where many of the cops knew me. If I had trouble navigating the streets, the New York City police would pick me up. I'd identify myself and they'd laugh and bring me home.

"The writer. The true crime guy. He's had a snootful," they'd laugh. They'd bring me home and deliver me to my apartment door.

Whatever private misgivings I had about cops, the New York cops liked me. They were good guys. More than once a green and white squad car would bring me to my door and deliver me to my wife. They were all noble Hibernians, the guys I knew. Mulrooney. Sullivan. O'Casey. Hearn. Ryan. And the occasional son of Italy. Ricci. Tedeschi. Sanpietro. I didn't deserve favored treatment and I quite profited by getting it. At Christmas, I'd send a case of Jameson to each of the local precincts, and on Columbus Day boxes of pastries from Ferrara's down on Mulberry Street. The boys in the precincts never declined any of it.

I was very much a privileged soul. But there were demons tormenting me. I'd seen too much over the years. Nassau was serving only as the icing as a very bad cake. In a way, being distant from it made me see if with a different and more horrifying perspective. I knew I didn't want to return. I knew I was going to have to. And I knew that my drinking days would have to end.

I had a wonderful friend named Herbert Ludwig Nossen. He was our family physician, a very bright man who had been born in German in 1895. He had emigrated to America in the 1920's and gone to medical school here. He had delivered my daughter, a priceless gift.

He had written an influential book titled *Twelve Against Alcohol*. The book comprised twelve true case histories of what was then called "dipsomania," with the alcoholic's own story in his or her own words. The work intended to present the realistic components of the problem. There were eleven instances of people being cured. There was one case where the patient did not want to be cured.

I read his book and contacted him through his publisher. We became friends. He started to counsel me about drinking. I went to work on the problem. God knew, the man had enough on his plate. He was a German Jew who had emigrated to America. His parents had tried to emigrate but been stopped by the Nazi regime. He hadn't heard from them for almost two years.

My magazine publisher, Fawcett Publications, was in a new building on West Forty-Fourth Street. I took a couple of meetings there, too, with my top editor Ken Gelb, the big boss at *True* Magazine, while I was back in Gotham, and my more immediate boss, Joe Verona, who was the Articles Editor

The famous Hippodrome Theatre had been just across Forty-Fourth Street. It had once been the world's largest theatre with a seating capacity of more than five thousand and a two-hundred-foot stage. In its day, the theatre had state-of-the-art theatrical technology, including a rising glass water tank. It had been home to some of the greatest vaudeville shows ever. When I was in my twenties, I saw Harry Houdini do his disappearing elephant act. There had also been silent movies. Chaplin. Jolson. Fatty Arbuckle and Lillian Gish.

The Hippodrome had been demolished in 1939 and replaced by an office building. I still missed the old place. In my editor's office on a Thursday afternoon, I looked out the window and saw wage slaves in other offices confined to their desks where trapeze artists had once flown through the air. But what could one do? The world changes whether one wants it to or not.

I looked from the window back to my Articles Editor. Joe Verona was the son of a cop from Naples. Joe had gone into the newspaper and magazine business with me in 1926, when we both were twenty-three. He was one of the first friends I'd made in New York and was still one of my best. He dished me bread-and-butter assignments and never let me down. I made a point to never let him down.

He was happy with the reports I was filing. He was publishing them himself, then farming out the reprint rights across the free part of the globe, mostly North America.

The company was making money. Joe was making money. I was making money. Nobody was complaining. But I couldn't get Alfred de Marigny out of my mind, flawed individual that he was, unjustly imprisoned as he remained.

Joe Verona and I went up to see the Yankees play at the stadium on Saturday, September 26th. We took our wives. The Yankees won the game and the pennant with a 2-1 victory over Detroit in fourteen innings. Bill Dickey bounced a single over the mound in the bottom of the fourteenth and the Yankees had their fourteenth pennant of the century. Rizzuto, my favorite, was gone to the war. DiMaggio didn't play. Spud Chandler pitched the complete game, as did the losing pitcher. The St. Louis Cardinals had run away with the National League, so the upcoming World Series would be a rematch of the 1942 classic, which the Cardinals had won.

I wondered about getting tickets to the Series. And that made me wonder how long I was staying.

I spent Sunday with my wife and daughter. My sister, Edythe, came in from New Jersey and we all had lunch. On Monday morning, my phone rang.

It was a representative of a man named Thomas Dewey, a former prosecutor in New York whose office I had worked with on many times. Dewey was now governor of New York State. He wanted to talk to me. That's right: the Governor of New York wanted to talk to me, alone and in private. There was a lunch meeting booked for the following Tuesday at The New York Yacht Club—a secure site, I knew—on West Forty-third Street.

I said I'd be there.

And while I had been en route to New York, yet another curious event had taken place.

A stranger had walked unannounced into the Schindler offices in New York. He introduced himself as Harry Phillips, formerly an investigator in the United States Treasury Department and no friend of Harold Christie. He obtained a meeting with Walter Schindler, Ray's younger brother who managed the agency. Phillips had, he said, been reading in the newspapers that Ray Schindler was working on the Oakes case.

"True, and so what?" asked Walter, who was pretty much a no-nonsense guy.

"Well," said Phillips, "I thought perhaps you would like to know something about this man, Harold Christie."

"What about him?" Walter asked, folding his arms before him.

"Well, for one thing," Phillips began, "Christie is something less than the lily-white holier-then-holy character that the upper bracket citizens of Nassau would have you think he is."

Christie, Phillips continued, had been a major rumrunner during Prohibition days, reputedly pals with the Capone mob in Chicago, and had been in some sort of trouble with the federal government in the early Nineteen Twenties. This we knew, but Phillips claimed he had much more. As Phillips recalled, there had been a body attachment in Boston—a legal process similar to a warrant for arrest—out for Christie about the false registry of a ship, but the attachment had never been served.

To say the least, Phillips now had Walter Schindler's attention.

The Boston offices of the Schindler organization examined the federal records there but drew a blank. Walter Schindler phoned Phillips and said that that he must be mistaken.

"The hell I am," said Phillips. "I'll go up to Boston and retrieve the record myself."

"You do that," Walter Schindler said. He dismissed Phillips from his office and shook his head, convinced that the man had wasted his time and was possibly a nut. There were plenty of them around.

CHAPTER 18

Thomas Dewey had graduated from Columbia University Law School two decades earlier and had been admitted to the New York Bar thereafter. Dewey was a credible Republican when there weren't many around—to my mind too many had been windbag isolationists and Nazi apologists. He served as chief assistant to the U.S. Attorney for the southern district of New York from 1930 to 1933. When he became the U.S. Attorney, he also served as special assistant to U.S. Attorney General Homer Stille Cummings, Ray Schindler's friend. It was a tight little world of legal eagles where, for better or worse, everyone knew everyone.

In 1935, Dewey was appointed the special prosecutor for a grand jury investigation into vice and racketeering in New York City. Dewey gained national attention by going after the hoodlums who controlled organized crime in New York. As a writer of true crime, I came to know him. I worked frequently with his office.

Dewey's crusade began with an attack on prostitution, gambling and loan sharks. FBI director J. Edgar Hoover labeled mobster "Dutch" Schultz, my old acquaintance from *Evening Graphic* days, Public Enemy No. 1. Schultz was a dangerous sorehead by this time and didn't much care for the compliment. With Dewey leading the investigation, Schultz set out to convince his mob associates that assassinating Dewey would be a great idea.

Word of the proposal traveled fast to the top shelf hoods: Lucky Luciano and Meyer Lanksy. Dutch's response backfired like a cheap twenty-two. Even with a $10,000 reward on Dewey's head, the mob's goon squad, Murder Inc., opted to get rid of Schultz instead. The syndicate's national board did not want the trouble that would come from snuffing a prominent prosecutor. It would be bad for business.

Schultz and three associates were whacked in at 10:15 p.m. on October 23, 1935 at the Palace Chophouse at 12 East Park Street in Newark, New Jersey, which he used as his new headquarters. Two bodyguards and Schultz's accountant were the other three unfortunate souls.

With Lucky Luciano now exposed to the public eye, Dewey brought him to trial for running prostitution rings all over New York City. Luciano kept clean records, so it was not easy to convict him— like his counterpart, Alfonse Capone of Chicago. Nevertheless, Dewey succeeded in convicting him on ninety counts of prostitution, and in 1936, Luciano was sent to prison for thirty to fifty years. Dewey obtained seventy-two convictions out of seventy-three prosecutions, a better batting average than the lordly Joe DiMaggio.

Following that mighty blow to the national crime syndicate, Dewey's was elected the New York District Attorney in 1937. He received credit for the convictions of numerous mobsters. Continuing his quest to put an end to organized crime, Dewey ran for governor of New York in 1938, but lost the election.

In 1940, Dewey made an unsuccessful bid for the Republican presidential nomination. The party instead turned to an insurance salesman from Ohio named Wendel Wilkie. Wilkie lost to Franklin Roosevelt's third term candidacy. But Dewey ran again for governor of New York in 1942 and won. So now Thomas Dewey was Governor, sitting across from me in a private booth in the dining room at the ritzy New York Yacht Club. There were plenty of trophies around, including the America's Cup, but no actual boats, other than some impressive models.

In smart circles in Manhattan and Long Island, a remark attributed to socialite Alice Roosevelt Longworth, the hard-living hard-drinking daughter of Theodore Roosevelt, skewered Tom Dewey as "the little man on the wedding cake." The remark targeted Dewey's neat mustache, tight proper collars and impeccably dapper dress. He did in fact look just like the little plastic man on millions of American wedding cakes. If ever there were a verbal bulls-eye in seven scathing words, this was it.

"Here we are at the N.Y.Y.C, Governor," I said when we met for lunch, "and I didn't know you owned a boat."

He looked at me for a second and then laughed out loud, which was unusual. Like most prosecutors, Dewey was a serious man, not given easily to merry thigh-slappers. "I don't, Alan. It's private in here," he said.

"No life preservers necessary?" I asked.

"Not here," he said affably. "But maybe down in Nassau Town."

"Ah," I said. "You've been keeping track of me."

"Very much so. I read your book, by the way. *Passport To Treason*. Well done! Nice work."

"Thank you."

"You're a Republican, I assume," he said, playing with me.

"I'm registered as one."

"I'm happy to have your continuing support."

"I'm always happy to vote for a great American," I said.

He took the compliment gracefully and gave a little nod.

He was not stupid. I wondered if he knew I was lying. The truth was, I had voted for Roosevelt three times. Dewey at his worst could be a stuffed shirt. There was something about him that was a little too pat. I didn't completely trust him. But unlike a lot of writers, I had never caused any problems for Mr. Dewey's office or ambitions. I received points for that.

A third man arrived. I didn't know him. He was introduced to me as Leonard Gaitskell, an assistant U.S. Attorney from the Southern District of New York. He was there to represent the current U.S. Attorney, James McNally, who was now in the job that Dewey had once held.

After exchanging greetings, I looked back to Dewey. I cocked my head. "So? Is Nassau what we're here to talk about?" I asked.

"Mostly, yes."

"On the record? Off the record?" I asked.

"Strictly off," he said. "All right?"

"All right," I said. I had a fountain pen and note pad on the table. I put them away.

"What do you think?" the governor asked. "Is de Marigny guilty?"

"That's not for me to decide."

"I asked you what you thought."

"I think the case against him is highly flawed," I said. "Whether they'll convict him or not is another matter."

"How is your pal Schindler doing?" Dewey asked. "Ray's not as smart as he thinks he is. In fact, he's a pretty much of a fraud, in my opinion. Silver hair to match his silver tongue. A charming fake, but a fake."

Gaitskell grinned.

"Ray's uncovering a few things," I said, playing my cards closely. "The existing powers are doing their best to make things difficult for him, but he has a way of pulling the rabbit out of the hat at the last minute."

All four eyes and ears were fixed on me.

"I'll say this, also," I added. "Ray's been ingratiating himself around town. He and Nancy de Marigny and that blonde, Marie af Tolle, they're winning a public relations battle which may be crucial. Sentiment on the island is turning toward the accused."

"Is that right?" Gaitskell said, intrigued.

"That's correct," I said.

"They control the press pretty tightly down there, don't they?" Dewey asked.

"They don't control the press so much as they control what the press has access to," I said. "Similar result."

"Ray is doing good public relations for the accused?" Dewey asked.

"It may not help," I said, "but it could. Jurors are jurors. In the end, they're perfectly free to accept or reject any evidence put before them and do whatever they damned feel like."

The two law school graduates exchanged a knowing glance.

"What do you hear about the Duke of Windsor?" Gaitskell asked.

"Quite a bit. None of it good." I paused. They waited. "He comes across as a bit of a featherhead," I said.

They laughed.

"He's a royal ass!" Dewey muttered. "Practically an out and out Nazi, as well as an idiot."

"Practically?"

All three of us shared a longer laugh. More small talk followed. Then Gaitskell moved the conversation along.

"Alan," he said, "if I may call you 'Alan,' here's what my office is curious about. Does the name Meyer Lansky come up? What about Lucky Luciano, also?"

"In what connection?" I asked.

"Oakes' death."

"Their names have come up. There's a lot of loose talk in Nassau. Rumors mostly. Wealthy people dealing with gangsters the same way they used to deal with the rum runners. Fill up their coffers on the sly with some dirty business. No one's going to prosecute their friends. Everyone's hand is in the same cookie jar as long as it's a white hand. The non-whites don't get anything. We all know that."

Gaitskell continued. "We hear stories that Cuba might not be so safe a bet for the Chicago boys after the war," the AUSA said. "Their boy there, Camacho, might lose the free election next year. Or he might get overthrown. We're hearing stories that the Miami and Chicago mob might want to hedge their bets and set up gambling in the Bahamas. See what I'm suggesting?"

It only took a few seconds. Then I did.

"But Sir Harry would have been a bluenose about such things," I said. "As the wealthiest man on the island, he wouldn't mind bedding the wives of several of his friends. But he was too much the moralist to want to hear a roulette ball clinking around a wheel or the shuffle of cards."

"It's just a theory," Dewey said.

"It could have accounted for his murder," Gaitskell suggested. "If Oakes was blocking the expansion of gambling into the Bahamas, now or in the future, there could have been a lot of people who'd stand to profit by his death."

"And the mob could have easily arranged a middle-of-the-night murder," Dewey said, his eyes tight.

I shrugged. "Possible," I said. "It's a working theory."

"Is Schindler working that angle?" Dewey asked.

"If so, I haven't seen it," I said.

"Why would he ignore that?" Gaitskell asked.

"Ray's job is to keep Nancy de Marigny's husband off the gallows," I told him. "Anything else is incidental."

"Ah. Okay," Gaitskell said.

"If you hear anything," Dewey said at length, "would you be good enough to advise Mr. Gaitskell?"

"Snitch my information with the prosecutors?" I said, with a smile. "You're asking an honest reporter to share information with a prosecutor?"

"Let's be high minded," Dewey said, never having trouble reaching for a platitude. "We need to keep a step ahead of these hoods. For the war effort. We wash your hand, you wash ours. Gentleman to gentleman." He paused. "It is a given, of course, that if we can help you or Ray in return, that will happen. Just call me at the Governor's office."

When I was in New York, there was no problem calling from a pay phone anywhere in the city. Just bring a fistful of nickels. But how I was supposed to get information to them from the Bahamas was not explained. Nor was it obvious. Every phone in Nassau was suspect these days. Western Union and Telex were monitored. Any regular mail to a noteworthy address was no-doubt read by a special office of the colonial post office before it got onto a boat or plane to head off the island.

But, "I'll see what I can do," I said, agreeing actually to nothing.

We shook hands and ordered lunch.

***

On the same afternoon in Boston, Harry Phillips, the former Treasury Department investigator who had come to see Walter Schindler with some backstory on Harold Christie, was in for a nasty surprise. There was nothing in the federal indexes in Boston to indicate that Harold Christie had ever been accused of any infraction of a federal law there at any time. Phillips was dead certain that an arrest warrant for Harold Christie had been issued in the early 1920's. He was dead certain because he had worked the case and held the paperwork in his own hands. This simply didn't add up.

All federal records of the day bore numbers that were recorded on federal indexes that give the names of persons accused. So now Phillips set himself to the tedious task of going through every number in the indexes beginning in 1920. What he hoped to find was that one number in the indexes was missing. And sure enough, the next day his persistence paid off. He found what he wanted.

Now Phillips asked to see the records that the missing number referred to.

The records related to Harold Christie and his alleged infraction of a federal statute. Included in the records was the unserved arrest warrant. Somebody had removed from the indexes the number leading to the warrant, a suspicious event right there. If it hadn't been for Phillips' search, the records in the Christie case might have been overlooked till doomsday.

Phillips made a copy of the federal record and took the train to New York late that afternoon. The next morning Walter Schindler took a photograph of it and mailed it to Raymond in Nassau.

The copy of the federal record could be an important piece of paper at the trial. If Christie, a principal witness for the Crown, were to be revealed as something less than a knight in armor by a detailed disclosure of his past, the Crown's case might begin to implode. But of course, it could have no effect whatsoever until it arrived.

CHAPTER 19

During my brief return to New York, my wife wanted to see Frank Sinatra perform live, but name a woman who didn't. I agreed to take her, ready to hold on tight if Frankie the notorious lounge lizard crept too close. Sinatra was married to his first wife, Nancy, back in those days, but the rumors were all over the city that he wasn't working too hard at it.

In Manhattan in September of 1943, there was a new night spot at 151 East 57th Street called the Riobamba. It was owned by one of Thomas Dewey's nemeses, American Mafia boss Louis "Lepke" Buchalter. Thanks to Dewey, Lepke was on death row awaiting execution, but that didn't interfere with his ownership of the club. His wife ran it along with a couple of mobbed-up managers.

While I was in Nassau, Frank Sinatra's people tried to book Blue Eyes at the Copacabana, which was then the hottest night club in New York. No go, Frankie. Yes, he was a star but he still struggled to get some of the top-line bookings. So Frank and his people settled for a three-week engagement at the Riobamba. At first, he was billed an extra act. He knocked the place out. Management moved him quickly to the main act in the middle of his first week. The wise guys always managed their clubs efficiently.

The Riobamba was a glitzy little jewel box of a joint, smaller and more intimate than the also-mobbed-up Copacabana ten blocks away. There was no stage at the Riobamba. Performers leaned on a piano or even the tables where the patrons sat. If you dared, and wanted to bump elbows with guys who had shoulder holsters under their jackets, there was a small dance floor. My wife and I dared a couple of times. Some of the hoods wanted to dance with my wife, and I said no but eventually we stopped going out on the floor.

Floor shows at the Riobamba were at 8:30 p.m., midnight, and two a.m. Dance troupes and relief bands performed at other times. Shows featured a stand-up comedian, dancers, and an orchestra in addition to the main act, usually a crooner. At the beginning of each show, a line of spectacular chorus girls came out singing a song called Riobamba. New York being a wonderfully decadent place in those days, the chorus girls had bare breasts for the two late shows. The Riobamba tune had been written by a young music guy named Leonard Bernstein who sold it to Lepke's club for fifty bucks. The next year he re-adapted the same music into a ballet called *Fancy Free*. Never sell something you wrote once if you can sell it more than once: that's an old writer's wisdom. Good deal for everyone.

The early shows at the Riobamba were sold out. We booked a table for eight for the two-a.m. show. That's right, two a.m., wartime blackouts be damned. A couple of the other writers from the pulp detective mags came along with us. Also in our group was a Newark police captain, Tommy Callahan, an old friend across the years. Captain Callahan went with us so we'd have some presence, an unofficial armed bodyguard. It was a good idea. There was no one at the show except magazine and newspaper people, cops, call girls and connected guys. Who the hell else is out at that hour?

Sinatra looked boyish and jittery, unnerved maybe by the small size of the performance area. He was in a dinner jacket, the focal point of a small narrow spotlight, and jammed right up next to a royal blue Steinway baby grand. He had a small curl that fell gently toward his right eye. With a twitching lip, in a breathless voice, he sang *That Old Black Magic, She's Funny That Way, Polka Dots and Moon Beams* and *Night and Day.*

My wife and I were so close that we could see Frankie's eyes get misty. He fiddled with his wedding ring. He unhooked his bow tie. Frankie worked the room, flirting with every female within twenty feet, avoiding the eyes of any men. In the gaze of my wife there was a glow of warmth and happiness. She put her hand on mine. When Sinatra finished and the lights went up, the applause and shrieking was deafening. I thought the paint on the ceiling was going to peel off and the upper floors of the building were going to crash down on us.

Sinatra bowed once, then eased away in a thin slouch and disappeared into the shadows. He came back out, nodded, and gave us one encore, *I'll Be Seeing You,* which had some extra poignancy for my wife and me. We knew a return to Nassau loomed in my near future. A few minutes later, we settled our bills and were out into the night. The club was only a few blocks from our home. My sister and her husband were staying with us, watching my daughter.

So it went in October of 1943. Some of us were out late at clubs, leading normal if privileged lives. Others were dying in trenches or prison camps or on death marches in the darker parts of the globe. It wasn't fair. It never would be.

***

A few evenings later, at an earlier and much saner hour, I was on my way back into the elevator at my apartment building, normally a safe and secure place. I heard footsteps behind me. They accelerated. Before I could turn I heard a gruff voice.

"Okay! Hold it right there you son of a bitch or I'll blow your damned head off!"

140

I entered the elevator but a hand was on my shoulder. I whirled and raised my own hands to defend myself, only to find myself staring into the face of a sturdy stocky dark-haired man with a square, bristly cut.

The butch haircut accentuated his crooked nose, giving him the look of a retired pugilist. He grinned and slapped my arm, all in good cheer. I gazed into the dancing eyes of my pal, Mike Todd, the Broadway producer. Mike was currently making a fortune with a show called *Stars and Garters*.

The elevator attendant didn't bat an eyelash. Nor did he ask which floors. It was a luxury Park Avenue building. He knew us both. He also knew how to listen without hearing anything.

"Mike!" I said with affection. "You bastard."

"You're a nervous fucker these days, Alan," he said amiably. "What's up, schnook? Haven't seen you for weeks!"

"I've been out of town covering a murder case. I'm only back for a few days."

"Which case?"

"Sir Harry Oakes. Bahamas."

"Whoa! No shit? That one?"

"That one."

"Who killed him?"

"Not the guy who's accused."

The elevator began to ascend. Mike lived on twelve.

"What about you?" I asked. "What are you messing with? Broadway? Hollywood? Booze? Gambling? Gorgeous women? The usual dull stuff?"

"Pretty much. All of the above."

"Details, Mike."

"Oh, I'm producing a little comedy on Broadway," he said. "It's called *The Naked Genius.*"

"Sounds like one of yours," I said. "You playing the lead?"

"Ha! I take that as a compliment coming from you, pal," he said. "But you're right. It's a straight up two-act comedy at the Plymouth Theatre. Should be a small show, but you know I can't control myself. I got forty-three cast members, seven dogs, a god damned rooster and a fucking monkey named Herman, the most charming damned simian you've ever seen. This mini-ape can actually smile on cue, I swear. You gotta see his teeth. And his balls. We should all have nuts that big, Alan! He's smarter than half the actors I'm paying. Gypsy Rose Lee wrote the show for me and it stars Joan Blondell. It's a story about a star stripper trying to lead a normal private life."

"Sounds very 'you', Mike," I said.

We arrived at the eighth floor. "God damned right it is!" Mike said. He walloped my arm again.

Mike was always a whirlwind. I always imagined that in school he'd never been able to sit still. I knew these days he couldn't. Mike was a married guy but I also knew Gypsy Rose Lee was a former paramour, and the top-secret rumor around town, known only to the millions of people who read the scandal sheets, was that Blondell was his current one, burnishing Todd's reputation around town as a skilled and inexhaustible stud.

I knew the rumor was true. I knew it was true because when we arrived at the eighth floor, Mike jammed his meaty forearm against the closing door, forced it to re-open and explained—right there in front of the elevator man—how Joan Blondell was struggling to extricate herself from a failing marriage to actor Dick Powell, one-time song-and-dance man and, according to Mike, soon-to-be celluloid tough guy in Raymond Chandler's *Murder, My Sweet*.

"If you're back in town when *The Naked Genius* opens, call me, you prick. Or kick in my door. Or send me a threatening note. I'll comp you with some house seats, you two-bit true crime hack, you know I'm kidding, Alan, right? I love the stuff you write."

"Right. Thanks, Mike. Always a pleasure."

"I imagine it is," he humbly conceded. "How's your wife?"

"She's wonderful. She's my second one and I'd like to keep her."

"That's great to hear. Say hello for me."

We shook hands and I exited.

I returned home out of breath from two minutes with Mike.

The next day I heard from Ray Schindler by Western Union.

Things were heating up again in Nassau. Two days later, on the twelfth of October, I kissed my wife good-bye, gave my daughter a long lingering hug and started the harsh three-day journey back to the Bahamas and into the depths of my soul.

CHAPTER 20

The evening that I arrived back in Nassau, I followed our game plan and met Ray Schindler again in Dirty Dick's. "There've been some new developments," Ray said ominously. "And they don't look good for de Marigny."

I asked what they were.

"The prosecution is taking testimony from five more people," Schindler said. "One of the new witnesses is a man named Thomas Lavelle. He's one of de Marigny's neighbors over on Victoria Avenue. He claims that there was more hostility between de Marigny and Oakes than anyone knew about. Money. Inheritance. Maybe women. I don't know. They don't tell me what he has to say, certainly."

"They're stacking the deck even higher against him," I said, half a question and half a statement.

"Well, that's pretty damned clear," Ray said with a rueful laugh. "Maybe they'll have the gallows rope reinforced also."

Then there was the issue of Colonel R. A. Erskine-Lindop, the Superintendent of Police and one of the first to reach the scene of the murder. Colonel Erskine-Lindop was one of the most scrupulously honest men in Nassau. He was also reputed to have his doubts about the guilt of the Count. De Marigny's attorney, Godfrey Higgs had been planning to call the colonel as a friendly witness. That would no longer be possible.

Colonel Erskine-Lindop had been transferred to the island of Trinidad. There he was to become Assistant Commissioner of Police.

"The Crown claims that the transfer has been in the works for months," Schindler said. "From long before the murder of Sir Harry Oakes."

"Nonetheless, it's rather queer that Erskine-Lindop won't be called as a witness at the trial," I said.

"That young lawyer Higgs better have some good stuff up his sleeve," Schindler said. "And he's going to have to come down hard on the fingerprint issue. Otherwise, de Marigny swings at the end of the rope. It's that simple."

He took a sip of whiskey.

"Think it's a lost cause?" I asked.

"It's never lost until the trap door opens and the victim drops through it," Ray said. "But it's getting pretty close."

"Then you agree with me that it's a frame up?" I asked.

"Who said that?" he said, turning on me quickly.

"You did," I said. "You used the word 'victim,'" I said.

He smiled.

"So I did, Alan," he allowed. "So I did."

"You know, my brother Walter was sending me some stuff about Harold Christie from New York. The envelope hasn't arrived."

"That's odd, too, isn't it?"

"It's par for the course," he said.

Schindler hadn't exactly expected fast delivery of the envelope containing the derogatory information on Harold Christie once it reached Nassau. The envelope, like all other mail arriving at the island, would have been subjected to wartime censorship...also meaning that someone who didn't like the contents could pick it off and destroy it.

Schindler knew it was against regulations to try to contact the censors directly. He could have contacted Harold Christie to see if Christie could inquire into the matter for him, since Christie, who in effect running the island, had power over the censors. But asking Christie to investigate the fate of an envelope loaded with a blast against himself was laughably out of the question.

"The defense has another problem, too," Ray said to me in a low voice. There was a night watchman Higgs was interviewing. The watchman and one of his friends were going to give evidence in favor of our French friend. He's disappeared."

"Who? The watchman? Or his friend?" I asked.

"Both."

"I'm not surprised," I said.

"I'm going to make a little trip on the island tomorrow in reference to that. I expect it to be unpleasant. Want to come along?"

"Why would I want to miss something unpleasant?"

He smiled. "Good man," he said. "Go into the New Providence Hotel at three p.m. tomorrow. Go out the fire door at the rear. I'll be there with a man named Kayo. We'll be in a panel truck. We'll go for a drive."

"No airplanes? No boats?"

"We'll be taking a small boat. But we won't be leaving the island."

"I'll be there," I said.

We laughed. Ray sipped his Dewar's. I sipped my rum and Coke. We exchanged a long glance. There was something on my mind, however, and I wanted to air it out.

"I'll tell you something, though, Ray," I began. "A lot of that stuff years ago at the *Graphic* was amusing. The fake pictures. The hokey dialogue. But it wore thin after a while. It's okay for a young man to be shameless, maybe. But I'm done with it. I'm looking to be a better writer and reporter in the future."

"Your bestseller has given you a touch of class," he said with a raised white eyebrow. "Is that it, Alan?"

"Maybe," I allowed. "Or maybe because I've turned forty. And have a family. And a reputation. Or maybe a combination of all of these."

"Fair enough," Ray allowed.

"Listen," I expanded over the drinks, "none of us are perfect. We make errors in reporting. Everyone does. Hopefully they're not big errors. But we have an obligation to try our best to get the facts straight. You don't invent facts as a detective, so we shouldn't invent them in what we write."

Ray opened his mouth to speak. I kept going.

"Maybe the Lindbergh case changed me," I said. "The case and ten years to think about it. I covered the investigation, the trial and Bruno Hauptmann's execution by the state of New Jersey. Hauptmann was innocent as charged, but no one wanted to hear about it. We have a higher obligation than the Hearst rags or tabloid media would have you believe. People's lives are at stake." I paused for a moment, trying not to sound too sanctimonious. "Every time an innocent man is convicted at least one guilty man walks free," I said. "There's that angle, too."

"I suppose that's what keeps both of us in business."

I poured more out of the bottle of rum that had been left on the table. I took a long sip. I reminded myself that I never cut down on the booze. Well, after the Oakes case, after I was back in the United States, I told myself. Later. Not now.

I looked back to Ray. In some ways, maybe I was subconsciously trying out my thoughts on him. He was twenty years my senior and twenty years my mentor. What I hadn't seen, what I hadn't learned, he probably had. Plus, while I might be involved in a case, I was still very much the observer, the person trying to view my way in and make sense of it. Ray was more the participant, the actor in the drama. I didn't force events, other than to report them and wait and see a reaction. Ray could force the issues.

He leaned forward and lowered his voice. "Sure. I agree with you. We're professionals. We have our pride. Most of us have standards. Pretty high ones, too. But let me ask you: Are you being paid to be here?"

"Of course, I am. You know that."

"And I am, also," Schindler said. "What's your assignment?"

"To report that case. As I see it."

"Not as your editor sees it? Not as your editor wants it?"

I grimaced. "That was the mistake I made on the Lindbergh case," I said. "And I suppose it's one I'm willing to make again. The situation is a little different. I'm way down here in the Bahamas. It's more difficult to call me back. In New Jersey I was just a day's drive in the auto from the editor's desk. Much easier and less expensive to replace me."

"So, fine! Your job is to file reports. As you see things?" he asked.

"Correct," I allowed.

"And Nancy de Marigny hired me," he said. "I receive her money. Now follow carefully. Nancy is convinced that her husband is innocent. At this point I am, too. Same as you, I reason. I accept her money to find evidence that acquits her husband. My job is to uncover

146

material that will be admissible in a British court that will vindicate him. That's what I've been trying to do." He paused. "And that's where it stops. I'm under no obligation to resolve the inquiry. But I'm also under no moral need to provide a guilty party or in any other way drag the culprit or culprits kicking and screaming to justice," Ray said. "Remember that, Alan."

After a moment, I finished my drink. "I'll try to," I said. I was finished with the booze for the evening. So was Ray, after a final gulp.

"You would be *wise* to," he advised. He leaned back. He glanced at his watch. His eyes checked the door. He side-glanced the other tables. "Let's stop fooling ourselves," he said. "Under current conditions there's no possibility of anyone being convicted other than de Marigny. Either he swings from that lovely new noose they ordered or no one swings. Those are the ground rules. That's where it's going. It's insanity to think otherwise."

"May I quote you?" I asked.

"Of course not," he laughed. "You think I'm crazy?"

"In some ways, you're the sanest man I know."

"Ha! Not always," he said. He slapped my arm. "And by the way, yes, you can quote me. Years from now. When we're safely off this island. Okay?"

A lovely vision intruded. Madame af Tolle appeared at the door, resplendent in a blue gown. Nancy Oakes was right behind her, and behind them both loomed their bodyguard: a handsome native man of about six feet three inches of muscle, threat and presumably under his jacket, a major firearm.

"Ah!" he said. "There's my ride. Can I give you a lift to your hotel?"

"It's just up the street," I said. "Maybe a block."

"A lot can happen in a block after dark in Nassau," Ray said.

"I don't mind stretching my legs," I said.

"Poor old Harry couldn't even get a safe final night's sleep in his own bed."

We stood and paid.

"You walk ahead to the British Colonial," Schindler said. "We'll follow slowly in the car and depart after you're safely in the lobby. How's that?"

"That sounds good," I said.

He slapped my arm.

"See you tomorrow," he said.

We left together and followed our plan. It was twelve past ten when I returned to my room at the British Colonial Hotel. I carefully locked the door. Just for the hell of it, I also wedged the back of the chair under the doorknob. I left the key in the inside slot for security.

I slept fitfully.

CHAPTER 21

I hadn't picked up on any continuing surveillance on me since my return to the islands. I attributed that to two factors, though I was mostly guessing.

First, with more writers and reporters pouring into Nassau with the approach of the trial, I figured that powers that were out there had more interesting people to follow. Second, they might have become a bit self-satisfied. How much damage could I really do them if the result in court was predetermined?

Not much. We both knew it.

Thus, I turned up at the New Providence Hotel the next day at 2:55 p.m. and moved quickly through the hotel to a narrow hot alley just behind it. There was a panel truck there as expected. The driver was a black man. He gave me a nod. I went to his window.

"I'm Alan," I said.

"Get in," he answered. He indicated the rear of his truck. "Sit low."

I obeyed.

There was no one else in the truck. The back was like an oven. I said nothing. We bounced over some side roads in eastern Nassau and he made two more deliveries of bread. Then, from what I could see and sense, we were on open but bumpy road that led out of the town proper. I timed the trip. It took seventeen minutes. I noted the direction of the sun. We were driving east.

Finally, we turned off the main road and were on dirt. We pulled up in front of a thatched hut. The truck stopped. The engine kept running.

The driver motioned with his head. I was to climb forward and get out. I did. My clothes were soaked with sweat.

From within the hut, Schindler appeared with a smaller darker man. The bread truck took off. Ray approached me, grinning.

"This is my friend, Kayo," Ray said to me, introducing me to his contact.

Kayo was a Bahamian with dark skin. He had a slightly Creole look and surprising blue eyes. His smile was nervous. I offered my hand, but Kayo ignored it. He either didn't see it or didn't want it.

"Kayo has something to show us," Ray said. "We're his guests. We do things his way."

Kayo nodded. His eyes zipped over the landscape behind us, making sure there were no followers. Quickly satisfied, he nodded in the direction in which we were to follow. We were going behind his hut.

As he walked, Kayo turned toward us and made a gesture to Ray of rubbing his fingers together. On the fly, Ray quickly produced and counted out five five-pound notes. Kayo took them, checked the sum, pocketed the cash, smiled and never missed a stride. Ray gave him a pat on the arm.

Kayo was not a man of few words. At this juncture, he was a man of no words. He motioned us along. He led us across a rocky pathway through a clump of twisted palms. I saw a small inlet of water with a small fishing skiff tied up and pulled up onto a strip of sand no more than twenty feet wide. The skiff itself was maybe twelve feet long.

Kayo held his small skiff steady on the beach and gestured for us to step in. Ray, older and less agile, stepped in first. I followed, careful not to unbalance the small craft. We settled onto a small board that ran across the midway of the boat. It's what passed for seating.

There were some bulky fisherman's hats and slickers on the floor of the boat. Native stuff, rugged, bulky and—I knew in advance—hot as hell.

Ray reached for one for each of us. "We're to put these on and sit low," Ray said. "Precautions. Don't wish to be recognized, right?"

"Right," I said.

Kayo pushed the boat into the water, guiding it while knee deep in the salt water. Then he gracefully lifted himself into the craft. He took the tiller at the square stern of the skiff. He sculled for a moment. He had a small Evinrude, maybe one of those new little five horsepower jobs, attached to rear. For whatever reason—noise, fuel economy—he chose not to use it here.

There was a sail that he could hoist but it was tied down. There were two oars. Kayo grabbed one and used it to pull toward the opening to the inlet. He managed a slow but steady pace, then broke out of the inlet into the surf, which was gentle. There was a current and Kayo let it take us. I knew from the sun that we were facing west. He turned the tiller sharply and we headed south. When we were about a hundred yards off shore, Kayo started his engine with a rope cord.

I glanced at my watch. I wanted to keep track of time. It was four-fifty.

The sun was lower in the sky but had lost none of its intensity. I opened my slicker but was still sweating like a pig. Fortunately, a slight breeze picked up. We continued south for fifteen minutes.

"Pleasant ride, don't you think, Alan?" Ray asked amiably. "Too far out for alligators, too far in for German U-boats."

"Peachy," I answered.

Ray laughed.

"You'll remember this trip, I promise you," he said. He patted my shoulder. "You can swim, right?" he asked.

"Only when my life depends on it," I answered.

"It won't," he said. "Or it shouldn't."

We followed the shoreline for fifteen minutes. I counted. Then Kayo passed a large coral stone that protruded from the water. He gave it a wide cautious turn and then steered around it toward a small cove. He looked in all directions, but mostly to see if there were any

150

other boats within view on the water. There were not. In another three minutes, we were well within the cove.

Further before us lay an inlet into a sandy coral beach. There was nothing significant within my sight. As we neared, I saw some native kids playing with a half-flat soccer ball. Several small fishing boats had been pulled up onto the sand. A noisy pack of gulls patrolled low over the surf. There was a cluster of lean-to shacks with tin roofs, plus one hut which was straw and had a doorway covered by a ragged yellow sheet. The sheet fluttered in a sharp inbound breeze. As we drew closer, a cluster of poorly dressed or naked black children stopped what they were doing to stare at us, unspeaking and wide-eyed as we neared the shoreline, then travelled parallel to it.

The children scattered as if they had heard something. After a half-moment, a tall broad man with ebony skin and no shirt emerged swiftly from the hut. He marched toward the shoreline.

"It's all right," Kayo said. "Just be still."

The man on the beach glared at us, shielding his eyes against the setting sun. He kept his other hand in his pants pocket. I assumed he had a weapon.

Kayo rose and half-stood on bow of our boat and waved to the man on the beach. The shirtless man recognized our skipper and relaxed. He waved back, assessed us, turned slowly and went back to his hut. I noticed that the children kept as far out of the man's way as possible.

"Almost there," Kayo said.

He cut his engine to a crawl. We were within fifty feet of the shoreline. The heat intensified. The flies from the land began to find us and swarm.

After a moment, Kayo revved his engine.

We travelled another few hundred yards. Then Kayo cut the boat sharply and followed a narrow inlet. The foliage grew thicker around the waterway until there was nothing but a green wall on each side of us, alive with insects and fauna. Then we were in the clear again and Kayo cut a small circle in the water.

He rose from his seat and in a somber voice said, "There!"

My eyes fastened on the horror within the space of his single word. I heard Ray let out a gasp. There was a gibbet standing over the water fifty feet in front of us. Beneath it, a pair of alligators, or maybe there were three, were splashing and occasionally leaping, their jaws extended. Above them were suspended the bodies of two black men, their clothing partly worn away. They had been hanged by the neck and left to swing and rot. The left foot of one of the dead men was missing. There was a pool of dark crimson on the remaining bone. It looked as if one of the gators had snacked.

I heard Kayo change positions. He leaned down and withdrew a bolt action rifle from under his bench.

"All right?" he asked Ray. "We go?"

Ray was holding a handkerchief to his mouth. Schindler didn't say anything. He gestured that he had seen enough. Certainly, I had also.

Kayo turned the boat. We left faster than we had arrived.

"Jesus," I muttered to myself. We broke into the clearing and were back on the salt water.

"Okay. What was that all about?" I asked.

"Remember the story about the two native men who worked on the Oakes estate?" Schindler asked. "The watchman and his friend who might have been witnesses for de Marigny?"

I did. "That's them?" I asked.

"That's what the people around here are saying," Ray said.

We rode in silence. It was finally getting dark. The water was getting choppy and I held on.

"A trail of tombstones," Ray Schindler said to me. "Or, more likely, unmarked graves. That's what this case will turn into."

We travelled the rest of the way back to Nassau in silence.

The start of the trial was thirty-six hours away.

CHAPTER 22

The next night, on the eve of the judicial proceedings, Ray and I wandered into Dirty Dick's at a few minutes past eight p.m. We stood at the crowded bar and took the temperature of the room and the town. There was more press interest in the Oakes murder case than in any since the trial of Bruno Hauptmann for kidnapping of the

Lindbergh baby a decade earlier. Maybe it was because of the war and the public need to have a story other than the war. I didn't know. I did know that as I scanned the room I saw many people I knew from New York, both crime and general interest writers.

I saw many other writers in the room, good ones.

There was Elizabeth Townsend for the *York Post*, and my friend Ruth Reynolds from the *New York Daily News*, a classy lady writer who was a kindred soul: she covered murders. I also knew Jeanne Bellamy for the *Miami Herald*. Henry Luce's *Time Magazine*, which we in the business called "the weekly fiction magazine." *Time* printed Henry's opinion more than straight news. *Time* was running regular features on the case. They had a team there. I was told that a special table had to be constructed just to accommodate the number of journalists in the courtroom. The hotels of Nassau jacked up their prices, something not popular with my editors back in New York. What did I care? I wasn't paying. But it wasn't lost on me that the trial was great for the local economy. Conspicuously absent from the room were the brothers Dupuch, Etienne and Eugene, who were covering the story not just for their own paper, the *Nassau Daily Tribune*, but also for the *New York Times*, Reuters, the *Daily Telegraph*, the racing and theatrical journal.

"Hey, there's a familiar local face," Ray said suddenly, tapping my arm. He indicated our windy friend Colonel Chalmers, drinking alone, halfway down the bar. We went over and joined him.

Chalmers, a fount of local gossip, seemed anxious to have an audience. We were happy to oblige and listen. I was honored to irrigate the colonel with another drink.

Finally, "So tell us, Colonel," I said, "what's going to happen tomorrow?"

"The wrong man is on trial, I'll tell that," he said. "That's how a lot of us feel here. I have friends. Police. They know the system here. The Frenchman is the patsy. The sacrificial lamb."

"Who *should* be on trial?" I asked.

"Harold Christie," he said.

"So Christie did it?" I asked.

"No, no. Not saying that," the colonel said. "No one will come out and say that. But he was sleeping in the next room? He didn't hear anything? Balderdash!"

"Christie was one of Sir Harry's best friends," I said. "Where's the motive?"

Chalmers' eyes slid in my direction. "There's talk of unpaid debts. There's gossip about gambling interests coming to the island. Sir Harry may have been moving to Mexico which, if true, would seriously have undermined Christie's ambitions as a realtor. When money, ambition and greed combine, the mixture proves combustible, right? Especially in Nassau. Here money is everything."

Chalmers drained his glass. He rattled some ice cubes in his mouth, then spit them back into his glass.

"Damn!" he finally said. "I'm not saying Harold shot Sir Harry or smashed his head or did it himself. No one's saying that. But people are keeping quiet. Self-interest, don't you know? Bay Street Boys. Power. But Christie must have known more. He must have at least smelled smoke. Or heard something."

"Oh, I can think of one reason why he didn't hear or smell something," I said.

"What's that?" he asked.

"He wasn't in the next room."

"Well, that's his alibi. That's where he says he was."

"I know," I said.

Chalmers looked critically at me. "Hrrmp," he said. "You've been reading too many of your own stories, perhaps."

"Perhaps," I said.

"Well, one thing's certain," Chalmers said. "The Frenchman's going to swing from the end of a rope. Do that little dance of death that men do on the gallows. Ever seen a man hang, Alan?"

"No," I said.

"Well, it happens around here. You'll see."

CHAPTER 23

The trial of Alfred de Marigny for the murder of Sir Harry Oakes, began on October 18, 1943, a cloudy day in the Bahamas. The summer's heat and humidity had broken. The day was at least tolerable.

Shortly before nine a.m., local constables escorted Alfred de Margigny on a walk from the Central Police Station to the courthouse. Nobody would have given much of a bet for his chances of surviving his trial. So much seemed efficiently rigged against him.

Crowds gathered around the impressive white marble portico of the courthouse. Spectators pushed in on the tight corridor of police escorting de Marigny. In another building not too far away, the rope that had been ordered to hang him sat under lock and key, waiting for its macabre moment.

Several people were notably absent. Thomas Lavelle, who had offered the most recent testimony against de Marigny had been allowed to travel, but his testimony had been taken. Erskine-Lindop, perhaps one of the only honest men in sight, had assumed his post in Trinidad and had been advised by counsel that any reappearance in Nassau would not be appreciated by the Crown.

And then there were the Duke and Duchess of Windsor. Or more accurately, there *weren't* the Duke and Duchess. Wallis Simpson had let it be known being that something as sordid as a murder trial was beneath her dignity. As for her husband, David, Duke of Windsor, he again proved that there was no important obligation from which he could not flee. The case in Nassau and the unseemly cast of characters that populated it was largely because of the Duke's incompetence, starting with his ersatz reporting of Oakes' "suicide" and his hiring of the two American cops who passed themselves off as able Miami detectives.

So naturally, the Windsors planned to visit friends in the United States for the duration of the trial, far from view, far from legal obligation, and far from responsibility. Never mind that an innocent man might have been accused. Never mind that the feeling on the streets of the Bahamian capital was that de Marigny was not guilty

Equally absent was the information that Schindler had requested in New York. He kept inquiring, yet somehow the dispatch had been held up in Bahamian customs and censors, considerably weakening the hand of the defense team

"Surprising?" I asked Ray the night before the trial started.

"Here?" he snorted. "Nothing is surprising."

Thus convened the tribunal that first morning. When de Marigny was seated, when the public gallery was packed to standing room, a legal spectacle began that reminded me of something out of Charles Dickens, with some Pirandello and Kafka sprinkled in.

At nine a.m., the doors opened to the public. There was a rush to fill the five benches in the courtroom that had been allocated to spectators. At half past ten, a crier, dressed in the British colonial garb of the 1700s, cracked a staff on the floor and called the court to be in session. "Oyez! Oyez! Oyez!" the living relic, the crier, bellowed. "All persons having anything to do before His Majesty's Supreme Court in the Bahamas draw near and you will be heard! God save the King!"

Then from a door that led from his private chambers, the Chief Justice, Sir Oscar Daly, emerged in a crimson gown and a shoulder-length white wig. The judge was an Irish King's Counsel who was also a former Great War intelligence officer. He arrived in the Bahamas after distinguished legal service in Kenya. The Irish lilt in his voice and impish humor marked him as a character among legal colleagues.

But it was the attire that struck everyone. I sat close enough to the visiting press corps to hear a few muffled snickers. The gowns, the arcane language, the wigs—also worn by all members of the court—the overly bloated courtesies and obsequies, made the spectacle look less like a 20th Century legal proceeding than a movie with Charlie Chaplin or the Marx Brothers.

But it commenced in earnest.

The high-ceilinged courtroom, notoriously oppressive and insect-infested, was cramped and stank of insecticide. De Marigny sat in the defendant's box in a lightweight grey suit and blue tie. From time to time, he winced. He was suffering not just from the indignities of being the accused, but from having spent two months in a hot fetid cell. Facing him across the room was the pew for the jury, not yet selected.

Although Adderley was nominally the prosecutor, the man who was expected to send de Marigny to the gallows was the Attorney General, a nasty ambitious man named Eric Hallinan. Hallinan was a barrister-at-law of the Irish and English Bars. He was also the former Crown counsel of Nigeria.

"The Brits have brought in their top colonial team, haven't they?" I whispered to Schindler, who sat next to me.

Ray nodded. "They've done all of that," he said. "They want no mistakes here. Just want to get this done."

In comparison, the defense team looked like a trio on law students. Godfrey Higgs, in his mid-thirties, was one of the youngest members of the Bahamas Bar. His assistant, Ernest Callender, was even younger, though he'd practiced criminal law for several years.

The trial began. De Marigny was given the opportunity to respond to the charges against him. "Are you guilty or not guilty?" asked the court registrar.

"Not guilty," replied the prisoner in a firm clear voice.

The games began.

First came the jury selection. There were challenges, legal exchanges, and a fistful of legalisms. Twelve men were quickly installed, including a few that Schindler described to me as "religious nuts." Nassau being a tiny incestuous place, everyone on the jury knew de Marigny, which did not mean that he had any friends. What defense lawyers needed to hope for was that none of them had an ulterior reason for stringing up the Count. The jury selected a foreman, a businessman named James Sands, a well-known local man best known for driving an agonizingly slow old Ford around Nassau. Sands, however, at least had the reputation of being fair-minded.

The presentation of the case thus began.

Adderley was out of the gate fast and effectively. He portrayed de Marigny as a near penniless con man with a grudge, and a flagrant womanizer as well. Adderley scored his points. On the day before the murder, he said, the accused had a substantial overdraft at the Royal

Bank of Canada. Adderley then went to work on the antagonisms between Sir Harry and his son-in-law. He joyously reminded the jury of de Marigny's elopement with Nancy Oakes, just two days after her eighteenth birthday. The prosecution's case was thus premised on de Marigny's thorough dislike of Sir Harry and a desire to solve his financial problems and sustain his status as one of the world's most successful freeloaders.

The jury listened. I watched them. They were buying it.

Adderley also hammered away on the collection of well-publicized comments de Marigny had allegedly made in the hours following Sir Harry's death. The comments deepened the Count's predicament.

But the prosecution's most crushing disclosure centered on that single fingerprint, found on the Chinese screen in Sir Harry's bedroom. Adderley recalled that de Marigny, by his own account, had said the last time he had visited Westbourne was three years before the murder. How, then, did his fingerprint appear on the screen? Here was the evidence that put him in Sir Harry's bedroom at the relevant time. It was enough to hang a man and everyone in the courtroom knew it. Schindler and I exchanged glances as Adderley worked the fingerprint angle. Ray blew out a long breath. He leaned over to me.

"Well, that's why we brought in our own experts," he whispered.

Next, Adderley made a pivot that raised my eyebrows. He maintained that any doubts that existed about the whereabouts of Harold Christie on the night Sir Harry was snuffed did not undercut the Crown's case.

As the trial proceeded over the following days, everybody in the courtroom wondered just how Harold Christie was going to do. He was finally called as a witness on October 20th, three days into the purported search for justice. Under the circumstances, he made out all right. For a while, at least.

Christie gave a simple account of his discovery of the murder. If there had been any commotion in Westbourne during the commission of the crime, he had not heard it. The tropical storm would have drowned out any disturbance in the chamber of his longtime friend and business associate, he explained.

In terms of his actual testimony, he did fine. In terms of his physical presentation, he flunked. The proceedings deeply unnerved him. Perspiration soaked and darkened his suit jacket. He gripped the rail in front of him, appearing for no reason to be on a white-knuckle ride to oblivion. Several writers in court were to dwell on his extraordinary demeanor. If Christie was not guilty of anything, he surely didn't look it.

The question arose whether Christie had spent the entire night of July seven and eight at Westbourne. If the evidence of others could establish that he was lying, and that he was up and about during the night of Sir Harry's murder, it would prove he had something to hide.

But what?

Attorney Higgs had done some homework. The first obstacle for Christie to overcome was the evidence of a woman named Mabel Ellis, a local housemaid. Mrs. Ellis made two points about Christie's car which contradicted his version of events.

According to Christie, he had driven off in his own car on the morning of July 7th to attend an Executive Council meeting, but Mrs. Ellis said he had left the auto at Sir Harry's. That evening, said Christie, he had asked his driver, Levi Gibson, to bring the car to Westbourne in case it was needed to ferry dinner guests.

What did it matter? Quite a bit. The position of the car on Westbourne's grounds, and whether Christie left it there during July 7th, were significant. It raised questions about whether the car was subsequently used for an illicit purpose, or at an unusual hour. Had Christie parked it away from the house, near the country club, instead of outside the main entrance?

But there was a bigger issue to be raised by the car.

The jurors knew Sears and knew him to be an honest man, beholden to no one. He said he believed he had seen Christie in a station wagon in George Street, in downtown Nassau, perhaps a few minutes past midnight in the first minutes of July eighth.

If Christie were to be believed, he was by that time already ensconced in his bedroom at Westbourne. But Sears insisted that he had seen Christie. Sears, it seemed, was doing his rounds at the time of this sighting. His vehicle passed the station wagon under a street light. There was no doubt in his mind that Christie was in the passenger seat, but he was unable to identify the driver.

"Perhaps you could explain that to the court," Higgs said.

"If Captain Sears said he saw me out that night, I would say that he was very seriously mistaken and should be more careful in his observations," replied Christie.

"No! I put it to you," insisted the attorney. "Captain Sears saw you in a station wagon in George Street around midnight that night."

"Captain Sears was mistaken," Christie shot back.

Under further questioning, the witness accepted that Captain Sears was a reputable person, but reputable persons made mistakes, too, he said.

The Sears testimony made Christie burn, but he was unable to refute it. And it had raised questions in the minds of the jurors on whether Christie, respected and feared as he was, was telling the whole truth or a variation on it. The court proceedings had raised a mountain of speculation and hearsay. Higgs' team kept hammering at the notion that Christie was holding back information. They questioned why he had parked his car some distance from Oakes' house, something Christie couldn't completely answer.

In concluding the cross-examination, Higgs led Christie through his actions immediately after discovering Sir Harry's body. The young attorney managed to unsettle the witness to such a degree that Christie blew up. As he stepped down from the witness-box at the end of his ordeal, he lumbered like a shaken old man. If Christie had been expected to add something to the sum of the prosecution's case, he had failed. Adderley's response to his evidence was to invite the jury to discount it. The Crown had flubbed it royally.

There followed the evidence of Dr. Hugh Quackenbush. Quackenbush had driven to Westbourne after receiving a telephone call early on July eighth. He had found Harold Christie in his pajamas in the hall, he said. He proceeded upstairs, where he found Sir Harry's burned mutilated corpse on his bed. There was a "perforating wound" in front of the left ear, he testified, large enough to admit the tip of his left index finger.

"I assessed that Sir Harry had been dead for two-and-a-half to five hours," Quackenbush told the court. "Most of the burning had occurred after death. Later, at the mortuary, I noted four head wounds that could not have been self-inflicted. This was obviously no suicide. All four were close to the left ear, of different depth and triangular in shape."

"Could you suggest what the murder weapon might have been?" Higgs asked.

The doctor theorized that the murder weapon had been a heavy blunt instrument with a well-defined edge. The victim's skull was fractured, probably by a series of quick blows. The blows, he believed, were struck before Sir Harry was burnt.

The trial lumbered into its sixth day. International film crews with cameras surged upon the trial location. They set up on the square outside the court, creating more public interest and more havoc. Cameramen strained to get the protagonists "in the can" as they made their way to court. Barristers preened themselves international exposure. Bit players in the trial readily gave interviews. A carnival atmosphere was creeping upon the Bahamian capital.

Then on that same day, Saturday, October 23, a new scandal broke on the front page of the local newspaper and rocked Nassau. Much of it was premised on the missing information that Ray Schindler had never received from New York.

The town's leading living citizen, Harold Christie, most recently seen on the witness stand trying to hold his composure, was a fugitive from American justice, the newspapers were saying. He had been for twenty years. His past was finally starting to catch up with him.

In 1923, the newspapers reported, Christie had been charged with illegally transferring a schooner from the American to the British registry of ships, in order to make it easier to smuggle alcohol into the United States. He had been indicted in Boston, but had fled and was still wanted by the authorities.

Even if Christie's days as a rum-runner were known by the "in crowd" and the older residents of Nassau, and remembered with an affable wink, this was still a sensational story. And now it was out in the open. It was enhanced by the fact that it was true and verifiable. The FBI's files showed that in the early 1920s Christie was regarded as a major player in the battle of the bottles and was one of the Bureau's main targets.

"Christie is one of the big guns in the rum-running game," one FBI agent had opined in a memo to J. Edgar Hoover. "It would be a significant victory for Prohibition to arrest him."

Christie had led a hide-and-seek existence, visiting the States in disguise or under an alias. Traps were set for him and he had eluded all of them. The files, according to the newspaper, was several hundred pages. Identifying Christie as "a mulatto," certain amount of time was even spent trying to ascertain how much "colored" blood he had, as if that explained something.

Ray and the defense team wouldn't be able to present an official document at the trial. But now, no juror could possibly not know Christie's background. He might still have been popular. But he was a lot less credible.

"The Good Lord," Schindler said to me with a wink during a break in the proceedings, "works in wonderful ways, does He not?"

CHAPTER 24

Whenever there's a big trial, there's invariably some local place, usually a bar, often a hotel bar, which becomes the hangout for the visiting press or others who want to talk about the events of the day. In the case of the de Marigny trial, the venue was the hotel bar at the British Colonial Hotel, a short walk from the courtroom.

When I entered on Saturday night, October thirtieth, I spotted Erle Stanley Gardner holding court at the far end of the bar.

The boisterous *New York Journal-American*, owned by William Randolph Hearst, always prided itself on its breathless treatment of such scandals. Hearst's rag had gone one better than its competitors by hiring Gardner, someone adapt at writing about sudden death.

Erle had a law degree and was still a practicing lawyer in California. But for more than ten years, Gardner's pulp novels, some of them featuring his creation Perry Mason, the mouthpiece who never lost a case, had been growing in popularity. Erle was into some great luck as a writer. During the trial, his fictional mouthpiece-detective was to find a much larger audience with the broadcast on CBS of the first radio serial of Mason's adventures.

Gardner, then fifty-four, had been given complete liberty by Hearst. He had as much space to fill as he wanted. He normally filed three to six pages. He knew what the public craved and he dished up generous helpings of it to the unwashed masses.

But any writer can have his or her little goofs. Erle had recently had a good one: Early in the proceedings, when the press was shown around Westbourne, Gardner noticed the game of Chinese checkers that Oakes had been playing with his dinner guests.

"Well, Major," he said breezily to one of the local police officials. "There's the checkers board! Just as it was on that fateful evening."

"Sorry to spoil your story, mate," the officer answered. "But the constables have actually been playing checkers there for the last four months."

"Not a problem," Gardner responded evenly, ever the realist. "Facts never get in the way in a Hearst paper."

Gardner was a guy who always had a keen eye on the profit and loss aspects of being a professional writer. He had once dropped one of the lasting pearls of wisdom about the art, philosophy and boundless spirit of creativity. When a literary critic asked him why his heroes always snuffed villains with the final bullet in their guns. Gardner elucidated, "At three cents a word, every time I say 'Bang' in the story I get three cents. If you think I'm going to finish the gun battle while my hero still has fifteen cents worth of unexploded ammunition in his gun, you're crazy."

I waved to Gardner when he caught my gaze. He was at the end of the bar where he was holding court with some of his adoring public. Erle, sometimes an arrogant soul, gave me a curt wave in return.

I mouthed the words "Chinese checkers" to him and he laughed.

I spotted Ray sitting with at a table for four with Captain O'Neil and Professor Keeler. They had saved me a seat. I slid onto a wooden chair, but it was under a ceiling fan so I had no complaints.

"Alan, do you know Ernest Hemingway?" Captain O'Neil asked.

"I met him once," I answered.

"In Paris in the Twenties?" Ray asked. "I know you were both there."

"It would make a better story," I said. "But Hemingway and I have had the same editors at *The Saturday Evening Post*," I said. "The *Post* is published in Philadelphia. We crossed paths there."

"De Marigny claims him as a friend," Keeler said. "Think there's truth to that?"

"There could be," I said. "They both like to hang out with wealthy famous people. Same as Ray here," I added, tossing a gentle dart at my friend.

"What your opinion?" O'Neil asked.

"Personally or professionally?" I asked.

"Either or both."

"I'm willing to keep an open mind for the future, but I'll tell you what I think right now. Ernie is a great writing talent. People will read his books for years, long after he's dead. But he is not a great person. He leaves massive amounts of human wreckage in his wake. His wives. Is there anyone who doesn't feel for poor Hadley, who financed him and truly loved the son of a bitch? His children. His ill-chosen lovers. His betrayed friends. More than one editor in New York has had his job on the line not because Ernie turns in bad copy, but because he overspends his budget and puts his editors in the crosshairs of their own bosses." I quaffed a rum and Coke as soon as it arrived. "Almost everyone who crosses his path suffers some degree of damage, be it professional or personal."

"Does that include you, Alan?" Ray asked. "Do we hear experience talking?"

"Honestly, no, Ray," I said. "I've kept my distance. You hear a reporter talking. I don't pass myself off as a friend or even an acquaintance. Just someone who's come close enough to draw some conclusions, all of which I just shared with you."

"And shared generously," he said.

"Generously," I agreed. "Even indulgently."

We all laughed.

Captain O'Neil took over the conversation. Through his contacts in the various police forces in the Old Confederacy, he had heard a few personal anecdotes about Hemingway. He had no reluctance to amuse us.

Hemingway had been living at his Cuban home, Finca Vigía, since the war began in 1939, Captain O'Neil related. Hemingway's first contribution to the Allied war-effort was to organize his own self-styled counter-intelligence force to root out any Axis spies operating in Havana in 1942. He had fifteen to twenty men with whom he had worked five years before during the Spanish Civil War, when they had all been on the anti-Franco side.

"The effort yielded no results, however," Captain O'Neil said, "which didn't surprise anyone. So, Hemingway shifted his attention to fighting the German U-boats operating in the Caribbean."

"*What?*" Schindler laughed.

"No, no, I swear this is true stuff," O'Neil said. "Hemingway got permission from the U.S, Ambassador to Cuba, Spruille Braden, to arm his fishing boat, the *Pilar*, for patrols against U-boats off the Cuban coast. So now Ernie is out there with machine guns, bazookas, and hand grenades."

"No!" I laughed.

"Yes. The *Pilar* has become something like a Q-ship, a heavily armed decoy. Hemmie sails around in what appears to be a harmless pleasure craft, inviting the Germans to surface and board, and when they do, the boarding party would be disposed of with the machine guns, and the U-boat would then be engaged with the bazookas and grenades. That's the plan, anyway."

"I'll believe it more when he claims to have sunk some German tonnage," Schindler said.

"Which have you read by our pal, Ernie?" O'Neil asked me.

"I read *For Whom The Bell Tolls* and *Death in The Afternoon*," I said.

"Which is the one about the man who got his balls shot off?" Keeler asked.

"What?" I asked, turning.

"That's *The Sun Also Rises*," said Schindler.

"That's what the book is about?" I asked. "Hemingway doesn't behave like a guy who lost his manhood."

"Oh, he didn't. And that's not entirely what the book's about," Schindler said. "When Ernie was an ambulance driver on the Italian Front at the end of the First World War, he got hit in his lower body by a trench mortar. Took a couple of hundred separate chunks of shrapnel wounds. Think about it, gentlemen. Must have been torture. His scrotum was pierced twice, and he had to be laid on a special pillow for weeks in a special military hospital in Italy for genital wounds. His testicles were undamaged and his penis intact. But he knew a man who had lost his entire manhood. He wondered what a man's life would have been like after that if his penis had been lost and his testicles and spermatic cord remained intact. So he wrote a book about this poor guy whose gonads had been blown away and what his problems would be when he was in love with someone who was in love with him and there was nothing that they could do about it."

"I might skip that one," I said.

"War is war, gentlemen," O'Neil said. "Sad, serious business."

"Read *A Farewell to Arms*, Alan," Ray said. "I think you might appreciate it."

"Duly noted," I said.

The conversation returned to the trial.

Nassau was percolating with rumors that Sunday night, mostly about the trial, and largely focused on Harold Christie. The story that Captain Sears had related in court was the centerpiece. Sears had insisted that he had seen Harold Christie away from Westbourne on the night of the murder. Curiously enough, nobody in court had brought out the fact that Christie had a brother who looked enough like him, in fact, to pass for a twin in the conditions under which the cop saw the man in the station wagon.

This evening, the gossip around Nassau was awash with rumors that the driver was, in fact, Christie's brother, Frank, and Harold was the other man in the car. This spin on purported events suggested that Harold and Frank Christie were out driving on a mission they wanted kept quiet at all costs. It also gave some credibility to the tale of the now-deceased night watchman who claimed he had seen Christie down at the piers welcoming some shady visitors.

For those locals who gave credence to the notion that Christie was somehow involved in Oakes' death, this was compelling supporting evidence. However, there was a corollary to the theory, favored by those who believed in Christie's innocence.

Christie was a personable, quietly attractive unmarried man about town with a bit of reputation for the ladies: especially married ladies whose husbands were off fighting the war. One of his rumored frequent conquests was, it seems, a British officer's wife who had been a dinner guest at Westbourne on the eve of the murder. The lady had been driven to her Eastern Road home by fellow guest Charles Hubbard. The suggestion was that Frank drove Harold to the woman's home for an assignation at an hour when her two children would be asleep. Meanwhile, Harold's car remained at Westbourne, where its presence would support his contention that he never left the house, and the British officer himself was off on a battlefield somewhere in Europe or Asia, not realizing that he was ceding valuable territory on the home front.

CHAPTER 25

On Monday October 25th, the courtroom proceedings continued.

Lt. John Douglas of the Bahamian police recalled a conversation with de Marigny in which the count supposedly said, "the old bastard should have been killed anyhow." While the statement may have reflected much public sentiment, it didn't do the defendant any good.

As the proceedings moved slowly forward, Harold Christie, still reeling from his tense performance on the witness stand, felt it necessary to give an interview to reporters, this time to crush more rumors about his whereabouts during the early morning of the murder.

Christie admitted to the Miami *Herald* that his story sounded implausible, but he couldn't help that because it was true.

The judge was not pleased with Christie giving outside interviews. He issued a warning about giving public statements, and then, as if on cue, another interview surfaced, this one by Captain Edward Melchen. It contained comments he had given to correspondent John B. McDermott of United Press. No sooner had the comments circulated than Melchen tried to walk back from them. He called McDermott a liar and denied giving an interview.

Thus arrived the first chink in Melchen's armor. No one imagined that McDermott had faked a story. Melchen was a liar. The defense was ready to pounce. The Count's junior counsel, Ernest Callender, cross-examined Melchen and capitalized fully on the officer's perceived dishonesty. In doing so, he exposed a major flaw in the prosecution's case.

Melchen staggered the court with an extraordinary statement about the fingerprint that his colleague Barker had supposedly lifted from the Chinese screen. Melchen admitted that he did not know about this fingerprint until Barker broke news of it to Lady Oakes in Bar Harbour, Maine at her husband's funeral.

The two Miami cops had been presumably working closely on the case since the early afternoon following Sir Harry's death. They had travelled together back to Miami, and then on to Maine. And not once was the fingerprint mentioned? They had discussed other aspects of the case, but Barker had not referred even fleetingly to the single most important piece of evidence against de Marigny?

Or so said Melchen on Monday.

On Tuesday in court, Melchen asked permission to change his testimony, explaining that he had been tired when he gave it. He had heard Barker mention lifting a print to Colonel Erskine-Lindop and that he was going to process it. At Bar Harbour, Barker told Lady Oakes about a print on which he was still working which he thought was de Marigny's.

An irritated Chief Justice said, "That is very different from what you said yesterday. Don't you know the very great importance of this piece of evidence? Have you a good memory?"

"A fairly good memory," Melchen answered.

"Tell me, now that you are not tired, have you talked to Barker about this matter since you gave evidence yesterday?"

"No," Melchen answered. "I talked about it in the Attorney General's office with the Attorney General in the presence of Captain Barker, after I gave evidence yesterday."

This remark suggested that, having blundered in the witness-box, Melchen went into deep discussions with the Attorney General and Barker, to see if his evidence was salvageable. The stench in the air suggested that something was very wrong.

Melcher's equivocation ignited a moment of panic for the prosecution. The defense tried to have the print withdrawn as evidence. They argued that the print was inadmissible, but the judge ruled against them.

Higgs might have been set back by the decision, but he wasn't. He wore a sly smile and looked like a man who had just gained some important ground. He shifted his attention to the authenticity of the fingerprint that Ray Schindler had originally questioned. Now everything would hinge on Barker's testimony, and especially his ability to withstand the dogged, penetrating interrogation of young Godfrey Higgs, who was gaining steam and confidence.

So the fingerprint, allegedly from de Marigny's right little finger, was formally admitted as evidence.

When Captain Barker, the Miami cop, hulked into the witness box, Godfrey Higgs started to blast away with double barrels, armed with ammunition supplied by Schindler, Captain O'Neil of the New Orleans Police Department, and Keeler, who all sat in the same hot pew with me. We tried to cool ourselves with hand fans as we watched the drama unfold.

Young Higgs was impressive. To shatter the opposition's case in court, lawyers often rely on circumstantial evidence. The traditional analogy is that each piece of evidence is a brick. No specific event by itself may prove or disprove a case. But once assembled, the individual bricks might build a wall, a solid brick wall, that provides a barrier to conviction or acquittal. Higgs was skillfully constructing such a wall.

Barker told the court he had taken rubber lifts from the top panel of the screen because his Scotch tape had run out. In the

169

magistrate's court, he had marked in blue pencil the area from which he thought the rubber lift of de Marigny's print was taken. Now he equivocated. He informed the court that, since re-examining the screen, he was not now prepared to say the print was lifted from that area. It did, however, come from the top panel, he asserted. The screen was carried to the witness-box so that Barker could see it more clearly.

Barker, working on his own crash-and-burn routine, blithely said, "I wish to inform the court that the blue line which I now see on the screen was not made by me. There has been an effort to trace a blue line over the black line that I made myself on August first in the presence of the Attorney General in the Central Police Station. That blue line is not my work."

Then, astonishingly, he said he wished to correct this statement. Following the inconsistencies of Melchen, this had a powerful effect. The prosecution's two-star witnesses, far from being stars, were coming off as a couple of incompetent clowns. First, they said one thing, then they said something else. They couldn't even seem to make up their mind on their own testimony. Jurymen shuffled their feet and exchanged glances.

Higgs was ready for his big moment.

Barker continued, "I am sorry I have caused the court this trouble. I wish to withdraw what I said about the alteration of the blue line. I find my initials where the blue line is."

He said the area marked by him had been indicated twice—the first time in black pencil, then in blue. He had dated the find on July ninth, but only recorded it on August first.

Higgs could barely contain his excitement.

"So, until August first there was nothing on that screen to show where the fingerprint came from?" asked Higgs.

"I relied on my memory only," Barker said,

Higgs displayed astonishment. Out of his view, so did the jurors.

"Yet on the third of August in the magistrate's court," Higgs reminded the witness, "you swore on your oath that, 'I marked the spot on the screen, where the latent impression above referred to was found, with pencil and it is now within the area marked with blue pencil and signified by *Number 5* and initialed and dated *8/3/43* by me.'"

"Yes. I did," Barker said.

"And you marked that area while giving evidence in the magistrate's court and said that was where the print came from?"

"I did."

"You were certain then that it came from that area, weren't you?"

"I was."

"And why are you not certain today, Captain Barker?"

"I re-examined the screen carefully last Sunday. I did not have sufficient evidence of ridges to enable us to say with certainty that it came from that area. I can only say now that it came from the top of the screen."

Higgs paused for a moment so that the implications could sink in for everyone in western hemisphere. If the fingerprint was to put de Marigny's neck in the noose, Barker needed to show beyond doubt that it came from the screen. De Marigny's fingerprint detached from its background was useless.

"Where would you say today that the print came from?" Higgs asked.

"I can only say now from my memory that it came from some part of the top of that panel. I did not feel justified in isolating any area."

Higgs, who had done some solid research on the witness, then asked Barker to give a rundown of his career.

Barker said he had been a street cop, then had worked as a clerk and then returned to uniformed duties before his eventual elevation to superintendent of the Bureau of Criminal Investigation. It was penny-ante stuff compared to his present responsibilities.

"Is it customary in Miami to appoint a superintendent with such small qualifications?"

"No," Barker said.

"You had only five months as a clerk before that?"

Barker answered, "Yes."

"You continued as superintendent of the BCI until March 1939, when you were ordered back to uniformed duty?"

"Yes."

"Why?"

Barker hesitated. "Insubordination," he said.

"And you remained out of that department for eleven months?"

"Yes."

Higgs closed in for the kill. "You term yourself a fingerprint expert?"

"As the term applies, yes."

"Have you ever introduced as evidence a lifted print without producing photographs of the actual raised print on the object on which it was found?"

"Yes."

"Will you give me the name of just one case in which you have done so."

Barker pondered it. "I can't do that."

"Not one?"

"I could by inspection of my records."

"This Chinese screen that is so important here?" Higgs asked. "Is the screen mobile?"

"It can be moved."

"Why didn't you produce this moveable object in this court with the print on it?"

"The only equipment I had on the 8th and 9th of July was a small dusting outfit and tape. The use of tape expedited the examination."

"But you came prepared to look for fingerprint evidence, did you not?"

"Yes."

"But you left your fingerprint camera behind?"

"I didn't know the nature of the case. I thought the kit I brought was sufficient to take care of the average situation, even a murder case. A camera would have been desirable, but I didn't know the conditions."

Again, Barker came off as an idiot, a professional hack who was prepared to take short-cuts even when a man's life was at stake.

Higgs ramped up the pummeling.

"I suggest, Captain Barker," Higgs said, "that there were numerous articles in Sir Harry's room that you never processed."

"I quite agree with you."

"If the accused had left a fingerprint on that screen, wouldn't it be likely that he left fingerprints on other objects?"

"Yes, under ordinary conditions. It is, however, my opinion that the nature of the crime and the extent of emotion or hurry would most likely prevent him from handling a lot of objects. In this case there was no necessity for the assailant to handle many objects."

"Well, why did you dust the powder room downstairs?" Higgs asked.

Barker answered, "We can't exclude anything in an investigation like this."

"But you did exclude a number of articles in the bedroom?"

"Yes."

If the defense had yet to put Barker's dishonesty beyond doubt, there was now no question. Higgs continued to hammer at Barker's credibility for two days. Eventually, he came right out and said what everyone in the courtroom was thinking: it was impossible for the print to be lifted from the screen without some of its ornate pattern being lifted, too. The print, in other words, had detached from its supposed original venue with no proof it had ever been there.

This revelation meant one of two things: that Barker was almost criminally incompetent or grossly dishonest. And it suggested another possibility: that the print had been lifted from another object unconnected with the murder scene to frame de Marigny.

Higgs slammed home exactly that point. "I suggest that Exhibit J never came from that screen."

"It did come from that screen! Number 5 panel!" Barker answered.

"You can show none of the scrollwork on Exhibit J, can you?"

"I cannot."

Higgs continued softly. "This is the most outstanding case in which your expert assistance has been required, is it not?"

"Well, it's developed into that."

"And I suggest that in your desire for personal gain and notoriety you have swept away truth and substituted fabricated evidence."

"I emphatically deny that!" Barker bellowed.

But it was too late to reverse the damage Barker's testimony had done to the prosecution's case.

***

On November 4, 1943, Alfred de Marigny was freed from his cage to give evidence in his own defense. After two weeks of silently observing proceedings, he was anxious to speak.

His lawyers questioned him on his movements on July 7th and 8th, his relationship with the Oakes family, and his financial affairs. He closed the day's testimony by denying that he was at Westbourne on the night of the killing or that he was responsible for the murder. Several more days of questioning followed. De Marigny continued smoothly. There were no surprises or inconsistencies. His friend the Count de Visdelou supported him with an alibi.

On November 5, de Marigny faced Eric Hallinan, the Attorney General whom he felt had made it his personal ambition to railroad him. Hallinan's inquiries revolved around his finances, his relationship with his former wife, and the elopement with Nancy Oakes, whom he had married two days after she became of legal age.

Hallinan also zeroed in on the fact that Nancy became pregnant when she was ill. This had been one of the Oakes' main bones of contention. Having set the scene, Hallinan then pivoted to the antipathy which had apparently developed between the two men. He referred to the hospital incident, when Sir Harry threatened to eject him, and the hauling of young Sydney out of de Marigny's house in Victoria Avenue, asking if these incidents left him feeling humiliated.

"No," de Marigny answered. "Everyone knew Sir Harry was a moody man and had a violent temper. He would lose his temper for nothing and might forget the whole thing the next day."

Hallinan asked, "Did he call you a sex maniac?"

"Quite possibly. But when he was angry he said things he didn't mean. I did not resent it."

De Marigny replied to every question with firm, unruffled authority. If Hallinan's objective had been to trick him into indiscretion, he had failed. Higgs had scored a victory.

***

The other telling defense evidence came from Captain Maurice O'Neil, supervisor of the New Orleans investigation bureau, who said the now famous Exhibit J, the print of de Marigny's right little finger, did not come from the screen in Sir Harry's bedroom, but an object with circular patterns on it. He also said he had never heard of a lifted print being accepted as evidence, unless it was photographed in its original position beforehand.

For the most part, the defense case went well. The final witness was the nineteen-year-old heiress, herself, Nancy Oakes de Marigny. She showed up in the witness box in a black designer dress and flat white beret. De Marigny, leaning forward in his cage, watched her intently as she took the oath in an almost inaudible voice. I watched de Marigny as his wife gave testimony. I did not see him did take his eyes off her.

Her evidence largely concerned family relationships, but also covered Barker's graphic account of the murder, an account which spared no one's feelings, least of all those of the distraught Lady Oakes. Higgs asked her, "Have you ever heard your husband use any expression of hatred towards your father?"

"Never," she said. "Not once in my life."

When she stepped from the box, Higgs said: "That is the case for the defense."

So now only the final speeches of the attorneys, and the judge's summing-up, stood between de Marigny and his fate. Nassau remained in a state of high tension. The trial was the only point for discussion in the bars and stores of Bay Street, and in the shanty communities over the hill. Barber shops were abuzz with nothing else.

Higgs opened his final address by saying that never in the history of the Bahamas had there been a crime of more sensational nature. It was a brutal and dastardly affair and it fell to the jury to decide whether de Marigny committed "the shocking deed." Never had a local jury been faced with greater responsibility. The rest of Higgs' address spotlighted deficiencies in the prosecution evidence. He focused on Lady Oakes' statement that de Marigny had never shown ill-will towards Sir Harry.

Higgs then, having dismissed most of the prosecution evidence as irrelevant, suggested the Crown's case would stand or fall on the reliability of Melchen and Barker and the reliability of the fingerprint that he had worked so hard to discredit. The case against de Marigny was, he said, purely circumstantial. There was nothing to show what weapon was used, how the killer entered the house, or how he committed the crime. Higgs was merciless in his treatment of Barker, whom he criticized for not bringing proper photographic equipment to the Bahamas, for not producing the contested print on the object on which it was found, and for changing his story when he realized his original testimony about the print and its location given at the preliminary hearing could not have been true. With the verbal beating of the Miami cop complete, Higgs rested his case.

Justice Daly spent five tedious hours on a summation of the case. Daly expressed the hope that the jury would reach a unanimous verdict. He noted that a unanimous verdict was required to hang a man under Bahamian law. The noose was ready and waiting.

The jury retired at 5:25 p.m.

They returned at 7:20 p.m.

They had reached their conclusion after less than two hours. Ray, our fingerprint experts, and I scrambled to get back to our seats.

De Marigny, who had been chatting with policemen during the interim, pacing the floor and smiling nervously, was called back into court. Nancy, who had been waiting tensely on the second floor of the nearby Central Police Station, took her seat. Her face was pale, her lips quivering.

Then the jury trooped in, their faces somber but inscrutable.

When the judge had taken his seat, the court registrar asked the jury if they had agreed on a verdict. Foreman Sands said: "Yes, we have."

The registrar asked, "How say you? Is the prisoner guilty or not guilty of the offence with which he is charged?"

The foreman, James Sands, stood. He addressed the court. In a firm, clear voice, he gave the answer that the world had been waiting for weeks to hear.

"Not guilty."

CHAPTER 26

In the courtroom, the acquittal of Alfred de Marigny sparked a tumultuous celebration. Windows rattled. Walls shook. Spectators bolted to their feet and cheered. Police tried to maintain order but for several minutes there wasn't any.

The judge discharged Alfred de Marigny. He jumped off the dock to embrace his wife. Immediately, they fled outside to the crowded square where crowds cheered and jostled to get close. They pushed their way through excited well-wishers. Flashbulbs popped. People wanted to touch them. Reporters, including myself, shouted questions. The only comment de Marigny made to waiting reporters was, "The judge is a fair man," which as it turned out was quite accurate.

I rushed over to the telegraph office which was jammed with other members of the press. I sent a bulletin to my editors in New York. I promised to follow up the next day with a thousand words. Then I sent a second Western Union telegram to my wife, advised her that at the trial was over and I loved her and would be home soon.

Thereafter, I turned my attention back to Nassau. I followed the celebrations that were breaking out in the streets, high spirits quickly met with a strong and ominous police and military presence.

Alfred de Marigny was, however, still not completely out of trouble, at least in Nassau. The jury had taken the highly questionable legal step of recommending his deportation, as well as the deportation of his pal, de Visdelou. But de Marigny had little desire to linger in Nassau at this point. He would most likely have been making his own plans to get out of town even if he weren't being kicked out.

But that night it was all revelry. There was a big party thrown at the estate of the Baron and Baroness af Trolle. Ray was invited and pulled me along. The Baroness was in a great mood since her friend's husband had just ducked a noose. No one objected to my presence. Leonarde Keeler was also there with his polygraph.

After everyone was suitably juiced with some of the best stuff from the Baroness's bar, Keeler, who had been a key to the acquittal, started to show off his lie detector.

"Say," de Marigny finally said to Keeler, "how about giving me a lie detector test about the murder of Sir Harry Oakes? I'd like to take such a test. You know, I asked the Crown for such a test when I was arrested, but was refused."

The test was made with a stenographer present. The key exchange went like this.

Keeler asked, "Is your name Alfred de Marigny?"

De Marigny answered. "Yes."

"Did you know Sir Harry Oakes?"

"Yes."

"Do you know who killed Sir Harry Oakes?"

"No."

"Have you had something to eat today?"

"Yes."

"Did you kill Sir Harry yourself?"

"No."

The needle never wavered. De Marigny's answers to the key questions brought no more of a reaction in the lie detector than his replies to a dozen unimportant queries. It was clear to even those who might have nursed a few doubts that de Marigny knew nothing about the murder of Oakes.

A throng of reporters and well-wishers had gathered outside de Marigny's home in Victoria Avenue. Rather than brave the crowd, the couple accepted Godfrey Higgs' offer of refuge. The evening passed in a spirit of relief and jubilation.

The prisoner's release also brought an unexpected explosion of joy from the public, and especially the blacks, who had carried him to his car outside the court. Hallinan had ordered the police to stand by with fire-hoses, expecting that conviction would spark riotous hostility towards de Marigny. But as the prosecution team vanished quietly into the night, the holiday mood spread through Nassau. The bars filled with revelers celebrating the count's victory over the establishment forces that had wished to hang him.

***

Later that same evening, in one of the bars, I found Leroy Stone, one of the jurors.

He was at the bar, staring into a whiskey but not touching it. He was fair, burley and pink-faced. A few beads of sweat were on his forehead just below the hairline. I walked over to him and put a hand on his shoulder. He flinched slightly in surprise, but calmed when he recognized me. "Hello, Alan," he said in a low voice. "How's tricks?"

"Congratulations," I said.

"On what?"

"You did the right thing," I said.

"Did we?"

"Yes. De Marigny is innocent. We all know that."

I ordered a quinine water over ice.

"Of course, we know that," he said. "Want to know how close he came to the gallows?"

"Sure. Tell me."

"Four of the jurymen were Plymouth Brethren," Stone began.

"Plymouth what?" I asked.

"Evangelical sect. Conservative, low church, nonconformist. There are a bunch of them on the island. They didn't like de Marigny for more reasons than I can count."

"They thought he murdered Oakes?"

Stone turned toward me. "It had nothing to do with Oakes," he said. "They figured he was French and thus suspect. They didn't like the stories they'd heard about him fornicating around town with various indulgent women. And, most of all, they disliked him because they said he had 'broken God's laws.'"

"Which laws? Adultery? Murder?"

"He was in the habit of going sailing on Sundays. The Sabbath."

I blinked.

"They were ready to hang him for that?" I asked.

"Good Christian men all," he said. He knocked back his drink with one deft toss. "They talk about forgiveness and Salvation, and they were ready to send the bloke to the gallows all out of their own righteous indignation of his way of living." He wiped a sleeve across his mouth. "I thought of the deportation order myself," he said. "I told these devout buggers that if they didn't like seeing the Frenchman around town there was a more charitably Christian way to get rid of him. Make him leave. One of the four of them went along with me. We avoided a hung jury which would have meant a new trial. A new trial, who knows? We would have had to do this all again. Anything could have happened. De Marigny could have swung."

Stone fell silent. I joined him with a whiskey. I thought about it.

"Jesus!" I said.

"If you'll excuse me now," he said, "I'm going out into the alley to vomit."

I examined my own thoughts. I started to put in order what I wanted to say in the report I would telegraph the next day. I had no shortage of thoughts. It wasn't like working on the *Evening Graphic* any more. I was forty years old and needed to file top notch material or I wouldn't be able to look myself in the mirror.

A body lurched up against the bar next to me.

"Thinking about what to write?"

I turned sharply. At first, I thought it was Stone, returning. But it was a man I'd never seen before, a gaunt white man with a fedora, a suit jacket and a tie.

"I'm always thinking about what to write," I allowed.

"You're Alan, aren't you?" he asked. "Ray's pal from New York?"

"Who are you?" I asked.

Instead of giving his name, he gave me mine, first and last, as if I didn't know it. Then he gave me my street address in New York and the names of the publications I wrote for. I could tell he was not a fan looking for me to autograph a book.

I glanced around. There were two other men at the door who were watching us. Quickly, it was intimidating and ominous.

"What can I do for you?" I asked. My eyes lowered for a split second. I found what I had suspected. Police shoes. My eyes came back up and met his.

"What did you think of the trial?" he asked. "The verdict?"

"You want an honest answer or a polite answer?" I asked.

"How about both?" he suggested.

I unloaded, speaking more out of indignation than courage. "You acquitted an innocent man," I said. "Bully for you. He should never have been accused in the first place. The real killer—or killers—is out there walking the streets right now while you and your two gorillas over there at the door are wandering around the bars looking for stragglers from the courtroom. That's not a very impressive episode of policework, but nothing here has been. Frankly, you guys should be ashamed of yourselves. Let's see if you ever go the next step and arrest the real killer. Let's see, but I suspect it'll be a cold day in hell when that happens."

I waited for a fist to find my nose. I'd badly overplayed my hand. But I had no choice but to stand my ground and go with it.

"When are you leaving Nassau?" he asked.

"As soon as I can."

"We'll see about that," he said.

"Let me phrase it differently," I said. "If Alfred de Marigny didn't kill Sir Harry, who did? Got a theory on that?"

He snuffed out his cigarette on the back of my hand. I flinched but went with it. I reasoned that if I betrayed my fear, I'd be dead. Over the years, I'd learned. Back up an inch for thugs like this and they'll push you for a lifetime.

He lifted the cigarette butt, hurled it behind the bar, turned and stalked to the door. His back-ups followed. I left via the back door, rather than walk out onto a dark street late in the evening. I might have found a reception committee brandishing weapons.

CHAPTER 27

The Nassau Tribune, in a postscript to the trial, read: "Today Bahamians are looking around for someone to scalp for the unsolved murder of Sir Harry Oakes. In this 'Tragedy of Errors', the question for the public to decide is who made the first and biggest error that led to the greatest fiasco in a criminal trial in this colony?"

That referenced only one individual, the person who had bollixed the case from the get-go, labeled it a suicide, imported a couple of incompetent corrupt American cops, and then started to point a finger at a man who was innocent. The individual's initials were H.R.H., The Duke of Windsor.

Typically, the ex-King missed the editorial. He was socializing with his friends in the United States on the evening that de Marigny was set free. But his Highness the Duke, the Royal Nitwit, still had a few tricks up his colonial sleeve for the man who had once called him, "not my favorite ex-King." Far from governing his ever-diminishing empire, the Duke and Mrs. The Duke were now cooling their royal heels in New York, waiting for the war and their obligations to end. But they still had some muscle with the administration of the islands.

Through the Colonial Secretary, a decree was issued that invited de Marigny and his pal Visdelou to leave the islands. The decree was very specific, saying that if de Marigny and Visdelou didn't accept the invitation, they would be forcibly deported to the first place that would accept them.

De Marigny argued that he couldn't be deported—he now had a British passport. Deportation only applied to foreigners. But there was a trump card in the recent law for folks like him, a law dating from Prohibition days, when good Nassau residents feared that Yankee gangsters could hide out among them. Oh, the horror of it! The law empowered the government to give the heave-ho to anyone, no hearing required. The Count was fair game to be sent adrift.

But deported? Who would take him? The war was still on.

The logical answer was to the United States. But the United States wouldn't grant a visa to a thrice-married spoiled adventurer, not even for transit. Pan Am Airways, the line with the only flights out, wouldn't sell him a ticket. Royal Air Force planes that the Duke might otherwise have been able to press into service had better business to attend to than to ferry around the world a lapsed-Frenchman who had just ducked a murder rap.

De Marigny sat tight in the island paradise, a modern-day Flying Dutchman with no port to sail to. In New York, Windsor inquired by telegraph as to how the deportation had gone and was enraged to discover de Marigny was still in Nassau. Windsor popped a royal knot.

"Why the hell is he still there?" he barked to his staff.

He was informed of the bothersome legal niceties. He told his people to think of something and think fast, thinking not being Windsor's stronger qualities.

They thought of something. A couple of mornings later, de Marigny was arrested a second time. The issue this time was lesser than homicide, but pesky all the same. The warrant cited four gasoline drums with RAF markings that were in his possession. De Marigny had mentioned these to the police the day he learned of his father-in-law's murder. No one had cared, though they were technically contraband due to wartime rationing. Now they were suddenly important. A local magistrate said the Count was on his way to a Bahamian jail if he didn't do everyone a favor and find his way out of the country, fast.

De Marigny sold his chicken farm to his foreman, John Anderson, who owed him several grand from gambling debts. They settled for pennies on the pound sterling. The Count and Nancy started to discuss their options for getting out of the Bahamas and beyond British jurisdiction.

I tried to wrap up my business in Nassau as quickly as possible. I did not see my acquaintance from the bar again, the police thug who'd put out his cigarette on the back of my hand. But I felt an uneasy presence near me. Just as I had when I arrived, I knew I was under surveillance. I tried to be careful and be conspicuous in public.

I stayed away from my friends of color on the island lest I bring the wrath of the powers in Nassau down upon them.

I made an air reservation to leave, and then the airline called me back and said my seat was no longer available. They had had to give it to a military man, they said. I made a new reservation. The same thing happened. Then it happened a third time.

Something was up. O'Neil and Keeler were already off the island, but Ray Schindler was still here, wrapping up and keeping company with Alfred and Nancy as they pondered their next moves and as Baroness af Tolle and Schindler made phone calls on their behalf.

De Marigny maybe have escaped the noose, but enemies were still out there and his troubles were far from over. I was starting to feel as if I were in a similar situation, myself.

Four nights after the trial ended, at around three a.m., there was a loud thump somewhere near where I slept. It was followed by a louder bang and the sound of the door to my hotel room jumping off its locking mechanism. I came awake fast but not quite fast enough. Or maybe it would never have mattered.

Harsh light slashed into my room from the hallway, accompanied by two figures moving quickly, one big, one small. The intruding yellow light from the hallway silhouetted. I couldn't see faces, but didn't need to.

The big heavy one was on me first. He was nimble for a large man. Worse, he'd gotten the drop on me. I tried to sit up quickly but he came right at me, pushed my shoulders back down, then jumped onto the bed. He shook me hard, violently slamming me against the mattress, then pressed his knee at the center of my chest to keep me pinned down. He said nothing but stank of whiskey, cigarettes and sweat.

The smaller man moved at a slower pace: much like a barracuda following in the wake of an oafish not-too-bright giant sea tortoise, looking for the chum that the bigger creature had missed. The silhouette told me everything: the ferret figure, the straw hat pushed back. The glasses. A sliver of reflected light caught the tone of the ever-present yellow tie.

"What the—?"

McBruey and Graywater. The Hardy and Laurel of nocturnal visits.

"Shut the hell up!" McBruey said. He slapped me across the face.

"We'll tell you when you can talk," Graywater said. "Right now, you listen!"

As ugly as it was, it was about to get uglier. With a fumbling motion, McBruey groped for something in a belt or a pocket. He kept his other hand on my throat. I had trouble breathing. His knee was on my heart, no coincidence, and most of his three hundred pounds was on it.

I figured the hand was going to come up with the truncheon and I was about to be treated to a few skull fractures and some dental work. Instead—worse. There was a flick, a snap and I could see the outline of a blade. He pressed the point of the knife to my right nostril and gave enough of a little tug to show he was ready to cut.

"Okay, listen up, you stupid nosy son-of-a-bitch!" McBruey grunted.

I didn't have much choice. Graywater came to me. He stooped down right next to me, his face a foot away from mine. He too stank of booze, tobacco and sweat. His breath was like gasoline. He glared. He studied me.

"Well, well, well," Graywater finally said. "Mr. Alan, our no-good friend. How are you sleeping?"

I grunted. "Just fine," I said. "Up until a minute ago."

"But you're a nosy fellow, aren't you?" Graywater asked. The tip of the dagger played with my nose again. I thought McBruey was ready to cut. I knew he wanted to. My arms were pinned. I was helpless. I was aware of rain hitting the glass of my slightly-opened window. There was a distant rumble of thunder and an even more distant sparkle of lightning. Tropical weather, the accoutrements of sudden death. On such a night was Sir Harry Oakes murdered.

"Let's maybe get to the issue," Graywater said. "You leave soon. Maybe. If we let you. You go home and write, right?"

"Yeah," I said.

"What are you going to write?"

"De Marigny was acquitted. What else? That's the story."

"Guilty man, de Marigny. Guilty man acquitted," he said. "That's your story. That's what you write."

"That's not how it looked," I said.

The bear on top of me moved his hand. The blade of the knife was now at my throat, keeping the jugular vein close company. With his other hand, he started to squeeze my throat.

"You be goddamned careful what you write, you stupid Yank bastard!" Graywater barked at me. He was livid. "We have ways in these islands! We find you. You write what's good for the islands or you never write anything again! You understand, you dumb American fuck? Yes?"

My brow exploded with sweat. The blade was pressing hard against my skin. I felt my pulse in the back of my mouth. My chest bone could barely support McBruey's suet-laden frame much longer.

"Yes," I sputtered. "Yes, sir. I understand."

"You write what we want, goddamn you!"

"I write what you want. Like you say, Graywater," I said. "What do I care, anyway, right? I get paid no matter what I write. Okay?"

The big man's head turned slowly toward his keeper. Through the round lenses of his glasses, Graywater glowered at me a few seconds longer. Then his dark eyes slid to the right and connected with his enforcer. There was a slight nod. I didn't know what it meant. It could just as easily have meant kill him as go get him a cup of coffee.

McBruey burped and grunted. He pulled back the knife. With effort, he steadied himself and hulked off me. My chest still ached. My cheeks stung from where he had wailed on me. My heart felt like a giant fan spinning in a hot room.

The yellow tie withdrew a little as the slim man leaned back. "Graywater? Who?" he asked me. "*Who* am I?" He slapped me. Hard.

"*Mister* Graywater," I said.

"Don't you ever fucking forget!" he barked. "We find you."

Graywater backed toward the door. His smelly ape gave me a final shove and followed him. They both withdrew while facing me, just in case, I suppose, that I caught a case of the crazies and tried to pull a gun. Yellow Tie disappeared first, then his brutal Hibernian. They left the door wide open, the hinges and lock shattered.

CHAPTER 28

Still shaken the next morning, I found Ray Schindler in the hotel dining room. In low confiding ones, out of earshot of any other tables, I told him what had happened. He listened quietly and attentively.

"Be casual about how you look around, Alan," he said softly. "But study the room."

I scanned. There was a team of security people watching us from a near corner. Another single cop was at a bar. Police shoes. I was good at spotting them and tired of seeing them.

"They're everywhere," Ray said.

I might have made visible pretenses of talking to Ray on a more casual subject, but that wasn't the way I was thinking. The way I calculated, Ray was one of the few people who could possibly bring pressure on the power structure of the Bahamas. He had the political swat, the American media adored him, he knew people in the New York-Miami-Palm Beach social circuits. Ray had juice. He also had balls.

"What are you planning to write?" he asked me.

I was too rattled for food. I was having a Chesterfield for breakfast. The calming blast of nicotine was good.

"I don't know," I said. "I'll decide when I get back to a free country. And I'll write what I damned well want to write."

"Be careful," he said. "They have short attention spans but long memories. Stupid but stubborn."

"For a 'free world' place," I said, "these islands bear a pretty good resemblance to a fascist state."

My comment made Ray laugh softly. "You noticed, did you? I suppose you can blame Windsor for that, too," he said. "God damn

Bosch sympathizer. What should we expect, right?" He looked at me. "When are you planning to get out of here?" he asked very softly.

"I'm already packed and ready," I said. "I've got an air ticket for this afternoon."

"What time?" he asked. "To where?"

"Three thirty," I said. "To Miami."

"Do they know?"

"They? Graywater and his bull?"

"Them. The others. Anyone," Schindler said.

"They know I'm leaving. Exactly when and to where, I don't know if they know."

"They've probably checked with the airlines," Ray said routinely. "They do it all the time. That way they know when to ambush people. I heard one story... Know how those small Eastern Airlines planes to Florida have straw mesh seats? There was someone who made himself unpopular down here. The man boarded and went to his seat. Someone came in, sat down behind him and put an icepick into his heart through the back of the seat. Then the killer left the aircraft. They didn't know someone was dead until they landed in the Keys. Or they didn't care to know. You choose." He paused. "A couple of other times, small planes departing have mysteriously exploded. Engine failure, also known as a bomb. Kill a dozen innocent people to get one victim. It happens, Alan."

I shuddered.

"But, good," Ray said, not skipping a beat. "We'll play along. We'll let them know. Now listen to me, Alan," he said softly, "and listen like you've never listened to anyone in your life."

I leaned forward.

"Keep your reservation and don't take it," he advised. "I'm paranoid, too, which is a healthy thing. I have a private flight arranged to the United States this afternoon at the same time from a private airfield. It's a small plane. It's cramped. Smuggler stuff. There's one extra place if you squeeze. Be on it with me. We'll get out of this damned place before these fools here know what happened. Do you trust me?"

"Sure," I said.

"You should."

"Not that I have much of a choice," I said with relief.

Ray gave me a friendly punch on the arm.

"You've been threatened before, you'll be threatened again," he said. "It's all grist for the mill. Writers need experiences, don't they? That's what our pal Hemingway says. Fitzgerald, too."

Ray picked up a copy of *The Nassau Tribune* and scanned it for a moment. He turned to the sports pages, found an American football story and pointed to the paper, as if he were indicating something interesting on the page.

He leaned close to me and raised a hand so that his lips couldn't be read across the room.

"Check out of the hotel at your normal time," he said. "How much luggage do you have?"

"Three bags. Two medium size, one small," I said.

"Good again. Put everything you need in the small bag. Your notes. Toiletries. Change of clothes," he said. "Passport too, even though you probably won't use it on the route we're going. When you check out, ask for a taxi. Put your two big bags in the lobby. Then tell them you need to visit the washroom. There's a washroom in the rear of the lobby. It's near the exit that the colored kitchen staff uses. Goes to an alley."

"I've seen it," I said.

"Take your small bag with you. Head to the lavatory and then bolt out the door to the alley. If you turn left it takes you to Cumberland Street. Speed is important, but don't run. It will attract attention. Go directly to the southwest corner of Cumberland and Marlborough, but for God's sake make sure your back is clean. I have a private driver. Carlos. He's a Cuban. Black as the ace of spades. A dear soul. He has a 1934 Chrysler. Dark green. I'll be in the back seat. We leave for the private airfield at 2:30. If you're not there, I leave without you. Our driver is also our pilot. Should be in the air by a few minutes past three. By the time Graywater's posse of homicidal imbeciles realizes they been skunked we'll be five thousand feet above the ocean, assuming the wings stay attached to the plane. We're flying in a fifteen-year-old taildragger and we're going to a private field on the coast near Orlando. Not many lights on the coastline. Wartime restrictions. We need to take off in daylight. Not sure our man Carlos has lights on his plane, by the way. Know what I mean? But he's a genius with a compass. We're skipping the whole obvious Miami and Palm Beach scene. Bring booze. You'll want it. Evening skies are choppy and visibility sometimes is a laugh. There'll be a barf bag under your seat."

I drew a breath and pointed to something else on the sports page, maintaining the ruse of a sports discussion.

"Got it?" Ray asked.

"Looking forward it," he said.

"You should be. Ever read *Vol de Nuit. Night Flight*. By the French guy, de Saint-Exupéry?"

"I saw Selznick's movie," I said. "Haven't read the book." He looked at me with disapproval. "Not yet, anyway," I corrected.

"You're still part philistine, Alan," he said. "That's what I like. Now wait here while I share our escape plan with our murderously corrupt pals."

"What?"

"Just play along."

He folded away the newspaper. We both put money on the table.

Ray lumbered to his feet and buttoned his sports jacket. He went toward the door, never looking at his followers, both of whom watched him. Near the door, he turned toward me. "Oh! Hey, Alan!" he called. "Same flight as me this afternoon? Three thirty to Miami?"

"That's the one," I said.

"I'll see you at the airport!" he said.

I gave him a wave. He gave me a nod.

CHAPTER 29

The late morning lumbered. I checked out of my room. I found my friend Felipe at his usual spot at the taxi stand. I tipped him twenty-five American dollars for his help and shook his hand. In his way, he was as fine a man as I'd met in Nassau, brimming with personal integrity and a sense of honor. I apologized for not using him to the airport that day, but told him that a friend had insisted on taking me. Felipe accepted graciously. I think he knew something was up.

I passed the interim time in the hotel lobby. The desk staff stashed my bags in a corner of the lobby near a porter. I was not inclined to be privately visited in my bedchamber again.

The hotel was happy to have the room free earlier for other arrivals, so that part was fine. A second wave of journalists was pouring in. I couldn't wait to pour myself out.

I counted two more teams of police shoes in the hotel lobby. They seemed as numerous as rats in the alley; sometimes the distinction was vague. Whether they were watching me, watching everyone or just watching, I didn't know, and it didn't matter. The powers that prevailed in Nassau liked to operate under darkness or in closed spaces. They could be blatant when they had to, but out in clear view I felt I was safe, at least to a degree.

Time crept along. Noon arrived. Then one o'clock. The slowest tick tocks I'd ever lived in my life. The humidity accelerated. Finally, it was near two p.m. I began the check-out charade.

I went to the desk and told them I was expecting a friend to pick me up in a brown Plymouth. "Tell me again where the men's room is," I asked.

They indicated down the back hall to the left. I thanked them.

"If my friend arrives, tell him he can load my bags," I said.

I indicated my two bags of luggage and had a porter bring them to the front entrance. I picked up my small bag. I noticed that one set of police shoes had followed me to the lobby. Coincidence? Like hell. So that's the way it is, huh? I was high up on their list, whether I wanted to be or not.

I walked calmly down the corridor toward the wash room. There was a final corner to turn where I would be out of view. I thanked God. I opened the men's room door and let it slam shut without entering. Then I ran. I passed the kitchen and then hit the service door, almost knocking over a pair of dishwashers.

I excused myself to their surprise, then was out into an alley that festered in the afternoon sun. I ran to the end of the alley. Some gulls squawked and fluttered aloft. I knew where I was on Cumberland Street. I caught my breath. I tried to slow to an inconspicuous walk. I looked at my watch. It was two minutes after two. I was good on time but still wondered if I'd ever see my wife and daughter again.

I went down the block toward the hack stand. I didn't see anyone.

No Carlos. No Thirty-four Chrysler. No dammed nothing.

I cursed. I suddenly realized I had no fallback plan.

I crossed to the designated corner at Marlborough. Sweat was pouring off me. Then I noticed a battered dark green Chrysler sliding into a spot away from the curb. I could see no passenger, only the driver.

The driver was a dark man with an applejack cap. Right hand drive. It was pick-up time but this didn't look quite right.

Cuban? Maybe.

I walked to the curb. He took pains to ignore me. I could smell rum and sweat.

I took a gamble. I leaned to his window.

"Carlos?" I asked.

He looked at me. I heard a voice from the back seat.

"Get in, damn it, Alan," said the voice. "Be quick now and let's move."

There was Schindler, squeezed low to one side. The car was a two-door. I hustled in.

"Back seat," Carlos said with an accent.

"Slump low," Schindler added. "You're not Black Jack Pershing and this isn't a ticker tape parade."

I obeyed. I left my bag on the front seat. Ray also had a bag on the floorboards. Carlos turned and we headed out of town. Immediately I felt better. We were moving.

"Give your people the slip?" Schindler asked.

"I'm pretty sure. You?"

"Of course. They're idiots, you know. What they lack in intelligence, they make up for in venality, however. There's the problem."

"One of the problems," I corrected.

"Yup."

"You bring booze?" he asked.

"No. Didn't have a chance."

The driver, Carlos, laughed. He thrust his hand under the seat and reached for something. His hand came up. He handed us a bottle of Bacardi's. The glass was filthy. It was beautiful. We were on our way.

He took a rough pot-holed road out of town, the opposite direction as the airport. He drove steadily, about a mile every two minutes. We passed agricultural fields and local people on bicycles. Carlos turned and watched every pretty girl. I didn't blame him. Every pretty girl responded with a smile. I didn't blame them, either. I was starting to feel better.

After a fifteen-minute drive, Carlos turned into a battered fuel station. He jumped out and told us to follow. A shirtless teenage boy with skin the color of mahogany raised a garage door with a chain. Carlos' eyes were scanning everything on the road that went past the station. But it was quiet. The kid pushed the Chrysler into the garage. We went around back. A path led through some trees. Carlos led us.

I swatted insects the whole way but had not a word of complaint. We came out in a small clearing. The aircraft was a small Cessna, a taildragger as promised, light blue with no lettering, so that it couldn't be seen easily on a watery horizon. It was under a canvas that was stretched across six poles, with foliage growing over it so that it couldn't be seen from the air. I looked at the sun to find my direction. We were on the northern part of the island. It was hazy from the heat, but clear.

Carlos turned to Schindler. He didn't say anything. Ray reached into his pocket and withdrew two hundred-dollar bills.

"May I contribute?" I asked.

"This one's on me, Alan," he said. "You're a good travelling companion. It's the least I can do."

"You're very generous."

"Treat me well when you write up the Oakes case," he said. "But I'll invoice Lady Oakes, anyway," he said. He winked. "She's very happy today. She has her husband back. How long her happiness will last is another question. Time will tell, won't it? It always does." He put away his wallet. Carlos pocketed the money. "Come on," Ray said.

The three of us pushed the taildragger out of its sleeping quarters. Carlos got the front propeller going and we piled in. He pushed a revolver into his belt. We closed the doors and buckled in. A smuggler's aircraft, indeed. There were a couple of bullet holes in the floor. There was another bottle of rum and a larger pistol. Carlos was not a man to be messed with.

The Cuban's little bird crept out on to a runway that was nothing more than a hundred-yard patch of grass. But it was enough. To my mind it was beautiful.

We started to accelerate and bounce down the runway. Then we climbed into the sky. We flew low. Ray and I passed the bottle of rum back and forth. The coastline of Florida was visible within twenty minutes. We had a few more bounces, but Carlos knew his way, and we landed seventy-six minutes after departure, finally back on the mainland of the United States. My heart was in my throat. God, it was good to be back on U.S. soil!

Carlos set us up with a local family. The parents spoke no English but they had a beautiful daughter who was bilingual in Spanish and English. She fed us. No phone. We stayed indoors. Precautions. We lay low for a couple of days.

On the third day, another driver appeared and took us to the sleepy naval city of Jacksonville. When I saw the American flag for the first time in weeks, waving free and proud over the airfield, I caught a lump in my throat that I would always remember. America may have had its flaws, but it was a damn sight better than a lot of other places.

From Jacksonville, we took a train to Atlanta. In the station, I went to one of the big telephone rooms and called my wife. I choked up again on the line when I heard her voice.

"Hello?" she asked twice. "Hello?"

"I'm in Atlanta," I said. "I'm back in a free country. I'm almost home." I added, "I'm safe and I love you."

Then it was her turn to choke up.

We stayed overnight at a hotel and we finally able to bathe. God knew what hell was happening in Nassau, but I sure knew there were folks unhappy with us.

"Tough crap for them," Schindler said over dinner before we took a morning train the next day that would eventually get us to New York's Pennsylvania Station. "Now," he then said. "Have you decided what you're going to write?"

"I have," I said.

"Good," he said. "I don't want to know in advance. Just spell my name right."

By the next evening we were back in New York City. I couldn't have been happier and more relieved. At majestic Pennsylvania Station, a creature of habit, I bought a box of chocolates for my wife, a Whitman Sampler, an expensive doll for my daughter, and a bunch of red roses for both.

I found a cab and gave the address.

I rang the doorbell and when my wife answered, I fell into her arms again or she fell into mine. I couldn't tell which and it made no difference.

CHAPTER 30

In November, the Nassau Yacht club gave de Marigny a big party. They presented him with all his trophies from the preceding season. Then they told him to put all the silverware in a sack and get off the island fast.

The distant royal cat's paw again? An official in the Cuban government invited Nancy and Alfred de Marigny to Cuba. Another wrinkle: There was no direct passage from Nassau to Havana. Every boat or plane now connected through Florida. Though de Marigny had visited the United States maybe two dozen times in the past, this time a transit visa was denied.

Time was running out. The Bahamian jail loomed. Once they had had a rope ready for de Marigny. Now there was a cement and iron cell, populated with spiders, mosquitoes and rats.

De Marigny contacted a local fisherman, or maybe it was a retired rum runner. On December sixth, he sailed to Cuba. There were winter seas. At least one big storm. Nonetheless, a week later, they arrived. It was not exactly a romantic sail into the sunset of happiness.

The Cuban government announced there had been a misunderstanding. There had been no actual invitation. But since de Marigny and his wife were there, they could stay anyway if they could find a place.

Before the war, de Marigny and his wife had crossed the Atlantic Ocean on the *Normandie*, before it had become a target for saboteurs in New York. On board, they had struck up a friendship with Ernest Hemmingway. Papa now continued to maintain his place a few miles east of Havana in San Francisco de Paula, where he was knocking out top drawer short stories about bullfights, social injustice and smuggling, all the while working on a manuscript about a fisherman stuck on Joe DiMaggio while chasing a big stubborn fish. So when Nancy and Alfred de Marigny found their way to Cuba, they eventually stayed on the estate of de Marigny's friend, Ernest Hemingway.

As about the same time, on December tenth, the Marquis de Visdelou left Nassau alone, bound for Haiti, one of the most backward places in North America, an untamed land of descendants of freed slaves, a toxic mix of French and African culture, voodoo rituals, staunch Catholicism and harsh rum.

The old French colony was not a happy venue for the displaced Marquis. Betty Roberts took a powder on following her Mauritian stud into exile. That was the last anyone heard of the Marquis. He vanished into the haze. I also heard Betty had gone to Europe and married a Russian count. Who knew? Not me, but I hoped she landed on her charming feet.

Thereupon, 1943 ended. Mercifully.

1944 began. Optimistically.

The tide of the Second World War had turned both in Europe and Asia. Allied troops were advancing northward through Italy, meeting resistance from Germans who were dug in and none from Italians who had wisely capitulated.

The Bahamas continued to fester in the Caribbean sun. And so did the aftermath of the Oakes murder trial.

It was impossible not to see the self-satisfied mug of the Duke of Windsor in the newspapers. His Former Highness tried to give the appearance of governing the islands during wartime, but seemed to make it to Florida and New York with the Duchess as often as he pleased. Official cameras would show him trying to look diligent at official meetings, but, as is usually the case, the truth lay far beneath the surface. There were parties, masked balls, golfing dates and the like. Any good reporter with his ear to the ground in New York picked up the stories. Most of them made him out to be an insensitive putz at best, a wealthy moron at worst.

I kept in touch with Ray Schindler and some of the other Americans who had worked on the case. It was difficult not to. Those of us who had been prevented from seeing any sort of justice for Sir Harry formed out own little press cabal. The Oakes case was like a train wreck. You hated it but couldn't take your eyes off it.

Ray continued his brilliant career out of his office on West 44th Street. But then even he couldn't resist another glimpse of the train wreck. Schindler's pal John Edgar Hoover had offered to send American FBI agents to Nassau to take the case to its next level and find the killer or killers of Sir Harry. Schindler again wrote to the Duke of Windsor and asked that Scotland Yard reopen the investigation. Ray offered his services for free.

Windsor replied that the Crown didn't think that was such a good idea. In fact, he labeled it an insult.

Schindler flew to Nassau, anyway. The day after his arrival, he was playing golf with an old friend when the friend was called to the clubhouse in mid-bogie. The friend vanished, then returned, looking shaken.

"What was that about?" Schindler asked.

"The call was from Government House," the friend said, referring to the Duke's private residence. "I'm to tell you that if you ask me or anyone else one question about the Oakes case, you'll be deported immediately."

Schindler remained for two or three more days. He was followed everywhere. Everyone he spoke to, everyone he knew, had received the same message. He took the hint and flew back to the United States, deeply frustrated.

197

And yet Schindler was not finished with the Oakes case. Nor, it turned out, was I.

Raymond Schindler, sitting in his office in New York in the months after the trial in Nassau, went through the whole business with his friend, former Attorney General Homer Cummings. Cummings pondered the matter, then wrote Schindler this letter:

From what I can see from the record, the police in Nassau fell into a mistake common to inexperienced officers everywhere. They found their logical suspect first and then proceeded to search for facts to fit him. From this first step, it was easy to fall into a state of mind where the investigator makes himself blind to every bit of evidence except that which he can apply to the preconceived theory he has created in his own mind.

Exactly what royal hand pointed to the "logical suspect" was something Cummings didn't address, at least not in writing.

Next Schindler dictated this letter to the Duke of Windsor:

Knowing your deep concern for the welfare of the citizens of the Bahamas, I take the liberty of addressing you on a matter of great importance. It is my considered opinion that the murderer of Sir Harry Oakes can be found, identified, convicted and brought to justice. During the incarceration and trial of Alfred de Marigny no adequate investigation was possible. Statements which failed to point toward the defendant were ignored. It goes without saying that I and my associate, Leonarde Keeler, would welcome an opportunity to work on the case. We would willingly offer our services without compensation.

President Franklin D. Roosevelt, a lifelong mystery fan, had been following the Oakes case, as well he could despite his declining health. The President had been a distinguished graduate of Columbia University Law School. He had formed his own theories about the legal proceedings and de Marigny was not his culprit.

The President, like practically everybody else in possession of the salient facts, had the definite feeling that the investigation into the scragging of the Baronet had been intentionally fouled up. Former Attorney General Cummings, in discussing the case with the President one day, received a tacit nod at his suggestion that the Federal Bureau of Investigation, busy as it was turning up spies, might be able to send a few men down to Nassau and take the mystery apart. Scotland Yard could have done the same thing.

But His Royal Highness the Duke of Windsor wanted none of it. One of his secretaries sent Schindler a form letter saying thank you, no.

The Duke had done one thing, though. He ordered an investigation of law enforcement in the islands. To no one's surprise, the probe accomplished approximately as much as a probe into the gambling situation in practically any American city.

The *Nassau Daily Tribune* blew some predictable smoke. A friend of mine mailed me a clipping:

Nassau can now relax after witnessing nearly a month of the tensest possible emotions engendered by the trial of Alfred de Marigny ...

Before the trial had progressed very far it was aptly described as "The Tragedy of Errors." The first and perhaps the greatest error was made when His Royal Highness the Governor called long distance and obviously got the wrong number. But in passing judgment on this action it must be conceded that His Royal Highness acted in good faith, doing what he be believed to be in the best interest of the Colony ...

It is pleasing that, in the closing chapter of this case, the cloud which threatened to obscure the life work and career of the Honorable Harold Christie was completely lifted by the defense, the prosecution and the bench. Mr. Christie has served this country well and its citizens owe him a large measure of good will.

When I read the above. I wanted to vomit.

Nancy Oakes de Marigny stayed in Cuba for a short while. She found Papa Ernie to be crude and obnoxious. No surprise there. But she was smitten by his son, Jack, with whom she started to share a bed. Thereafter, the de Marignys' problems as a couple multiplied, not that they needed adultery to give it a push. Nancy returned to the Bahamas.

When it was safe to travel again on or above the open seas, Nancy fled to the United States and left her husband behind. Still denied a visa to travel, Alfred couldn't follow. The U.S.A. was still off-limits. Rumors abounded that Windsor had put the fix in through some wealthy American friends. It may have been true.

Stranded in Cuba for several months, de Marigny eventually signed on as crew on a merchant ship carrying sugar from Havana to Halifax. He arranged to meet his wife in Montreal. He shouldn't have bothered. When she got there, Nancy Oakes announced that their marriage was over. She wanted nothing further to do with him. They were divorced in 1944.

At mid-life, having worked his way through three women, three fortunes, one poultry farm, one murder trial and who-knew-what-else, Alfred de Marigny was broke.

What next? Hitting bottom, he joined the Canadian Army as a private.

My old acquaintance Thomas Dewey ran for President as a Republican in 1944. He was a heavy underdog. Some nasty stories started to surface. One of the Hearst papers in New York, *The Daily Mirror,* ran stories claiming that Dewey sent top-ranking Murder Incorporated man Louis Lepke, the late owner of the Riobamba, to the electric chair in 1944 with a direct connection to a payoff from the mob.

The *Mirror* speculated that Lepke, in an attempt to save his own life, offered Dewey information that would link President Franklin D. Roosevelt and his cabinet members to several crimes, including a homicide. Lepke tried to convince Dewey that it would make him an unbeatable presidential candidate. Dewey granted Lepke a 48-hour reprieve, but with the consequences being too explosive, he did not make a deal. Lepke went to the hot seat in Sing Sing.

I have no idea if the *Mirror*'s story was true. But I was coming around to the opinion, shared by millions, that Dewey was a snake. There was also something about the man that just seemed fake. Or shady. A lot of people agreed. My vote went again for FDR. The nation re-elected an ailing Roosevelt, frail, weak, and aged beyond his years. Beyond the knowledge of most Americans, Roosevelt, a chain-smoker, had been in quickly declining physical health since at least 1940. By1944 he was terminally fatigued. In March 1944, shortly after his 62nd birthday, he underwent testing at Bethesda Hospital and was found to have high blood pressure, atherosclerosis, coronary artery disease causing angina pectoris, and congestive heart failure. He was now in the last six months of his life.

The President died in Warm Springs, George on April 12th, 1945. The war in Europe ended less than a month later. The Duke of Windsor resigned his duties as governor of the Bahamas the day the war in Europe ended. The war in Asia ended ninety days afterward.

Thank God. Twenty million people had been killed worldwide in World War Two. Why? If you wanted to believe there was no God, this was a good time for it. If you wanted to think mankind was evil, it was an easy sell. At least Fascism and Hitler had been defeated and most of the crazy little corporal's henchman would swing from nooses in Nuremberg. But Bolshevism was triumphant, living to imprison people and contaminate the world for the decades to follow.

In the days after Roosevelt's passing, an editorial by *The New York Times* declared, "Men will thank God on their knees a hundred years from now that Franklin D. Roosevelt was in the White House." At the time, most Americans would have agreed. Whatever else the criticisms of the thirty-second President, and there were many legitimate ones, the United States had come out of the war as a victorious.

There was a sad and sobering note for me, however. The parents of my dear friend Herbert Nossen, the doctor who had helped me stop drinking, had been murdered by the Nazis in Auschwitz.

Murdered. There was no other word for it.

*****

I had a new hardcover book out at the end of 1945. It was called *The Giant Killers*. It was about the U.S. Treasury agents who brought down Capone and some of the other big shot bad guys of the Prohibition era. I worked with a guy named Elmer Irey, a friend and a legend in law enforcement till he dropped dead suddenly in 1948. The book sold well. At the same time, RKO studios turned my second book, *Betrayal From The East*, into a quickie Hollywood movie starring Nancy Kelly and Lee Tracy. It was a second feature job, a propaganda piece, with a cast of loyal Chinese American actors playing evil Japanese because American audiences wouldn't notice. It was best left forgotten.

By 1946, my friend Mike Todd had left New York and moved to Los Angeles, where, so that he could be close to the high stakes gambling he craved, he bought the Del Mar Racetrack in San Diego. I saw Mike occasionally, usually at Romanoff's or The Brown Derby.

The Todd-Blondell affair was also full speed ahead. For Todd, that meant a permanent split from Bertha, his wife of the most recent nineteen years, would have to be arranged. The first Mrs. Todd, Bertha, wanted no part of said split, Mike's adulterous behavior notwithstanding.

Mike filed for divorce. A day or two after the filing, Bertha confronted her husband in his rented home in Rancho Santa Fe and lunged at him with a knife. She missed, hit a wall or a door frame, and sliced a tendon between two of her fingers.

Or maybe she sliced her hand cutting a piece of fruit. It depended on whose version of the events were to be believed. Bertha was taken by ambulance to St. John's Hospital in Santa Monica for minor surgery to repair the tendon. And there she died from an allergic reaction to anesthesia, much to the delight of the tabloids and gossip rags which were not-undeservedly all over Mike.

But by the hand of God, or whoever had wielded that knife, Mike was now free to marry Joan Blondell. The couple thus drove from Los Angeles to Las Vegas on a steamy July evening in 1947. They got married in the banquet room of the El Rancho Vegas on the Strip. Pictures in the press show the three kids of the newly blended family looking miserable. Joan wore a tense smile.

Meanwhile, things continued well for me.

My son was born in 1947. I had a book out titled *Murder* in 1947. No compendium of ordinary situations of those whose chips were forcibly cashed, the focus was on the human heart in its darkest, strangest most violent moments. They were great cases.

It was heady stuff.

It didn't get too much better than that.

Tenacious and unwavering, however, Thomas Dewey just wouldn't go away. Governor Dewey was nominated for President again in 1948, this time running against President Harry S. Truman.

202

His aggressive campaign and backing led his supporters to believe that he would be the next President of the United States. The problem with people who have no vices is that generally you can be pretty sure they're going to have some very annoying virtues.

Over time, he also stopped talking about crime. True, he hadn't prosecuted for years, but there seemed to be something he was avoiding. Or hiding. A federal investigative committee decided to question him. The investigators wanted to talk about the Luciano pardon. Dewey didn't want to discuss that or much else. His lack of response to the committee left more people to wonder about the complexity of his relationship to mobsters.

To the surprise of many, but not those of us who knew him, he lost again.

CHAPTER 31

In the last week of 1948, I heard that Bill McCoy, the gentleman smuggler whom I'd written about in the 1930's, had died of a heart attack. He bit the dust where he was happiest—at sea aboard his private yacht *Blue Lagoon*. He had made it to the ripe old age of seventy-one. Well, it seemed like ripe and old at the time. Bill was perhaps best remembered by his brother Ben when he simply wrote, "When the country went dry, Bill irrigated it".

I wrote a punchy hard-hitting book called *We Are The Public Enemies*. It was an account of the Depression era bandits who swaggered and shot their paths through the sweltering American Midwest before J. Edgar Hoover sent out well-armed Gestapo-style squads under the direction of G-Man Melvin Purvis to assassinate them. A new line of paperback books called Gold Medal was hitting the newsstands and book shops across America. *We Are The Public Enemies* was Gold Medal's prominent lead-off title, Numero 101 on a list that started with 101. There was no such thing as a paperback best seller list at the time, but Gold Medal told me that no other non-fiction was selling as fast.

The public enemies in question were: Dillinger. Karpis. Pretty Boy Floyd. Bonnie and Clyde. Ma Barker. The dirty little secret about these bandits was that they had a huge public following. They were more popular than the cops who had tracked them down and killed them. The dirtier secret was that they were, for the most part, vile human beings who had no use for anyone other than themselves. They would murder a cop as easily as other people might change their underwear. But they had their fans. And the book sold well.

And they were all conveniently dead, thanks to J. Edgar's hit squads.

The magazine stuff flowed, also: the police magazines, *The Saturday Evening Post. True. Liberty. Look. Coronet. The American Mercury.* In the very top magazines, the A-plus ones, I often had to take second billing to the old pain, Ernie Hemingway and some bull fight bull crap. In the A-Minus mags, I was Numero Uno.

Hemingway's patrols against German U-boats turned out to be just as unsuccessful as his counter-intelligence operation. As the months passed, and as no U-boat appeared, the *Pilar's* patrols turned into fishing trips, and the grenades were thrown into the sea as "drunken sport." After adding his sons Patrick and Gregory to the crew, Hemingway acknowledged that his U-boat hunting venture had turned into an excuse to go out to sea with friends and booze. But he never admitted it to his adoring public. He had an image to maintain, as we all do, I suppose. Years later, the Cuban naval officer Mario Ramirez Delgado, who sank U-176, said Hemingway was a playboy who hunted submarines off the Cuban coast as a whim.

I was glad to be out of Nassau, to have all that behind me, though I had no reluctance about sharing my thoughts as to what had happened. Why should I have?

Radio was a now a big thing. I developed some friends who had radio shows in New York. My ex-wife even had a radio show, not that she invited me. I'd go on the air and gab about crime. People still wanted to know about, and hear about, the Lindbergh case. And the Ponzi case. And the gangsters. And always the Oakes case, which remained unsolved.

Talk was cheap. I talked.

I kept an ear to the ground. I kept hearing things about the Bahamas.

I knew that down in Nassau there were several theories as to who murdered Sir Harry Oakes. There was a motive to fit each theory, a suspect for everyone's tastes. But the only theory that was openly discussed in Nassau, even as the years started to glide by is the one that was officially embraced. All other theories were discussed guardedly, if at all. It was not healthy in Nassau to talk too freely.

From what I hoped would be a safe distance, I kept tabs on what was going on. I gabbed on the radio about what I was doing. I wrote another article or two, questioning why the investigation had never continued after de Marigny's acquittal. No one had a good answer to that question.

The Oakes case wouldn't go away. And not just for those of us who were under the dark shadow of the case. Occasionally, I'd open the *New York Times* or the *Herald Tribune* or see something in the *New York Daily News* or *The New York Mirror*. I would always read it.

First there was the outright screwball stuff.

In 1950, a California shoe store clerk named George Boyle confessed to the murder, saying that he had committed it on a fishing trip while drunk.

That same year, a journeyman cook named Edward Majava, who worked on a Nassau-registered tanker, told the Bahamian cops that two women were involved in blackmailing the killer, whom he hinted was Harold Christie. He claimed the name had been passed on to him by a society portrait painter in Florida who was well-acquainted with the Oakes family's Palm Beach friends. Majava was vacationing in California at the time of his utterances. The local police took the unusual step of taking him seriously. They phoned Augustus Robinson, then the Nassau police chief, who travelled to California to interview the man. Majava named Harold Christie as the killer. No action followed in the Bahamas.

One would have been tempted to crumple up Majava's tale and toss it into the surf at Cable Beach, except a few months later, after a quiet legal process, a local taxi driver named Nicholas

Musgrave landed in jail for writing extortion letters to Lady Oakes. He was asking for forty thousand pounds' sterling.

Musgrave, something less than a master criminal, never saw the free light of day again. He died in jail of unexplained causes.

A few days later, a Canadian woman also told the FBI that Christie was implicated and had plotted Sir Harry's death with a powerful accomplice, a man who was the trusted family lawyer. The lawyer had also done his best to assist in the destruction of Alfred de Marigny.

While Christie had possible motives for murdering Oakes, the lawyer's motives were murkier. He was already a well-paid retainer. Unless he had somehow engineered Oakes' will to include legacies to himself, what was the point? And Oakes' will revealed no such language. I wasn't buying it. Yet it was conceivable that he alone outside the family, except for Christie, would know the whereabouts of any cache of bullion or precious coins or metals that Sir Harry might have stashed around the islands. Hence, I thought back to the attractive female snitch who had bent Schindler's ear in Nassau seven years earlier.

Who knew? Not me.

Then more ominously, there was the case of an American woman named Bettie Renner, a nice-looking lady in her late thirties. I'm told she had a law degree and had worked for the FBI. She flew into Nassau from Washington and began to make inquiries among locals, starting from the ground up, same as I did, same as Ray Schindler did. This was still in 1950.

She played short the feelings aroused by the case in Nassau, where fear and intimidation had now become part of national life. It was even possible that she was working on the misassumption that foreigners were relatively safe from intimidation and reprisal.

Whatever the truth of it was, instead of going undercover and posing as a tourist, Bettie Renner said she was going to "crack" the Oakes mystery.

Such a mission had its merits. Notoriety and stardom beckoned for anyone producing solid evidence leading to Sir Harry's killer. But Bettie's mission didn't turn out so well. Riding a bicycle outside of Nassau two days after her arrival, she was followed by an assailant. She was bludgeoned to death, dragged across some coral and dumped upside-down half-naked in an irrigation well in some limestone rocks by the road, not far from a grove of poisonous manchineel trees. The location was only three miles from Westbourne, where on July 8, 1943, Harry Oakes was found bludgeoned and his body burned. Her body was battered and beaten. Her clothing had been torn off above the waist, her breasts traumatized and exposed. It looked like a sexual assault, but the coroner noted that she hadn't been raped.

Nonetheless, dead was dead.

The unfortunate lady's death sent another shock wave through Nassau and encouraged the growing suspicion that the Oakes murder plot was a local affair, and that certain people were intent on keeping the lid on the truth at whatever cost.

Someone else hatched out a local account of the crime: a man of hot blood and dark skin had followed Bettie from where she had been looking to make some contacts. The attacker had followed her to the remote roadside spot near the manchineels and sexually assaulted her.

I wasn't buying this for an instant, either. I'd seen too many cases where an anonymous man of color was blamed for a crime when there was something bigger and more nefarious going on. The conspiracy of silence made many people uneasy. Nassau took on an even more sinister air. Not that anyone would talk publicly, but the common feeling was that powerful local people were being protected, or protecting themselves, in an extraordinarily brutal take-no-prisoners manner. Since working-class blacks of the day had no power, no equal status and no say over anything, I was guessing that the plot, the ongoing cover-up, the continued chain of strange deaths and disappearances had nothing to do with them. Only the ruling white power structure had the juice to keep things hot for anyone who wanted to kick open the hornets' nest of Oakes questions.

I frequently used to run into my friends Mike Todd, the Broadway producer, Aaron Fairstein, the radio producer and Ray Schindler at the bar of the Algonquin Hotel in those days. The bar was in the rear of the lobby, not far from the famous Round Table, which was in the Oak Room, formerly the Pergola Room. My magazine publisher was just upstairs on 44th Street and Ray's office was down the block on the same street. Mike Todd was showing up less often as he'd made his bundle on Broadway but was working more in Hollywood. Anyway, it was an obvious watering hole.

As usual, we would sit and people watch, sip drinks and talk about crime, music, Broadway, business, detective work and literature.

One day I confessed that I had been so busy recently that I hadn't been reading very much.

"It shows," said Ray, who could be a scold from time to time. "You should catch up on your reading now that you're doing well and back in the States," he said.

"Ray," I said, "I write so much that I don't have time to read much."

"That's a mistake, Alan. Reading is part of writing. Just like re-writing."

I laughed. "I need a wealthy detective to tell me that?"

"You need a friend to tell you that."

"So, what should I read?" I challenged.

"Start at the top. Read some Hemingway. Let's face it. He's the author of our age, no offense to true crime guys such as yourself who've been on the bestseller lists, also."

"No offense taken." Actually, a small one had been. "I'm still a little more partial to Steinbeck. Or Fitzgerald," I said.

"Ha!" Ray scoffed, curling a lip and waving away my suggestion. "Fitzgerald. Over and out. Fitzgerald was famous at twenty-four, dead and now forgotten at forty-four. He's an American type, Alan. Don't become it. The big fireworks display with a couple of jazz age books. Then complacence, followed by decades of indulgence and then silence. Reminds me of Bix Beiderbecke, the jazz trumpeter, remember him?"

"Sure. Played with Paul Whiteman's Orchestra in the 1920's."

"He made sublime music and died at twenty-eight. Stephen Crane wrote one perfect book, *The Red Badge of Courage*. Orson Welles' career in Hollywood began with two great movies and we'll see if he does anything worthwhile again. He's gaining weight you know. I saw him in Palm Springs last year and he looks like a small blimp. Your man Fitzgerald may have been right about no second acts in American life."

"I'm not sure that was Fitzgerald's point," I said. "The line has lost its original point, which is that there is no room for the graceful intermediate development of themes before the catastrophe arrives. If you're a writer, second acts are where the hard work is. That's where the slow stuff happens. That's where we are in the Oakes case right now."

"You have an answer for every literary potshot I can throw at you, right?"

"I try to."

He lifted his glass.

"Second acts exist, Ray," I said. "So do solid third acts. And epilogues can go on forever."

"Ah, all right!" he said. "I'll concede the point. Listen. You're maybe halfway through your life, I'm more than that far through mine. Let's be sure we have solid final acts, all right?"

"All right," I said.

We clicked our glasses.

I took Ray's advice and read some more Hemingway, the volume I hadn't yet caught up with, *A Farewell to Arms*. I still didn't care much for Ernie the man, but it was mostly table manners and his personal behavior which I found boorish. Or maybe I was just jealous of his enormous financial success. When we were in the same magazines, he had the top billing, drew the big checks, and his name on the upper right side on the cover. I might have had two or three articles in the same edition but I was always father back in the book.

"The world breaks everyone and afterward many are strong at the broken places," Hemingway wrote toward the end of his novel. "But those that will not break it kills. It kills the very good and the very gentle and the very brave impartially. If you are none of these you can be sure that it will kill you too but there will be no special hurry."

It seemed to me that he was speaking of the Oakes case, as well as life in general.

"...it will kill you too but will be in no special hurry."

Eventually, those words would haunt me.

I ran into Ray at the Algonquin again about a month after Bettie Renner's death. I mentioned it to him. He knew about it. He only shrugged and shook his head.

"It's the Bahamas, Alan," he said, as if that explained everything. "What the hell do you expect?"

"Maybe some semblance of justice?" I asked.

"Ha!" he laughed. "For a working-class kid from New Jersey who covered the Lindbergh case you still have an element of naiveté to you."

"Maybe," I said.

"Grow a pair, pal," he said, punching my arm. "Embrace the real world."

"I just would have liked to see some justice for poor old Harry," I said. "I mean, what the hell were we all in Nassau for, if not that?"

"Selling magazines, newspapers and books?" Ray offered, ever the cynic.

"Maybe," I said again.

CHAPTER 32

By that time, coming close to a decade after the acquittal of Alfred de Marigny in Nassau, the case had taken its place as one of the most baffling mysteries in the annals of crime. Not since the kidnapping of the Lindbergh baby had there been a crime that, for its strange and bewildering aspects, compared with the murder of Sir Harry Oakes.

Although the Oakes case was officially dormant, many reputable law enforcement authorities who had studied the evidence felt that the mystery remained wide open and that the mastermind was still walking the streets of Nassau. Just as the investigation of the Lindbergh kidnapping was bungled by the New Jersey State Police, then an organization chiefly concerned with traffic regulations, so was the Oakes case messed up by a police department that didn't even possess modern fingerprint equipment and a Crown governor who, for one reason or another, was intent on sending every mechanism of investigation in the wrong direction.

The specific weapon used to kill Sir Harry was never located, never identified in court and was only guessed at several years later. A man was officially accused of the crime and tried for it. The case against him turned out to be as full of holes as a screen door. But as far as the local authorities were concerned, the case ended there anyway. The trial, in short, posed more questions than it answered.

I wrote an incisive summary article. Its title was *Who Killed Sir Harry Oakes?* I accused no one, just laid out the events and the facts as I saw them. An innocent man was accused, an innocent man was acquitted. Thereafter, no one in any position of authority had any interest in finding the real killer. Or specifically, I wrote,

One thing is officially certain. Marie Alfred Fouquereaux de Marigny was not guilty of the murder. Another thing is equally certain. The powers that be down in the Bahamas have demonstrated that they don't want Schindler, or anybody else, to prove guilty the real killer of Sir Harry Oakes. Whoever did in the old boy is probably still walking the streets.

My article was published around the world in a dozen languages, first in magazines, later in several books. Predictably, the reaction in Nassau was far from enthusiastic. I found myself officially banned from the island. *Persona non grata, summa cum laude,* to coin a new legal term.

I got a phone call from Raymond Schindler a few days after the article appeared.

"Alan, have you won an uncontested divorce from your common sense?" he asked.

"Probably, Ray," I answered. "Why do you ask?"

"The Oakes case. I'd shut the hell up if I were you," Ray said.

"I'm fifteen hundred miles away, Ray. What are they going to do?"

"Come after you," he said.

"I'm not buying it," I said. "I'm not that easy to find. I'll be fine."

"I warned you," he said. "Let it drop. Don't mess with them."

I put the phone down. Ray's advice was ominous and not to be taken lightly. I vowed to be more careful, if possible.

I had a radio friend in those days named John Zimmerman. He would produce some spot shows in New York. He was a big guy, maybe six four, but never weighed more than one sixty. A bean pole. A smart bean pole. He later got his own show and called himself, "Long John Nebel." He had serious writers, kooks and nuts and was eventually on all night: from midnight to five thirty a.m. when normal people started to wake up.

I'd go on his show and talk. I'd talk about my many cases, including Oakes. I'd elaborate on my theories. Why not? It was a free country. In many parts of the world, where the Reds had taken over, you couldn't say what you wanted on radio. God bless America. It was safe to say anything, or so I thought.

By now I had moved the family to Connecticut. It was 1951. I had rented a great house in a section of Fairfield called Greenfield Hill. My kids were in school. I had my morning coffee in our kitchen, I was the only coffee drinker in the house. Then I went to my study to work on a new book. There was something, it seemed, a little "off" about the coffee. It had a strange peppery subtlety to it, with an undertone of sweetness. A little unusual. But coffee batches were inconsistent in those days. I didn't think much about it. It didn't even taste bad.

In the late morning, I started to not feel so good. I went to lie down. I felt worse. My wife was with me. She called the doctor who made an emergency house call. He stayed till evening. I began to sweat. My heart began to race. I wanted to vomit, but couldn't. Gradually, there was a burning, tearing sensation and tightness in my throat. The doctor tried to give me water but I could barely swallow liquid or solid food because of the excruciating pain I was in.

Just before I passed out, the doctor called an ambulance. I was taken to Bridgeport Hospital. My last thoughts as they put me into the ambulance were borderline hallucinatory. It seemed as if they were putting me in a dark green hearse. I was thinking about the trip to the cemetery. I pictured my own tombstone and pictured it in a hot tropical place.

That would have been appropriate. I was convinced that I was dying. I wasn't far wrong. After I'd been at the hospital for an hour, one of the emergency room doctors came out and told my wife that things didn't look for good for survival. Vital signs were failing. But they were doing what they could.

She nodded. She cried.

Then he asked my wife if I'd recently been in the Bahamas.

"Not for several years," she answered.

"How many is several?"

"Seven. Almost eight."

"Strange."

"Why?"

"It looks like poisoning from manchineel bark," the doctor said. "That's the theory of one of our doctors who's from the West Indies. Maybe manchineel concealed in another substance. Those are the symptoms. We can't figure anything else so we're applying manchineel antidotes."

She nodded. "Is there anything I can do?" she asked.

"There's a chapel down the hall," he said gently. "I'd wait there if I were you. And be at peace. There's only so much we can do."

I woke up a day later, eyes fluttering into consciousness and out of it. My midsection was in agony. I felt as if I had been stabbed or shot. I was in an oxygen tent. The tent was over my entire body, a strange clear plastic canopy that attempted to provide oxygen at a higher level than normal.

I remembered the trouble I had had breathing when they had brought me in here. That difficulty was gone, but I was still wincing with each breath at the extreme pain in my chest. It was much like the tightness associated with a heart attack.

There were figures moving around me. Gradually, they came into focus. I discovered that I was looking straight into the eyes of an Episcopal priest.

He had white hair and a kindly smile.

I could hear him through the canvas of the tent and the low hum of my oxygen supply. "Hello," he said.

I tried to raise a hand to acknowledge.

"I'm alive?" I asked.

He nodded. "Apparently," he said. "And against the odds, if you don't mind my saying."

I glanced around the hospital room. The shades were drawn.

"Remind me. Where am I?" I asked.

"Bridgeport General Hospital," he said.

"Oh," I whispered. "Of course. Right."

I took a few moments to look around the room. I only hazily remembered arriving.

"Why are the shades drawn?" I asked, indicating the windows.

"There was a fire across the street," the priest replied. "We didn't want you to wake up, see the fire, and think you'd gone to the 'other place.'"

"Oh," I said again. I'm not sure, but I think I managed a weak laugh.

He smiled and touched my hand. "I'll summon your wife," he said. "You're going to survive. You'll be okay."

CHAPTER 33

It took almost two years, but gradually I recovered from my "illness."

That's what everyone called it. An illness. But I knew better and so did my doctors. So did my editors, so did my wife, so did Ray Schindler and so did a lot of other folks.

No longer did I ever feel completely safe. I knew another attempt on my life could happen again. I knew deep in my heart that the same people who had killed Harry Oakes had come after me. They didn't like what I had written.

Sometimes I had deeply depressive mood spells during the daylight hours, only to be followed by savage nightmares at night. I saw Harry in his bed being set aflame more times than I could count, more times than any man could sanely tolerate. I could hear the metal instrument, whatever it was, crashing into his skull. I can hear his initial anguish, his pain, his screams, his cries and then I see the final spasms. Then the blood, the fire, the smoke.

I saw Harry in my mind's eye. But I also knew it was me.

I think part of my memory disappeared forever, surrendered or compromised in my illness. Perhaps part of my past went with it, along with the final tiny pieces of any idealism or good intentions I might have had. My daughter forever afterwards told me about things we did together when she was younger, in Short Hills, New Jersey, days at the beaches, flying kites, and I do not remember these things.

Nor do I admit that I do not remember. I take her hand, try to be strong and be a father. There are things no child should know or see. And yet, there is an irony: I cannot completely remember and I cannot completely forget.

Nonetheless, I was back in some of the better magazines by 1953 and 1954. *The Saturday Evening Post. Colliers. True.* Plus many of the smaller magazines, *True Detective, Official Detective, Master Detective.* It wasn't classy but it was bread and butter. And I still had some book contracts. A new book came out, in fact. Ironically, it was titled *Alan Hynd's Murder.* It was a collection of murder cases, originally published in magazines. People wondered from the title, however: had I murdered someone or had I been murdered? The phraseology was too close for comfort.

Speaking of crime, Thomas Dewey was back in the news around that time, too.

Dewey's third term as governor ended in 1955. Leaving the political arena at the end of his term as governor, Dewey marched back to his lucrative law practice. I kept my eye on him but had no direct contact ever again. It appeared to many that Dewey had suddenly begun to accommodate the very people he used to put in jail, notably gangsters and their casinos.

Dewey eventually became a major stockholder in Mary Carter Paints, which held an interest in gambling in the Bahamas. In addition, Carter's chief assistant was none other than Meyer Lansky, who was directly associated with the mafia commission, thus leading to more suspicions about Thomas E. Dewey and his dealings with the Mob. When I read this, our whole meeting in October of 1943 came back to me, but with a viciously different spin.

In the fall of that year, my darkest suspicions about my "illness" were confirmed to me. I was in New York at the bar of the Algonquin Hotel. It was late afternoon. I had stopped drinking, but would come by for a Coke and leave the booze to other men. I was more interested in running into old friends. I was with my wife, but she had ducked away to the washroom.

I was sipping a Coke when two men accosted me.

I felt a powerful pair of hands hold both my arms from behind. Then someone slid into place beside me at the bar.

"Hello, you schnook," said a familiar gruff voice. I turned to my left. I was looking into the eyes of my old friend, Mike Todd, the producer. "What are you doing here, you lousy scribbler? I thought you lived in Connecticut, no?" Mike asked.

The other man released me from behind. It was Aaron Fairstein, the radio producer. My two pals had gotten the drop on me from a remote table.

I pumped Aaron's hand. I embraced Mike. "I'm in town to take my wife to see *Silk Stockings*."

"I wish I had known," Mike said. "I would have gotten you house seats for tonight."

"We just saw the show this afternoon. The matinee."

"The matinee? Only pimps go to matinees," Mike answered.

"Maybe so. Pimps and suburbanites. That would include me in the latter, but not the former, all right? What hell are you raising?" I asked.

Mike had emerged from his most recent bankruptcy in grand style. From somewhere he had begged, borrowed and cajoled another pile of other people's money. He had also plucked a script off the bookshelf of British producer Alexander Korda. It was a cinematic take on *Around the World in 80 Days,* the durable Nineteenth Century Jules Verne novel. Korda had been trying to find a way to film the story for years. Orson Welles had, too, after he'd produced a disastrous Broadway version that crashed and burned faster than Phileas Fogg's balloon. Todd had lost a fistful of money on the Broadway show and, stubborn as ever, was looking to recoup his losses. Now, Mike had an expensive film in pre-production.

"That's good, Mike," I said. "I'm pleased for you."

"I know you are. Thanks." His expression changed. "Say, listen, old friend," he said. "We're glad we spotted you."

"That right?" I asked.

"Yeah," Fairstein said. "I want to talk some business with you. Private like."

I looked my friends back and forth. I sensed something was up.

"Sure," I said. "Okay."

Aaron draped an arm around me. We left Mike at the bar.

"I need to talk to you," Aaron said. I expected a pitch about a radio project. He pulled me away from everyone else and lowered his voice. "What was all this shit with you and the Sir Harry Oakes case?"

"What do you mean?" I asked. "I wrote—"

"Yeah, yeah," he said, interrupting me, "I read what you wrote. And I heard you popping off on Long John Nebel's show a few times. Alan, Listen to me. I was just down in Puerto Rico a few weeks ago. I ran into some unpleasant people from the Bahamas at the Hilton Casino. They asked me if I knew you. I said, yes, but they knew the answer before they asked because you and me had the radio show together, know what I mean?"

"I know what you mean."

"One of these bastards started with some pretty venal threats. He was the smallest one but he looked like he was in charge. You know how a fucked-up little man can strut even while he's sitting down? This sawed-off little runt says, 'Well, tell him we hope he feels better. Because the next time we fix him a Bahamian cocktail with manchineel juice we'll finish off the son-of-a-bitch.' Then they all laughed."

I felt what I could only describe as a surge of renewed fear. I waited again.

"Does that crap mean anything to you?" Aaron asked.

"Yes. It does. What did they look like?"

"Bunch of obnoxious Brit colonials on a low-class holiday. Booze and tacky hookers. There was a big stupid fat one and a little monkey with a hat and a yellow tie. Know them?"

"Yes."

217

"Do you own pistol?"

"No."

"Of course, you do. You showed it to me one time when we were doing *Wanted: Armed and Dangerous!*"

"I got rid of it. I stopped drinking, also."

"Well, you should get a new piece. Maybe something military. Want me to send you one?"

"I have kids in the house, Aaron. No. No gun."

"Okay, okay, okay. Just be careful. These guys were serious shitbirds and they were mad as hell with you." He paused. "I told them that you were pals with J. Edgar Hoover and Dwight Eisenhower from the war, and if anything no-good happened to you again, I was going to rat them out and they could expect a fucking bomb to fall on them!"

"Jesus, Aaron. None of that's true!"

"Yeah, I know. But they got all quiet. They might have believed me. You got to take care of yourself."

"I'll watch after myself," I said. "I promise."

"Do that, kiddo," Aaron said. "I don't worry about too many people but I worry about you."

"Thanks."

Our hands clasped. My wife returned from the ladies' room. She said hello to Mike. He cleaned up his lexicon and returned the gracious greeting. Mike was always a gentleman around other men's wives unless he was planning to make a move on one. I introduced her to Aaron whom she had never met. He was cordial. My wife and I didn't linger. I knew better. We went for our 6:02 train to Westport.

"What did Mike have to say?" my wife asked.

"Nothing much," I said. "He's got a new film project."

"That other guy, the little one, gave me the creeps," she said.

"He does that sometimes."

"You know some strange people."

"I suppose I do."

I disappeared to my safe home in Westport, Connecticut. Mike went back to California and other points around the globe to make his movie. *Around the World in 80 Days* would be the ultimate Todd extravaganza, shot in thirteen countries and costing a then-astronomical six million dollars.

Around the World in 80 Days told the story of a Victorian Englishman, Phileas Fogg, played by David Niven, who wagered everything he owned that he could circle the world in eighty days. What followed was a rambling chronicle of the exploits of Fogg and his French valet, Passepartout, played to the loopy hilt by the Mexican star, Cantinflas, as they journey by balloon, boat, train and elephant through locations beyond the imagination of most American viewers. What was unique, however, were the cameos of more than forty stars that dazzled from minute to minute: Peter Lorre as a stateroom attendant, Buster Keaton as a train conductor, Noel Coward as a banker, Frank Sinatra on piano and Marlene Dietrich as a leggy San Francisco saloon keeper. The voyage was pure kitsch, pure spectacle and pure Mike.

But just as important for Mike was what had happened off the set. He had met a young woman of twenty-four named Elizabeth Taylor. She was less than half his age and three years younger than Mike's son. Inconveniently, she was married to someone else, but stuff like that never stopped Mike. Their high-profile romance was tabloid stuff in the extreme. Eventually, Todd and Taylor were married in a lavish ceremony in Acapulco; a huge fireworks display, a gift from Cantinflas, lit up their names against the night sky.

A few weeks later, *Around the World in 80 Days* lit up the night sky in Los Angeles. Todd's film won five Oscars, including Best Picture, besting an impressive field: *Giant, The Ten Commandments, The King and I,* and *Friendly Persuasion.*

Mike was back on top. I was again happy for him. But there was a personal casualty around then, also, a victim of changing times. *The Boston Post*, where I had begun my career in crime writing, went out of business. People were starting to get their news from television. Newspapers were in trouble and so were the men and women employed by them.

CHAPTER 34

Ten years before Sir Harry took it in the head, there was a young sergeant in the Cuban army who was good at organizing people and things. When the repressive government of General Gerardo Machado collapsed in 1933 the young sergeant, Fulgenio Batista, organized a rebellion of non-commissioned officers. The so-called Sergeant's Rebellion grabbed control of the entire armed forces. Battista created alliances with student groups and unions. He was a charming guy in those years. Good-looking, slick. They called him *El Mulatto Lindo* because he was a mutt: a mix of Spanish, African and Chinese. All that mixed blood must have made him a smart guy, in addition to a good-looking guy.

Batista ruled the country. He eventually broke with the student groups because they were pink and a pain. A student activist group called the Revolutionary Directorate became his enemy.

In 1938, Batista ordered a new constitution. He ran for president. In 1940, he was elected. The balloting was rigged. His party won a majority in Congress. Everything was rigged.

Batista soon legalized a pro-fascist organization linked to Hitler's buddy in Spain, Francisco Franco, in Spain. Uncle Sam saw him a possible headache. Would the handsome sergeant align his country with the Axis or the Allies?

An Axis alliance would have played poorly in El Caribe. Fulgencio sent the British army a few shiploads of sugar as a gift. Later, Batista travelled to Washington to suggest to the United States that Cuba launch a joint US-Latin American invasion of Spain to overthrow Franco and his regime. Washington didn't buy it. The wartime plate was already full.

Batista kept thinking. The United States was ninety-miles away. Europe was twenty-five hundred miles away. In February 1941, Battista ordered all German and Italian consular officials to leave his country. Cuba entered the war on December 8, 1941, by declaring war on Japan, which a day before had attacked Pearl Harbor, Hawaii. Then Cuba declared war on Germany and Italy on December 11, 1941 and broke relations with Vichy France on November 10, 1942.

Batista signed an agreement with the United States that gave permission to build airfields in Cuba for the protection of the Caribbean Sea lanes. He also signed a mutual defense pact with Mexico for the defense against enemy submarines in the Gulf of Mexico. The United States sent Cuba modern military aircraft, which were vital for coastal defense and anti-submarine operations. The American taxpayers also refitted the Cuban Navy with modern weapons and other equipment.

The Cuban Navy escorted hundreds of Allied ships through hostile waters, sailed nearly 400,000 miles on convoy and patrol duty, flew over 83,000 hours on convoy and patrol duty, and rescued over 200 U-boat victims from the sea, all without losing a single warship or aircraft to enemy action. It was a no-brainer: Cuba's military was the most cooperative and helpful of all the Caribbean states during the world war. Its navy was "small but efficient" in its fight against German U-boats. Then came 1944. There was another election. This one wasn't rigged. Battista lost.

The handsome one raided the treasury and took off for the United States, where he had made many friends. He bought a plush place in Daytona Beach. He took a snazzy long-term suite at the Waldorf Astoria in New York, again financed by the hard-pressed American taxpayers who didn't know they were paying for it. He prepared to sit things out in luxury and plot a return when the proper time and circumstances presented themselves.

He knew they would.

After the war, Batista returned to Cuba, while maintaining his residences and contacts in the United States. He ran for president in 1952. Soon, it became apparent that he would lose. So, he did the next best thing to being elected. Batista and his allies in the military staged a coup in the early hours of March 10, 1952 and took over the government.

Batista quickly reasserted himself, placing his old cronies back in positions of power. A young Cuban lawyer named Fidel Castro tried to bring Batista to court to answer for the illegal takeover, but nothing came of it. Many Latin American countries quickly recognized the Batista government. On May 27 of the same year, the United States also extended formal recognition.

And so, the big deal was done: for the next several years, Havana would flourish as a center of gambling, sex shows, whoring, and drug dealing, with the American Mafia raking in millions on top of millions of post-war dollars. Control of gambling in the Caribbean was like a license to print money.

Castro, who would likely have been elected to Congress had the elections taken place, quickly saw that there was no way of legally removing Batista. On July 26, 1953, Castro and a handful of rebels attacked the army barracks at Moncada, igniting the Cuban Revolution. The attack failed and Fidel and Raúl Castro were jailed, but it brought them a great deal of attention.

Many captured rebels were executed on the spot, resulting in a lot of negative press for the government. In prison, Fidel Castro began organizing the 26th of July movement, named after the date of the Moncada assault. Six and a half years later, Castro's revolutionary army marched into Havana. The mob grip on the city was broken, the casinos were looted, smashed and closed. Those who controlled them fled if they weren't shot.

Gambling interests moved quickly to the Bahamas.

Casinos are a way of mugging the public without an arrest.

The late Sir Harry Oakes would have been horrified.

I always wondered, conjuring up images of Meyer Lansky and Lucky Luciano and their heirs, whether this was the final shoe dropping in the murder case of Sir Harry Oakes.

CHAPTER 35

On the first anniversary of the release of *Around the World in 80 Days,* the film was still playing in first run theatres coast to coast. Mike Todd continued to rake in the money. To keep the film in the public eye, Todd and his wife Elizabeth Taylor invited eighteen thousand of their "close friends" to a Madison Square Garden extravaganza. Boasting a long list of celebrities, an enormous cake and music from Boston Pops conductor Arthur Fiedler, Todd conned the CBS program *Playhouse 90* into covering the tacky spectacle live.

He induced the executives at CBS to pay him three hundred thousand dollars to televise his publicity stunt. Inevitably, the crowd got out of control, a giant food fight ensued and the party turned into one of early television's most memorably vulgar events.

My wife and I were invited. We didn't go. But that didn't mean the party didn't cause my phone to ring. Shortly after the television show, I received a call from a senior editor at *Look* Magazine. Todd was hotter than ever.

"Alan," he said, "you're an old acquaintance of Mike Todd, aren't you?"

"We go back to about 1940," I said. "Seventeen years."

"We're hearing a lot of stories about Mike that have never hit the press," the editor said. "Dicey contacts. Shady deals. How he may have strong-armed people in Hollywood to vote for his move for Best Picture. Interested in doing a three-part exposé on your old buddy?"

"It sounds like a hatchet job," I said. "Is that what you're asking?"

"Mike Todd. The Real Story. Everything. Good and bad," he said.

"A hatchet job," I said again.

"If you don't do it, someone else will."

They offered twenty thousand dollars, a fortune for a magazine work.

"Interested?"

I needed the money. "I'm interested," I said.

I put the phone down. Sure, I needed the money. But I also wanted one more big assignment. I knew things about Mike that no one knew. Mike could be a bastard. There were things he'd done that I hated him for. But I also considered him, warts and all, a friend. If I had to tell the bad, I would also tell the good, and hope that it didn't get edited out.

I was damned tempted. But I didn't want to write it from a bunker or ambush the man. Like anyone else, Mike deserved the opportunity to defend himself.

I gave *Look* a tentative yes. I made some phone calls. I wanted to meet with Mike to tell him what was being offered.

As it happened, Mike and Elizabeth had taken a summer rental three miles away. It was on the Westport-Fairfield line in Connecticut across from the polo field of the Fairfield County Hunt Club.

I called. Mike graciously said he'd see me. I drove over with my daughter, who was a teenager, and wanted to catch a glimpse of the now-grown-up little girl who had ridden horses in *National Velvet.*

Mike was cordial. We sat down in the living room of a sprawling home where the brilliant composer Richard Rodgers had once lived. A maid brought sandwiches and sodas. I told Mike what *Look* asking for.

"Oh, yeah? It's a hatchet piece, right?" he laughed. "They want you to trash me."

"I wouldn't make stuff up, Mike, like some of the others would."

"You wouldn't need to," he said, amused. "Anything you wrote would be at least partially true."

"Anything I write would be completely true," I said. "I can make errors like any other man with a typewriter. But I won't submit anything false."

"How much are they offering you?"

"Twenty thousand dollars."

He whistled low. "Wow. That's good money for scribbling." His eyes drifted away for a moment. Then he looked back to me. "Listen, schnook. I'll give you forty grand *not* to write it."

I was stunned. "That's an outright bribe, Mike," I said.

"Yeah. A pretty good one."

"That's true, too," I said.

"Think about it," he said.

There was an uneasy silence between us.

"I'll think about it," I said. "I've know you for a long time. You're a charming bastard. A lot of the stuff you've done is disgraceful. But I don't dislike you."

He laughed. "Join the club," he said. "Sounds like an interesting article. I might read it."

I rounded up my daughter and we departed.

Several weeks later, Mike was back on the West Coast with his wife. Liz was in the throes of bronchitis and a 102-degree fever.

Mike walked over to her bed and hugged her. His twin-engine Lockheed Lodestar, *The Lucky Liz,* was on a Burbank airstrip, waiting to take him to New York, where the Friars Club was to honor him the next night as Showman of the Year.

Mike reported to the Burbank airstrip an hour later. He boarded the Lockheed Lodestar he had named for her, Todd picked up the air-to-ground telephone to say goodbye to Liz one last time. "I'll call you when we stop in Tulsa to re-fuel," he told her.

Across the aisle from him sat the newspaper columnist Art Cohn, a screenwriter and former columnist for *The Oakland Tribune.* Cohn was writing Todd's authorized biography.

The plane's interior was pure Mike: plush, with an oak conference table, a couch, a bar, thick carpeting, and bronze ashtrays. The toiletries were engraved LIZ and HIS. The pilot radioed in from the cockpit. Despite the bad weather, it was clear above the clouds. There was a pilot and a co-pilot. Everyone was expecting a smooth flight.

At 10:41 p.m. on March 21, 1958, its lights flashing through the downpour, *The Lucky Liz* zipped down the airstrip, wheeled up and headed to New York.

At six a.m. on March 22, 1958, the West Coast correspondent for the Associated Press, a man named Jim Bacon, got a phone call. A fellow AP reporter near Albuquerque had found Bacon's name on the passenger list of a Lockheed Lodestar that had crashed into a mountain in bad weather. Bacon had agreed to go with Todd on his trip to New York but hadn't been able to make it.

"Is anyone injured?" Bacon asked.

"Everyone's dead," the reporter said.

Mike had never made the call from Tulsa. The aircraft crashed that night in bad weather in the Zuni Mountains near Grants, New Mexico.

Dick Hanley, Todd's personal secretary, took a call from Elizabeth Taylor early that morning; she was worried that she hadn't yet heard from Mike. Rex Kennamer, her physician, and Hanley went to the house in Coldwater Canyon to break the news. As the pair opened the door to Taylor's bedroom, she shrieked, "No!"

In New York, Eddie Fisher was walking into the Essex House, where he'd been staying as a guest of Chesterfield cigarettes, one of the sponsors of his television show, but a product I no longer consumed. Eddie had just finished a sixteen-verse parody of the theme song to *Around the World in 80 Days*, which he planned to sing at the Friars roast. Jim Mahoney, his press agent, intercepted him. Fisher went into his hotel room, closed the door, and collapsed into tears.

The funeral was held on a cold day in Chicago. Howard Hughes provided Liz his private plane to transport the funeral party. Press and gawkers swarmed like gnats. The trashy *Los Angeles Mirror News* erroneously reported that Taylor had thrown herself on top of the coffin. It seemed almost fitting that Mike Todd's last show degenerated into spectacle. There wasn't much in the coffin, by the way. Mike had been incinerated in the plane crash.

"Kids were sitting there eating ice cream cones," Eddie Fisher later remembered. "They were howling yelling to see Elizabeth. There was all kinds of noise. It was awful."

By that time, the editors at *Look* had already contacted me. No profit in speaking ill of the dead, they said. The contract to write the story, which I had never actually signed, was cancelled.

Tough break for me. Tougher break for Mike. Somehow, I had never really wanted to write this one, anyway. And it started me to thinking about the murder of Sir Harry Oakes for a final time.

CHAPTER 36

A few months after Mike Todd's death, I picked up the telephone and phoned Raymond Schindler. I knew Ray still maintained his agency in New York and went to work every day. I also knew that sometimes after a busy day at his desk, he sat pondering the strange geometry of the Oakes case. Schindler had made several public statements saying that he still believed that he could crack the mystery of the killer's identity if he went down to Nassau and were given a free hand. But time was running out.

Raymond Schindler was well into his seventies and no one was offering him a free hand.

Ray had moved to Tarrytown, New York, Washington Irving's old haunt, and lived not far from the legendary Sleepy Hollow. That would have been enough to spook lesser men.

But not Mr. Schindler. And not me.

"Hello, Alan," Ray said, sounding not the least any weaker than the last time we had spoken, maybe five years earlier.

"Hello, Ray. I'm hoping we can have a conversation."

"For you, always, old pal. What's on your mind?"

"A conversation in person," I said.

"Oh," he said. There was a pause on the line. "The Oakes murder case." His words did not carry the intonation of a question.

"None other," I said. "May I drive up and see you sometime soon?"

"You know where to find me?"

"I have a map," I said.

He laughed. The same laugh I used to hear in the Bahamas, the one that punctuated so many late nights in bars and hotel lobbies.

It was a crisp fall day when I took off. I drove up the Merritt Parkway and arrived at Raymond's estate in mid-afternoon. He had done well for himself. He had a big sprawling place in Duchess County, an estate with high walls and a long driveway. I drove a two-year-old De Soto. Ray had three cars in his driveway, one an antique.

He had household help. A cook made us some sandwiches, we exchanged small talk and then went to his den. He eased heavily into a leather chair by a lattice window. His appearance would not have given away his age, but his movements did. He labored like an old man. I was saddened. I was only in my mid-fifties myself but aging was a specter that never escaped a man after the mid-century mark, even if he hid it well.

"I see you have a new book coming out this Christmas," he said. "*Murder, Mayhem, and Mystery*. Do I have the title right?"

"You have it, Mr. Detective," I said.

"Congratulations."

"It's a compendium of my best cases," I said. "About fifty of them. A life's work, you could call it."

"I assume your take on the Oakes case is in there," he said.

"Lindbergh and Oakes. Ponzi, too. And maybe fifty others."

"So? A few are unsolved?"

"Lindbergh and Oakes," I said.

We were playing verbal chess. I knew the game.

"Drink?" he finally asked.

"My drinking days or over," I said. "I'm better off for it."

He nodded. "Glad to hear it," he said. A slight beat and he added, "Don't touch the booze much myself anymore," he said. "Don't blame you. Not healthy. What's on your mind, Alan?"

"I'm wondering how much more you can tell me about the Oakes case," I said.

"Ha! Not much. Not anything, in fact."

"Come on, Ray," I said. "Level with me."

"Whoever did in the old boy is still wielding a lot of power on that hot little sandbar."

"And?" I asked.

"And nothing. That's where it ends."

There was an uneasy silence between us. He fixed me in that gaze that I knew so well from so many cases. I hesitated, then knew there was no point to trying to conceal the truth from one of the greatest detectives our country had ever produced.

"I haven't had a bestseller since 1943, Ray," I said. "Same year as the Oakes case. That's fifteen years. I could use another big book."

"How's your wife?" he asked.

"She's fine."

"You had a daughter," he said.

"Fine, also. Lovely young woman now. She's at a private school in New York City.'"

"And a son."

"You've kept tabs on me, haven't you?" I said.

"Any reason why I shouldn't?"

"None. I appreciate it. My son is doing well. Ten years old. Private school in Fairfield, Connecticut."

"You're a wealthy man," he said.

"Not in terms of finances."

228

"You're a wealthy man."

"Talk to me about Oakes, Ray. Who do you think did it? Who killed him?"

"A well-placed and prominent person in the Bahamas," Schindler answered. "A man, or men, with huge financial interests."

"Harold Christie?"

"No."

"Mob people?"

"No."

"Local people? A sex angle? A racial angle?"

"No," he said.

"Are you going to tell me anything?" I asked.

"No," he said.

"I need a bestseller, Ray."

"Listen, Alan," he said, leaning forward. "You made yourself unpopular in the Lindbergh case, too, didn't you?"

"Yes, I did."

"You have that habit."

"Yes, I do."

Schindler leaned back and sipped his iced tea.

"This case has obsessed you, hasn't it?" he asked.

"For more reasons than I can count, yes," I said.

"Well," he said. "I can't say it hasn't had the same effect on me, damn it," he said. "I get it. I understand. Look, if I could go down to Nassau again, follow up on everything that was left hanging, I'm damned sure I could get to the resolution of the case. But I'm not going. I'm not doing that. And you're not either."

Then he continued.

"There's a big reason for you to lay off, Alan," he said. "You have a lovely wife. A fine family. A few words to remember if you ever take any of God's blessings for granted again: *The manchineel tree*. And what it did to you. And nearly did. Most men don't get second chances after something like that. God smiled on you."

"I know," I said gently.

"Do you?"

"If I didn't," I said, "I do now. You just reminded me."

"Good."

There followed an awkward pause between us, the most awkward moment that ever existed in the four decades we had known each other.

"Come on, Ray," I finally urged. "Tell me something I don't know."

After more silence, he replied. "All right," he said. "I will. But if I tell you something off the record. You're not to print it. But, now that I consider it, I don't want to take it to the grave with me. So? Ready?"

"Okay," I said.

"A few years ago, a man told me a story," Ray began. "He said that Frank Christie drove into Westbourne's grounds late on the murder night in a vehicle with two or three men who had arrived by boat in the storm from off the island. They ran up the outer staircase of Harry's home and, according to the story, into Sir Harry's bedroom. There were voices. Angry ones. There was a fight. Flames flickered briefly, before being extinguished, maybe by the wind. Then the men rushed away. Let's suppose this story is true. Did the killers include Harold Christie? Or would he have been there to guide along the intruders? Harold was never named by the gentleman who told me this story. And the man who told me this was an underworld figure with something to sell. Who knows if the story is true? Perhaps Harold was in bed with his lady friend when the murder took place. Maybe there was thunder and a driving rain at exactly that time. Either way, it was important for Harold Christie to insist that he remained in his bedroom all night, that he was completely innocent and that he had heard nothing to suggest his friend was being butchered by killers just a few feet away. Whether an adulterer or killer, it was so important to Christie that his real whereabouts remained a mystery that he was prepared to lie about it, and declare that Captain Sears was mistaken."

"Is that story true?" I asked.

"I have no way of knowing, Alan. The source was not reputable, as I said. And it seems a trifle convenient. Make of it what you will and hold onto it for fifty years. Happy?"

"Not very."

"Good. I'm not, either."

I opened my mouth to speak and he kept talking. I knew enough to shut up.

"Listen to me. I'll now tell you something else. A few years ago, I was having a drink with an old friend," Ray began, "a man who's been in publishing for many years here in New York. Paperback books. Newspapers. Some girlie smut mags. Gets his stuff on all the newsstands. Does well. Makes a lot of money. Let's call him Norman." Schindler's eyes found me. "Norman does a lot better than his competitors. His competitors sometimes have acid thrown on their newspapers and paperbacks."

"So, he's a connected guy?"

Schindler shrugged but his eyes said yes. He kept talking.

"The subject of the Lindbergh kidnapping came up. I don't know how. Or why. I'm a detective, Norman's a publisher. These subjects come up. I guess we were talking crime. Norman told me that he had some friends in New Jersey. People in positions of influence, let's say. Trucking industry. Norman referenced the Lindbergh boy and the kidnapping and one of these goombah wise guys turned to him and said, 'Norman, would you actually like to know what happened? Who really did it? Where the money went? Who did the job? Who killed the kid? Where the body went?'"

"And?"

"And Norman gave the only wise answer," Schindler said. "He said, 'No. Don't tell me. I don't want to know.'" Schindler paused for a long time. "It's not worth it, sometimes, Alan," he concluded, shaking his head. "It's just not worth it."

I sighed. I knew right there that I would no sooner get the Sphinx to get up and do a song and dance than I'd get Raymond Schindler to tell me anything more. Our meeting was cordial. But it appeared to be over.

"You're a good man, Alan. You tried. Take care of yourself," Ray said.

"You, too."

We stood. We shook hands. I walked back to my car and slid into the driver's seat. For a moment, I took time to glance around Ray's gorgeous estate. I turned the key in the ignition, backed up and turned. I drove through the high gate. It closed behind me.

I drove home. There was a crackle in the air and suddenly a hint of winter.

There would be no big best seller for me on the Oakes case. And not for Ray, either, although many books on the case came and went. Occasionally, Ray would give an interview in the papers or magazines. He was right about many things. Foremost among them, no one in the Bahamas wanted the case solved.

I read an interview with Ray in early 1959 and he was still banging the same drum. He could solve the case if he would be allowed to visit the islands. But the Bahamian government wouldn't grant him a visit. Finally, in May of 1959, Nassau finally asked him to submit in writing any new evidence that he had and "the proper authorities" would review it.

I doubt that he ever submitted anything. The late investigation was a potential whitewash. We all knew it. A few weeks later, Ray Schindler had a massive heart attack sitting in that same green leather chair where I had left him. He died that same afternoon at the local hospital.

Four days later. I went to the funeral. I saw people I knew. I didn't linger. I didn't chat with anyone. No point. Nothing good could have come from it. It just wasn't worth it.

CHAPTER 37

As the 1970's arrived, I began looking backward. Often what I wrote about over the course of a half century was brutal stuff, stories filled with men and women driven to extremes of human behavior. They were possessed by greed, passion, despair, loneliness, or just the general rottenness and meanness of a cold empty world and the need to survive in it.

There was no shortage of that in the case of Sir Harry Oakes, but here there were extra spins: a framed man, a distinguished victim, vast wealth, a forbidden romance, royals, an unusual venue, and racial antagonisms. All this played out against wartime. Keep in mind, the world of 1943 was one where the fate of the world was still in doubt.

Hitler might have won. Tojo might have won. America might have lost. The Soviet Union might have occupied all of Western Europe. The bad guys might have gotten the nukes first. A dunderhead like Windsor might have climbed back into power and sold out Europe to the people running the concentration camps.

Think about that next time you toss back a drink or two.

Ray Schindler, much as he mentored me, much as I respected the man, much as I loved our conversations about books, people and murder, Ray was a hired gun. He had his detractors. There were people who said Nancy Oakes overpaid, but put yourself in her size seven heels: Your dad's been murdered and your husband, whom you know to be incapable of the crime is arrested and locked in a black hole by people so intent on framing him that they had already hired the hangman and bought the rope.

You have an unlimited bank account. Wouldn't you have gone to New York and hired the best detective money could buy?

If you say, no, you wouldn't have, you don't understand. We don't think alike.

In the years immediately preceding his death, Raymond Schindler wrote or gave his name to several articles about the Oakes case. One of them speculated on the voodoo aspects of the case and earned Nancy Oakes' enmity. The article suggested there was a curse on anyone who dabbled in the Oakes murder too long or who was in any way associated with it.

I don't believe in curses any more than I believe that an evil pixie few into my home and put poison in my morning coffee. More likely, some bastard probably slipped me something on my travels in New York. But one does wonder about the evil star that seemed to twinkle upon this case. A disproportionate number of people involved either intimately or tangentially suffered great and painful misfortune.

Others fared even worse.

Leonarde Keeler, the polygraph expert, was never quite the same shortly after the case. On the surface of things, in the public view, things continued to go well for him. He remained instrumental in the popularization of modern polygraphs in criminal investigation and job screenings. He went as far as appearing in person in the 1948 film noir docudrama, *Call Northside 777* with

Jimmy Stewart and Lee J. Cobb. He was a minor celebrity and played himself.

Much like a crime on a stormy night, however, the truth was well hidden. In 1930, he had married a fellow psychology student, a smart pretty lady named Katherine Applegate. Kay, as she was called, was also trained as a forensic expert and became the nation's first female handwriting analyst. At about the time of the Oakes investigation, Kay left Keeler for another man, a swaging USO paratrooper named Rene Dussaq. Kay joined the WASPS, the Women's Auxiliary Service Pilots. She died in 1944 near Patterson Field in Ohio while flying solo across the country to help halt the disbanding of the WASPs. Devastated by the betrayal and death of the only woman he had ever loved, Keeler buried his sorrow in alcohol, cigarettes, anxiety and depression. Keeler died of a stroke in 1949, at the age of forty-five.

Captain Edward Melchen was still an officer in the Miami force when he died of a sudden and massive heart attack on July 5, 1948, almost five years to the day after being called to Nassau. Melchen never quite lived down the Oakes case. The lingering suspicion that he had conspired with Barker to trick de Marigny into leaving his print on a drinking glass, followed him to the moment he drew his last breath. And even afterward. To try to hang an innocent man, it wasn't cricket, even for a corrupt no-good cop. By eerie coincidence, he was succeeded as Miami Chief of Detectives by his discredited buddy. James Barker. But not for long.

James Barker, the other compromised detective, whose false evidence sabotaged the prosecution case against de Marigny, went back to Miami. Word reached me that he and his equally corrupt buddy Melchen were suspected of being stoolies in the pay of Meyer Lansky, the sunshine state godfather. Suspected? That was the word being used. It made me laugh. Everyone knew that the Miami police force was the most corrupt in the United States, mainly because of the powerful Mafia presence on Miami Beach and the willingness of bulls like Barker to accept Mob money. Most corrupt? That took some doing after Chicago, New York and New Orleans.

One story reached me that Barker had even tried enlisting police colleagues to fall in with Lansky and his henchmen.

Then it became academic, at least for Barker. On December 26, 1952, the holiday went off the rails for the nasty old ex-cop. He was shot dead by his own son, James Duane Barker, also a Miami cop with the service revolver Barker had used during his police days, the same piece of artillery that he waved at me in Nassau. Call it professional courtesy. The story had it that there was a family brawl and Barker senior had been making passes at his son's wife. Ka-BOOM! A coroner's jury later concluded justifiable homicide. Public opinion called it a civic improvement.

The lofty local mouthpiece, Alfred Adderley, whose legal skills in the prosecution team were rightly feared by de Marigny, was a man who must have known a lot of the inside skivvy. The Royal family needed some black faces from the colonies to give a light salt and pepper effect to Coronation of Queen Elizabeth II in 1953. So, Adderley flew from Nassau to London in 1953. He dropped dead on the return flight.

The Chief Justice, Sir Oscar Daly, returned to Ireland when his days as a colonial judge were over. He must have had some private opinions as to what had happened at Westbourne that night. He died quickly and quietly. Meanwhile, that other fine product of the Hibernian bar, Sir Eric Hallinan, who led the prosecution case against de Marigny, achieved the promotion he desired and ended his colonial service career as Chief Justice of the old West Indies Federation. When questioned about the Oakes case after the fact, Hallinan always was reluctant to discuss it. He even told one reporter in 1949 that he had already forgotten most of the details. I never bought that. The case was the biggest trial of Hallinan's career. It had also been a humiliation. The de Marigny affair had been an embarrassing failure for him, made more irksome by his unshakeable belief in the Mauritian count's guilt and his determination to see him hang.

He and the Duke appeared to share that view—but no one else, apart from the distraught Lady Oakes, believed it for a second, and nor do I. Hallinan lived to be eighty-four, dying in County Cork, Ireland.

As for Lieutenant Colonel Erskine-Lindop, whose rapid transfer to Trinidad in the early days of the investigation raised many eyebrows, especially as he was never called to give evidence at de

Marigny's trial, he did okay. He was probably the only man who knew for sure who killed Sir Harry Oakes, but said he would never discuss it. It was during a conversation in Trinidad some time afterwards that Erskine-Lindop revealed that he had a suspect on the verge of a tearful confession at the time of his transfer and expressed dismay that the killer was still mixing in Nassau society.

One of Sir Harry's three guests on the night of his murder, Charles Hubbard, didn't hang around long. Road crash, wouldn't you know it? Single car, late at night. He ran smack into a casuarina tree on West Bay Street. The tree must have jumped out in the middle of the road to get him, as there didn't seem to be any reason for the accident. But it killed him instantly.

There was no proof of foul play, or none reported, anyway. The Nassau police took care of it. But inevitably there was talk. Jinxes. Coincidences.

There was also a cloud hanging over the earthly demise of Assistant Superintendent Bernard J. Nottage, the senior detective in the de Marigny affair. He died relatively young from massive bleeding after having his teeth pulled by a Nassau dentist. It was always thought that Superintendent Nottage knew far more than he let on, and that he was among the select few who knew the whole truth about the Oakes murder.

Superintendent Nottage was a remarkable man, the first black to reach such heights in the Bahamas force and well-regarded by colleagues of all shades. His appointment with the dentist should have been a routine matter. He was a healthy, active man and his death shook the Nassau community. It came at a time when suspicion was growing about Oakes-related conspiracies, and it was inevitable that his demise was one more example of evil scheming. The feeling was that he fell victim to powerful forces in Nassau at the time, and that his death was no accident.

All those deaths. All those people dropping like flies on a hot August afternoon on Paradise Island. They put a charley horse in the long arm of coincidence. Even two of Nancy Oakes' two siblings died suspiciously young:

Sir Sydney Oakes, Second Baronet of Nassau, inherited his title from his father. He died in a single-car accident in Nassau in

1966 when a utility pole jumped out into the middle of the street one dark night, just like the casuarina tree that had killed Charles Hubbard, and ran into his sports car. He was thirty-nine years old.

Another brother, William Pitt Oakes, got himself hooked on heroin and went stark raving nuts. For some months, he ran around his home behaving like a canine, urinating on the rug and the furniture and barking—Arf! Arf!—like a dog. He was visiting New York City on business and staying at the Westbury Hotel when he fell ill to coronary thrombosis complicated by liver failure. He was taken to a Bronx nursing home where he died shortly after arrival. He was buried with his father, Sir Harry Oakes. It was 1956 and he was twenty-eight.

A sister, Shirley Oakes, seemed for a while to escape the contagious misfortune. But only for a while. She went to Vassar and Yale Law, then later also had a vehicular accident that left crippled and in a coma for the remaining years of her life. If any loudmouth ever tries to tell you that money buys happiness, tell him to pipe down so you can tell him about Eunice Oakes, Harry's widow.

She was once married to the wealthiest man in the British Empire. And what did it buy her? Not only did her husband get murdered, but two of her three children predeceased her.

But let's get back to Sir Harry.

I'll come right out and say it. I ended up liking the man and liking his family. Maybe more than anything, that was what drove me onward in the case and prevented me from ever letting the case drop.

I had started out at best indifferent to Sir Harry, or even not liking him, seeing him as a bit of a parvenu bore: an intense crude man with a questionable moral compass. Then I began to understand him, particularly when I assembled the facts on his life, through the early failures in Maine and Australia. He had his quirks, his blemishes, his demons.

He had enemies. But he deserved better than to be heinously murdered as he slept.

I came to think of him as a rough-hewn Jay Gatsby, Fitzgerald's anti-hero, exiled to the Bahamas as a quasi-colonial. Gatsby was a crook, of course. Harry wasn't. But there was a kindred spirit, or maybe I only imagined it.

I'm tempted to say that Sir Harry was no better and no worse than any other man and that he deserved justice, even in death. But then I re-assess and I do admit that after he was murdered, he won me over. Dare I say, I even admired him, flaws and all, the way he would go banging around town in his old mining gear. He was a self-made man as so many of the lions of his generation were. One had to admire that: his dynamism. His frontier mentality. I grew to like him and wanted to help bring justice to his case. I couldn't.

Oddly, he formed a strange triumvirate of self-made men in the case, men I liked and respected. Harry seemed like a distant great uncle, wealthy and cantankerous. Ray Schindler seemed like a wise cousin to me, a man of experience in a rough world. And Mike Todd, peripheral to the case but in and out of my orbit during the Forties and Fifties, seemed like an irascible big brother. As the years passed, I liked all three of them even more. The world was a smaller place without such outsized men.

Over the years, Harold Christie became very wealthy. Property values boomed in the Bahamas. Gambling and new hotels brought tourists. Tourists brought money. Westbourne, where Harry Oakes was murdered, became the site of the Playboy Casino, part of the Ambassador Beach Hotel. Creepily, the casino building bore a shocking resemblance to Harry's old estate.

For all his good work in bringing prosperity to the Bahamas, Harold Christie was knighted in 1964 by Queen Elizabeth II, the niece of Edward VIII. Not long thereafter, white colonial rule gradually ended in the Bahamas and the country inched toward its independence, which it gained in June of 1973, a month after my seventieth birthday.

A few months later, Sir Harold Christie was on a business trip to West Germany. He suffered a heart attack. He died the same day. He was seventy-seven.

When I read the news in *The New York Times*, the Oakes case had a final echo. Christie's obituary mentioned that on the night forty years earlier when the millionaire baronet was burned and beaten to death Harold Christie "had heard nothing but the sounds of a severe rainstorm."

There it would forever remain.

I read the obituary twice. I angrily folded the newspaper and threw it away.

Alfred de Marigny did not kill Sir Harry Oakes.

Apparently, no one did.

END

Alan Hynd in 1943

Notes and Acknowledgements

The primary source for the story contained in this book was the years of conversations that I had with my father as I was growing up. We spoke many times on the subjects that he wrote about, including what he wrote and published on the Oakes case.

In attempting to recreate Alan Hynd's narrative voice with as much accuracy as possible, I've even incorporated some of his text in the Oakes case into this book. As noted previously, as a true crime reporter he covered more than a thousand true crime cases in a long career. I'm more than familiar with most of them. Our conversations on cases frequently included what couldn't be printed at the time, mostly due to the invasion of privacy laws as well as the libel laws.

Alan Hynd was in fact a friend of Raymond Schindler and a friend of Mike Todd. Their inclusion here is an affectionate nod. The apparent attempt on his life in 1951 happened as it is portrayed here. He was no friend, of course, of many of the main players in the Bahamas, who didn't care much for his reporting. I was four years old at the time and my father left our home in an ambulance during the right. It's a vivid memory and not a pleasant one. The Duke of Windsor was not a fan, either, and feelings were mutual. I remember it quite well.

The Oakes case, the Lindbergh case and the Ponzi case were always foremost of what he covered, but he was equally an authority on the desperado outlaws of the Great Depression, notably John Dillinger. He even struck up an acquittance with John Wilson Dillinger, Johnny's dad, when the bank robber's father went on the vaudeville circuit in the late 1930's. But that's another story for another day….

Alan Hynd really was a *New York Times* Best Selling author with a book titled *Passport To Treason* in 1943. All of his newspaper and work in the true crime field is accurately portrayed here.

THE NEW YORK TIMES BOOK REVIEW, *May 30, 1943.*

The Best Selling Books, Here and Elsewhere

This chart is based upon the reports from book-sellers in fourteen cities which appear each Monday on the book page of The New York Times. The order in which the titles are listed is based upon the number of cities which report them as among the best-sellers. The numerals indicate their relative standing.

Fiction

	NEW YORK	BOSTON	PHILADELPHIA	WASHINGTON	BALTIMORE	ATLANTA	CLEVELAND	DETROIT	CHICAGO	ST. LOUIS	NEW ORLEANS	DALLAS	SAN FRANCISCO	LOS ANGELES
The Robe, by Lloyd C. Douglas.	1	1	1	1	1	1	1	1	1	1		1	1	1
The Human Comedy, by William Saroyan.	2	2	2	2	2	2	2	2		2		1	1	2
The Valley of Decision, by Marcia Davenport.	2	2		2	2	2	2	2	2					2
Gideon Planish, by Sinclair Lewis.	2	2	2	2		2	2	2					2	2
The Forest and the Fort, by Hervey Allen.		3		4	2	2		2	2			2	2	
Capricornia, by Xavier Herbert.				2					2					
Mrs. Parkington, by Louis Bromfield.						.				2	2			
Wide Is the Gate, by Upton Sinclair.										2	2			
The Story of Dr. Wassell, by James Hilton.			2			2								
Mama's Bank Account, by Kathryn Forbes.												2	2	
The Choice, by Charles Mills.						2								
Rivers of Glory, by F. Van Wyck Mason.									2					
Citizen Tom Paine, by Howard Fast.	2													
Crescent Carnival, by Frances Parkinson Keyes.														
The Song of Bernadette, by Franz Werfel.														2

General

	NEW YORK	BOSTON	PHILADELPHIA	WASHINGTON	BALTIMORE	ATLANTA	CLEVELAND	DETROIT	CHICAGO	ST. LOUIS	NEW ORLEANS	DALLAS	SAN FRANCISCO	LOS ANGELES
One World, by Wendell L. Willkie.	1	1	1	1	1	1	1	1	1		1	1	1	
On Being a Real Person, by Harry Emerson Fosdick.	2	2	2	2	2	2	2	2	2			2	2	
Between the Thunder and the Sun, by Vincent Sheean.	2	2	2		2	2		2	2			2	2	
Guadalcanal Diary, by Richard Tregaskis.								2	2				2	
Journey Among Warriors, by Eve Curie.	2	2		2		2			2	2			2	
George Washington Carver, by Rackham Holt.	2								2	2				
Lee's Lieutenants, Vol. 2, by Douglas Southall Freeman.			2			2							2	
They Call It Pacific, by Clark Lee.						2							2	
They Were Expendable, by W. L. White.										2			2	
Seven Came Through, by Captain Eddie Rickenbacker.						2			2				2	
Life in a Putty-Knife Factory, by H. Allen Smith.										2			2	
See Here, Private Hargrove, by Marion Hargrove.													2	
Battle for the Solomons, by Ira Wolfert.													2	
Appeasement's Child, by Thomas J. Hamilton.							2							
Our Hearts Were Young and Gay, by Skinner & Kimbrough.							2							
Suez to Singapore, by Cecil Brown.														
Young Lady Randolph, by Rene Kraus.		2												
Passport to Treason, by Alan Hynd.									2					
Henry Ford, by William A. Simonds.										2				
Elisabet Ney, by Fortune & Burton.														2
Father and Glorious Descendant, by Pardee Lowe.														2

Crime Corner

By ISAAC ANDERSON

THE RAT BEGAN TO GNAW THE ROPE. By C. W. Grafton. 243 pp. New York; Farrar & Rinehart. $2.

Setting: Somewhere in Kentucky

The Crime: William Jasper Harper, rich industrialist, is murdered in his own home shortly after a stormy interview with Tim McClure, one of his employes. Tim is charged with the crime and can give no satisfactory account of himself.

Sleuth: Gil Henry, a young lawyer who starts out by trying to discover why Mr. Harper wants to pay Ruth McClure four times the market value of the Harper stock she inherited from her father.

Finding: Action swift enough and violent enough to satisfy the most exacting reader, plus a crisp narrative style that wastes no words. This is the prize winner in the 1943 Mary Roberts Rinehart Mystery Contest, and well merits that distinction.

THE BLACK RUSTLE. By Constance and Gwenyth Little. 214 pp. New York: Published for The Crime Club, Inc., by Doubleday, Doran & Co. $2.

Setting: The home of as wacky a family as ever populated the pages of a mystery novel.

Clues: A disappearing doll dressed in black; a gadget whose original purpose is never explained; a taffeta bedspread; a tress of black hair; a marriage certificate; a volume of Poe; noises in the attic; a spot of blood.

Sleuth: Marina Hays, a house guest.

Finding: Goofy dialogue; strange happenings that appear to make no sense — until one learns the explanation; baffling mystery and excellent enter-

---

Research on this book, however, included many further sources. Many books have been written on the Oakes case. Some of them contain passages remarkably similar to Alan Hynd's own final account which appeared in 1958 in a big compendium of true crime titled, *Murder, Mayhem and Mystery.* I've looked at all of them. They are remarkable in the sense that no two arrive at exactly the same conclusion over who-dun-it. In any case, I used them for sources on Nassau in 1943, the

trial, and many of the players in the drama. In chronological order, the books are as follows:

> *The Life and Death of Sir Harry Oakes*. Geoffrey Bocca. 1959
> *Who Killed Sir Harry Oakes?* Marshall Houts, 1972 and 1976.
>
> *Who Killed Sir Harry Oakes?* James Leasor, 1983
> *King of Fools* John Parker 1988
> *The Duchess of Windsor: The Secret Life* Charles Higham,
2005
> *A Conspiracy of Crowns*, Alfred de Marigny and Mickey
Herskowitz 1990
> *Carnal Hours: A Nathan Heller Mystery*, Max Allan Collins
1994
> *Any Human Heart,* William Boyd 2002
> *A Question of Evidence: The Casebook of Great Forensic
Controversies, from Napoleon to O.J. 2003,* Colin Evans   2003
> *Blood and Fire: the Duke of Windsor and the Strange Murder
of Sir Harry Oakes*, John Marquis. 2005
> *A Serpent in Eden*, James Owen 2006

It was more than amusing to find that two of the books above took their titles from the title of Alan Hynd's 1958 article which appeared in *Murder, Mayhem and Mystery* and one took a title, *The Carnal Hours*, from a phrase he used in the third line of his account of the case.

Who Killed Sir Harry Oakes?

Here's the fascinating account of the murder that set the glamorous international set on its ear—the story for which the author has been banned from the Bahamas.

Sometime between the dark and the daylight, known in the Bahama Islands as the carnal hours, a murder was committed in Nassau, the Bahama capital, in about some of the less well publicized aspects of the mystery of Sir Harry Oakes' death. A man was officially accused of the crime and tried for it. The

Having said that, I'm particularly indebted to James Leasor's *Who Killed Sir Harry Oakes?* for its fine description of wartime Nassau and to James Owen's *A Serpent in Eden* for its detailed account of the legal proceedings in which Albert de Marigny was accused of murder. Specific credit is gratefully acknowledged here. Both are commendable works and, let's face it, the question posed in the title *Who Killed Sir Harry Oakes?* is a pretty good one and not the province of any single writer. I also used *The New York Times, The Guardian, The Nassau Tribune, The Hollywood Reporter* and *Wikipedia* for various further details, including background on Ernest Hemingway, The Duke and Duchess of Windsor, Joe Schenk, Meyer Lansky, Lucky Luciano, Thomas Dewey, Mike Todd, Bill McCoy and Fulgencio Battista. I should also note that Herbert Nossen was a real person and his parents did die in something very real known as "the Holocaust," something we should never forget.

On a lighter note, may I confirm that there really was a joyously disreputable New York tabloid named *The New York Evening Graphic?* I wouldn't overexaggerate the type of illustrations they used on their front pages, such as the one of Rudolph Valentino and Enrico Caruso meeting in Heaven. I wouldn't and I couldn't. My only question would have been whether Rudy and Caruso spoke English or Italian. For better or worse, they were pioneers in what might be called "junk journalism" and those Jesus-is-in-my-toast moments.

Nor can I underestimate what a valuable experience it was for me to pick up some assignments that my father didn't want in 1968 when I was twenty years old. My start in professional writing was in true crime for a small press syndicate based in Oslo, Norway. I filed American police cases to them, about 2000 words each, four reports a month, and they set them up in the foreign true crime mags of the era. I figured the job was temporary. It was, but it ran for eighteen years, long after I'd started writing spy stories like *Flowers From Berlin.*

All of which brings us to a final bonus article from
Prescription Murder, Volume One by Alan Hynd, which along with
several of Alan Hynd's other works, is available on Kindle.

Enjoy.

Noel Hynd

October 2017

Readers can reach Noel Hynd at NH1212f@yahoo.com.

Arsenic, Old Lace and Sister Amy Archer

By Alan Hynd, re-edited by Noel Hynd in 2014

The eerie sound of the hearse creaking to a stop in front of The Archer Home for old folks and chronic invalids in the ink-black pre-dawn hours of the steaming August night awakened the two old maids who lived in the snug brick house across the street.

"Heavens!" said Mabel Bliss to her sister, Patricia, as she drew the bedroom curtain aside and peered out. "That's the third time somebody's died over there in less than a month! And always in the middle of the night."

A light went on in the vestibule of The Archer Home and the front door opened to admit two burly men who had jumped down from the driver's seat of the death wagon, opened the rear door and dragged out a box six feet long. They weren't inside very long when they reappeared with the box, which now seemed to be more of a burden to carry. They shoved it into the hearse and clattered into the gloom.

Now a light went on in the parlor and the Bliss sisters could see Sister Amy Archer, founder of the home bearing her name, wearing nothing but a very fancy nightgown, settling herself at a little organ. (The "Sister" was a title she had bestowed on herself. It had nothing to do with any religious order.) The windows were open and presently there wafted across the narrow street the sweet sad strains of *Nearer, My God, To Thee,* accompanied by Sister Amy's pleasant soprano.

Sister Amy Archer, one of the few arch-murderesses in criminal history who could quote passages from the Bible from Genesis to Exodus, was only half way through the hymn when a second figure appeared, a brooding giant of a man with a red puffy face and walrus moustache, in nightshirt and bare feet. This was Big Jim Archer, Sister Amy's fifth spouse, a coarse type in his forties who

247

seemed to be an odd sort of a mate for our heroine. Sister Amy, though in her late thirties, looked a good decade younger, and, though sharp-featured, was a very attractive little woman with snow-white skin, jet-black hair and a divine form that even the starch in her professional uniform simply couldn't hide. Not that she was hiding much that August night after the hearse left, nor was Big Jim hiding anything, either, when the music stopped and the lights went out.

It was Sister Amy's views on sex that puzzled the Bliss sisters. For somebody who was so devout and stern, and who was so unalterably opposed to alcohol and tobacco in any form, Sister Amy was simply mad about sex. Nor did she make any bones about it.

"One man in bed at night when the lights are out," she had said to the Bliss sisters after coming up from New York six months previously to establish The Archer Home in an abandoned rich man's mansion in the tree-shaded village of Windsor, just outside of Hartford, Connecticut, "is worth ten on the street in broad daylight."

After breakfast in the morning, when the twenty residents of The Archer Home, assorted widows and widowers who were, in one way or another, breaking up and coming apart at the joints, were out on a veranda that swept across the front and ran around one side of the big gray frame ramshackle Home, Big Jim clumped across the street and knocked on the front door of the Bliss house. Sister Amy, a simply superb cook, had sent him over with some of her hotcakes and maple syrup. He was both a comic and tragic figure, Big Jim, none too bright, and turned out in brown derby, baggy light-brown suit and heavy black shoes.

"We see you lost another one during the night, Jim," said Mabel Bliss.

"Yeah," said Big Jim, "another heart case."

"That's what the other two died from, isn't it, Jim?"

"Yeah. It's gettin' to be a regular epidemic."

"They always seem to die during the night, don't they?"

"Yeah, don't they! Well, I gotta to be goin'."

Six nights later, that hearse was there again, and in the morning, Big Jim was over with something tasty from Sister Amy for the two spinsters.

"Who was it this time, Jim?" asked Mabel Bliss.

"A woman. First woman we've lost."

"What was it this time, Jim?"

Big Jim, who had a flair for the dramatic gesture, didn't reply with words but, raising his eyes toward the ceiling, pointed to his heart.

There was a total of three doctors who had staked out the village of Windsor in the year of 1908, all driving up from their offices in Hartford. None of the three, luckily enough for Sister Amy, was a wizard in the field of diagnostics. And, since all of the deaths in the Home were sudden, and in the dead of the night, none of the physicians was ever able to be at the bedside when the Grim Reaper appeared. It was never until morning, when the corpse was already embalmed, that Sister Amy phoned one of the physicians to get his name on the death certificate.

"What was it, Sister Amy?" the doctor would inquire. The physician, realizing that Sister Amy had been a head nurse in New York's Bellevue Hospital, where Big Jim had been an orderly before coming to Connecticut, had such complete respect for Sister Amy's knowledge in the field of diagnostics, that he would never question her word when she said, "The heart," or, "A general breaking up due to the infirmities of age."

There were ten bedrooms for the residents of The Home, each a double, and the residents, who averaged sixty years of age or more, which was old age in that period, were kept equally divided as to sex, so that there could always be two residents in each room. Sister Amy's deal was a unique one for the day: one lump of money or property, anywhere from $5,000 to $15,000, depending on the resident's age, physical condition and what the fiscal traffic would bear. For that sum, the resident was to receive a lifetime contract from Sister Amy, including everything from food and lodging and medical care, with a fine plot in Windsor's leading cemetery thrown in as a cheerful after-death bonus.

"I'm going to take such good care of my charges," Sister Amy told the Bliss sisters shortly after founding The Home, and explaining her plan, "that they'll be eating me into the poor house, praise the Good Lord!"

The Archer Home had been functioning for about a year and a half, and that hearse had been there in the night nineteen times, when Big Jim Archer, who did all the chores around the place, from emptying the bedpans to sweeping up, began to feel himself breaking up. There was a fine Irish saloon, Paddy's, just three blocks from The Home and Big Jim, despite Sister Amy's strict ban on booze, began to sneak around to it when he got the chance. After a few shots, he'd pop some cloves into his mouth.

As time went on, Paddy, a discerning man, saw that Big Jim was beset by troubles of some sort and one night he asked him just what was wrong.

Big Jim, wiping the foam from a beer chaser from his walrus moustache, looked levelly at Paddy for a little while. Then he said, in a voice filled with sorrow:

"It's my wife, Paddy."

"Sister Amy? Why, is she ill or somethin'?"

"Far from that, my friend."

"What is it, then?"

Big Jim looked around him to make sure none of the other men at the bar were within earshot, then said,

"It's her demands at night."

"You mean they're more than you can handle, Jim?"

"More than I can handle now. I used to be able to handle things fine but her demands have increased since we came up here from New York."

"If I'm not asking too much, Jim, just how great are her demands?"

"Two and three times."

"A week?"

"No, a night."

"Good God, Jim, that's enough to put a man in an early grave!"

As the months wore on, and that hearse continued to stop at The Archer Home on an average of once a month, always at night, Jim continued to confide in Paddy. He was now patronizing a quack doctor down in New York, who was fixing him up with an aphrodisiac. The pills worked for a time. Then one night Jim appeared in Paddy's with simply woeful tidings.

"The old clock," he confided to his friend, "has not only run down, it's stopped altogether."

"You mean…?"

"The very worst," said Big Jim, almost breaking into a fit of sobbing, "has happened."

"And Sister Amy? Is she complainin'?"

"That's just it," came the reply. "She don't say nothin' when we go to bed and I lay there useless. In the mornin', when it's daylight, she has a funny way of lookin' at me. I'd give a year of my life to know what's goin' on in that mind of hers. There's an awful lot about Sister Amy that I could tell you if I wanted to."

One day, when Jim was sweeping out the dirt at the back door, there appeared a redheaded, baggy-pants stranger carrying a knapsack on a stick over his shoulder.

"The name's Gilligan, Michael Gilligan," he announced to Big Jim in a deep, cheerful voice, "and I'm lookin' for work."

"There's no work here for you," snapped Big Jim, who was later to tell Paddy that instinct told him that, what with his dried-up condition, Gilligan would be a dangerous man to have around his wife. "Beat it. And beat it quick."

Big Jim had just ordered Gilligan off the property when he was conscious of Gilligan's eyes meeting those of somebody who had come up silently behind him. Turning, he saw Sister Amy. She was looking straight at the stranger, tall, handsome, and obviously bursting with what it took when the lights were out. He shuddered, he was to tell Paddy that night, for he hadn't seen Sister Amy with that light in her eyes since the first time she had laid eyes on him.

Within an hour, Michael Gilligan, having been fed enough for three men by Sister Amy, who overruled her spouse in important matters, was addressing himself to assorted repair chores around The Home.

It was less than a month after Gilligan had first appeared that Sister Amy dropped in on the Bliss sisters one morning far from her usual bubbling self.

"What on earth's wrong, Sister Amy?" asked Mabel Bliss.

"Jim."

"Jim? Why, what's the matter with Jim?"

"He's not long for this world, may the Lord bless his soul."

"But just what's wrong with the man?"

"Complications."

The Christmas season was coming on, nearing the end of the third year of Sister Amy's functioning in Windsor, when the hearse called in the night and took Big Jim Archer away. Sister Amy appeared to be inconsolable… for a while. Then she appeared to brighten very suddenly. The Bliss sisters couldn't figure out what was up until spring came and the windows were open.

Then, on those occasions when Sister Amy forgot to douse the lights, the two old maids could see history repeating itself, with one exception. When Archer had divested himself of his nightshirt he had been clothed only in his birthday suit. Gilligan, though, no matter whether he was vertical or horizontal, never seemed to divest himself of his socks and garters.

It was in early summer that Sister Amy bounced over to the Bliss place one morning with the news. "My heart has been broken since Jim was called to Heaven but now Michael Gilligan has mended it. It is God's will that Michael and I become one."

Gilligan and Sister Amy got married by a local Justice of the Peace but were too busy with various matters to go off on a honeymoon. Gilligan wasn't the friendly type to the Bliss sisters that Archer had been. And he seemed to drink a bit, always having a pint in his pants pockets as he roamed the property making repairs.

Sister Amy explained to the Bliss sisters why she made an exception to liquor in Gilligan's case. "My Michael," she said, "uses alcohol for medicinal purposes."

One morning, after the second stiff in forty-eight hours had been carried away in the night, Gilligan was out front sweeping the porch when the sisters, who couldn't stand the suspense, decided to call over to him.

"What'd the last two residents die of, Mr. Gilligan?" asked Mabel.

Gilligan stopped to take a swig out of the bottle before answering. Then he bellowed out, loudly enough to be heard in the next block:

"None of yer goddam business!"

That, as it was eventually to turn out, was a mistake. The Bliss sisters were furious. They sat down and got off a letter to *The Hartford Courant,* then, as today, a great New England newspaper. They had been counting the number of people who left in that box during the night for more than four years now and it added up to one a month.

"I think," the letter to *The Courant* concluded, "that that's a lot of people dying and that there is something mighty strange going on over there."

The next day there popped up at the Bliss front door a very appropriately named man named Mike Toughy, the youthful star reporter of *The Courant,* a walking, talking symbol of the front-page scribes of the era: battered hat, dangling cigarette, whiskey breath and side-of-the-mouth talk.

"And now," he began, as he settled himself on a green chair in the Bliss parlor, "suppose you tell me just why you ladies are so suspicious of that place across the street."

The Bliss sisters didn't have anything to impart to Mike but suspicion. But, as they went into details about that hearse that had been calling in the night all those years, there was something so earnest about them that Mike decided to look into things. So he dug into the records of a few of Sister Amy's recent losses, got the names of the three physicians who had signed the death certificates, and sought out the doctors.

True, all three doctors told Toughy, an average of a death a month at The Archer Home did, at first glance, seem high, considering that such an average would completely decimate the Home and repopulate it every twenty months. But the doctors pointed out to Mike that Sister Amy's patients were all breaking up from the infirmities of age when they came to The Home and had a short time to live at best. Then, too, all three doctors pointed out, Sister Amy, having come out of Bellevue Hospital with practically as much knowledge of the human system as a physician, was more than capable of seeing that everything possible was done for any of her charges.

Toughy wasn't satisfied, though. He had a friend who was an actuary, one of those statistics wizards who figure out how long people are going to live, employed by The Greater New England Life Insurance Company, and he dropped in on the man. After filling him in on the death rate at Sister Amy's establishment, he made some notes, and asked Mike to come back in a few days.

The news that awaited Mike was mixed. The death rate was high, but, considering the condition of Sister Amy's charges when they checked in, a lot was accounted for.

"So," concluded the actuary, a good man with double talk, "the picture doesn't look all black and it isn't all white, either."

Mike Toughy didn't do anything now but hire a couple of grave diggers and an intern from Hartford General Hospital, dig up one of Sister Amy's most recent check-outs, take the man's insides out, put him back and cover the grave. Then Mike took the insides to the state toxicologist right in Hartford. The news from the toxicologist wasn't what Mike was after: not the slightest trace of any kind of poison. Mike, the persistent one, dug up a second stiff but got the same kind of a report. A third stiff got him nowhere, nor did a fourth.

Mike had just gone back to the city room of his newspaper after getting his fourth negative report when who telephoned him but Sister Amy.

"Mr. Toughy," came the sweet voice of the lady who mixed sex and murder, "I'm wondering if you can stop over to see me as soon as you can."

Sitting in Sister Amy's parlor half an hour later, Toughy found himself looking at a very confident lady.

"Well, Mr. Toughy," she began, smiling sweetly, "were you disappointed?"

"Disappointed? Disappointed at what?"

"Disappointed," said Sister Amy, her voice taking on some harshness now, "at not finding any poison in the four bodies."

For once, Mike couldn't come up with an answer.

"No wonder you can't answer me," said Sister Amy, her voice now dripping icicles, "you no good son of a bitch. Dig up one more body and try to blacken my fine reputation and I'll see that you wind up in jail and, besides, I'll sue that paper of yours for the last desk in that room where you write your lies."

Mike had no sooner returned to the city room when the city editor beckoned him.

"Mike," said the city editor, "I can guess what Sister Amy said to you."

"Why?"

"She's hired the sharpest shyster lawyer this side of the Rockies, a scoundrel from New York, and he's just been in here threatening the very future of this paper."

"Anything else?" Toughy asked.

"Yes. This: maybe that woman is one of the greatest criminals since Bluebeard. But if she is, we'll never prove it. Let the law find out and dig into the facts. Drop this thing."

Mike Toughy, though, was practically fearless. On his days off, he ran down to New York and began to poke around Bellevue Hospital. There was a coffee house near Bellevue where the doctors, interns and nurses hung out. It was from a young physician who had been an intern when Sister Amy had been a nurse who gave Toughy some idea of Sister Amy's sexual demands.

"I've had quite a few women in my life," the doctor told the scribe, "but never anybody to come anywhere near Amy Archer. I know for a fact that she had three other fellows besides myself one day when she was here within a twelve-hour period."

Gilligan seems to have been a very talented man, for as long as he was to last. On most nights, he preferred to perform with the lights on and the shades up in a front room of the second floor. The Bliss sisters, with that wonderful show going on, lost so much sleep that they were seldom awake during the day. Every month or so, in the middle of the night, there would be a change of scene: that hearse.

It hadn't taken Gilligan long, of course, to become something of a fixture at Paddy's saloon. Being a boastful man, he regaled Paddy and some of the barflies of stories of why Big Jim Archer had failed as a husband and why he himself was such a success, going into all the details.

Then one night, some three years after his marriage to Sister Amy, Gilligan walked into Paddy's a man with terror in his face.

"Good God, Mike," said Paddy, "you look like you've seen a ghost."

"It's worse than that, Paddy. I've just seen somebody *makin'* a ghost."

"Whaddya you mean?"

Gilligan had been hitting it up before he came into Paddy's and was about two sheets to the ozone. Now, though, as if suddenly realizing that he had let out something that should never have been mentioned, he clammed up. Looking at a shot Paddy had poured for him, he shoved it back, without a word, and hustled out of the joint.

"I wonder what he meant by what he just said?" one of the barflies could hear Paddy muttering to himself. Paddy thought for a while, then shrugged and went back to pouring booze for the customers.

Two nights later, that hearse was at Sister Amy's again. When Paddy's opened in the morning, the word was there before the first spigot was turned on: Brother Gilligan had conked out during the night. Heart attack.

Sister Amy, always a lady who looked ahead, had Gilligan's successor all lined up, a classy-looking gentleman answering to the name of Harold Q. Knight, who had been in residence for several months now.

Knight was a small man of about fifty, with very white skin, very red lips, and jet-black hair that the other residents were certain had been dyed. Nobody knew where he had come from and, as he passed the other residents at any hour of the day or night, he was always quoting to himself from a book of poetry he carried.

On the night of the day that Sister Amy's seventh husband had been buried, one of the residents, a new arrival named Charles W. Andrews, happened to be passing Sister Amy's bedroom when he heard the voices of Sister Amy and Harold Q. Knight.

"I asked you to come into my room," Andrews could hear Sister Amy saying to Knight, "because I thought maybe we could get together."

"I don't quite understand," Knight replied. There was silence, then Andrews heard Knight saying: "But why are you taking your nightgown off?"

"Can't you guess, Mr. Knight?"

"Why, no."

"I'm a woman," Sister Amy was saying, "and I no longer have a husband. You are a man and you do not have a wife. We can have a lot of fun together."

"Sister Amy," Knight said, "I thought you knew."

"Knew what?"

"That I prefer men to women." There was a stony silence. Then Andrews heard Sister Amy say in the terminology of the day, "You mean you're a fairy?"

"Well," replied Knight, "I guess you can call it that."

It wasn't long afterward when Knight left in the night.

All this time, of course, Mike Toughy had been biting his nails and tearing out his hair because *The Hartford Courant,* not wanting to find itself without a press to print on, had admonished him to lay off Sister Amy. Sister Amy had, of course, cut down on that one-a-month hearse call. But the old boys and girls were still going away in the night.

Sister Amy, who had, up to now, as she began her seventh year operating The Home, always appeared in The Home starched out in a nurse's white uniform and appeared on the street in regular pedestrian attire. Now, though, for street wear, she appeared in the semi-religious garb of the Quaker, flowing gray cape and little gray bonnet. As she minced along the streets of Windsor, out purely for exercise and air, she was never without her Bible, glancing at it as she walked, then quoting it as she looked skyward with a holy light in her eyes.

Our girl sure knew what she was doing. Some citizens regarded her as something of a nut. Others respected her as a devout little character. But nobody, nobody but Mike Toughy, had the slightest idea that she was one of the great killers of criminal history.

It was along about now that Sister Amy, in her middle forties, entered that phase that women call change of life. With the normal woman, sex becomes pretty important. With Sister Amy, the demand was out of this world. To make matters worse, there wasn't a stalwart male on the premises. So Sister began to pay for it. Windsor was filled with stalwart young workmen, plumbers and carpenters and jacks of all trades. So now there was always a leak that developed somewhere in The Home, after dark, and a plumber called to plug it up.

One day, Mike Toughy happened to be lifting a few in Paddy's saloon when who walked in but Charley Andrews, the old boy who had heard that dialogue between Sister Amy and the gay resident. Toughy and Andrews happened to fall into conversation and when Mike heard the story of how Knight had conked out so quickly after not being able to rise to Sister's demands, he began to throb with suspicion again.

So Mike Toughy, without his paper being any the wiser, decided to play for all or nothing. He scouted around Hartford until he found an old couple, smart folks in their sixties named Flanagan, and he coached them in the part they were to play in a lethal plot.

A few days later, then, Mr. and Mrs. Michael Flanagan appeared at the front door of The Archer Home.

"We're from Massachusetts," Flanagan said to Sister Amy, "and we've heard about your wonderful home."

"Come in," said Sister Amy. The Flanagans looked like prosperous people and Sister Amy sat there for quite a while, sizing them up and feeling them out. The Home, she divulged, was all filled but she'd be glad to put them on the waiting list.

"Oh," said Flanagan, uttering words that Toughy had put in his mouth, "isn't that too bad you can't take us right away. Now we'll have to hunt around for someplace else because we want to get into a Home somewhere right away."

"Yes," piped up Mrs. Flanagan. "And money is no object."

"Oh," said Sister Amy, "I just remembered: there will be two vacancies here in a week or so."

"Oh? You have residents who are very ill?"

"Yes. Two cases of heart trouble, poor souls." Amy dabbed at her eyes. "They're unaware of what's wrong with them, God bless them," she said.

"We'll be back," said Flanagan. "We're staying with relatives down in New York."

When the Flanagans told Toughy about the vacancies, Mike was afraid he'd have two murders on his conscience. So he had the Flanagans go right back and tell Sister Amy they'd changed their minds.

Unbeknown to Mike, though, there was another couple, people named the Chester Watsons, who had popped up at the Bliss home, of all places, asking the two old maids what they knew about the residence.

"We're looking for some place to spend our last years," Mrs. Watson told Mabel Bliss, "and we've heard a lot about the Archer Home."

Mabel Bliss, having been told by Mike Toughy that Sister Amy would have the law on anybody who said a bad word about her, was afraid, unfortunately, as it turned out, to open her mouth. And so she and her sister saw the Chester Watsons walking across the street, rapping on the front door of The Home, and being graciously received by Sister Amy.

Two nights later, not one but two residents of The Archer Home left in boxes. One dead one was an old lady; the other was Brother Andrews.

And that did it, the double departure in the gloom of the night. There was room now for the Watsons. When the Bliss sisters dropped the word to Mike Toughy, he got busy. Toughy had always thought that Sister Amy had learned about those four bodies he had had dug up by spotting him when he had visited the Bliss home originally and somehow having him shadowed when he went to the cemetery at nights. Now, though, he to take his chances.

The body that Toughy had disinterred this time, long enough to get out of the cemetery with the stomach, was that of Charley Andrews. Toughy was in better luck this time. Andrews had been poisoned.

The next day Mike Toughy was sitting in the office of State's Attorney Hugh M. Alcorn. Toughy had, while the state toxicologist had been analyzing Andrews' stomach, been doing some fast poking around the region. He learned that Sister Amy had insured Andrews for $4,000. He learned that on the occasion that he had had the actuary look into the insurance records for him that the actuary had not looked far enough.

True, Sister Amy had not at that time been carrying insurance on any of the departed ones. Not that she hadn't tried. She had tried to take out policies on most of them but they had all failed to pass their medical tests.

But Toughy had discovered something even more vital to the future of The Archer Home. In digging into the poison books of the drugstores, which he had done previously without results, it occurred to him that Sister Amy might not have used her own name when buying arsenic. And he struck luck there, too. A little woman answering Sister Amy's description had, over a period of years, put in occasional appearances at a drug store in Hartford. And when Mike Toughy sneaked the druggist around to the Bliss house under cover of night and had him get a gander at Sister Amy when she came out the front door next morning, the druggist just nodded.

Now Toughy sat there telling State's Attorney Alcorn the whole lethal story of Sister Amy's seven years of bad luck for Windsor. Alcorn saw the black light. But, to make assurance doubly sure, he had the bodies of four of Sister's most recent victims dug up. Two of them were filled with arsenic. Two of them had been smothered. That answered a lot, that smothering; it explained why most of Sister Amy's victims were walking around after supper and leaving in a box a few hours later. And a smothering job didn't leave any trace in a victim's stomach.

Finally, The Hartford Courant ran the big story.

The Hartford Courant

POLICE BELIEVE ARCHER HOME FOR AGED A MURDER FACTORY
MRS. ARCHER - GILLIGAN ACCUSED OF MURDER OF INMATE
AUTOPSY SHOWS TWO WHO DIED WERE KILLED BY POISON

U.S. ACCEPTS GERMAN PROMISE; NO CONDITION TO BE CONSIDERED

Wilson, in Brief Note Cabled Last Night, Informs Berlin Government That Differences With Other Belligerents Cannot Form Subject of Discussion With Germany.

FOUR MORE IRISH LEADERS EXECUTED

Mrs. Gilligan, Arrested at Her Home Late Yesterday Afternoon, Withstands Grilling by State Police---Body of Franklin R. Andrews, Whom She is Accused of Killing, Disinterred from its Resting Place in Cheshire Cemetery at Night, Shows Death Was Caused by Arsenic, Not Gastric Ulcers, as Stated in Death Certificate---Another Body Also Shows Death by Poison.

MAY BE 20 WHO HAVE BEEN POISONED

Old Folks Have Come to the Home From All Parts of the State---Woman Has Had Two Husbands---Startling Number of Deaths at Home---Purchases of Arsenic at Windsor Drug Store---Woman Waives Examination ---Bodies Taken Away at Night in Violation of Law

Sister Amy was charged with the murder-for-profit of Brother Andrews. A bad case of "prison psychosis" made it seem unlikely that she'd come to trial, but on June 18, 1917, the woman suspected of at least a score of murders faced the jury. After a four-week trial and four hours of deliberation, they found her guilty and sentenced her to die on the gallows in November. But State's Attorney Alcorn, in his enthusiasm, had made a slip in the first trial and had told the jury about twenty-three other arsenic jobs that the State had linked to Sister Amy. That got her a new trial in June 1919.

At the second trial, a curious thing was noticeable. Sister Amy, though only in her forties, had suddenly aged. At the first trial, where she had appeared with a daughter from one of the five marriages she had gone through before darkening the Connecticut landscape, she had retained her remarkable youth.

Now, though, she had suddenly become an old woman, with evil written all over her face. She reminded some court observers of a female Jekyll-Hyde. All through the seven years while she was writing criminal history she had kept her innocent, youthful face. Now, overnight, it seemed, the evil and age had wiped out the innocence and the youth.

Insanity was her defense the second time around, with defense lawyers declaring her crazy. Her 19-year-old daughter, Mary E. Archer, testified that her mother was a morphine addict. The second trial ended on July 1, 1919, with a plea of guilty of murder in the second degree, which carried a life sentence. She was a model prisoner until 1924, when she was declared hopelessly insane and transferred to a mental hospital.

End of story? Not quite.

An aspiring young writer heard of Amy's story in the 1930's and wrote it up as a stage play. His name was Joseph Otto Kesselring, and the original title of his word was *Bodies in Our Cellar*. The title changed, however, and the play found its way to Broadway as *Arsenic and Old Lace*.

Written in 1939, it opened on Broadway at the Fulton Theater, on January 10, 1941, to rave reviews. The original production featured Boris Karloff playing a killer who looked like the Boris Karloff of *Frankenstein* fame and made the idea of wholesale slaughter simply hilarious.

Frank Capra later made it into a film, starring Cary Grant. As one critic proclaimed,

"You wouldn't believe homicidal mania could be such fun!"

Sister Amy was still alive for both the play and the movie. But it is not known if she saw either. Nonetheless, she starred in the original cast and became a celebrity patient, of sorts, in the nut house where she resided. Ironically, she outlived just about everyone she ever met until a day April 1962, when she died quietly at the ripe old age of ninety-two.

The End

Also by Alan Hynd

Alan Hynd's '"Til Death Do Us Part" Volume 1: 5 Spicy Classic Tales of Adultery, Murder and Marriage
by Alan Hynd et al.
Link: http://amzn.com/B00QMIUYP0

Prescription: Murder! Volume 1: Authentic Cases From The Files of Alan Hynd by Alan Hynd
Link: http://amzn.com/B00NG77JSK

 Prescription: Murder! Volume 2: Authentic Cases From the Files of Alan Hynd by Alan Hynd
Link: http://amzn.com/B00PBYTIE4

 Prescription: Murder! Volume 3: Authentic Cases From the Files of Alan Hynd by Alan Hynd
Link: http://amzn.com/B00Q1X5ZCI

CPSIA information can be obtained
at www.ICGtesting.com
Printed in the USA
BVHW030449160219
540451BV00001B/55/P